THE

HISTORY

OF

EMILY

MONTAGUE

D1295945

Frances Brooke

THE
HISTORY
OF
EMILY
MONTAGUE

Introduction—Carl F. Klinck

General Editor—Malcolm Ross

New Canadian Library No. 27

MCCLELLAND AND STEWART

The Canadian Publishers
McClelland and Stewart Limited
25 Hollinger Road, Toronto

0-7710-9127-3

Manufactured in Canada by Webcom Limited

NOTE ON THE TEXT

The History of Emily Montague, in four volumes, was first
printed in 1769 for T. Dodsley in Pall Mall, London. Another
edition, that of 1784, may be regarded as a slightly corrected
version; it has been accepted here as the standard text. The
publishers of this reprint in the New Canadian Library have
made some further adjustments, chiefly because of errors and
inconsistencies in spelling and punctuation. In the early editions,
for example, there were two quite separate letters numbered 112,
and two numbered 113; in this reprint the numbering has been
made properly consecutive and the total now reaches 228 letters.
Old spellings such as 'chear,' 'aukward,' 'rasberries,' 'plumbs,'
'meer,' 'surprized,' 'inclose,' and the French *'tems'* and
'sçai' have been retained. Some spellings have been altered to
conform to the prevailing usage in the original text. Accents
have been added to French words in cases where they were
missing. Roman numerals have been replaced by Arabic ones.
The flavour of the eighteenth century has been easily preserved
in a text which required no modernization for the reader of
our day.

THE HISTORY OF EMILY MONTAGUE

AN EARLY NOVEL

1769

Although Mrs Brooke's *Emily Montague* was published in England, it has a unique place in the literary history of North America. The action is set in Quebec City in the 1760's, the brief period between Wolfe's conquest of Canada in 1759 and the American War of Independence of the 1770's. French Canada had been added to Britain's intact and growing New World empire; the colonies soon to be the United States had not yet seceded. *Emily Montague* may be described as the first Canadian novel, and indeed the first American one. Such claims are not unreasonable for a book of fiction written almost two hundred years ago. Even in old England, the earliest group of authors satisfying our modern demands and definitions of the novel had not long been in their graves. Fielding had died in 1754, Richardson in 1761, and Sterne in 1768; Smollett was still alive, Fanny Burney had not yet published *Evelina*. Mrs Brooke, born Frances Moore in Stubton, Lincolnshire, in 1724, had been sixteen when Samuel Richardson had published *Pamela* (1740–1741), and thirty-seven when he died. She had known him as a personal friend about the time when he was publishing *Sir Charles Grandison* (1754). Her *Emily Montague* was constructed like one of his own novels, in the epistolary fashion, made up wholly of letters passing between the characters. The novel was thus transplanted into America by a member of the second generation, writing in the manner of the first.

The book has not gone unrecognized; it has long been in the canon of Canadian literature as an inheritance from the days when only the Lower colony and then the Upper one—but not the Maritime provinces—bore the name of Canada. If scholars had to blow some dust off the book, the job was done at least a hundred years ago; Henry J. Morgan described it for his *Bibliotheca Canadensis* (1867), a survey of literary activity before Confederation. The novel fits naturally into Morgan's extensive list, and also into J. M. LeMoine's record of historical features, *Picturesque Quebec* (1882). Here there is even a hint of popular interest antedating Morgan's scholarly notice. "It is stated in all old Quebec Guide-Books," LeMoine said, "that the house in which the 'divine' Emily then dwelt stood on the foot of Sillery Hill, close to Mrs Graddon's property at Kilmarnock." Legend, indeed, spanned the whole two centuries of the novel's career, for it kept alive the report, handed on by LeMoine, that Colonel Henry Caldwell, Wolfe's Assistant Quarter-Master General, was the original of Colonel Rivers in *Emily Montague*.

Mrs Brooke's connection with Canada was solidly based on residence in Quebec from 1763 to 1768, broken perhaps by one short visit to England in 1764. She certainly knew Colonel Caldwell and other officers of General Wolfe's army who remained in the colony after the Conquest. She was also associated with the administrators who organized British rule, including Governor James Murray; Guy Carleton, his successor, and Francis Maseres, the Attorney General. Dr John Brooke, her husband, was Chaplain of the garrison and deputy to the Auditor General. A letter from Murray to his wife in England, dated November 6, 1763, mentioned "Mrs Brookes who arrived here some time ago." For nearly five years she lived in Quebec or neighbouring Sillery, contemplating the scenery, people, and activities, and perhaps making some social history of her own. Letters of Governor Murray on January 8 and October 30, 1764, expressed his complaints against Dr Brooke for making an issue of a dispute between a Captain Brown and Miss Moore, Mrs Brooke's sister, who had accompanied her to Quebec. The trouble was described as "engaging in the idle, very idle disputes of a tea table conversation"; Murray had seen Dr Brooke "perpetually interfere with things that do not concern him." "I was in hopes," he added, "the Ladys would have wrought a change, but on the contrary they meddle more than he does." Mrs Brooke had apparently settled into the life of the colony. In her time, when Englishwomen in Quebec were few, fewer still had a prior right to be called residents. More complete identification with the country, advertised by a Canadian imprint on *Emily Montague*, was not to be hoped for; there was no publisher for novels in Canada.

Nor was there anything in Mrs Brooke's training or circumstances to make her look southward for publication. Although one of her letters in *Emily Montague* advised prudent handling of English restraints upon American trade (133), the Revolution had not yet occurred; and independence for American fiction was not yet a popular goal. The novels read in the New World in the English language were imported from London. Not a single title dated as early as 1709 appears today in the standard bibliographies of the American novel; the book lists of American fiction by Oscar Wegelin, Arthur H. Quinn, and Lyle H. Wright lead off with a short political satire in 1774. A case can be made for some earlier prose fiction, but not, it appears, for earlier novels. In such surveys no claims are found for emigrés like Mrs Charlotte Lennox, a native of New York State, who moved at the age of fifteen to England, and there, in the literary London of Samuel Richardson and Samuel Johnson, published a number of novels—of which her first, *The Life of Harriott Stuart* (1751), had an opening scene in America. Mrs Lennox and Mrs Brooke (Miss Moore at the time) began to write under similar influences proceeding from Samuel Richardson and from the French sentimental romances of the Abbé Prévost. American literary historians appear to be content without Mrs Lennox; by ignoring Mrs Brooke, Canadians could lose the principal artistic attempt to recreate life in the early northern colonies. Commonwealth literature could lose its first novel.

FRENCH CANADA

Emily Montague consists of two hundred and twenty-eight letters which follow one another without division into chapters and without narrative links. They concern mainly the fortunes of two pairs of lovers who meet, spend their period of courtship in Quebec, and then marry before or after leaving for permanent residence in England; these couples are Colonel Ed. Rivers and Emily Montague, and Captain Fitzgerald and Arabella Fermor. Another pair, the Colonel's sister Lucy and John Temple, Rivers's friend, have meanwhile remained in their homeland. Had the letters of all these lovers and their closest friends actually been sent, the mails in and out of Quebec City, and back and forth across the Atlantic, would have been busy indeed, without the addition of other notes which were represented as travelling, artificially enough, only from door to door, or room to room. Such minor peculiarities of the epistolary novel emphasize its conventional nature: the differences between it and naturalistic fiction, as well as the affinity between it and modern books which shape life into patterns for the purpose of revealing more clearly relationships, forms, and values. *Emily Montague* can be read today as if it were an experimental novel, set in an outmoded pattern of society. Rapport and aesthetic distance can both be achieved—a classical-modern mood congenial to art.

"Society" refers to the life of the eighteenth-century gentlemen and gentlewomen, those people in England, France, or French Canada who could regard themselves as especially endowed by birth and training to enjoy wealth, luxury, ease, honours, and privileges. Mrs Brooke's attitude toward such matters was not radical; no one could claim that she was republican before the United States framed its constitution, or egalitarian two decades before France had its Revolution. Class consciousness, rarely defended now in America, made it possible for her to write a novel then. The structure and customs of society as she knew it provided a frame for her picture. With so much given and understood, she was free to develop her special interest in the niceties of courtship and love. Like other masters of comedy and of manners, she thought "no politics worth attending to," as her Arabella says, "but those of the little commonwealth of woman" (45). No one knew better, of course, than she, that men also were citizens or subjects in this realm. By narrowing her topic, she enlarged it, for she was concentrating on something permanent in what her generation delighted to call the "general nature" of mankind and womankind.

For such a novel London would have seemed an appropriate setting. But what could Mrs Brooke do with Quebec in the 1760's? Was society there sophisticated enough, and "general nature" suitably refined? The truth is that class-consciousness and its etiquette were international, and that French Canada had its own gentry long before the British officers arrived. Mrs Brooke uses two letters of Arabella Fermor to dispel Lucy's mistaken "idea of the society here." On December 1, with winter setting in, Arabella is sufficiently gloomy to say that Quebec "is like a third or fourth rate country town in England; much hospitality, little society; cards, scandal, dancing, and good chear" (45). When a busy winter, a short spring and a pleasant summer have brought her to June 30, she has changed her mind: "I had rather live at Quebec, take it for all in all, than in any town in England, except London; the manner of living here is uncommonly agreeable; the scenes about us are lovely, and the mode of amusements makes us taste those scenes in full perfection" (157). Mrs Brooke's knowledge of the Continental French was an asset. She had read French romances with the Richardson circle in her *Old Maid* days. Later, when Richardson and Fielding had disciples among French writers, she had enjoyed reciprocal influences found in the works of Madame Marie Jeanne Riccoboni, whose *Letters from Lady Juliet Catesby* she had turned into English and published in 1760. Her own novels, *Julia Mandeville* and *Emily Montague*, translated by other hands, appeared in French. In 1770, after her return from Canada, she would publish *Memoirs of the Marquis of St Forlaix*, and in 1771 her translation of the Abbé Milot's *Ele-*

ments of the History of England. Her social view bridged the Atlantic as it bridged the Channel.

English-French Canada was ideal for a writer with her experience; it taught her new kinds of entertainment, more stimulating—at least in *Emily Montague*—than the life she pictures when her couples return to English scenes of wealth, luxury, and rigid convention. "Here [in Quebec] are some very estimable persons," writes Arabella Fermor's father to the Earl, "and the spirit of urbanity begins to diffuse itself from the centre" (159). The French gentry were invited to the parties, or gave the parties, and Mrs Brooke was quite certain that the "Canadian" ladies vied with scenery as the principal charms of Quebec. Her Arabella Fermor, apparently named for the lady whose misfortunes were celebrated in *The Rape of the Lock,* is an English coquette, possessing the good nature and the arts which Pope's Belinda lost. This Arabella could have graced Hampton Court, but she was also admirably suited to make the Quebec social world come alive. She—or Mrs Brooke—was the first articulate English-Canadian gentlewoman.

Colonel Rivers described the French-Canadian ladies, Arabella's counterparts, as "gay, coquet, and sprightly; more gallant than sensible; more flatter'd by the vanity of inspiring passion, than capable of feeling it themselves; and, like their European countrywomen, prefer[ring] the outward attentions of unmeaning admiration to the real devotion of the heart. There is not perhaps on earth a race of females," he added, as Mrs Brooke let him get in deeper, "who talk so much, or feel so little, of love as the French; the very reverse is in general true of the English: my fair countrywomen seem ashamed of the charming sentiment to which they are indebted for all their power" (4). He lived to see Arabella and even Emily upset his neat definitions, and to have Madame Des Roches, a sprightly "Canadian" widow, give him first-hand lessons about Frenchwomen. Mrs Brooke smiles at her own maxims; there is femininity and whimsicality, rather than heavy irony, in her handling of such affairs. She allows Fitzgerald to win Arabella, but not to tame the coquette; and she shows the French widow taking an "English" turn toward "the romantic style of love." "Your little Bell," says Arabella, "seems in point of love, to have changed countries with Madame Des Roches" (172).

Social life in her Quebec is exceptionally well described against a notable background of what Mrs Brooke called the *great sublime* in natural scenery. Her word-pictures of early Canada rival Cornelius Krieghoff's paintings of Quebec scenes which were done about seventy-five years later. Colonel Rivers's first letter pays tribute both to the vivacity and beauty of the French belles and to the majesty of the St Lawrence. Other letters throughout the book vividly refer to Indian women, a cottage at Sillery, religious institutions, towns and villages, the Chaudière and Montmorenci falls, aboriginal customs, autumn evenings, squaws on vacation, the crops, cold weather, carriages and sleighs, winter cheer, cloaks and furs, the seigniorial system, a ride over the frozen river, fishing through the ice, the breaking of the ice bridge, the rapid course of spring, summer parties, picnicking on islands in the St Lawrence, and sailing out to sea. William Fermor, a man much older than Rivers, writes letters in this novel to the Earl of ——; it is chiefly he who shows regard for the French-Canadian problems of reconstruction and adjustment to British rule. Through him Mrs Brooke reveals some prejudices which may be classified as conservatively English, imperialistic, Anglican, and characteristic of her time and social position. Convent life, for example, was not likely to suit her or her book.

The modern reader will know how to be tolerant of her conventional intolerance because the "Canadians" genuinely had her sympathy and her admiration. A few years earlier even Pitt could ask the House of Commons, "Some are for keeping Canada, some Guadeloupe, who will tell me which I shall be hanged for not keeping?" And in 1763, when she had written *Julia Mandeville*, Mrs Brooke had given her informal vote in favour of Canada "if population is encouraged; the waste lands settled; and a whale fishery set on foot" (II, 49). Five years later she knew more than all but a few officials in the British government about this new country, but she was probably content to leave politics, the handling of racial problems, and everything except love and women to Murray, Carleton, and Dr Brooke. Like her Arabella, she may have said, "they are squabbling at Quebec, I hear, about I cannot tell what, therefore shall not attempt to explain . . . we new comers have certainly nothing to do with these matters, you can't think how comfortable we feel at Silleri, out of the way" (45). *Emily Montague* is a *tour de force* in describing, not in defining, Canadian life; Mrs Brooke attempts definition only in affairs of the heart.

EPISTOLARY FICTION

The special qualities of *Emily Montague* as a novel of sentiment, composed entirely of letters, may be brought out in a comparison with *Evelina*, published nine years later (1778) by Fanny Burney. Mrs Brooke was twenty-eight years older than

Miss Burney; old enough indeed to have known Richardson, the father of that kind of novel, and yet young enough (in her late 'twenties, still Miss Moore) to have fluttered about with his female admirers and to have received poetic tributes from his gentlemen, notably Thomas Edwards and John Duncombe, Jr. All around her had been signs that women were threatening to capture the world of letters. Miss Moore had pioneered as a journalist by publishing *The Old Maid*, attributed to "Mary Singleton, Spinster." When the essays had appeared in book form, and she had become Mrs Brooke, she had confessed that "a late Nobleman, well known in the literary world" had contributed the pieces marked "L.C."

It is unlikely that she knew Dr Samuel Johnson as well as young Fanny Burney did. There is an anecdote, probably apocryphal, which has the Doctor kissing Miss Moore (presumably our Frances) in private; but Miss More (Hannah) may have been the lady so highly favoured. The latter certainly had closer ties with Johnson's friend, David Garrick. The great actor, who would not produce Mrs Brooke's tragedy *Virginia* in 1756, or another of her plays several years later, came under attack in her novel *The Excursion* in 1777. Hannah More sprang to Garrick's defence in the August issue of *The Monthly Review*. It is reported in John Nicol's *Literary Anecdotes* that Mrs Brooke repented of her severity and retracted. She was, apparently, in this late period a person of some consequence in London : a translator and author of popular epistolary novels, and a partner with Mrs Mary Ann Yates, a great tragic actress, in theatrical enterprises which would culminate in remarkable success for Mrs Brooke's light opera *Rosina* (1782), "with music by William Shield." Even *The Excursion* of 1777, a less happy effort, received a review extending to two or three columns by "Sylvanus Urban" in *The Gentleman's Magazine*. Austin Dobson, biographer of Fanny Burney, wryly observes that this was "a far longer notice than he [Sylvanus] afterwards, and very tardily, accorded to *Evelina*," Miss Burney's first and most famous novel, published in 1778. The paths of the elder and younger Frances crossed several times, and Miss Burney enriched her *Diary* with a characteristic description of Mrs Brooke : "[She] is very short and fat, and squints, but has the art of showing agreeable ugliness. She is very well bred, and expressed herself with much modesty upon all subjects; which in an *authoress*, a woman of *known* understanding, is extremely pleasing."

Wit of this kind helps to keep the eighteenth century alive after didacticism and sentimentality have done their worst The pathetic and the moralistic were then marks of literary attainment. Mrs Brooke came by these early and honestly—one did not need to steal from Richardson. He himself had acted upon a hint from Dr Johnson and in 1755 had gathered his pearls into *A Collection of the Moral and Instructive Sentiments, Maxims, Cautions and Reflexions, Contained in the Histories of Pamela, Clarissa, and Sir Charles Grandison. Digested under Proper Heads.* . . . (395 pages, small print, plus an index). Mrs Brooke also has this ability to toss off maxims, but with the difference that being a woman makes. Her sex has long had its own way of managing sentiment, both in life and letters. When she wishes to indulge in moralizing, she lets a male character, Colonel Rivers, handle the bulk of the product; then she introduces relief by practising this bit of her own wisdom: "it is the interest of virtue to be represented as she is, lovely, smiling, and ever walking hand in hand with pleasure; we were formed to be happy, and to contribute to the happiness of our fellow-creatures; there are no real virtues but the social ones" (135). The saving grace of women appears in Arabella's *joie de vivre* and Mrs Brooke's common sense. Yet the author felt that men, rather than women, would be her readers. The British Museum has a letter to Dodsley, her publisher, dated August 29, 1769, in which she says: "one of the best judges of Literature I know, a man of exquisite taste, told me soon after it was publish'd that it would be lik'd by literary people, but that it wou'd not be so popular a book by much as *Julia Man[deville]*. That it wou'd be better lik'd by men than women; it has prov'd so I am afraid. Now a novel to sell shou'd please women because women are the chief readers of novels & perhaps the best judges."

The texture of Mrs Brooke's novel is different from that of Fanny Burney's. The author of *Evelina* makes her letter writers tell her story for her, recording dialogue and incident, as it were, in lieu of the author's third person narration. Mrs Brooke's *Emily Montague* is almost devoid of ordinary dialogue; the brevity of the epistles, however, makes allowance for something of the give-and-take of conversation. Looked at in this way, the letters are speeches at once formal, because they are written, and progressive, because they reveal interaction. Or they are like speeches in classical drama, calling for quick discrimination regarding character, mood, and motives. The reader is aware that reciprocity of thought and feeling is demanded of him: he has to concern himself with thinking and feeling, not merely with being a spectator of what someone else, in the story, has seen and heard. Mrs Brooke relies, more than Miss Burney does, on analysis of sentiment, and less on incident and characterization. Her novel is witty rather than comic; the art of good letter-writing is not wholly subordinated to the narrative function. Her essays also are lively as essays. In anatomizing human beings she puts her trust chiefly in language.

Her words are designed to do what epistles uniquely do —to annihilate space, and to link minds and hearts directly, by means of nothing more than ink spots on paper. A certain timelessness also results, as long as the words retain the author's meanings. In twentieth-century fiction there have been many experiments in direct mental communication; and Mrs Brooke may be given some credit for having a similar aim, to avoid lags and irrelevancies while verbally awakening the reader's conscious ness of thoughts and sentiments which he presumably shares with all men and women. This technique appears to be well adjusted to the intention, and indeed to the temper, of Mrs Brooke's age of reason; the neo-classical purpose of avoiding particularities in feelings of fictional individuals is carried out. What is conveyed is of general concern and consistent within the prescribed terms of reference of conventionalized society. It is a rarefied world but, as Mrs Brooke's Arabella shows, it can still be a delightful one.

While she thus demands her reader's co-operation, Mrs Brooke—like Arabella—contrives to render his progress enjoyable. Perhaps she felt all along, as she did when she wrote to Dodsley some months after publication, that she had a special problem in this four-volume novel: "it's [sic] having," as she said to Dodsley, "too little variety of story for the length of it." The criticism will be felt by every reader of the third, and perhaps the fourth quarter, of *Emily Montague*. As he grows correspondingly colder to the repetition of sentimental observations, he may also grow more conscious of the trouble Mrs Brooke has taken as hostess-novelist. Her epistles are short, her paragraphs of minimum length; her transitions telepathic; her sentences either balanced or uncomplicated; her flow rapid; and her diction wholly modern, familiar, requiring no footnotes. Her wit is not mere affectation; it shows itself in brevity and aptness. She does not make her moral tale a moral trial; her aphorisms arise naturally enough out of the context and, being flavoured with whimsy, are reasonably digestible. She does not confuse the sensuous with the sensitive; the reader must be willing, for the time being, to contemplate love alchemized into "an intellectual pleasure" (14). She will not repeat the failure of her *Julia Mandeville* by resorting to horror and violence; she risks singularity among the sentimental novelists in that her characters suffer only mild embarrassments, honourable renunciations, and temporary losses. No one is seduced, harmed or persecuted; there is no villain; no one is in mortal danger. She even hesitates to interrupt the course of true love: the rhythm of excitement, undeniably there, is carried along by normality and gaiety—the charm of enjoying the day and looking forward to the next, because virtue and conventionality are pleasurable. Only a writer of considerable literary talent would have dared to stir such ripples rather than waves.

CARL F. KLINCK

The University of
Western Ontario.

TO HIS EXCELLENCY GUY CARLETON, ESQ.
GOVERNOR AND COMMANDER IN CHIEF OF
HIS MAJESTY'S PROVINCE OF QUEBEC,
ETC., ETC., ETC.

SIR,

As the scene of so great a part of the following work is laid in Canada, I flatter myself there is a peculiar propriety in addressing it to your excellency, to whose probity and enlightened attention the colony owes its happiness, and individuals that tranquillity of mind, without which there can be no exertion of the powers of either the understanding or imagination.

Were I to say all your excellency has done to diffuse, through this province, so happy under your command, a spirit of loyalty and attachment to our excellent Sovereign, of chearful obedience to the laws, and of that union which makes the strength of government, I should hazard your esteem by doing you justice.

I will, therefore, only beg leave to add mine to the general voice of Canada; and to assure your excellency, that
I am,
With the utmost esteem
and respect,
Your most obedient servant,

FRANCES BROOKE

London,
March 22, 1769.

THE HISTORY OF EMILY MONTAGUE

LETTER 1 COWES, APRIL 10, 1766: After spending two or three very agreeable days here, with a party of friends, in exploring the beauties of the Island, and dropping a tender tear at Carisbrook Castle on the memory of the unfortunate Charles the First, I am just setting out for America, on a scheme I once hinted to you, of settling the lands to which I have a right as a lieutenant-colonel on half-pay. On enquiry and mature deliberation, I prefer Canada to New York for two reasons, that it is wilder, and that the women are handsomer: the first, perhaps, every body will not approve: the latter, I am sure, *you* will.

You may perhaps call my project romantic, but my active temper is ill-suited to the lazy character of a reduc'd officer: besides that I am too proud to narrow my circle of life, and not quite unfeeling enough to break in on the little estate which is scarce sufficient to support my mother and sister in the manner to which they have been accustom'd.

What you call a sacrifice, is none at all; I love England, but am not obstinately chain'd down to any spot of earth; nature has charms every where for a man willing to be pleased: at my time of life, the very change of place is amusing; love of variety, and the natural restlessness of man, would give me a relish for this voyage, even if I did not expect, what I really do, to become lord of a principality which will put our large-acred men in England out of countenance. My subjects indeed at present will be only bears and elks, but in time I hope to see the *human face divine* multiplying around me; and, in thus cultivating what is in the rudest state of nature, I shall taste one of the greatest of all pleasures, that of creation, and see order and beauty gradually rise from chaos.

The vessel is unmoor'd; the winds are fair; a gentle breeze agitates the bosom of the deep; all nature smiles: I go with all the eager hopes of a warm imagination; yet friendship casts a lingering look behind.

Our mutual loss, my dear Temple, will be great. I shall never cease to regret you, nor will you find it easy to replace the friend of your youth. You may find friends of equal merit; you may esteem them equally; but few connexions form'd after five-and-twenty strike root like that early sympathy, which united us almost from infancy, and has increas'd to the very hour of our separation.

What pleasure is there in the friendships of the spring of life, before the world, the mean unfeeling selfish world, breaks in on the gay mistakes of the just-expanding heart, which sees nothing but truth, and has nothing but happiness in prospect!

I am not surpriz'd the heathens rais'd altars to friendship: 'twas natural for untaught superstition to defy the source of every good; they worship'd friendship, which animates the moral world, on the same principle as they paid adoration to the sun, which gives life to the world of nature.

I am summon'd on board. Adieu!

ED. RIVERS

TO MISS RIVERS, CLARGES STREET

LETTER *2* QUEBEC, JUNE 27: I have this moment your letter, my dear; I am happy to hear my mother has been amus'd at Bath, and not at all surpriz'd to find she rivals you in your conquests. By the way, I am not sure she is not handsomer, not-withstanding you tell me you are handsomer than ever: I am astonish'd she will lead a tall daughter about with her thus, to let people into a secret they would never suspect, that she is past five-and-twenty.

You are a foolish girl, Lucy: do you think I have not more pleasure in continuing to my mother, by coming hither, the little indulgencies of life, than I could have had by enjoying them myself? pray reconcile her to my absence, and assure her she will make me happier by jovially enjoying the trifle I have assign'd to her use, than by procuring me the wealth of a Nabob, in which she was to have no share.

But to return; you really, Lucy, ask me such a million of questions, 'tis impossible to know which to answer first; the country, the convents, the balls, the ladies, the beaux—'tis a history, not a letter, you demand, and it will take me a twelve-month to satisfy your curiosity.

Where shall I begin? certainly with what must first strike a soldier: I have seen then the spot where the amiable hero expir'd in the arms of victory; have traced him step by step with equal astonishment and admiration: 'tis here alone it is possible to form an adequate idea of an enterprize, the difficulties of which must have destroy'd hope itself had they been foreseen.

The country is a very fine one: you see here not only the *beautiful* which it has in common with Europe, but the *great sublime* to an amazing degree; every object here is magnificent: the very people seem almost another species, if we compare them with the French from whom they are descended.

On approaching the coast of America, I felt a kind of religious veneration, on seeing rocks which almost touch'd the clouds, cover'd with tall groves of pines that seemed coeval with the world itself: to which veneration the solemn silence not a little contributed; from Cap Rosières, up the river St Lawrence, during a course of more than two hundred miles, there is not the least appearance of a human foot-step; no objects meet the eye but mountains, woods, and numerous rivers, which seem to roll their waters in vain.

It is impossible to behold a scene like this without lamenting the madness of mankind, who, more merciless than the fierce inhabitants of the howling wilderness, destroy millions of their own species in the wild contention for a little portion of that earth, the far greater part of which remains yet unpossest, and courts the hand of labour for cultivation.

The river itself is one of the noblest in the world; its breadth is ninety miles at its entrance, gradually, and almost imperceptibly, decreasing; interspers'd with islands which give it a variety infinitely pleasing, and navigable near five hundred miles from the sea.

Nothing can be more striking than the view of Quebec as you approach; it stands on the summit of a boldly-rising hill, at the confluence of two very beautiful rivers, the St Lawrence and St Charles, and, as the convents and other public buildings first meet the eye, appears to great advantage from the port. The island of Orleans, the distant view of the cascade of Montmorenci, and the opposite village of Beauport, scattered with a pleasing irregularity along the banks of the river St Charles, add greatly to the charms of the prospect.

I have just had time to observe, that the Canadian ladies have the vivacity of the French, with a superior share of beauty: as to balls and assemblies, we have none at present, it being a kind of interregnum of government: if I chose to give you the political state of the country, I could fill volumes with the *pours* and the *contres*; but I am not one of those sagacious observers, who, by staying a week in a place, think themselves qualified to give, not only its natural, but its moral and political history:

besides which, you and I are rather too young to be very pro-
found politicians. We are in expectation of a successor from
whom we hope a new golden age; I shall then have better subjects for a letter to a lady.

Adieu! my dear girl! say every thing for me to my
mother. Yours,

ED. RIVERS

TO COL. RIVERS, AT QUEBEC

LETTER 3 LONDON, APRIL 30: Indeed! gone to people
the wilds of America, Ned, and multiply the *human face divine?*
'tis a project worthy a tall handsome colonel of twenty-seven:
let me see; five feet, eleven inches, well made, with fine teeth,
speaking eyes, a military air, and the look of a man of fashion:
spirit, generosity, a good understanding, some knowledge, an
easy address, a compassionate heart, a strong inclination for the
ladies, and in short every quality a gentleman should have: excellent all these for colonization: *prenez garde, mes chères
dames.* You have nothing against you, Ned, but your modesty;
a very useless virtue on French ground, or indeed on any
ground: I wish you had a little more consciousness of your own
merits: remember that *to know one's self* the oracle of Apollo
has pronounced to be the perfection of human wisdom. Our fair
friend Mrs H— says, "Colonel Rivers wants nothing to make
him the most agreeable man breathing but a little dash of the
coxcomb."

For my part, I hate humility in a man of the world; 'tis
worse than even the hypocrisy of the saints: I am not ignorant,
and therefore never deny, that I am a very handsome fellow; and
I have the pleasure to find all the women of the same opinion.

I am just arriv'd from Paris: the divine Madame
De—— is as lovely and as constant as ever; 'twas cruel to leave
her, but who can account for the caprices of the heart? mine
was the prey of a young unexperienc'd English charmer, just
come out of a convent.

"The bloom of opening flowers—"

Ha, Ned? But I forget; you are for the full-blown rose: 'tis a
happiness, as we are friends, that 'tis impossible we can ever be
rivals; a woman is grown out of my taste some years before she

20

comes up to yours: absolutely, Ned, you are too nice; for my part, I am not so delicate; youth and beauty are sufficient for me; give me blooming seventeen, and I cede to you the whole empire of sentiment.

This, I suppose, will find you trying the force of your destructive charms on the savage dames of America; chasing females wild as the winds thro' woods as wild as themselves: I see you pursuing the stately relict of some renown'd Indian chief, some plump squaw arriv'd at the age of sentiment, some warlike queen dowager of the Ottawas or Tuscaroras.

And pray, *comment trouvez vous les dames sauvages?* all pure and genuine nature, I suppose; none of the affected coyness of Europe: your attention there will be the more obliging, as the Indian heroes, I am told, are not very attentive to the charms of the *beau sexe*.

You are very sentimental on the subject of friendship; no one has more exalted notions of this species of affection than myself, yet I deny that it gives life to the moral world; a gallant man, like you, might have found a more animating principle.

O Vénus! O Mère de l'Amour!

I am most gloriously indolent this morning, and would not write another line if the empire of the world (observe I do not mean the female world) depended on it.

Adieu!

J. TEMPLE

TO JOHN TEMPLE, ESQ; PALL MALL

LETTER 4 QUEBEC, JULY I: 'Tis very true, Jack; I have no relish for *the Misses*; for puling girls in hanging sleeves, who feel no passion but vanity, and, without any distinguishing taste, are dying for the first man who tells them they are handsome. Take your boarding-school girls; but give me *a woman*; one, in short, who has a soul; not a cold inanimate form, insensible to the lively impressions of real love, and unfeeling as the wax baby she has just thrown away.

You will allow Prior to be no bad judge of female merit; and you may remember his Egyptian maid, the favourite of the luxurious King Solomon, is painted in full bloom.

By the way, Jack, there is generally a certain hoity-toity

inelegance of form and manner at seventeen, which in my opinion is not balanc'd by freshness of complexion, the only advantage girls have to boast of.

I have another objection to girls, which is, that they will eternally fancy every man they converse with has designs; a coquet and a prude *in the bud* are equally disagreeable; the former expects universal adoration, the latter is alarm'd even at that general civility which is the right of all their sex; of the two however the last is, I think, much the most troublesome; I wish these very apprehensive young ladies knew their *virtue* is not half so often in danger as they imagine, and that there are many male creatures to whom they may safely shew politeness without being drawn into any concessions inconsistent with the strictest honour. We are not half such terrible animals as mammas, nurses, and novels represent us; and, if my opinion is of any weight, I am inclin'd to believe those tremendous men, who have designs on the whole sex, are, and ever were, characters as fabulous as the giants of romance.

Women after twenty begin to know this, and therefore converse with us on the footing of rational creatures, without either fearing or expecting to find every man a lover.

To do the ladies justice however, I have seen the same absurdity in my own sex, and have observed many a very good sort of man turn pale at the politeness of an agreeable woman.

I lament this mistake, in both sexes, because it takes greatly from the pleasure of mix'd society, the only society for which I have any relish.

Don't, however, fancy that, because I dislike *the Misses*, I have a taste for their grandmothers; there is a golden mean, Jack, of which you seem to have no idea.

You are very ill-inform'd as to the manners of the Indian ladies; 'tis in the bud alone these wild roses are accessible; liberal to profusion of their charms before marriage, they are chastity itself after: the moment they commence wives, they give up the very idea of pleasing, and turn all their thoughts to the cares, and those not the most delicate cares, of domestic life: laborious, hardy, active, they plough the ground, they sow, they reap; whilst the haughty husband amuses himself with hunting, shooting, fishing, and such exercises only as are the image of war; all other employments being, according to his idea, unworthy the dignity of man.

I have told you the labours of savage life, but I should observe that they are only temporary, and when urg'd by the sharp tooth of necessity: their lives are, upon the whole, idle beyond any thing we can conceive. If the Epicurean definition of happiness is just that it consists in indolence of body and tranquillity of mind, the Indians of both sexes are the happiest people on earth; free from all care, they enjoy the present moment, forget the past, and are without solicitude for the future: in summer, stretch'd on the verdant turf, they sing, they laugh, they play, they relate stories of their ancient heroes to warm the youth to war; in winter, wrap'd in the furs which bounteous nature provides them, they dance, they feast, and despise the rigours of the season, at which the more effeminate Europeans tremble.

War being however the business of their lives, and the first passion of their souls, their very pleasures take their colours from it; every one must have heard of the war dance, and their songs are almost all on the same subject: on the most diligent enquiry, I find but one love song in their language, which is short and simple, tho' perhaps not inexpressive.

> "I love you,
> "I love you dearly,
> "I love you all day long."

An old Indian told me, they had also songs of friendship, but I could never procure a translation of one of them: on my pressing this Indian to translate one into French for me, he told me with a haughty air, the Indians were not us'd to make translations, and that if I chose to understand their songs I must learn their language. By the way, their language is extremely harmonious, especially as pronounced by their women, and as well adapted to music as Italian itself. I must not here omit an instance of their independent spirit, which is, that they never would submit to have the service of the church, tho' they profess the Romish religion, in any language but their own; the women, who have in general fine voices, sing in the choir with a taste and manner that would surprize you, and with a devotion that might edify more polish'd nations.

The Indian women are tall and well-shaped; have good eyes, and before marriage are, except their colour, and their coarse greasy black hair, very far from being disagreeable; but the laborious life they afterwards lead is extremely unfavourable to beauty; they become coarse and masculine, and lose in a year or two the power as well as the desire of pleasing. To compensate however for the loss of their charms, they acquire a new empire in marrying; are consulted in all affairs of state, chuse a chief on every vacancy of the throne, are sovereign arbiters of peace and war, as well as of the fate of those unhappy captives that have the misfortune to fall into their hands, who are adopted

23

as children, or put to the most cruel death, as the wives of the conquerors smile or frown.

A Jesuit missionary told me a story on this subject, which one cannot hear without horror: an Indian woman with whom he liv'd on his mission was feeding her children, when her husband brought in an English prisoner; she immediately cut off his arm, and gave her children the streaming blood to drink: the Jesuit remonstrated on the cruelty of the action, on which, looking sternly at him, "I would have them warriors," said she, "and therefore feed them with the food of men."

This anecdote may perhaps disgust you with the Indian ladies, who certainly do not excel in female softness. I will therefore turn to the Canadian, who have every charm except that without which all other charms are to me insipid, I mean sensibility: they are gay, coquet, and sprightly; more gallant than sensible; more flatter'd by the vanity of inspiring passion, than capable of feeling it themselves; and, like their European countrywomen, prefer the outward attentions of unmeaning admiration to the real devotion of the heart. There is not perhaps on earth a race of females, who talk so much, or feel so little, of love as the French; the very reverse is in general true of the English: my fair countrywomen seem ashamed of the charming sentiment to which they are indebted for all their power.

Adieu! I am going to attend a very handsome French lady, who allows me the honour to drive her *en calache* to our Canadian Hyde Park, the road to St Foix, where you will see forty or fifty calashes, with pretty women in them, parading every evening: you will allow the apology to be admissible.

Ed. Rivers

LETTER 5 QUEBEC, JULY 4: What an inconstant animal is man! do you know, Lucy, I begin to be tir'd of the lovely landscape round me? I have enjoy'd from it all the pleasure meer inanimate objects can give, and find 'tis a pleasure that soon satiates, if not relieved by others which are more lively. The scenery is to be sure divine, but one grows weary of meer scenery; the most enchanting prospect soon loses its power of pleasing, when the eye is accustom'd to it: we gaze at first transported on the charms of nature, and fancy they will please for ever; but, alas! it will not do; we sigh for society, the conversation of those dear to us; the more animated pleasures of the heart. There are fine women, and men of merit here; but, as the affections are not in our power, I have not yet felt by heart gravitate towards any of them. I must absolutely set in earnest about my settlement, in order to emerge from the state of vegetation into which I seem falling.

But to your last: you ask me a particular account of the convents here. Have you an inclination, my dear, to turn nun? if you have, you could not have applied to a properer person; my extreme modesty and reserve, and my speaking French, having made me already a great favourite with the older part of all the three communities, who unanimously declare Colonel Rivers to be *un très aimable homme*, and have given me an unlimited liberty of visiting them whenever I please: they now and then treat *me* with a sight of some of the young ones, but this is a favour not allow'd to all the world.

There are three religious houses at Quebec, so you have choice; the Ursulines, the Hôtel Dieu, and the General Hospital. The first is the severest order in the Romish church, except that very cruel one which denies its fair votaries the inestimable liberty of speech. The house is large and handsome, but has an air of gloominess, with which the black habit, and the livid paleness of the nuns, extremely corresponds. The church is, contrary to the style of the rest of the convent, ornamented and lively to the last degree. The superior is an Englishwoman of good family, who was taken prisoner by the savages when a child, and plac'd here by the generosity of a French officer. She is one of the most amiable women I ever knew, with a benevolence in her countenance which inspires all who see her with affection: I am very fond of her conversation, tho' sixty and a nun.

The Hôtel Dieu is very pleasantly situated, with a view of the two rivers, and the entrance of the port: the house is chearful, airy, and agreeable; the habit extremely becoming, a circumstance a handsome woman ought by no means to overlook; 'tis white with a black gauze veil, which would shew your complexion to great advantage. The order is much less severe than the Ursulines, and I might add, much more useful, their province being the care of the sick: the nuns of this house are sprightly, and have a look of health which is wanting at the Ursulines.

The General Hospital, situated about a mile out of town, on the borders of the river St Charles, is much the most agreeable of the three. The order and the habit are the same with the Hôtel Dieu, except that to the habit is added the cross, generally worn in Europe by canonesses only: a distinction procur'd for them by their founder, St Vallier, the second bishop of Quebec. The house is, without, a very noble building; and neatness, elegance and propriety reign within. The nuns, who are all of the noblesse, are many of them handsome, and all genteel, lively, and well-bred; they have an air of the world, their conversation is easy, spirited, and polite: with them you almost forget the recluse in the woman of condition. In short, you have the best nuns at the Ursulines, the most agreeable women at the General Hospital: all however have an air of chagrin, which they in vain endeavour to conceal; and the general eagerness with which they tell you unask'd they are happy, is a strong proof of the contrary.

Tho' the most indulgent of all men to the follies of others, especially such as have their source in mistaken devotion; tho' willing to allow all the world to play the fool their own way, yet I cannot help being fir'd with a degree of zeal against an institution equally incompatible with public good, and private happiness; an institution which cruelly devotes beauty and innocence to slavery, regret, and wretchedness; to a more irksome imprisonment than the severest laws inflict on the worst of criminals.

Could any thing but experience, my dear Lucy, make it be believ'd possible that there should be rational beings, who think they are serving the God of mercy by inflicting on themselves voluntary tortures, and cutting themselves off from that state of society in which he has plac'd them, and for which they were form'd? by renouncing the best affections of the human heart, the tender names of friend, of wife, of mother? and, as far as in them lies, counter-working creation? by spurning from them every amusement however innocent, by refusing the gifts of that beneficent power who made us to be happy, and destroying his most precious gifts, health, beauty, sensibility, chearfulness, and peace!

My indignation is yet awake, from having seen a few days since at the Ursulines, an extreme lovely young girl, whose countenance spoke a soul form'd for the most lively, yet delicate, ties of love and friendship, led by a momentary enthusiasm, or perhaps by a childish vanity artfully excited, to the foot of those altars, which she will probably too soon bathe with the bitter tears of repentance and remorse.

The ceremony, form'd to strike the imagination, and seduce the heart of unguarded youth, is extremely solemn and affecting; the procession of the nuns, the sweetness of their voices in the choir, the dignified devotion with which the charming enthusiast received the veil, and took the cruel vow which shut her from the world for ever, struck my heart in spite of my reason, and I felt myself touch'd even to tears by a superstition I equally pity and despise.

I am not however certain it was the ceremony which affected me thus strongly; it was impossible not to feel for this amiable victim; never was there an object more interesting; her form was elegance itself; her air and motion animated and graceful; the glow of pleasure was on her cheeks, the fire of enthusiasm in her eyes, which are the finest I ever saw: never did I see joy so livelily painted on the countenance of the happiest bride; she seem'd to walk in air; her whole person look'd more than human.

An enemy to every species of superstition, I must however allow it to be least destructive to true virtue in your gentle sex, and therefore to be indulg'd with least danger; the superstition of men is gloomy and ferocious; it lights the fire, and points the dagger of the assassin; whilst that of women takes its colour from the sex; is soft, mild, and benevolent; exerts itself in acts of kindness and charity, and seems only substituting the love of God to that of man.

Who can help admiring, whilst they pity, the foundress of the Ursuline convent, Madame de la Peltrie, to whom the very colony in some measure owes its existence? young, rich, and lovely; a widow in the bloom of life, mistress of her own actions, the world was gay before her, yet she left all the pleasures that world could give, to devote her days to the severities of a religion she thought the only true one: she dar'd the dangers of the sea, and the greater dangers of a savage people; she landed on an unknown shore, submitted to the extremities of cold and heat, of thirst and hunger, to perform a service she thought acceptable to the Deity. To an action like this, however mistaken the motive, bigotry alone will deny praise: the man of candour will only lament that minds capable of such heroic virtue are not directed to views more conducive to their own and the general happiness.

I am unexpectedly call'd this moment, my dear Lucy, on some business to Montreal, from whence you shall hear from me.

Adieu!

ED. RIVERS

LETTER 6 MONTREAL, JULY 9: I am arriv'd, my dear, and have brought my heart safe thro' a continued fire as never poor knight errant was exposed to; waited on at every stage by blooming country girls, full of spirit and coquetry, without any of the village bashfulness of England, and dressed like the shepherdesses of romance. A man of adventure might make a pleasant journey to Montreal.

The peasants are ignorant, lazy, dirty, and stupid beyond all belief; but hospitable, courteous, civil; and, what is particularly agreeable, they leave their wives and daughters to do the honours of the house: in which obliging office they acquit themselves with an attention, which, amidst every inconvenience apparent (tho' I am told not real) poverty can cause, must please every guest who has a soul inclin'd to be pleas'd: for my part, I was charm'd with them, and eat my homely fare with as much pleasure as if I had been feasting on ortolans in a palace. Their conversation is lively and amusing; all the little knowledge of Canada is confined to the sex; very few, even of the seigneurs, being able to write their own names.

The road from Quebec to Montreal is almost a continued street, the villages being numerous, and so extended along the banks of the river St Lawrence as to leave scarce a space without houses in view; except where here or there a river, a wood, or mountain intervenes, as if to give a more pleasing variety to the scene. I don't remember ever having had a more agreeable journey; the fine prospects of the day so enliven'd by the gay chat of the evening, that I was really sorry when I approach'd Montreal.

The island of Montreal, on which the town stands, is a very lovely spot; highly cultivated, and tho' less wild and magnificent, more smiling than the country round Quebec: the ladies, who seem to make pleasure their only business, and most of whom I have seen this morning driving about the town in calashes, and making what they call, the *tour de la ville*, attended by English officers, seem generally handsome, and have an air of sprightliness with which I am charm'd; I must be acquainted with them all, for tho' my stay is to be short, I see no reason why it should be dull. I am told they are fond of little rural balls in the country, and intend to give one as soon as I have paid my respects in form.

I am just come from dining with the —— regiment, and find I have a visit to pay I was not aware of, to two English ladies who are a few miles out of town: one of them is wife to the major of the regiment, and the other just going to be married to a captain in it, Sir George Clayton, a young handsome baronet, just come to his title and a very fine estate, by the death of a distant relation: he is at present at New York, and I am told they are to be married as soon as he comes back.

I have been making some flying visits to the French ladies; tho' I have not seen many beauties, yet in general the women are handsome; their manner is easy and obliging, they make the most of their charms by their vivacity, and I certainly cannot be displeas'd with their extreme partiality for the English officers; their own men, who indeed are not very attractive, have not the least chance for any share in their good graces.

I am just setting out with a friend for Major Melmoth's, to pay my compliments to the two ladies: I have no relish for this visit; I hate misses that are going to be married; they are always so full of the dear man, that they have not common civility to other people. I am told however both the ladies are agreeable.

Agreeable, Lucy! she is an angel: 'tis happy for me she is engag'd; nothing else could secure my heart, of which you know I am very tenacious: only think of finding beauty, delicacy, sensibility, all that can charm in woman, hid in a wood in Canada!

You say I am given to be enthusiastic in my approbations, but she is really charming. I am resolv'd not only to have a friendship for her myself, but that *you* shall, and have told her so; she comes to England as soon as she is married; you are form'd to love each other.

But I must tell you; Major Melmoth kept us a week at his house in the country, in one continued round of rural amusements; by which I do not mean hunting and shooting, but such pleasures as the ladies could share; little rustic balls and parties round the neighbouring country, in which parties we were joined by all the fine women at Montreal. Mrs Melmoth is a very pleasing, genteel brunette, but Emily Montague—you will say I am in love with her if I describe her, and yet I declare to you I am not: knowing she loves another, to whom she is soon to be united, I see her charms with the same kind of pleasure I do yours; a pleasure, which, tho' extremely lively, is by our situation without the least mixture of desire.

I have said, she is charming; there are men here who do not think so, but to me she is loveliness itself. My ideas of beauty are perhaps a little out of the common road: I hate a woman of whom every man coldly says, *she is handsome*; I adore beauty, but it is not meer features or complexion to which I give that name; 'tis life, 'tis spirit, 'tis animation, 'tis—in one word, 'tis Emily Montague—without being regularly beautiful, she charms every sensible heart; all other women, however lovely, appear marble statues near her; fair; pale (a paleness which gives the idea of delicacy without destroying that of health), with dark hair and eyes, the latter large and languishing, she seems made to feel to a trembling excess the passion she cannot fail of inspiring: her elegant form has an air of softness and languor, which seizes the whole soul in a moment; her eyes, the most intelligent I ever saw, hold you enchain'd by their bewitching sensibility.

There are a thousand unspeakable charms in her conversation; but what I am most pleas'd with, is the attentive politeness of her manner, which you seldom see in a person in love; the extreme desire of pleasing one man generally taking off greatly from the attention due to all the rest. This is partly owing to her admirable understanding, and partly to the natural softness of her soul, which gives her the strongest desire of pleasing. As I am a philosopher in these matters, and have made the heart my study, I want extremely to see her with her lover, and to observe the gradual increase of her charms in his presence; love, which embellishes the most unmeaning countenance, must give to her's a fire irresistible: what eyes! when animated by tenderness!

The very soul acquires a new force and beauty by loving; a woman of honour never appears half so amiable, or displays half so many virtues, as when sensible to the merit of a man who deserves her affection. Observe, Lucy, I shall never allow you to be handsome till I hear you are in love.

Did I tell you Emily Montague had the finest hand and arm in the world? I should however have excepted yours. Her tone of voice too has the same melodious sweetness, a perfection without which the loveliest woman could never make the least impression on my heart; I don't think you are very unlike upon the whole, except that she is paler. You know, Lucy, you have often told me I should certainly have been in love with you if I had not been your brother: this resemblance is a proof you were right. You are really as handsome as any woman can be whose sensibility has never been put in motion.

I am to give a ball to-morrow; Mrs Melmoth is to have the honours of it, but as she is with child, she does not dance. This circumstance has produc'd a dispute not a little flattering to my vanity: the ladies are making interest to dance with me; what a happy exchange have I made! what man of common sense would stay to be overlook'd in England, who can have rival beauties contend for him in Canada? This important point is not yet settled; the *etiquette* here is rather difficult to adjust; as to me, I have nothing to do in the consultation; my hand is destin'd to the longest pedigree; we stand prodigiously on our noblesse at Montreal.

Four o'clock

After a dispute in which two French ladies were near drawing their husbands into a duel, the point of honour is yielded by both to Miss Montague; each insisting only that I should not dance with the other: for my part, I submit with a good grace, as you will suppose.

Saturday morning

I never passed a more agreeable evening; we have our amusements here, I assure you: a set of fine young fellows, and handsome women, all well dress'd, and in humour with themselves, and with each other: my lovely Emily like Venus amongst the Graces, only multiplied to about sixteen. Nothing is, in my opinion, so favourable to the display of beauty as a ball. A state of rest is ungraceful; all nature is most beautiful in motion; trees agitated by the wind, a ship under sail, a horse in the course, a fine woman dancing: never any human being had such an aversion to still life as I have.

I am going back to Melmoth's for a month; don't be alarm'd, Lucy! I see all her perfections, but I see them with the cold eye of admiration only: a woman engaged loses all her attractions as a woman; there is no love without a ray of hope: my only ambition is to be her friend; I want to be the confidant of her passion. With what spirit such a mind as hers must love!
Adieu! my dear!
Yours,

ED. RIVERS

LETTER 7 MONTREAL, AUGUST 15: By Heavens, Lucy, this is more than man can bear; I was mad to stay so long at Melmoth's; there is no resisting this little seducer: 'tis shameful in such a lovely woman to have understanding too; yet even this I could forgive, had she not that enchanting softness in her manner, which steals upon the soul, and would almost make ugliness itself charm; were she but vain, one had some chance, but she will take upon her to have no consciousness, at least no apparent consciousness, of her perfections, which is really intolerable. I told her so last night, when she put on such a malicious smile—I believe the little tyrant wants to add me to the list of her slaves; but I was not form'd to fill up a train. The woman I love must be so far from giving another the preference, that she must have no soul but for me; I am one of the most unreasonable men in the world on this head; she may fancy what she pleases, but I set her and all her attractions at defiance: I have made my escape, and shall set off for Quebec in an hour. Flying is, I must acknowledge, a little out of character, and unbecoming a soldier; but in these cases, it is the very best thing man or woman either can do, when they doubt their powers of resistance.

I intend to be ten days going to Quebec. I propose visiting the priests at every village, and endeavouring to get some knowledge of the nature of the country, in order to my intended settlement. Idleness being the root of all evil, and the nurse of love, I am determin'd to keep myself employed; nothing can be better suited to my temper than my present design; the pleasure of cultivating lands here is as much superior to what can be found in the same employment in England, as watching the expanding rose, and beholding the falling leaves: America is in infancy, Europe in old age. Nor am I very ill-qualified for this agreeable task: I have studied the Georgicks, and am a pretty enough kind of a husbandman as far as theory goes; nay, I am not sure I shall not be, even in practice, the best *gentleman* farmer in the province.

You may expect soon to hear of me in the *Museum Rusticum*; I intend to make amazing discoveries in the rural way; I have already found out, by the force of my own genius, two very uncommon circumstances: that in Canada, contrary to what we see every where else, the country is rich, the capital poor; the hills fruitful, the vallies barren. You see what excellent dispositions I have to be an useful member of society: I had always a strong bias to the study of natural philosophy.

Tell my mother how well I am employ'd, and she cannot but approve my voyage: assure her, my dear, of my tenderest regard.

The chaise is at the door.

Adieu!

ED. RIVERS

The lover is every hour expected; I am not quite sure I should have lik'd to see him arrive: a third person, you know, on such an occasion, sinks into nothing; and I love, wherever I am, to be one of the figures which strike the eye; I hate to appear on the back ground of the picture.

TO MISS RIVERS

LETTER 8 QUEBEC, AUGUST 24: You can't think, my dear, what a fund of useful knowledge I have treasur'd up during my journey from Montreal. This colony is a rich mine yet unopen'd; I do not mean of gold and silver, but of what are of much more real value, corn and cattle. Nothing is wanting but encouragement and cultivation; the Canadians are at their ease even without labour; nature is here a bounteous mother, who pours forth her gifts almost unsolicited: bigotry, stupidity, and laziness, united, have not been able to keep the peasantry poor. I rejoice to find such admirable capabilities where I propose to fix my dominion.

I was hospitably entertained by the curés all the way down, tho' they are in general but ill-provided for: the parochial clergy are useful every where, but I have a great aversion to monks, those drones in the political hive, whose study seems to be to make themselves as useless to the world as possible. Think too of the shocking indelicacy of many of them, who make it a point of religion to abjure linen, and wear their habits till they drop off. How astonishing that any mind should suppose the Deity an enemy to cleanliness! the Jewish religion was hardly any thing else.

I paid my respects wherever I stopped, to the *seigneuress* of the village; for as to the seigneurs, except two or three, if they had not wives, they would not be worth visiting.

33

I am every day more pleased with the women here; and, if I was gallant, should be in danger of being a convert to the French style of gallantry; which certainly debases the mind much less than ours.

But what is all this to my Emily? How I envy Sir George! what happiness has Heaven for him, if he has a soul to taste it!

I really must not think of her; I found so much delight in her conversation, it was quite time to come away; I am almost ashamed to own how much difficulty I found in leaving her: do you know I have scarce slept since? This is absurd, but I cannot help it; which by the way is an admirable excuse for any thing.

I have been come but two hours, and am going to Silleri, to pay my compliments to your friend Miss Fermor, who arrived with her father, who comes to join his regiment, since I left Quebec. I hear there has been a very fine importation of English ladies during my absence. I am sorry I have not time to visit the rest, but I go to-morrow morning to the Indian village for a fortnight, and have several letters to write to-night.

Adieu! I am interrupted.

Yours,

ED. RIVERS

TO MRS MELMOTH, AT MONTREAL

LETTER 9   QUEBEC, AUGUST 24: I cannot, Madam, express my obligation to you for having added a postscript to Major Melmoth's letter: I am sure he will excuse my answering the whole to you; if not, I beg he may know that I shall be very pert about it, being much more solicitous to please you than him, for a thousand reasons too tedious to mention.

I thought you had more penetration than to suppose me indifferent: on the contrary, sensibility is my fault; though it is not your little every-day beauties who can excite it: I have admirable dispositions to love, though I am hard to please: in short, *I am not cruel, I am only nice*: do but you, or your divine friend, give me leave to wear your chains, and you shall soon be convinced I can love *like an angel*, when I set in earnest about it. But, alas! you are married, and in love with your husband; and your friend is in a situation still more unfavourable to a lover's hopes. This is particularly unfortunate, as you are the only two of your bewitching sex in Canada, for whom my heart feels the least sympathy. To be plain, but don't tell the little Major, I am more than half in love with you both, and, if I was the grand Turk, should certainly fit out a fleet, to seize, and bring you to my seraglio.

There is one virtue I admire extremely in you both; I mean, that humane and tender compassion for the poor men, which prompts you to be always seen together; if you appeared separate, where is the hero who could resist either of you?

You ask me how I like the French ladies at Montreal: I think them extremely pleasing; and many of them handsome; I thought Madame L—— so, even near you and Miss Montague; which is, I think, saying as much as can be said on the subject.

I have just heard by accident that Sir George is arrived at Montreal. Assure Miss Montague, no one can be more warmly interested in her happiness than I am: she is the most perfect work of Heaven; may she be the happiest! I feel much more on this occasion than I can express: a mind like hers must, in marriage, be exquisitely happy or miserable: my friendship makes me tremble for her, notwithstanding the worthy character I have heard of Sir George.

I will defer till another time what I had to say to Major Melmoth.

I have the honour to be,
Madam,
Yours etc.

ED. RIVERS

LETTER 10 SILLERI, AUGUST 24: I have been a month arrived, my dear, without having seen your brother, who is at Montreal, but I am told is expected to-day. I have spent my time however very agreeably. I know not what the winter may be, but I am enchanted with the beauty of this country in summer; bold, picturesque, romantic, nature reigns here in all her wanton luxuriance, adorned by a thousand wild graces which mock the cultivated beauties of Europe. The scenery about the town is infinitely lovely; the prospect extensive, and diversified by a variety of hills, woods, rivers, cascades, intermingled with smiling farms and cottages, and bounded by distant mountains which seem to scale the very Heavens.

The days are much hotter here than in England, but the

heat is more supportable from the breezes which always spring up about noon; and the evenings are charming beyond expression. We have much thunder and lightening, but very few instances of their being fatal: the thunder is more magnificent and aweful than in Europe, and the lightening brighter and more beautiful; I have even seen it of a clear pale purple, resembling the gay tints of the morning.

The verdure is equal to that of England, and in the evening acquires an unspeakable beauty from the lucid splendour of the fire-flies sparkling like a thousand little stars on the trees and on the grass.

There are two very noble falls of water near Quebec, la Chaudière and Montmorenci: the former is a prodigious sheet of water, rushing over the wildest rocks, and forming a scene grotesque, irregular, astonishing: the latter, less wild, less irregular, but more pleasing and more majestic, falls from an immense height, down the side of a romantic mountain, into the river St Lawrence, opposite the most smiling part of the island of Orleans, to the cultivated charms of which it forms the most striking and agreeable contrast.

The river of the same name, which supplies the cascade of Montmorenci, is the most lovely of all inanimate objects: but why do I call it inanimate? It almost breathes; I no longer wonder at the enthusiasm of Greece and Rome; 'twas from objects resembling this their mythology took its rise; it seems the residence of a thousand deities.

Paint to yourself a stupendous rock burst as it were in sunder by the hands of nature, to give passage to a small, but very deep and beautiful river; and forming on each side a regular and magnificent wall, crowned with the noblest woods that can be imagined; the sides of these romantic walls adorned with a variety of the gayest flowers, and in many places little streams of the purest water gushing through, and losing themselves in the river below: a thousand natural grottoes in the rock make you suppose yourself in the abode of the Nereids; as a little island, covered with flowering shrubs, about a mile above the falls, where the river enlarges itself as if to give it room, seems intended for the throne of the river goddess. Beyond this, the rapids, formed by the irregular projections of the rock, which in some places seem almost to meet, rival in beauty, as they excel in variety, the cascade itself, and close this little world of enchantment.

In short, the loveliness of this fairy scene alone more than pays the fatigues of my voyage; and, if I ever murmur at having crossed the Atlantic, remind me that I have seen the river Montmorenci.

I can give you a very imperfect account of the people here; I have only examined the landscape about Quebec, and have given very little attention to the figures; the French ladies are handsome, but as to the beaux, they appear to me not at all dangerous, and one might safely walk in a wood by moonlight with the most agreeable Frenchman here. I am surpriz'd the Canadian ladies take such pains to seduce our men from us; but I think it a little hard we have no temptation to make reprisals.

I am at present at an extreme pretty farm on the banks of the river St Lawrence; the house stands at the foot of a steep mountain covered with a variety of trees, forming a verdant sloping wall, which rises in a kind of regular confusion,

"Shade above shade, a woody theatre,"

and has in front this noble river, on which the ships continually passing present to the delighted eye the most charming moving picture imaginable; I never saw a place so formed to inspire that pleasing lassitude, that divine inclination to saunter, which may not improperly be called, the luxurious indolence of the country. I intend to build a temple here to the charming goddess of laziness.

A gentleman is just coming down the winding path on the side of the hill, whom by his air I take to be your brother. Adieu! I must receive him: my father is at Quebec.

Yours,

ARABELLA FERMOR

Your brother has given me a very pleasing piece of intelligence: my friend Emily Montague is at Montreal, and is going to be married to great advantage; I must write to her immediately, and insist on her making me a visit before she marries. She came to America two years ago, with her uncle Colonel Montague, who died here, and I imagined was gone back to England; she is however at Montreal with Mrs Melmoth, a distant relation of her mother's. Adieu! *ma très chère!*

LETTER 11   QUEBEC, SEPTEMBER 10: I find, my dear, that absence and amusement are the best remedies for a beginning passion; I have passed a fortnight at the Indian village of Lorette, where the novelty of the scene, and the enquiries I have been led to make into their ancient religion and manners, have been of a thousand times more service to me than all the reflection in the world would have been.

I will own to you that I staid too long at Montreal, or rather at Major Melmoth's; to be six weeks in the same house with one of the most amiable, most pleasing of women, was a trying situation to a heart full of sensibility, and of a sensibility which has been hitherto, from a variety of causes, a good deal restrained. I should have avoided the danger from the first, had it appeared to me what it really was; but I thought myself secure in the consideration of her engagements, a defence however which I found grow weaker every day.

But to my savages: other nations talk of liberty, they possess it; nothing can be more astonishing than to see a little village of about thirty or forty families, the small remains of the Hurons, almost exterminated by long and continual war with the Iroquoise, preserve their independence in the midst of an European colony consisting of seventy thousand inhabitants; yet the fact is true of the savages of Lorette; they assert and they maintain that independence with a spirit truly noble. One of our company having said something which an Indian understood as a supposition that they had been *subjects* of France, his eyes struck fire, he stop'd him abruptly, contrary to their respectful and sensible custom of never interrupting the person who speaks, "You mistake, brother," said he: "we are subjects to no prince; a savage is free all over the world." And he spoke only truth; they are not only free as a people, but every individual is perfectly so. Lord of himself, at once subject and master, a savage knows no superior, a circumstance which has a striking effect on his behaviour; unawed by rank or riches, distinctions unknown amongst his own nation, he would enter as unconcerned, would possess all his powers as freely in the palace of an oriental monarch, as in the cottage of the meanest peasant: 'tis the species, 'tis man, 'tis his equal he respects, without regarding the gaudy trappings, the accidental advantages, to which polished nations pay homage.

I have taken some pains to develop their present, as well as past, religious sentiments, because the Jesuit missionaries have boasted so much of their conversion; and find they have rather engrafted a few of the most plain and simple truths of Christianity on their ancient superstitions, than exchanged one faith for another; they are baptized, and even submit to what they themselves call the *yoke* of confession, and worship according to the outward forms of the Romish church, the drapery of which cannot but strike minds unused to splendour; but their belief is very little changed, except that the women seem to pay great reverence to the Virgin, perhaps because flattering to the sex. They anciently believed in one God, the ruler and creator of the universe, whom they called the *Great Spirit* and the *Master of Life*; in the sun as his image and representative; in a multitude of inferior spirits and demons; and in a future state of rewards and punishments, or, to use their own phrase, in *a country of souls*. They reverenced the spirits of their departed heroes, but it does not appear that they paid them any religious adoration. Their morals were more pure, their manners more simple, than those of polished nations, except in what regarded the intercourse of the sexes: the young women before marriage were indulged in great libertinism, hid however under the most reserved and decent exterior. They held adultery in abhorrence, and with the more reason as their marriages were dissolvable at pleasure. The missionaries are said to have found no difficulty so great in gaining them to Christianity, as that of persuading them to marry for life: they regarded the Christian system of marriage as contrary to the laws of nature and reason; and asserted that, as the *Great Spirit* formed us to be happy, it was opposing his will, to continue together when otherwise.

The sex we have so unjustly excluded from power in Europe have a great share in the Huron government; the chief is chose by the matrons from amongst the nearest male relations, by the female line, of him he is to succeed; and is generally an aunt's or sister's son; a custom which, if we examine strictly into the principle on which it is founded, seems a little to contradict what we are told of the extreme chastity of the married ladies.

The power of the chief is extremely limited; he seems rather to advise his people as a father than command them as a master: yet, as his commands are always reasonable, and for the general good, no prince in the world is so well obeyed. They have a supreme council of ancients, into which every man enters of course at an age fixed, and another of assistants to the chief on common occasions, the members of which are like him elected by the matrons: I am pleased with this last regulation, as women are, beyond all doubt, the best judges of the merit of men; and I should be extremely pleased to see it adopted in England: canvassing for elections would then be the most agreeable thing in the world, and I am sure the ladies would give their votes on much more generous principles than we do. In the true sense of the word, *we* are the savages, who so impolitely deprive you of the common rights of citizenship, and leave you no power but that of which we cannot deprive you, the resistless power of your charms. By the way, I don't think you are obliged in conscience to obey laws you have had no share in making; your plea would certainly be at least as good as that of the Americans, about which we every day hear so much.

The Hurons have no positive laws; yet being a people not numerous, with a strong sense of honour, and in that state of equality which gives no food to the most tormenting passions of the human heart, and the council of ancients having a power to punish atrocious crimes, which power however they very seldom find occasion to use, they live together in a tranquillity and order which appears to us surprizing.

In more numerous Indian nations, I am told, every village has its chief and its councils, and is perfectly independent on the rest; but on great occasions summon a general council, to which every village sends deputies.

Their language is at once sublime and melodious; but, having much fewer ideas, it is impossible it can be so copious as those of Europe: the pronunciation of the men is guttural, but that of the women extremely soft and pleasing; without understanding one word of the language, the sound of it is very agreeable to me. Their style even in speaking French is bold and metaphorical: and I am told is on important occasions extremely sublime. Even in common conversation they speak in figures, of which I have this moment an instance. A savage woman was wounded lately in defending an English family from the drunken rage of one of her nation. I asked her after her wound; "It is well," said she; "my sisters at Quebec (meaning the English ladies) have been kind to me; and piastres, you know, are very healing."

They have no idea of letters, no alphabet, nor is their language reducible to rules: 'tis by painting they preserve the memory of the only events which interest them, or that they think worth recording, the conquests gained over their enemies in war.

When I speak of their paintings, I should not omit that, though extremely rude, they have a strong resemblance to the Chinese, a circumstance which struck me the more, as it is not the style of nature. Their dances also, the most lively pantomimes I ever saw, and especially the dance of peace, exhibit

40

variety of attitudes resembling the figures on Chinese fans; nor have their features and complexion less likeness to the pictures we see of the Tartars, as their wandering manner of life, before they became christians, was the same.

If I thought it necessary to suppose they were not natives of the country, and that America was peopled later than the other quarters of the world, I should imagine them the descendants of Tartars; as nothing can be more easy than their passage from Asia, from which America is probably not divided; or, if it is, by a very narrow channel. But I leave this to those who are better informed, being a subject on which I honestly confess my ignorance.

I have already observed, that they retain most of their ancient superstitions. I should particularize their belief in dreams, of which folly even repeated disappointments cannot cure them: they have also an unlimited faith in their *powawers*, or conjurers, of whom there is one in every Indian village, who is at once physician, orator, and divine, and who is consulted as an oracle on every occasion. As I happened to smile at the recital a savage was making of a prophetic dream, from which he assured us of the death of an English officer whom I knew to be alive, "You Europeans," said he, "are the most unreasonable people in the world; you laugh at our belief in dreams, and yet expect us to believe things a thousand times more incredible."

Their general character is difficult to describe; made up of contrary and even contradictory qualities; they are indolent, tranquil, quiet, humane in peace; active, restless, cruel, ferocious in war: courteous, attentive, hospitable, and even polite, when kindly treated; haughty, stern, vindictive, when they are not; and their resentment is the more to be dreaded, as they hold it a a point of honour to dissemble their sense of an injury till they find an opportunity to revenge it.

They are patient of cold and heat, of hunger and thirst, even beyond all belief when necessity requires, passing whole days, and even three or four days together, without food, in the woods, when on the watch for an enemy, or even on their hunting parties; yet indulging themselves in their feasts even to the most brutal degree of intemperance. They despise death, and suffer the most excruciating tortures not only without a groan, but with an air of triumph; singing their death song, deriding their tormentors, and threatening them with the vengeance of their surviving friends: yet hold it honourable to fly before an enemy that appears the least superior in number or force.

Deprived by their extreme ignorance, and that indolence which nothing but their ardour for war can surmount, of

41

all the conveniences, as well as elegant refinements of polished life; strangers to the softer passions, love being with them on the same footing as amongst their fellow-tenants of the woods; their lives appear to me rather tranquil than happy: they have fewer cares, but they have also much fewer enjoyments, than fall to our share. I am told, however, that, though insensible to love, they are not without affections, are extremely awake to friendship, and passionately fond of their children.

They are of a copper colour, which is rendered more unpleasing by a quantity of coarse red on their cheeks; but the children, when born, are of a pale silver white; perhaps their indelicate custom of greasing their bodies, and their being so much exposed to the air and sun even from infancy, may cause that total change of complexion, which I know not how otherwise to account for: their hair is black and shining, the women's very long, parted at the top, and combed back, tied behind, and often twisted with a thong of leather, which they think very ornamental: the dress of both sexes is a close jacket, reaching to their knees, with spatterdashes, all of coarse blue cloth; shoes of deer-skin, embroidered with porcupine quills, and sometimes with silver spangles; and a blanket thrown across their shoulders, and fastened before with a kind of bodkin, with necklaces, and other ornaments of beads or shells.

They are in general tall, well made, and agile to the last degree; have a lively imagination, a strong memory; and, as far as their interests are concerned, are very dextrous politicians.

Their address is cold and reserved; but their treatment of strangers, and the unhappy, infinitely kind and hospitable. A very worthy priest, with whom I am acquainted at Quebec, was some years since shipwrecked in December on the island of Anticosti: after a variety of distresses, not difficult to be imagined on an island without inhabitants, during the severity of a winter even colder than that of Canada; he, with the small remains of his companions who survived such complicated distress, early in the spring, reached the main land in their boat, and wandered to a cabbin of savages; the ancient of which, having heard his story, bid him enter, and liberally supplied their wants: "Approach, brother," said he; "the unhappy have a right to our assistance; we are men, and cannot but feel for the distresses which happen to men"; a sentiment which has a strong resemblance to a celebrated one in a Greek tragedy.

You will not expect more from me on this subject, as my residence here has been short, and I can only be said to catch a few marking features flying. I am unable to give you a picture at full length.

Nothing astonishes me so much as to find their manners so little changed by their intercourse with the Europeans; they seem to have learnt nothing of us but excess in drinking.

The situation of the village is very fine, on an eminence, gently rising to a thick wood at some distance, a beautiful little serpentine river in front, on which are a bridge, a mill, and a small cascade, at such a distance as to be very pleasing objects from their houses; and a cultivated country, intermixed with little woods lying between them and Quebec, from which they are distant only nine very short miles.

What a letter have I written! I shall quit my post of historian to your friend Miss Fermor; the ladies love writing much better than we do; and I should perhaps be only just, if I said they write better.

Adieu!

ED. RIVERS

TO MISS RIVERS, CLARGES STREET

LETTER 12 QUEBEC, SEPTEMBER 12: I yesterday morning received a letter from Major Melmoth, to introduce to my acquaintance Sir George Clayton, who brought it; he wanted no other introduction to me than his being dear to the most amiable woman breathing; in virtue of that claim, he may command every civility, every attention in my power. He breakfasted with me yesterday: we were two hours alone, and had a great deal of conversation; we afterwards spent the day together very agreeably, on a party of pleasure in the country.

I am going with him this afternoon to visit Miss Fermor, to whom he has a letter from the divine Emily, which he is to deliver himself.

He is very handsome, but not of my favourite style of beauty: extremely fair and blooming, with fine features, light hair and eyes; his countenance not absolutely heavy, but inanimate, and to my taste insipid: finely made, not ungenteel, but without that easy air of the world which I prefer to the most exact symmetry without it. In short, he is what the country ladies in England call *a sweet pretty man*. He dresses well, has the finest horses and the handsomest liveries I have seen in

Canada. His manner is civil but cold, his conversation sensible but not spirited; he seems to be a man rather to approve than to love. Will you excuse me if I say, he resembles the form my imagination paints of Prometheus's man of clay, before he stole the celestial fire to animate him?

Perhaps I scrutinize him too strictly; perhaps I am prejudiced in my judgment by the very high idea I had form'd of the man whom Emily Montague could love. I will own to you, that I thought it impossible for her to be pleased with meer beauty; and I cannot even now change my opinion; I shall find some latent fire, some hidden spark, when we are better acquainted.

I intend to be very intimate with him, to endeavour to see into his very soul; I am hard to please in a husband for my Emily; he must have spirit, he must have sensibility, or he cannot make her happy.

He thank'd me for my civility to Miss Montague: do you know I thought him impertinent? and I am not yet sure he was not so, though I saw he meant to be polite.

He comes: our horses are at the door. Adieu!

Yours,

ED. RIVERS

Eight in the evening

We are return'd: I every hour like him less. There were several ladies, French and English, with Miss Fermor, all on the rack to engage the Baronet's attention; you have no notion of the effect of a title in America. To do the ladies justice however, he really look'd very handsome; the ride, and the civilities he receiv'd from a circle of pretty women, for they were well chose, gave a glow to his complexion extremely favourable to his desire of pleasing, which, through all his calmness, it was impossible not to observe; he even attempted once or twice to be lively, but fail'd: vanity itself could not inspire him with vivacity; yet vanity is certainly his ruling passion, if such a piece of still life can be said to have any passions at all.

What a charm, my dear Lucy, is there in sensibility! 'Tis the magnet which attracts all to itself: virtue may command esteem, understanding and talents admiration, beauty a transient desire; but 'tis sensibility alone which can inspire love.

Yet the tender, the sensible Emily Montague—no, my dear, 'tis impossible: she may fancy she loves him, but it is not in nature; unless she extremely mistakes his character. His *approbation* of her, for he cannot feel a livelier sentiment, may at present, when with her, raise him a little above his natural vegetative state, but after marriage he will certainly sink into it again.

If I have the least judgment in men, he will be a cold, civil, inattentive husband; a tasteless, insipid, silent companion; a tranquil, frozen, unimpassion'd lover; his insensibility will secure her from rivals, his vanity will give her all the drapery of happiness; her friends will congratulate her choice; she will be the envy of her own sex; without giving positive offence, he will every moment wound, because he is a stranger to all the fine feelings of a heart like hers; she will seek in vain the friend, the lover, she expected; yet, scarce knowing of what to complain, she will accuse herself of caprice, and be astonish'd to find herself wretched with *the best husband in the world*.

I tremble for her happiness; I know how few of my own sex are to be found who have the lively sensibility of yours, and of those few how many wear out their hearts by a life of gallantry and dissipation, and bring only apathy and disgust into marriage. I know few men capable of making her happy; but this Sir George—my Lucy, I have not patience.

Did I tell you all the men here are in love with your friend Bell Fermor? The women all hate her, which is an unequivocal proof that she pleases the other sex.

TO MISS FERMOR, AT SILLERI

LETTER 13 MONTREAL, SEPTEMBER 2: My dearest Bell will better imagine than I can describe, the pleasure it gave me to hear of her being in Canada; I am impatient to see her, but as Mrs Melmoth comes in a fortnight to Quebec, I know she will excuse my waiting to come with her. My visit however is to Silleri; I long to see my dear girl, to tell her a thousand little trifles interesting only to friendship.

You congratulate me, my dear, on the pleasing prospect I have before me; on my approaching marriage with a man young, rich, lovely, enamour'd, and of an amiable character.

Yes, my dear, I am oblig'd to my uncle for his choice; Sir George is all you have heard; and, without doubt, loves me, as he marries me with such an inferiority of fortune. I am very happy certainly; how is it possible I should be otherwise?

I could indeed wish my tenderness for him more lively, but perhaps my wishes are romantic. I prefer him to all his sex, but wish my preference was of a less languid nature; there is something in it more like friendship than love; I see him with pleasure, but I part from him without regret; yet he deserves my affection, and I can have no objection to him which is not founded in caprice.

You say true; Colonel Rivers is very amiable; he pass'd six weeks with us, yet we found his conversation always new; he is the man on earth of whom one would wish to make a friend; I think I could already trust him with every sentiment of my soul; I have even more confidence in him than in Sir George whom I love; his manner is soft, attentive, insinuating, and particularly adapted to please women. Without designs, without pretentions; he steals upon you in the character of a friend, because there is not the least appearance of his ever being a lover; he seems to take such an interest in your happiness, as gives him a right to know your every thought. Don't you think, my dear, these kind of men are dangerous? Take care of yourself, my dear Bell; as to me, I am secure in my situation.

Sir George is to have the pleasure of delivering this to you, and comes again in a few days; love him for my sake, though he deserves it for his own. I assure you, he is extremely worthy.

Adieu! my dear.

Your affectionate

EMILY MONTAGUE

TO JOHN TEMPLE, ESQ; PALL MALL

LETTER 14 QUEBEC, SEPTEMBER 15: Believe me, Jack, you are wrong; this vagrant taste is unnatural, and does not lead to happiness; your eager pursuit of pleasure defeats itself; love gives no true delight but where the heart is attach'd, and you do not give yours time to fix. Such is our unhappy frailty, that the tenderest passion may wear out, and another succeed, but the love of change merely as change is not in nature; where it is a real taste, 'tis a depraved one. Boys are inconstant from vanity and affectation, old men from decay of passion; but men, and particularly men of sense, find their happiness only in that lively attachment of which it is impossible for more than one to be the object. Love is an intellectual pleasure, and even the senses will be weakly affected where the heart is silent.

You will find this truth confirmed even within the walls of the seraglio; amidst this crowd of rival beauties, eager to please, one happy fair generally reigns in the heart of the sultan; the rest serve only to gratify his pride and ostentation, and are regarded by him with the same indifference as the furniture of his superb palace, of which they may be said to make a part.

With your estate, you should marry; I have as many objections to the state as you can have; I mean, on the footing marriage is at present. But of this I am certain, that two persons at once delicate and sensible, united by friendship, by taste, by a conformity of sentiment, by that lively ardent tender inclination which alone deserves the name of love, will find happiness in marriage, which is in vain sought in any other kind of attachment.

You are so happy as to have the power of chusing; you are rich, and have not the temptation to a mercenary engagement. Look round you for a companion, a confidante; a tender amiable friend, with all the charms of a mistress: above all, be certain of her affection, that you engage, that you fill her whole soul. Find such a woman, my dear Temple, and you cannot make too much haste to be happy.

I have a thousand things to say to you, but am setting off immediately with Sir George Clayton, to meet the lieutenant-governor at Montreal; a piece of respect which I should pay with the most lively pleasure, if it did not give me the opportunity of seeing the woman in the world I most admire. I am not however going to set you the example of marrying: I am not so happy; she is engaged to the gentleman who goes up with me. Adieu!

Yours,

ED. RIVERS

TO MISS MONTAGUE, AT MONTREAL

LETTER 15 SILLERI, SEPTEMBER 16: Take care, my dear Emily, you do not fall into the common error of sensible and delicate minds, that of refining away your happiness.

Sir George is handsome as an Adonis; you allow him to be of an amiable character; he is rich, young, well born, and loves you; you will have fine clothes, fine jewels, a fine house, a coach and six: all the *douceurs* of marriage, with an extreme pretty fellow, who is fond of you, whom *you see with pleasure, and prefer to all his sex*; and yet you are discontented, because you have not for him at twenty-four the romantic passion of fifteen, or rather that ideal passion which perhaps never existed but in imagination.

To be happy in this world, it is necessary not to raise one's ideas too high: if I loved a man of Sir George's fortune half as well as by your own account you love him, I should not hesitate one moment about marrying; but sit down contented with ease, affluence, and an agreeable man, without expecting to find life what it certainly is not, a state of continual rapture. 'Tis, I am afraid, my dear, your misfortune to have too much sensibility to be happy.

I could moralize exceedingly well this morning on the vanity of human wishes and expectations, and the folly of hoping for felicity in this vile sublunary world: but the subject is a little exhausted, and I have a passion for being original. I think all the moral writers, who have set off with promising to shew us the road to happiness, have obligingly ended with telling us there is no such thing; a conclusion extremely consoling, and which if they had drawn before they set pen to paper, would have saved both themselves and their readers an infinity of trouble. This fancy of hunting for what one knows is not to be found, is really an ingenious way of amusing both one's self and the world: I wish people would either write to some purpose, or be so good as not to write at all.

I believe I shall set about writing a system of ethics myself, which shall be short, clear, and comprehensive; nearer the Epicurean perhaps than the Stoic; but rural, refined, and sentimental; rural by all means; for who does not know that virtue is a country gentlewoman? all the good mammas will tell you, there is no such being to be heard of in town.

I shall certainly be glad to see you, my dear; though I foresee strange revolutions *in the state of Denmark* from this event; at present I have all the men to myself, and you must know I have a prodigious aversion to divided empire: however, 'tis some comfort they all know you are going to be married. You may come, Emily; only be so obliging to bring Sir George along with you: in your present situation, you are not so very formidable.

The men here, as I said before, are all dying for me; there are many handsomer women, but I flatter them, and the dear creatures cannot resist it. I am a very good girl to women, but naturally artful (if you will allow the expression) to the other sex; I can blush, look down, stifle a sigh, flutter my fan, and seem so agreeably confused—you have no notion, my dear, what fools men are. If you had not got the start of me, I would have had your little white-haired baronet in a week, and yet I don't take him to be made of very combustible materials; rather mild, composed, and pretty, I believe; but he has vanity, which is quite enough for my purpose.

Either your love or Colonel Rivers will have the honour to deliver this letter; 'tis rather cruel to take them both from us at once; however, we shall soon be made amends; for we shall have a torrent of beaux with the general.

Don't you think the sun in this country vastly more chearing than in England? I am charmed with the sun, to say nothing of the moon, though to be sure I never saw a moonlight night that deserved the name till I came to America.

Mon cher père desires a thousand compliments; you know he has been in love with you ever since you were seven years old; he is vastly better for his voyage, and the clear air of Canada, and looks ten years younger than before he set out.

Adieu! I am going to ramble in the woods, and pick berries, with a little smiling civil captain, who is enamoured of me: a pretty rural amusement for lovers!

Good morrow, my dear Emily,

Yours,

A. FERMOR

TO MISS RIVERS, CLARGES STREET

LETTER 16 SILLERI, SEPTEMBER 18: Your brother, my dear, is gone to Montreal with Sir George Clayton, of whom I suppose you have heard, and who is going to marry a friend of mine, to pay a visit to *Monsieur le General*, who is arrived there. The men in Canada, the English I mean, are eternally changing place, even when they have not so pleasing a call: travelling is cheap and amusing, the prospects lovely, the weather inviting; and there are no very lively pleasures at present to attach them either to Quebec or Montreal, so that they divide themselves between both.

This fancy of the men, which is extremely the mode, makes an agreeable circulation of inamoratos, which serves to vary the amusement of the ladies; so that upon the whole 'tis a pretty fashion, and deserves encouragement.

You expect too much of your brother, my dear; the

summer is charming here, but with no such very striking difference from that of England, as to give room to say a vast deal on the subject; though I believe, if you will please to compare our letters, you will find, putting us together, we cut a pretty figure in the descriptive way; at least if your brother tells me truth.

You may expect a very well-painted frost-piece from me in the winter; as to the present season, it is just like any fine autumn in England: I may add, that the beauty of the nights is much beyond my power of description: a constant *Aurora borealis*, without a cloud in the heavens; and a moon so resplendent that you may see to read the smallest print by its light; one has nothing to wish but that it was full moon every night. Our evening walks are delicious, especially at Silleri, where 'tis the pleasantest thing in the world to listen to soft nonsense.

"Whilst the moon dances through the trembling leaves"

(A line I stole from Philander and Sylvia): But to return:

The French ladies never walk but at night, which shews their good taste; and then only within the walls of Quebec, which does not: they saunter slowly, after supper, on a particular battery, which is a kind of little Mall: they have no idea of walking in the country, nor the least feeling of the lovely scene around them; there are many of them who never saw the falls of Montmorenci, though little more than an hour's drive from the town. They seem born without the smallest portion of curiosity, or any idea of the pleasures of the imagination, or indeed any pleasure but that of being admired; love, or rather coquetry, dress, and devotion, seem to share all their hours: yet, as they are lively, and in general handsome, the men are very ready to excuse their want of knowledge.

There are two ladies in the province, I am told, who read; but both of them are above fifty, and they are regarded as prodigies of erudition.

Eight in the evening

Absolutely, Lucy, I will marry a savage, and turn squaw (a pretty soft name for an Indian princess!): never was any thing delightful as their lives; they talk of French husbands, but commend me to an Indian one, who lets his wife ramble five hundred miles, without asking where she is going.

I was sitting after dinner with a book, in a thicket of hawthorn near the beach, when a loud laugh called my attention to the river, where I saw a canoe of savages making to the shore; there were six women, and two or three children, without one man amongst them: they landed, tied the canoe to the root of a tree, and finding out the most agreeable shady spot amongst the bushes with which the beach was covered, which happened to be very near me, made a fire, on which they laid some fish to broil, and, fetching water from the river, sat down on the grass to their frugal repast.

I stole softly to the house, and ordering a servant to bring some wine and cold provisions, returned to my squaws: I asked them in French if they were of Lorette; they shook their heads: I repeated the question in English, when the oldest of the women told me, they were not; that their country was on the borders of New England; that, their husbands being on a hunting party in the woods, curiosity, and the desire of seeing their brethren the English who had conquered Quebec, had brought them up the great river, down which they should return as soon as they had seen Montreal. She courteously asked me to sit down, and eat with them, which I complied with, and produced my part of the feast. We soon became good company, and *brighten'd the chain of friendship* with two bottles of wine, which put them into such spirits, that they danced, sung, shook me by the hand, and grew so very fond of me, that I began to be afraid I should not easily get rid of them. They were very unwilling to part with me; but, after two or three very ridiculous hours, I with some difficulty prevailed on the ladies to pursue their voyage, having first replenished their canoe with provisions and a few bottles of wine, and given them a letter of recommendation to your brother, that they might be in no distress at Montreal.

Adieu! my father is just come in, and has brought some company with him from Quebec to supper.

Yours ever,

A. FERMOR

Don't you think, my dear, my good sisters the squaws seem to live something the kind of life of our gypsies? The idea struck me as they were dancing. I assure you, there is a good deal of resemblance in their persons: I have seen a fine old seasoned female gypsy, of as dark a complexion as a savage: they are all equally marked as children of the sun.

LETTER 17   REPENTIGNY, SEPT. 18, TEN AT NIGHT: I study my fellow traveller closely; his character, indeed, is not difficult to ascertain; his feelings are dull, nothing makes the least impression on him; he is as insensible to the various beauties of the charming country through which we have travelled as the very Canadian peasants themselves who inhabit it. I watched his eyes at some of the most beautiful prospects, and saw not the least gleam of pleasure there: I introduced him here to an extreme handsome French lady, and as lively as she is handsome, the wife of an officer who is of my acquaintance; the same tasteless composure prevailed; he complained of fatigue, and retired to his apartment at eight: the family are now in bed, and I have an hour to give to my dear Lucy.

He admires Emily because he has seen her admired by all the world, but he cannot taste her charms of himself; they are not of a style to please him: I cannot support the thought of such a woman's being so lost; there are a thousand insensible good young women to be found, who would doze away life with him and be happy.

A rich, sober, sedate, presbyterian citizen's daughter, educated by her grandmother in the country, who would roll about with him in unwieldy splendour, and dream away a lazy existence, would be the proper wife for him. Is it for him, a lifeless composition of earth and water, to unite himself to the active elements which compose my divine Emily?

Adieu! my dear! we set out early in the morning for Montreal.

Your affectionate

ED. RIVERS

LETTER 18   MONTREAL, SEPT. 19, ELEVEN O'CLOCK: No, my dear, it is impossible she can love him; his dull soul is ill-suited to hers; heavy, unmeaning, formal; a slave to rules, to ceremony, to *etiquette*, he has not an idea above those of a gentleman usher. He has been three hours in town without seeing her; dressing, and waiting to pay his compliments first to the general, who is riding, and every minute expected back. I am all impatience, though only her friend, but think it would be indecent in me to go without him, and look like a design of reproaching his coldness. How differently are we formed! I should have stole a moment to see the woman I loved from the first prince in the universe.

The general is returned. Adieu! till our visit is over; we go from thence to Major Melmoth's, whose family I should have told you are in town, and not half a street from us. What a soul of fire has this *lover*! 'Tis to profane the word to use it in speaking of him.

One o'clock

I am mistaken, Lucy; astonishing as it is, she loves him; this dull clod of uniformed earth has touched the lively soul of my Emily. Love is indeed the child of caprice; I will not say of sympathy, for what sympathy can there be between two hearts so different? I am hurt, she is lowered in my esteem; I expected to find in the man she loved, a mind sensible and tender as her own.

I repeat it, my dear Lucy, she loves him; I observed her when we entered the room; she blushed, she turned pale, she trembled, her voice faltered; every look spoke the strong emotion of her soul.

She is paler than when I saw her last; she is, I think, less beautiful, but more touching than ever; there is a languor in her air, a softness in her countenance, which are the genuine marks of a heart in love; all the tenderness of her soul is in her eyes.

Shall I own to you all my injustice? I hate this man for having the happiness to please her: I cannot even behave to him with the politeness due to every gentleman.

I begin to fear my weakness is greater than I supposed.

22nd in the evening

I am certainly mad, Lucy; what right have I to expect! —you will scarce believe the excess of my folly. I went after dinner to Major Melmoth's; I found Emily at piquet with Sir George; can you conceive that I fancied myself ill-used, that I scarce spoke to her, and returned immediately home, though strongly pressed to spend the evening there. I walked two or three times about my room, took my hat, and went to visit the handsomest Frenchwoman at Montreal, whose windows are directly opposite to Major Melmoth's; in the excess of my anger,

I asked this lady to dance with me to-morrow at a little ball we are to have out of town. Can you imagine any behaviour more childish? It would have been scarce pardonable at sixteen.

Adieu! my letter is called for. I will write to you again in a few days.

Yours,

ED. RIVERS

Major Melmoth tells me, they are to be married in a month at Quebec, and to embark immediately for England. I will not be there; I cannot bear to see her devote herself to wretchedness: she will be the most unhappy of her sex with this man; I see clearly into his character; his virtue is the meer absence of vice; his good qualities are all of the negative kind.

TO MISS FERMOR, AT SILLERI

LETTER 19 MONTREAL, SEPT. 24: I have but a moment, my dear, to acknowledge your last; this week has been a continual hurry.

You mistake me; it is not the romantic passion of fifteen I wish to feel, but that tender lively friendship which alone can give charms to so intimate a union as that of marriage. I wish a greater conformity in our characters, in our sentiments, in our tastes.

But I will say no more on this subject till I have the pleasure of seeing you at Silleri. Mrs Melmoth and I come in a ship which sails in a day or two; they tell us, it is the most agreeable way of coming: Colonel Rivers is so polite, as to stay to accompany us down: Major Melmoth asked Sir George, but he preferred the pleasure of parading into Quebec, and shewing his fine horses and fine person to advantage, to that of attending his mistress: shall I own to you that I am hurt at this instance of his neglect, as I know his attendance on the general was not expected? His situation was more than a sufficient excuse; it was highly improper for two women to go to Quebec alone; it is in some degree so that any other man should accompany me at this time: my pride is extremely wounded. I expect a thousand times more attention from him since his acquisition of fortune; it is with pain I tell you, my dear friend, he seems to shew me much less. I will not descend to suppose he presumes on this increase of fortune, but he presumes on the inclination he supposes I have for him; an inclination, however, not violent enough to make me submit to the least ill-treatment from him.

In my present state of mind, I am extremely hard to please; either his behaviour or my temper have suffered a change. I know not how it is, but I see his faults in a much stronger light than I have ever seen them before. I am alarmed at the coldness of his disposition, so ill-suited to the sensibility of mine; I begin to doubt his being of the amiable character I once supposed: in short, I begin to doubt of the possibility of his making me happy.

You will, perhaps, call it an excess of pride, when I say, I am much less inclined to marry him than when our situations were equal. I certainly love him; I have a habit of considering him as the man I am to marry, but my affection is not of that kind which will make me easy under the sense of an obligation.

I will open all my heart to you when we meet: I am not so happy as you imagine: do not accuse me of caprice; can I be too cautious, where the happiness of my whole life is at stake?

> Adieu!
>> Your faithful

>>> EMILY MONTAGUE

TO MISS RIVERS, CLARGES STREET

LETTER 20   SILLERI, SEPT. 24: I declare off at once; I will not be a squaw; I admire their talking of the liberty of savages; in the most essential point, they are slaves: the mothers marry their children without ever consulting their inclinations, and they are obliged to submit to this foolish tyranny. Dear England! where liberty appears, not as here among these odious savages, wild and ferocious like themselves, but lovely, smiling, led by the hand of the Graces. There is no true freedom any where else. They may talk of the privilege of chusing a chief; but what is that to the dear English privilege of chusing a husband?

I have been at an Indian wedding, and have no patience. Never did I see so vile an assortment.

> Adieu! I shall not be in good humour this month.
>> Yours,

>>> A. FERMOR

LETTER 21 MONTREAL, SEPT. 24: What you say, my dear friend, is more true than I wish it was; our English women of character are generally too reserved; their manner is cold and forbidding; they seem to think it a crime to be too attractive; they appear almost afraid to please.

'Tis to this ill-judged reserve I attribute the low profligacy of too many of our young men; the grave faces and distant behaviour of the generality of virtuous women fright them from their acquaintance, and drive them into the society of those wretched votaries of vice, whose conversation debases every sentiment of their souls.

With as much beauty, good sense, sensibility, and softness, at least, as any women on earth, no women please so little as the English: depending on their native charms, and on those really amiable qualities which envy cannot deny them, they are too careless in acquiring those enchanting nameless graces, which no language can define, which give resistless force to beauty, and even supply its place where it is wanting.

They are satisfied with being good, without considering that unadorned virtue may command esteem, but will never excite love; and both are necessary in marriage, which I suppose to be the state every woman of honour has in prospect; for I own myself rather incredulous as to the assertions of maiden aunts and cousins to the contrary. I wish my amiable countrywomen would consider one moment, that virtue is never so lovely as when dressed in smiles: the virtue of women should have all the softness of the sex; it should be gentle, it should be even playful, to please.

There is a lady here, whom I wish you to see, as the shortest way of explaining to you all I mean; she is the most pleasing woman I ever beheld, independently of her being one of the handsomest; her manner is irresistible: she has all the smiling graces of France, all the blushing delicacy and native softness of England.

Nothing can be more delicate, my dear Temple, than the manner in which you offer me your estate in Rutland, by way of anticipating your intended legacy: it is however impossible for me to accept it; my father, who saw me naturally more profuse than became my expectations, took such pains to counterwork it by inspiring me with the love of independence, that I cannot have such an obligation even to you.

Besides, your legacy is left on the supposition that you

are not to marry, and I am absolutely determined you shall; so that, by accepting this mark of your esteem, I should be robbing your younger children.

I have not a wish to be richer whilst I am a batchelor, and the only woman I ever wished to marry, the only one my heart desires, will be in three weeks the wife of another; I shall spend less than my income here: shall I not then be rich? To make you easy, know I have four thousand pounds in the funds; and that, from the equality of living here, an ensign is obliged to spend near as much as I am; he is inevitably ruined, but I save money.

I pity you, my friend; I am hurt to hear you talk of happiness in the life you at present lead; of finding pleasure in possessing venal beauty; you are in danger of acquiring a habit which will vitiate your taste, and exclude you from that state of refined and tender friendship for which nature formed a heart like yours, and which is only to be found in marriage: I need not add, in a marriage of choice.

It has been said that love marriages are generally unhappy; nothing is more false; marriages of meer inclination will always be so; passion alone being concerned, when that is gratified, all tenderness ceases of course; but love, the gay child of sympathy and esteem, is, when attended by delicacy, the only happiness worth a reasonable man's pursuit, and the choicest gift of heaven: it is a softer, tenderer friendship, enlivened by taste, and by the most ardent desire of pleasing, which time, instead of destroying, will render every hour more dear and interesting.

If, as you possibly will, you should call me romantic, hear a man of pleasure on the subject, the Petronius of the last age, the elegant, but voluptuous St Evremond, who speaks in the following manner of the friendship between married persons:

"I believe it is this pleasing intercourse of tenderness, this reciprocation of esteem, or, if you will, this mutual ardour of preventing each other in every endearing mark of affection, in which consists the sweetness of this second species of friendship.

"I do not speak of other pleasures, which are not so much in themselves as in the assurance they give of the intire possession of those we love: this appears to me so true, that I am not afraid to assert, the man who is by any other means certainly assured of the tenderness of her he loves, may easily support the privation of those pleasures; and that they ought not to enter into the account of friendship, but as proofs that it is without reserve.

" 'Tis true, few men are capable of the purity of these

sentiments, and 'tis for that reason we so very seldom see perfect friendship in marriage, at least for any long time: the object which a sensual passion has in view cannot long sustain a commerce so noble as that of friendship."

You see, the pleasures you so much boast are the least of those which true tenderness has to give, and this in the opinion of a voluptuary.

My dear Temple, all you have ever known of love is nothing to that sweet consent of souls in unison, that harmony of minds congenial to each other, of which you have not yet an idea.

You have seen beauty, and it has inspired a momentary emotion, but you have never yet had a real attachment; you yet know nothing of that irresistible tenderness, that delirium of the soul, which, whilst it refines, adds strength to passion.

I perhaps say too much, but I wish with ardour to see you happy; in which there is the more merit, as I have not the least prospect of being so myself.

I wish you to pursue the plan of life which I myself think most likely to bring happiness, because I know our souls to be of the same frame: we have taken different roads, but you will come back to mine. Awake to delicate pleasures; I have no taste for any other; there are no other for sensible minds. My gallantries have been few, rather (if it is allowed to speak thus of one's self even to a friend) from elegance of taste than severity of manners; I have loved seldom, because I cannot love without esteem.

Believe me, Jack, the meer pleasure of loving, even without a return, is superior to all the joys of sense where the heart is untouched: the French poet does not exaggerate when he says.

——*Amour;*
Tous les autres plaisirs ne valent pas tes peines.

You will perhaps call me mad; I am just come from a woman who is capable of making all mankind so. Adieu!
Yours,

Ed. Rivers

58

LETTER **22** SILLERI, SEPT. 25: I have been rambling about amongst the peasants, and asking them a thousand questions, in order to satisfy your inquisitive friend. As to my father, though, properly speaking, your questions are addressed to him, yet, being upon duty, he begs that, for this time, you will accept of an answer from me.

The Canadians live a good deal like the ancient patriarchs; the lands were originally settled by the troops, every officer became a seigneur, or lord of the manor, every soldier took lands under his commander; but, as avarice is natural to mankind, the soldiers took a great deal more than they could cultivate, by way of providing for a family : which is the reason so much land is now waste in the finest part of the province : those who had children, and in general they have a great number, portioned out their lands amongst them as they married, and lived in the midst of a little world of their descendents.

There are whole villages, and there is even a large island, that of Coudre, where the inhabitants are all the descendents of one pair, if we only suppose that their sons went to the next village for wives, for I find no tradition of their having had a dispensation to marry their sisters.

The corn here is very good, though not equal to ours; the harvest not half so gay as in England, and for this reason, that the lazy creatures leave the greatest part of their land uncultivated, only sowing as much corn of different sorts as will serve themselves; and being too proud and too idle to work for hire, every family gets in its own harvest, which prevents all that jovial spirit which we find when the reapers work together in large parties.

Idleness is the reigning passion here, from the peasant to his lord; the gentlemen never either ride on horseback or walk, but are driven about like women, for they never drive themselves, lolling at their ease in a calash : the peasants, I mean the masters of families, are pretty near as useless as their lords.

You will scarce believe me, when I tell you, that I have seen, at the farm next us, two children, a very beautiful boy and girl, of about eleven years old, assisted by their grandmother, reaping a field of oats, whilst the lazy father, a strong fellow of thirty-two, lay on the grass, smoking his pipe, about twenty yards from them : the old people and children work here; those in the age of strength and health only take their pleasure.

A propos to smoking, 'tis common to see here boys of

three years old, sitting at their doors, smoking their pipes, as grave and composed as little old Chinese men on a chimney.

You ask me after our fruits: we have, as I am told, an immensity of cranberries all the year; when the snow melts away in spring, they are said to be found under it as fresh and as good as in autumn: strawberries and rasberries grow wild in profusion; you cannot walk a step in the fields without treading on the former: great plenty of currants, plumbs, apples, and pears; a few cherries and grapes, but not in much perfection: excellent musk melons, and water melons in abundance, but not so good in proportion as the musk. Not a peach, nor any thing of the kind; this I am however convinced is less the fault of the climate than of the people, who are too indolent to take pains for any thing more than is absolutely necessary to their existence. They might have any fruit here but gooseberries, for which the summer is too hot; there are bushes in the woods, and some have been brought from England, but the fruit falls off before it is ripe. The wild fruits here, especially those of the bramble kind, are in much greater variety and perfection than in England.

When I speak of the natural productions of the country, I should not forget that hemp and hops grow every where in the woods; I should imagine the former might be cultivated here with great success, if the people could be persuaded to cultivate any thing.

A little corn of every kind, a little hay, a little tobacco, half a dozen apple trees, a few onions and cabbages, make the whole of a Canadian plantation. There is scarce a flower, except those in the woods, where there is a variety of the most beautiful shrubs I ever saw; the wild cherry, of which the woods are full, is equally charming in flower and in fruit; and, in my opinion, at least equals the arbutus.

They sow their wheat in spring, never manure the ground, and plough it in the slightest manner; can it then be wondered at that it is inferior to ours? They fancy the frost would destroy it if sown in autumn; but this is all prejudice, as experience has shewn. I myself saw a field of wheat this year at the governor's farm, which was manured and sown in autumn, as fine as I ever saw in England.

I should tell you, they are so indolent as never to manure their lands, or even their gardens; and that, till the English came, all the manure of Quebec was thrown into the river.

You will judge how naturally rich the soil must be, to produce good crops without manure, and without ever lying fallow, and almost without ploughing; yet our political writers in England never speak of Canada without the epithet of *barren*.

They tell me this extreme fertility is owing to the snow, which lies five or six months on the ground. Provisions are dear, which is owing to the prodigious number of horses kept here; every family having a carriage, even the poorest peasant; and every son of that peasant keeping a horse for his little excursions of pleasure, besides those necessary for the business of the farm. The war also destroyed the breed of cattle, which I am told however begins to increase; they have even so far improved in corn, as to export some this year to Italy and Spain.

Don't you think I am become an excellent farmeress? 'Tis intuition; some people are born learned: are you not all astonishment at my knowledge? I never was so vain of a letter in my life.

Shall I own the truth? I had most of my intelligence from old John, who lived long with my grandfather in the country; and who, having little else to do here, has taken some pains to pick up a competent knowledge of the state of agriculture five miles round Quebec.

Adieu! I am tired of the subject.

Your faithful,

A. Fermor

Now I think of it, why did you not write to your brother? Did you chuse me to expose my ignorance? If so, I flatter myself you are a little taken in, for I think John and I figure in the rural way.

TO MISS RIVERS, CLARGES STREET

LETTER **23** SILLERI, SEPT. 29, 10 O'CLOCK: O to be sure! we are vastly to be pitied: no beaux at all with the general; only about six to one; a very pretty proportion, and what I hope always to see. We, the ladies I mean, drink chocolate with the general to-morrow, and he gives us a ball on Thursday; you would not know Quebec again; nothing but smiling faces now; all so gay as never was, the sweetest country in the world; never expect to see me in England again; one is really somebody here: I have been asked to dance by only twenty-seven.

On the subject of dancing, I am, as it were, a little embarrassed: you will please to observe that, in the time of scarcity, when all the men were at Montreal, I suffered a foolish little captain to sigh and say civil things to me, *pour passer le tems*, and the creature takes the airs of a lover, to which he has not the least pretensions, and chuses to be angry that I won't dance with him on Thursday, and I positively won't.

It is really pretty enough that every absurd animal, who takes upon him to make love to one, is to fancy himself entitled to a return: I have no patience with the men's ridiculousness: have you, Lucy?

But I see a ship coming down under full sail; it may be Emily and her friends: the colours are all out, they slacken sail; they drop anchor opposite the house: 'tis certainly them; I must fly to the beach: music as I am a person, and an awning on the deck: the boat puts off with your brother in it. Adieu for a moment: I must go and invite them on shore.

2 o'clock

'Twas Emily and Mrs Melmoth, with two or three very pretty Frenchwomen; your brother is a happy man: I found tea and coffee under the awning, and a table loaded with Montreal fruit, which is vastly better than ours; by the way, the colonel has bought me an immensity; he is so gallant and all that: we regaled ourselves, and landed; they dine here, and we dance in the evening; we are to have a syllabub in the wood: my father has sent for Sir George and Major Melmoth, and half a dozen of the most agreeable men, from Quebec: he is enchanted with his little Emily, he loved her when she was a child. I cannot tell you how happy I am; my Emily is handsomer than ever; you know how partial I am to beauty: I never had a friendship for an ugly woman in my life.

Adieu! *ma très chère*.

Yours,

A. Fermor

Your brother looks like an angel this morning; he is not drest, he is not undrest, but somehow, easy, elegant and enchanting: he has no powder, and his hair a little *dégagée*, blown about by the wind, and agreeably disordered; such fire in his countenance; his eyes say a thousand agreeable things; he is in such spirits as I never saw him: not a man of them has the least chance to-day. I shall be in love with him if he goes on at this rate: not that it will be to any purpose in the world; he never would even flirt with me, though I have made him a thousand advances.

My heart is so light, Lucy, I cannot describe it: I love Emily at my soul: 'tis three years since I saw her, and there is something so romantic in finding her in Canada: there is no saying how happy I am: I want only you, to be perfectly so.

3 o'clock

The messenger is returned; Sir George is gone with a party of French ladies to Lake Charles: Emily blushed when the message was delivered; he might reasonably suppose they would be here to-day, as the wind was fair: your brother dances with my sweet friend; she loses nothing by the exchange; she is however a little piqued at this appearance of disrespect.

12 o'clock

Sir George came just as we sat down to supper; he did right, he complained first, and affected to be angry she had not sent an express from *Point au Tremble*. He was however gayer than usual, and very attentive to his mistress; your brother seemed chagrined at his arrival; Emily perceived it, and redoubled her politeness to him, which in a little time restored part of his good humour: upon the whole, it was an agreeable evening, but it would have been more so, if Sir George had come at first, or not at all.

The ladies lie here, and we go all together in the morning to Quebec; the gentlemen are going.

I steal a moment to seal, and give this to the colonel, who will put it in his packet to-morrow.

TO MISS RIVERS, CLARGES STREET

LETTER 24 QUEBEC, SEPT. 30: Would you believe it possible, my dear, that Sir George should decline attending Emily Montague from Montreal, and leave the pleasing commission to me? I am obliged to him for the three happiest days of my life, yet am piqued at his chusing me for a *cecisbeo* to his mistress: he seems to think me a man *sans conséquence*, with whom a lady may safely be trusted; there is nothing very flattering in such a kind of confidence: let him take care of himself, if he is impertinent, and sets me at defiance, I am not vain, but set our fortunes aside, and I dare enter the lists with Sir George Clayton. I cannot give her a coach and six; but I can give her, what is more conducive to happiness, a heart which knows how to value her perfections.

I never had so pleasing a journey; we were three days coming down, because we made it a continual party of pleasure, took music with us, landed once or twice a day, visited the French families we knew, lay both nights on shore, and danced at the seigneur's of the village.

This river, from Montreal to Quebec, exhibits a scene perhaps not to be matched in the world: it is settled on both sides, though the settlements are not so numerous on the south shore as on the other: the lovely confusion of woods, mountains, meadows, corn-fields, rivers (for there are several on both sides, which lose themselves in the St Lawrence), intermixed with churches and houses breaking upon you at a distance through the trees, form a variety of landscapes, to which it is difficult to do justice.

This charming scene, with a clear serene sky, a gentle breeze in our favour, and the conversation of half a dozen fine women, would have made the voyage pleasing to the most insensible man on earth: my Emily too of the party, and most politely attentive to the pleasure she saw I had in making the voyage agreeable to her.

I every day love her more; and, without considering the impropriety of it, I cannot help giving way to an inclination, in which I find such exquisite pleasure; I find a thousand charms in the least trifle I can do to oblige her.

Don't reason with me on this subject: I know it is madness to continue to see her; but I find a delight in her conversation, which I cannot prevail on myself to give up till she is actually married.

I respect her engagements, and pretend to no more from her than her friendship; but, as to myself, will love her in whatever manner I please: to shew you my prudence, however, I intend to dance with the handsomest unmarried Frenchwoman here on Thursday, and to shew her an attention which shall destroy all suspicion of my tenderness for Emily. I am jealous of Sir George, and hate him; but I dissemble it better than I thought it possible for me to do.

My Lucy, I am not happy; my mind is in a state not to be described; I am weak enough to encourage a hope for which there is not the least foundation: I misconstrue her friendship for me every moment; and that attention which is merely gratitude for my apparent anxiety to oblige. I even fancy her eyes understand mine, which I am afraid speak too plainly the sentiments of my heart.

I love her, my dear girl, to madness; these three days——
I am interrupted. Adieu!

Yours,

ED. RIVERS

'Tis Capt. Fermor, who insists on my dining at Silleri. They will eternally throw me in the way of this lovely woman: of what materials do they suppose me formed?

TO MISS RIVERS, CLARGES STREET

LETTER **25** SILLERI, OCT. 3, TWELVE O'CLOCK: An enchanting ball, my dear; your little friend's head is turned. I was more admired than Emily, which to be sure did not flatter my vanity at all: I see she must content herself with being beloved, for without coquetry 'tis in vain to expect admiration.

We had more than three hundred persons at the ball; above three-fourths men; all gay and well dressed, an elegant supper; in short, it was charming.

I am half inclined to marry; I am not at all acquainted with the man I have fixed upon, I never spoke to him till last night, nor did he take the least notice of me, more than of other ladies, but that is nothing; he pleases me better than any man I have seen here; he is not handsome, but well made, and looks like a gentleman; he has a good character, is heir to a very pretty estate. I will think further of it: there is nothing more easy than to have him if I chuse it: 'tis only saying to some of his friends, that I think Captain Fitzgerald the most agreeable fellow here, and he will immediately be astonished he did not sooner find out I was the handsomest woman. I will consider this affair seriously; one must marry, 'tis the mode; every body marries; why don't you marry, Lucy?

This brother of yours is always here; I am surprized Sir George is not jealous, for he pays no sort of attention to me, 'tis easy to see why he comes; I dare say I shan't see him next week: Emily is going to Mrs Melmoth's where she stays till tomorrow seven-night; she goes from hence as soon as dinner is over.

Adieu! I am fatigued; we danced till morning; I am but this moment up.

Yours,

A. Fermor

Your brother danced with Mademoiselle Clairaut; do you know I was piqued he did not give me the preference, as Emily danced with her lover? not but that I had perhaps a partner full as agreeable, at least I have a mind to think so.

I hear it whispered that the whole affair of the wedding is to be settled next week; my father is in the secret, I am not. Emily looks ill this morning; she was not gay at the ball. I know not why, but she is not happy. I have my fancies, but they are yet only fancies.

Adieu! my dear girl; I can no more.

TO MISS RIVERS, CLARGES STREET

LETTER **26** QUEBEC, OCT. 6: I am going, my Lucy. —I know not well whither I am going, but I will not stay to see this marriage. Could you have believed it possible—But what folly! Did I not know her situation from the first? Could I suppose she would break off an engagement of years, with a man who gives so clear a proof that he prefers her to all other women, to humour the frenzy of one who has never even told her he loved her?

Captain Fermor assures me all is settled but the day, and that she has promised to name that to-morrow.

I will leave Quebec to-night; no one shall know the road I take; I do not yet know it myself; I will cross over to Point Levi with my valet de chambre, and go wherever chance directs me. I cannot bear even to hear the day named. I am strongly inclined to write to her; but what can I say? I should betray my tenderness in spite of myself, and her compassion would perhaps disturb her approaching happiness: were it even possible she should prefer me to Sir George, she is too far gone to recede.

My Lucy, I never till this moment felt to what an excess I loved her.

Adieu! I shall be about a fortnight absent: by that time she will be embarked for England. I cannot bring myself to see her the wife of another. Do not be alarmed for me; reason and the impossibility of success will conquer my passion for this angelic woman; I have been to blame in allowing myself to see her so often.

Yours,

ED. RIVERS

LETTER 27 BEAUMONT, OCT. 7: I think I breathe a freer air now I am out of Quebec. I cannot bear wherever I go to meet this Sir George; his triumphant air is insupportable; he has, or I fancy he has, all the insolence of a happy rival; 'tis unjust, but I cannot avoid hating him; I look on him as a man who has deprived me of a good to which I foolishly fancy I had pretensions.

My whole behaviour has been weak to the last degree: I shall grow more reasonable when I no longer see this charming woman; I ought sooner to have taken this step.

I have found here an excuse for my excursion; I have heard of an estate to be sold down the river; and am told the purchase will be less expence than clearing any lands I might take up. I will go and see it; it is an object, a pursuit, and will amuse me.

I am going to send my servant back to Quebec; my manner of leaving it must appear extraordinary to my friends; I have therefore made this estate my excuse. I have written to Miss Fermor that I am going to make a purchase; have begged my warmest wishes to her lovely friend, for whose happiness no one on earth is more anxious; but have told her Sir George is too much the object of my envy, to expect from me very sincere congratulations.

Adieu! my servant waits for this. You shall hear an account of my adventures when I return to Quebec.

Yours,

ED. RIVERS

LETTER 28 QUEBEC, OCT. 7, TWELVE O'CLOCK:
I must see you, my dear, this evening; my mind is in an agitation
not to be expressed; a few hours will determine my happiness
or misery for ever; I am displeased with your father for pre-
cipitating a determination which cannot be made with too much
caution.

I have a thousand things to say to you, which I can say
to no one else.

Be at home, and alone; I will come to you as soon as
dinner is over.

Adieu!
Your affectionate
EMILY MONTAGUE

LETTER 29 I will be at home, my dear, and denied to
every body but you.

I pity you, my dear Emily; but I am unable to give you
advice.

The world would wonder at your hesitating a moment.
Your faithful
A. FERMOR

LETTER 30 QUEBEC, OCT. 7, THREE O'CLOCK: My
visit to you is prevented by an event beyond my hopes. Sir
George has this moment a letter from his mother, desiring him
earnestly to postpone his marriage till spring, for some reasons
of consequence to his fortune, with the particulars of which she
will acquaint him by the next packet.

He communicated this intelligence to me with a grave

air, but with a tranquillity not to be described, and I received it with a joy I found it impossible wholly to conceal.

I have now time to consult both my heart and my reason at leisure, and to break with him, if necessary, by degrees.

What an escape have I had! I was within four and twenty hours of either determining to marry a man with whom I fear I have little chance to be happy, or of breaking with him in a manner that would have subjected one or both of us to the censures of a prying impertinent world, whose censures the most steady temper cannot always contemn.

I will own to you, my dear, I every hour have more dread of this marriage: his present situation has brought his faults into full light. Captain Clayton, with little more than his commission, was modest, humble, affable to his inferiors, polite to all the world; and I fancied him possessed of those more active virtues, which I supposed the smallness of his fortune prevented from appearing. 'Tis with pain I see that Sir George, with a splendid income, is avaricious, selfish, proud, vain, and profuse; lavish to every caprice of vanity and ostentation which regards himself, coldly inattentive to the real wants of others.

Is this a character to make your Emily happy? We were not formed for each other; no two minds were ever so different; my happiness is in friendship, in the tender affections, in the sweets of dear domestic life; his in the idle parade of affluence, in dress, in equipage, in all that splendour, which, whilst it excites envy, is too often the mark of wretchedness.

Shall I say more? Marriage is seldom happy where there is a great disproportion of fortune. The lover, after he loses that endearing character in the husband, which in common minds I am afraid is not long, begins to reflect how many more thousands he might have expected; and perhaps suspects his mistress of those interested motives in marrying, of which he now feels his own heart capable. Coldness, suspicion, and mutual want of esteem and confidence, follow of course.

I will come back with you to Silleri this evening; I have no happiness but when I am with you. Mrs Melmoth is so fond of Sir George, she is eternally persecuting me with his praises; she is extremely mortified at this delay, and very angry at the manner in which I behave upon it.

Come to us directly, my dear Bell, and rejoice with your faithful.

EMILY MONTAGUE

LETTER **31** I congratulate you, my dear; you will at least have the pleasure of being five or six months longer your own mistress; which, in my opinion, when one is not violently in love, is a consideration worth attending to. You will also have time to see whether you like any body else better; and you know you can take him if you please at last.

Send him up to his regiment at Montreal with the Melmoths; stay the winter with me, flirt with somebody else to try the strength of your passion, and, if it holds out against six months absence, and the attention of an agreeable fellow, I think you may safely venture to marry him.

A propos to flirting, have you seen Colonel Rivers? He has not been here these two days. I shall begin to be jealous of this little impertinent Mademoiselle Clairaut. Adieu!

Yours,

A. FERMOR

Rivers is absurd. I have a mighty foolish letter from him; he is rambling about the country, buying estates: he had better have been here, playing the fool with us; if I knew how to write to him I would tell him so, but he is got out of the range of human beings, down the river, Heaven knows where; he says a thousand civil things to you, but I will bring the letter with me to save the trouble of repeating them.

I have a sort of an idea he won't be very unhappy at this delay; I want vastly to send him word of it.

Adieu! *ma chère*.

LETTER **32** KAMARASKAS, OCT. 10: I am at present, my dear Lucy, in the wildest country on earth; I mean of those which are inhabited at all: 'tis for several leagues almost a continual forest, with only a few straggling houses on the river side; 'tis however of not the least consequence to me, all places are equal to me where Emily is not.

I seek amusement, but without finding it: she is never one moment from my thoughts; I am every hour on the point of returning to Quebec; I cannot support the idea of her leaving the country without my seeing her.

'Tis a lady who has this estate to sell: I am at present at her house; she is very amiable; a widow about thirty, with an agreeable person, great vivacity, an excellent understanding, improved by reading, to which the absolute solitude of her situation has obliged her; she has an open pleasing countenance, with a candour and sincerity in her conversation which would please me, if my mind was in a state to be pleased with any thing. Through all the attention and civility I think myself obliged to shew her, she seems to perceive the melancholy which I cannot shake off: she is always contriving some little party for me, as if she knew how much I am in want of amusement.

Oct. 12

Madame Des Roches is very kind; she sees my chagrin, and takes every method to divert it: she insists on my going in her shallop to see the last settlement on the river, opposite the Isle of Barnaby; she does me the honour to accompany me, with a gentleman and lady who live about a mile from her.

Isle of Barnaby, Oct. 13

I have been paying a very singular visit; 'tis to a hermit, who has lived sixty years alone on this island; I came to him with a strong prejudice against him; I have no opinion of those who fly society; who seek a state of all others the most contrary to our nature. Were I a tyrant, and wished to inflict the most cruel punishment human nature could support, I would seclude criminals from the joys of society, and deny them the endearing sight of their species.

I am certain I could not exist a year alone: I am miserable even in that degree of solitude to which one is confined in a ship; no words can speak the joy which I felt when I came to America, on the first appearance of something like the chearful haunts of men; the first man, the first house, nay the first Indian fire of which I saw the smoke rise above the trees, gave me the most lively transport that can be conceived; I felt all the force of those ties which unite us to each other, of that social love to which we owe all our happiness here.

But to my hermit: his appearance disarmed my dislike; he is a tall old man, with white hair and beard, the look of one who has known better days, and the strongest marks of benevolence in his countenance. He received me with the utmost hospitality, spread all his little stores of fruit before me, fetched me fresh milk, and water from a spring near his house.

After a little conversation, I expressed my astonishment, that a man of whose kindness and humanity I had just had such proof, could find his happiness in flying mankind: I said a good deal on the subject, to which he listened with the politest attention.

"You appear," said he, "of a temper to pity the miseries of others. My story is short and simple: I loved the most amiable of women; I was beloved. The avarice of our parents, who both had more gainful views for us, prevented an union on which our happiness depended. My Louisa, who was threatened with an immediate marriage with a man she detested, proposed to me to fly the tyranny of our friends: she had an uncle at Quebec, to whom she was dear. The wilds of Canada, said she, may afford us that refuge our cruel country denies us. After a secret marriage, we embarked. Our voyage was thus far happy; I landed on the opposite shore, to seek refreshments for my Louisa; I was returning, pleased with the thought of obliging the object of all my tenderness, when a beginning storm drove me to seek shelter in this bay. The storm increased, I saw its progress with agonies not to be described; the ship, which was in sight, was unable to resist its fury: the sailors crowded into the boat; they had the humanity to place my Louisa there; they made for the spot where I was, my eyes were wildly fixed on them; I stood eagerly on the utmost verge of the water, my arms stretched out to receive her, my prayers ardently addressed to Heaven, when an immense wave broke over the boat; I heard a general shriek; I even fancied I distinguished my Louisa's cries; it subsided, the sailors again exerted all their force; a second wave—I saw them no more.

"Never will that dreadful scene be absent one moment from my memory: I fell senseless on the beach; when I returned to life, the first object I beheld was the breathless body of my Louisa at my feet. Heaven gave me the wretched consolation of rendering to her the last sad duties. In that grave all my happiness lies buried. I knelt by her, and breathed a vow to Heaven, to wait here the moment that should join me to all I held dear. I every morning visit her loved remains, and implore the God of mercy to hasten my dissolution. I feel that we shall not long be separated; I shall soon meet her, to part no more."

He stopped, and, without seeming to remember he was not alone, walked hastily towards a little oratory he has built on the beach, near which is the grave of his Louisa; I followed him a few steps, I saw him throw himself on his knees; and, respecting his sorrow, returned to the house.

Though I cannot absolutely approve, yet I more than

forgive, I almost admire, his renouncing the world in his situation. Devotion is perhaps the only balm for the wounds given by unhappy love; the heart is too much softened by true tenderness to admit any common cure.

Seven in the evening

I am returned to Madame Des Roches and her friends, who declined visiting the hermit. I found in his conversation all which could have adorned society; he was pleased with the sympathy I shewed for his sufferings; we parted with regret. I wished to have made him a present, but he will receive nothing.

A ship for England is in sight. Madame Des Roches is so polite to send off this letter; we return to her house in the morning.

Adieu! my Lucy.

Yours,

ED. RIVERS

TO MISS RIVERS, CLARGES STREET

LETTER **33** QUEBEC, OCT. 12: I have no patience with this foolish brother of yours; he is rambling about in the woods when we want him here: we have a most agreeable assembly every Thursday at the General's, and have had another ball since he has been gone on this ridiculous ramble; I miss the dear creature wherever I go. We have nothing but balls, cards, and parties of pleasures; but they are nothing without my little Rivers.

I have been making the tour of the three religions this morning, and, as I am the most constant creature breathing; am come back only a thousand times more pleased with my own. I have been at mass, at church, and at the presbyterian meeting: an idea struck me at the last, in regard to the drapery of them all; that the Romish religion is like an over-dressed, tawdry, rich citizen's wife; the presbyterian like a rude aukward country girl; the church of England like an elegant well-dressed woman of quality, "plain in her neatness" (to quote Horace, who is my favourite author). There is a noble, graceful simplicity both in the worship and the ceremonies of the church of England, which, even if I were a stranger to her doctrines, would prejudice me strongly in her favour.

Sir George sets out for Montreal this evening, so do the house of Melmoth; I have however prevailed on Emily to stay a month or two longer with me. I am rejoiced Sir George is going away; I am tired of seeing that eternal smile, that countenance of his, which attempts to speak, and says nothing. I am in doubt whether I shall let Emily marry him; she will die in a week, of no distemper but his conversation.

They dine with us. I am called down. Adieu!

Eight at night

Heaven be praised, our lover is gone; they parted with great philosophy on both sides; they are the prettiest mild pair of inamoratoes one shall see.

Your brother's servant has just called to tell me he is going to his master. I have a great mind to answer his letter, and order him back.

TO MISS RIVERS, CLARGES STREET

LETTER 34 OCT. 12: I have been looking at the estate Madame Des Roches has to sell; it is as wild as the lands to which I have a right; I hoped this would have amused my chagrin, but am mistaken: nothing interests me, nothing takes up my attention one moment: my mind admits but one idea. This charming woman follows me wherever I go; I wander about like the first man when driven out of paradise: I vainly fancy every change of place will relieve the anxiety of my mind.

Madame Des Roches smiles, and tells me I am in love; 'tis however a smile of tenderness and compassion; your sex have great penetration in whatever regards the heart.

Oct. 13

I have this moment a letter from Miss Fermor, to press my return to Quebec; she tells me Emily's marriage is postponed till spring. My Lucy! how weak is the human heart! In spite of myself, a ray of hope—I set off this instant: I cannot conceal my joy.

LETTER **35**   LONDON, JULY 23: You have no idea, Ned, how much your absence is lamented by the dowagers, to whom, it must be owned, your charity has been pretty extensive.

It would delight you to see them condoling with each other on the loss of the dear charming man, the man of sentiments, of true taste, who admires the maturer beauties, and thinks no woman worth pursuing till turned of twenty-five: 'tis a loss not to be made up; for your taste, it must be owned, is pretty singular.

I have seen your last favourite, Lady H——, who assures me, on the word of a woman of honour, that, had you staid seven years in London, she does not think she should have had the least inclination to change: but an absent lover, she well observed, is, properly speaking, no lover at all. "Bid Colonel Rivers remember," said she, "what I have read somewhere, the parting words of a French lady to a bishop of her acquaintance, Let your absence be short, my lord; and remember that a mistress is a benefice which obliges to residence."

I am told, you had not been gone a week before Jack Willmott had the honour of drying up the fair widow's tears.

I am going this evening to Vauxhall, and to-morrow propose setting out for my house in Rutland, from whence you shall hear from me again.

Adieu! I never write long letters in London. I should tell you, I have been to see Mrs Rivers and your sister; the former is well, but very anxious to have you in England again; the latter grows so very handsome, I don't intend to repeat my visits often.

Yours,

J. TEMPLE

LETTER **36**   QUEBEC, OCT. 14: I am this moment arrived from a ramble down the river; but, a ship being just going, must acknowledge your last.

You make me happy in telling me my dear Lady H—— has given my place in her heart to so honest a fellow as Jack

Willmott; and I sincerely wish the ladies always chose their favourites as well.

I should be very unreasonable indeed to expect constancy at almost four thousand miles distance, especially when the prospect of my return is so very uncertain.

My voyage ought undoubtedly to be considered as an abdication: I am to all intents and purposes dead in law as a lover; and the lady has a right to consider her heart as vacant, and to proceed to a new election.

I claim no more than a share in her esteem and remembrance, which I dare say I shall never want.

That I have amused myself a little in the dowager way, I am very far from denying; but you will observe, it was less from taste than the principle of doing as little mischief as possible in my few excursions to the world of gallantry. A little deviation from the exact rule of right we men all allow ourselves in love affairs; but I was willing to keep as near it as I could. Married women are, on my principles, forbidden fruit; I abhor the seduction of innocence; I am too delicate, and (with all my modesty) too vain, to be pleased with venal beauty: what was I then to do, with a heart too active to be absolutely at rest, and which had not met with its counterpart? Widows were, I thought, fair prey, as being sufficiently experienced to take care of themselves.

I have said married women are, on my principles, forbidden fruit: I should have explained myself; I mean in England, for my ideas on this head change as soon as I land at Calais.

Such is the amazing force of local prejudice, that I do not recollect having ever made love to an English married woman, or a French unmarried one. Marriages in France being made by the parents, and therefore generally without inclination on either side, gallantry seems to be a tacit condition, though not absolutely expressed in the contract.

But to return to my plan: I think it an excellent one; and would recommend it to all those young men about town, who, like me, find in their hearts the necessity of loving, before they meet with an object capable of fixing them for life.

By the way, I think the widows ought to raise a statue to my honour, for having done my *possible* to prove that, for the sake of decorum, morals, and order, they ought to have all the men to themselves.

I have this moment your letter from Rutland. Do you know I am almost angry? Your ideas of love are narrow and pedantic; custom has done enough to make the life of one half of our species tasteless; but you would reduce them to a state of still greater insipidity than even that to which our tyranny has doomed them.

You would limit the pleasure of loving and being beloved, and the charming power of pleasing, to three or four years only in the life of that sex which is peculiarly formed to feel tenderness; women are born with more lively affections than men, which are still more softened by education: to deny them the privilege of being amiable, the only privilege we allow them, as long as nature continues them so, is such a mixture of cruelty and false taste as I should never have suspected you of, notwithstanding your partiality for unripened beauty.

As to myself, I persist in my opinion, that women are most charming when they join the attractions of the mind to those of the person, when they feel the passion they inspire; or rather, that they are never charming till then.

A woman in the first bloom of youth resembles a tree in blossom, when mature in fruit; but a woman who retains the charms of her person till her understanding is in its full perfection, is like those trees in happier climes, which produce blossoms and fruit together.

You will scarce believe, Jack, that I have lived a week *tête à tête*, in the midst of a wood, with just the woman I have been describing; a widow extremely my taste, *mature*, five or six years more so than you say I require, lively, sensible, handsome, without saying one civil thing to her; yet nothing can be more certain.

I could give you powerful reasons for my insensibility; but you are a traitor to love, and therefore have no right to be in any of his secrets.

I will excuse your visits to my sister; as well as I love you myself, I have a thousand reasons for chusing she should not be acquainted with you.

What you say in regard to my mother, gives me pain; I will never take back my little gift to her; and I cannot live in England on my present income, though it enables me to live *en prince* in Canada.

Adieu! I have not time to say more. I have stole this half-hour from the loveliest woman breathing, whom I am going to visit; surely you are infinitely obliged to me. To lessen the obligation, however, my calash is not yet come to the door.

Adieu once more.

Yours,

ED. RIVERS

LETTER 37   SILLERI, OCT. 15: Our wanderer is returned, my dear, and in such spirits as you can't conceive: he passed yesterday with us; he likes to have us to himself, and he had yesterday; we walked *à trio* in the wood, and were foolish; I have not passed so agreeable a day since I came to Canada: I love mightily to be foolish, and the people here have no taste that way at all: your brother is divinely so upon occasion. The weather was, to use the Canadian phrase, *superbe et magnifique*. We shall not, I am told, have much more in the same *magnifique* style, so we intend to make the most of it: I have ordered your brother to come and walk with us from morning till night; every day and all the day.

The dear man was amazingly overjoyed to see us again; we shared in his joy, though my little Emily took some pains to appear tranquil on the occasion: I never saw more pleasure in the countenances of two people in my life, nor more pains taken to suppress it.

Do you know Fitzgerald is really an agreeable fellow? I have an admirable natural instinct; I perceived he had understanding, from his aquiline nose and his eagle eye, which are indexes I never knew fail. I believe we are going to be great; I am not sure I shall not admit him to make up a *partie quarrée* with your brother and Emily: I told him my original plot upon him, and he was immensely pleased with it. I almost fancy he can be foolish; in that case, my business is done: if with his other merits he has that, I am a lost woman.

He has excellent sense, great good nature, and the true princely spirit of an Irishman: he will be ruined here, but that is his affair, not mine. He changed quarters with an officer now at Montreal; and, because the lodgings were to be furnished, thought himself obliged to leave three months wine in the cellars.

His person is pleasing; he has good eyes and teeth (the only beauties I require), is marked with the small pox, which in men gives a sensible look; very manly, and looks extremely like a gentleman.

He comes, the conqueror comes.

I see him plainly through the trees; he is now in full view, within twenty yards of the house. He looks particularly well on horseback, Lucy; which is one certain proof of a good education. The fellow is well born, and has ideas of things: I think I shall admit him of my train.

Emily wonders I have never been in love: the cause is clear; I have prevented any attachment to one man, by constantly flirting with twenty: 'tis the most sovereign receipt in the world. I think too, my dear, you have maintained a sort of running fight with the little deity: our hour is not yet come. Adieu!

Yours,

A. FERMOR

TO MISS RIVERS, CLARGES STREET

LETTER 38 QUEBEC, OCT. 15, EVENING: I am returned, my dear, and have had the pleasure of hearing you and my mother are well, though I have had no letters from either of you.

Mr Temple, my dearest Lucy, tells me he has visited you. Will you pardon me a freedom which nothing but the most tender friendship can warrant, when I tell you that I would wish you to be as little acquainted with him as politeness allows? He is a most agreeable man, perhaps too agreeable, with a thousand amiable qualities; he is the man I love above all others; and, where women are not concerned, a man of the most unblemished honour; but his manner of life is extremely libertine, and his ideas of women unworthy the rest of his character; he knows not the perfections which adorn the valuable part of your sex, he is a stranger to your virtues, and incapable, at least I fear so, of that tender affection which alone can make an amiable woman happy. With all this, he is polite and attentive, and has a manner, which, without intending it, is calculated to deceive women into an opinion of his being attached when he is not: he has all the splendid virtues which command esteem; is noble, generous, disinterested, open, brave; and is the most dangerous man on earth to a woman of honour, who is unacquainted with the arts of man.

Do not however mistake me, my Lucy; I know him to be as incapable of forming improper designs on you, even were you not the sister of his friend, as you are of listening to him if he did: 'tis for your heart alone I am alarmed; he is formed to please; you are young and inexperienced, and have not yet loved; my anxiety for your peace makes me dread your loving a man whose views are not turned to marriage, and who is therefore incapable of returning properly the tenderness of a woman of honour.

I have seen my divine Emily: her manner of receiving me was very flattering; I cannot doubt her friendship for me; yet I am not absolutely content. I am however convinced, by the easy tranquillity of her air, and her manner of bearing this delay of their marriage, that she does not love the man for whom she is intended: she has been a victim to the avarice of her friends. I would fain hope—yet what have I to hope? If I had even the happiness to be agreeable to her, if she was disengaged from Sir George, my fortune makes it impossible for me to marry her, without reducing her to indigence at home, or dooming her to be an exile in Canada for life. I dare not ask myself what I wish or intend: yet I give way in spite of me to the delight of seeing and conversing with her.

I must not look forward; I will only enjoy the present pleasure of believing myself one of the first in her esteem and friendship, and of shewing her all those little pleasing attentions so dear to a sensible heart; attentions in which her *lover* is astonishingly remiss: he is at Montreal, and I am told was gay and happy on his journey thither, though he left his mistress behind.

I have spent two very happy days at Silleri, with Emily and your friend Bell Fermor: to-morrow I meet them at the governor's, where there is a very agreeable assembly on Thursday evening. Adieu!

Yours,

ED. RIVERS

I shall write again by a ship which sails next week.

TO JOHN TEMPLE, ESQ; PALL MALL

LETTER **39** QUEBEC, OCT. 18: I have this moment a letter from Madame Des Roches, the lady at whose house I spent a week, and to whom I am greatly obliged. I am so happy as to have an opportunity of rendering her a service, in which I must desire your assistance.

'Tis in regard to some lands belonging to her, which, not being settled some other person has applied for a grant of at home. I send you the particulars, and beg you will lose no time in entering a *caveat*, and taking other proper steps to prevent what would be an act of great injustice: the war and the incursions of the Indians in alliance with us have hitherto prevented these lands from being settled, but Madame Des Roches is actually in treaty with some Acadians to settle them immediately. Employ all your friends as well as mine if necessary; my lawyer will direct you in what manner to apply, and pay the expences attending the application. Adieu!

Yours,

ED. RIVERS

TO MISS RIVERS, CLARGES STREET

LETTER 40 SILLERI, OCT. 20: I danced last night till four o'clock in the morning (if you will allow the expression), without being the least fatigued: the little Fitzgerald was my partner, who grows upon me extremely; the monkey has a way of being attentive and careless by turns, which has an amazing effect; nothing attaches a woman of my temper so much to a lover as her being a little in fear of losing him; and he keeps up the spirit of the thing admirably.

Your brother and Emily danced together, and I think I never saw either of them look so handsome; she was a thousand times more admired at this ball than the first, and reason good, for she was a thousand times more agreeable; your brother is really a charming fellow, he is an immense favourite with the ladies; he has that very pleasing general attention, which never fails to charm women; he can even be particular to one, without wounding the vanity of the rest: if he was in company with twenty, his mistress of the number, his manner would be such, that every woman there would think herself the second in his esteem; and that, if his heart had not been unluckily pre-engaged, she herself would have been the object of his tenderness.

His eyes are of immense use to him; he looks the civilest things imaginable; his whole countenance speaks whatever he wishes to say; he has the least occasion for words to explain himself of any man I ever knew.

Fitzgerald has eyes too, I assure you, and eyes that know

how to speak; he has a look of saucy unconcern and inattention, which is really irresistible.

We have had a great deal of snow already, but it melts away; 'tis a lovely day, but an odd enough mixture of summer and winter; in some places you see half a foot of snow lying, in others the dust is even troublesome.

Adieu! there are a dozen or two of beaux at the door.

Yours,

A. FERMOR

LETTER 41 NOV. 10: The savages assure us, my dear, on the information of the beavers, that we shall have a very mild winter; it seems, these creatures have laid in a less winter stock than usual. I take it very ill, Lucy, that the beavers have better intelligence than we have.

We are got into a pretty composed easy way; Sir George writes very agreeable, sensible, sentimental, gossiping letters, once a fortnight, which Emily answers in due course, with all the regularity of a counting-house correspondence; he talks of coming down after Christmas: we expect him without impatience; and in the mean time amuse ourselves as well as we can, and soften the pain of absence by the attention of a man that I fancy we like quite as well.

With submission to the beavers, the weather is very cold, and we have had a great deal of snow already; but they tell me 'tis nothing to what we shall have: they are taking precautions which make me shudder beforehand, pasting up the windows, and not leaving an avenue where cold can enter.

I like the winter carriages immensely; the open carriole is a kind of one-horse chaise, the covered one a chariot, set on a sledge to run on the ice; we have not yet had snow enough to use them, but I like their appearance prodigiously; the covered carrioles seem the prettiest things in nature to make love in, as there are curtains to draw before the windows: we shall have three in effect, my father's, Rivers's, and Fitzgerald's; the two latter are to be elegance itself, and entirely for the service of the ladies: your brother and Fitzgerald are trying who shall be ruined first for the honour of their country. I will bet three to one upon Ireland. They are every day contriving parties of pleasure, and making the most gallant little presents imaginable to the ladies.

Adieu! my dear.

Yours,

A. FERMOR

TO MISS RIVERS

LETTER 42 QUEBEC, NOV. 14: I shall not, my dear, have above one more opportunity of writing to you by the ships; after which we can only write by the packet once a month.

My Emily is every day more lovely; I see her often, and every hour discover new charms in her; she has an exalted understanding, improved by all the knowledge which is becoming in your sex; a soul awake to all the finer sensations of the heart, checked and adorned by the native loveliness of woman: she is extremely handsome, but she would please every feeling heart if she was not; she has the soul of beauty: without feminine softness and delicate sensibility, no features can give loveliness; with them, very indifferent ones can charm: that sensibility, that softness, never were so lovely as in my Emily. I can write on no other subject. Were you to see her, my Lucy, you would forgive me. My letter is called for.

Adieu!

Yours,

ED. RIVERS

Your friend Miss Fermor will write you every thing.

TO MISS MONTAGUE, AT SILLERI

LETTER 43 MONTREAL, NOV. 14: Mr Melmoth and I, my dear Emily, expected by this time to have seen you at Montreal. I allow something to your friendship for Miss Fermor; but there is also something due to relations who tenderly love you, and under whose protection your uncle left you at his death.

83

I should add, that there is something due to Sir George, had I not already displeased you by what I have said on the subject.

You are not to be told, that in a week the road from hence to Quebec will be impassable for at least a month, till the rivers are sufficiently froze to bear carriages.

I will own to you, that I am a little jealous of your attachment to Miss Fermor, though no one can think her more amiable than I do.

If you do not come this week, I would wish you to stay till Sir George comes down, and return with him; I will entreat the favour of Miss Fermor to accompany you to Montreal, which we will endeavour to make as agreeable to her as we can.

I have been ill of a slight fever, but am now perfectly recovered. Sir George and Mr Melmoth are well, and very impatient to see you here.

Adieu! my dear.

Your affectionate

E. MELMOTH

TO MRS MELMOTH, AT MONTREAL

LETTER 44   SILLERI, NOV. 20: I have a thousand reasons, my dearest Madam, for entreating you to excuse my staying some time longer at Quebec. I have the sincerest esteem for Sir George, and am not insensible of the force of our engagements; but do not think his being there a reason for my coming: the kind of suspended state, to say no more, in which those engagements now are, call for a delicacy in my behaviour to him, which is so difficult to observe without the appearance of affectation, that his absence relieves me from a very painful kind of restraint: for the same reason, 'tis impossible for me to come up at the time he does, if I do come, even though Miss Fermor should accompany me.

A moment's reflexion will convince you of the propriety of my staying here till his mother does me the honour again to approve his choice; or till our engagement is publicly known to be at an end. Mrs Clayton is a prudent mother, and a woman of the world, and may consider that Sir George's situation is changed since she consented to his marriage.

I am not capricious; but I will own to you, that my

esteem for Sir George is much lessened by his behaviour since his last return from New York: he mistakes me extremely, if he supposes he has the least additional merit in my eyes from his late acquisition of fortune: on the contrary, I now see faults in him which were concealed by the mediocrity of his situation before, and which do not promise happiness to a heart like mine, a heart which has little taste for the false glitter of life, and the most lively one possible for the calm real delights of friendship, and domestic felicity.

Accept my sincerest congratulations on your return of health; and believe me,

My dearest Madam,

Your obliged and affectionate

EMILY MONTAGUE

TO MISS RIVERS, CLARGES STREET

LETTER **45** SILLERI, NOV. 23: I have been seeing the last ship go out of the port, Lucy; you have no notion what a melancholy sight it is: we are now left to ourselves, and shut up from all the world for the winter: somehow we seem so forsaken, so cut off from the rest of human kind, I cannot bear the idea: I sent a thousand sighs and a thousand tender wishes to dear England, which I never loved so much as at this moment.

Do you know, my dear, I could cry if I was not ashamed? I shall not absolutely be in spirits again this week.

'Tis the first time I have felt any thing like bad spirits in Canada: I followed the ship with my eyes till it turned Point Levi, and, when I lost sight of it, felt as if I had lost every thing dear to me on earth. I am not particular: I see a gloom on every countenance; I have been at church, and think I never saw so many dejected faces in my life.

Adieu! for the present: it will be a fortnight before I can send this letter; another agreeable circumstance that: would to Heaven I were in England, though I changed the bright sun of Canada for a fog!

Dec. 1

We have had a week's snow without intermission: happily for us, your brother and the Fitz have been weather-bound all the time at Silleri, and cannot possibly get away.

We have amused ourselves within doors, for there is no stirring abroad, with playing at cards, playing at shuttlecock, playing the fool, making love, and making moral reflexions: upon the whole, the week has not been very disagreeable.

The snow is when we wake constantly up to our chamber windows; we are literally dug out of it every morning.

As to Quebec, I give up all hopes of ever seeing it again: but my comfort is, that the people there cannot possibly get to their neighbours; and I flatter myself very few of them have been half so well entertained at home.

We shall be abused, I know, for (what is really the fault of the weather) keeping these two creatures here this week; the ladies hate us for engrossing two such fine fellows as your brother and Fitzgerald, as well as for having vastly more than our share of all the men: we generally go out attended by at least a dozen, without any other woman but a lively old French lady, who is a flirt of my father's, and will certainly be my mamma.

We sweep into the general's assembly on Thursdays with such a train of beaux as draws every eye upon us; the rest of the fellows crowd round us; the misses draw up, blush, and flutter their fans; and your little Bell sits down with such a fancy impertinent consciousness in her countenance as is really provoking: Emily on the contrary looks mild and humble, and seems by her civil decent air to apologize to them for being so much more agreeable than themselves, which is a fault I for my part am not in the least inclined to be ashamed of.

Your idea of Quebec, my dear, is perfectly just; it is like a third or fourth rate country town in England; much hospitality, little society; cards, scandal, dancing, and good chear; all excellent things to pass away a winter evening, and peculiarly adapted to what I am told, and what I begin to feel, of the severity of this climate.

I am told they abuse me, which I can easily believe, because my impertinence to them deserves it: but what care I, you know, Lucy, so long as I please myself, and am at Silleri out of the sound?

They are squabbling at Quebec, I hear, about I cannot tell what, therefore shall not attempt to explain: some dregs of old disputes, it seems, which have had not time to settle: however, we new comers have certainly nothing to do with these matters: you can't think how comfortable we feel at Silleri, out of the way.

My father says, the politics of Canada are as complex

and as difficult to be understood as those of the Germanic system.

For my part, I think no politics worth attending to but those of the little commonwealth of woman: if I can maintain my empire over hearts, I leave the men to quarrel for every thing else.

I observe a strict neutrality, that I may have a chance for admirers amongst both parties. Adieu! the post is just going out.

Your faithful

A. FERMOR

TO MISS MONTAGUE, AT SILLERI

LETTER 46 MONTREAL, DEC. 18: There is something, my dear Emily, in what you say as to the delicacy of your situation; but, whilst you are so very exact in acting up to it on one side, do you not a little overlook it on the other?

I am extremely unwilling to say a disagreeable thing to you, but Miss Fermor is too young as well as too gay to be a protection—the very particular circumstance you mention makes Mr Melmoth's the only house in Canada in which, if I have any judgment, you can with propriety live till your marriage takes place.

You extremely injure Sir George in supposing it possible he should fail in his engagements: and I see with pain that you are more quicksighted to his failings than is quite consistent with that tenderness, which (allow me to say) he has a right to expect from you. He is like other men of his age and fortune; he is the very man you so lately thought amiable, and of whose love you cannot without injustice have a doubt.

Though I approve your contempt of the false glitter of the world, yet I think it a little strained at your time of life: did I not know you as well as I do, I should say that philosophy in a young and especially a female mind, is so out of season as to be extremely suspicious. The pleasures which attend on affluence are too great, and too pleasing to youth, to be overlooked, except when under the influence of a livelier passion.

Take care, my Emily; I know the goodness of your heart, but I also know its sensibility; remember that, if your situation requires great circumspection in your behaviour to Sir George, it requires much greater to every other person: it is even more delicate than marriage itself.

I shall expect you and Miss Fermor as soon as the roads are such that you can travel agreeably; and, as you object to Sir George as a conductor, I will entreat Captain Fermor to accompany you hither.

> I am, my dear,
>> Your most affectionate

>>> E. Melmoth

LETTER 47 SILLERI, DEC. 26: I entreat you, my dearest Madam, to do me the justice to believe I see my engagement to Sir George in as strong a light as you can do; if there is any change in my behaviour to him, it is owing to the very apparent one in his conduct to me, of which no one but myself can be a judge. As to what you say in regard to my contempt of affluence, I can only say it is in my character, whether it is generally in the female one or not.

Were the cruel hint you are pleased to give just, be assured Sir George should be the first person to whom I would declare it. I hope however it is possible to esteem merit without offending even the most sacred of all engagements.

A gentleman waits for this. I have only time to say, that Miss Fermor thanks you for your obliging invitation, and promises she will accompany me to Montreal as soon as the river St Lawrence will bear carriages, as the upper road is extremely inconvenient.

> I am,
>> My dearest Madam,
>>> Your obliged
>>>> and faithful

>>>> EMILY MONTAGUE

LETTER 48   SILLERI, DEC. 27: After a fortnight's snow, we have had near as much clear blue sky and sunshine: the snow is six feet deep, so that we may be said to walk on our own heads; that is, speaking *en philosophe*, we occupy the space we should have done in summer if we had done so; or, to explain it more clearly, our heels are now where our heads should be.

The scene is a little changed for the worse: the lovely landscape is now one undistinguished waste of snow, only a little diversified by the great variety of evergreens in the woods: the romantic winding path down the side of the hill to our farm, on which we used to amuse ourselves with seeing the beaux serpentize, is now a confused, frightful, rugged precipice, which one trembles at the idea of ascending.

There is something exceedingly agreeable in the whirl of the carrioles, which fly along at the rate of twenty miles an hour; and really hurry one out of one's senses.

Our little coterie is the object of great envy; we live just as we like, without thinking of other people, which I am not sure *here* is prudent, but it is pleasant, which is a better thing.

Emily, who is the civilest creature breathing, is for giving up her own pleasure to avoid offending others, and wants me, every time we make a carrioling-party, to invite all the misses of Quebec to go with us, because they seem angry at our being happy without them: but for that very reason I persist in my own way, and consider wisely, that, though civility is due to other people, yet there is also some civility due to one's self.

I agree to visit every body, but think it mighty absurd I must not take a ride without asking a hundred people I scarce know to go with me: yet this is the style here; they will neither be happy themselves, nor let any body else. Adieu!

Dec. 29

I will never take a beaver's word again as long as I live: there is no supporting this cold; the Canadians say it is seventeen years since there has been so severe a season. I thought beavers had been people of more honour.

Adieu! I can no more: the ink freezes as I take it from the standish to the paper, though close to a large stove. Don't expect me to write again till May; one's faculties are absolutely congealed this weather.

Yours,

A. FERMOR

LETTER 49   SILLERI, JAN. I: It is with difficulty I breathe, my dear; the cold is so amazingly intense as almost totally to stop respiration. I have business, the business of pleasure, at Quebec; but have not courage to stir from the stove.

We have had five days, the severity of which none of the natives remember to have ever seen equalled: 'tis said, the cold is beyond all the thermometers here, tho' intended for the climate.

The strongest wine freezes in a room which has a stove in it; even brandy is thickened to the consistence of oil: the largest wood fire, in a wide chimney, does not throw out its heat a quarter of a yard.

I must venture to Quebec to-morrow, or have company at home: amusements are here necessary to life; we must be jovial, or the blood will freeze in our veins.

I no longer wonder the elegant arts are unknown here; the rigour of the climate suspends the very powers of the understanding: what then must become of those of the imagination? Those who expect to see

"A new Athens rising near the pole,"

will find themselves extremely disappointed. Genius will never mount high, where the faculties of the mind are benumbed half the year.

'Tis sufficient employment for the most lively spirit here to contrive how to preserve an existence, of which there are moments that one is hardly conscious: the cold really sometimes brings on a sort of stupefaction.

We had a million of beaux here yesterday, notwithstanding the severe cold: 'tis the Canadian custom, calculated I suppose for the climate, to visit all the ladies on New-year's-day, who sit dressed in form to be kissed: I assure you, however, our kisses could not warm them; but we were obliged, to our eternal disgrace, to call in rasberry brandy as an auxiliary.

You would have died to see the men; they look just like so many bears in their open carrioles, all wrapped in furs from head to foot; you see nothing of the human form appear, but the tip of a nose.

They have intire coats of beaver skin exactly like Friday's in Robinson Crusoe, and casques on their heads like the old knights errant in romance; you never saw such tremendous figures; but without this kind of clothing it would be impossible to stir out at present.

The ladies are equally covered up, tho' in a less unbecoming style; they have long cloth cloaks with loose hoods, like those worn by the market-women in the north of England. I have one in scarlet, the hood lined with sable, the prettiest ever seen here, in which I assure you I look amazingly handsome; the men think so, and call me the *Little red riding-hood*; a name which becomes me as well as the hood.

The Canadian ladies wear these cloaks in India silk in summer, which, fluttering in the wind, look really graceful on a fine woman.

Besides our riding-hoods, when we go out, we have a large buffaloe's skin under our feet, which turns up, and wraps round us almost to our shoulders; so that, upon the whole, we are pretty well guarded from the weather as well as the men.

Our covered carrioles too have not only canvas windows (we dare not have glass, because we often overturn), but cloth curtains to draw all round us; the extreme swiftness of these carriages also, which dart along like lightening, helps to keep one warm, by promoting the circulation of the blood.

I pity the Fitz; no tiger was ever so hard-hearted as I am this weather: the little god has taken his flight, like the swallows. I say nothing, but cruelty is no virtue in Canada; at least at this season.

I suppose Pygmalion's statue was some frozen Canadian gentlewoman, and a sudden warm day thawed her. I love to expound ancient fables, and I think no exposition can be more natural than this.

Would you know what makes me chatter so this morning? Papa has made me take some excellent *liqueur*; 'tis the mode here; all the Canadian ladies take a little, which makes them so coquet and agreeable. Certainly brandy makes a woman talk like an angel. Adieu!

Yours,

A. FERMOR

LETTER 50 SILLERI, JAN. 4: I don't quite agree with you, my dear; your brother does not appear to me to have the least scruple of that foolish false modesty which stands in a man's way.

He is extremely what the French call *awakened*; he is modest, certainly; that is, he is not a coxcomb, but he has all that proper self-confidence which is necessary to set his agreeable qualities in full light: nothing can be a stronger proof of this, than that, wherever he is, he always takes your attention in a moment, and this without seeming to solicit it.

I am very fond of him, though he never makes love to me, in which circumstance he is very singular: our friendship is quite platonic, at least on his side, for I am not quite so sure on the other. I remember one day in summer we were walking *tête à tête* in the road to Cape Rouge, when he wanted me to strike into a very beautiful thicket: "Positively, Rivers," said I, "I will not venture with you into that wood." "Are you afraid of *me*, Bell?" "No, but extremely of *myself*."

I have loved him ever since a little scene that passed here three or four months ago: a very affecting story, of a distressed family in our neighbourhood, was told him and Sir George; the latter preserved all the philosophic dignity and manly composure of his countenance, very coldly expressed his concern, and called another subject: your brother changed colour, his eyes glistened; he took the first opportunity to leave the room, he sought these poor people, he found, he relieved them; which we discovered by accident a month after.

The weather, tho' cold beyond all that you in England can form an idea of, is yet mild to what it has been the last five or six days; we are going to Quebec, to church.

Two o'clock

Emily and I have been talking religion all the way home: we are both mighty good girls, as girls go in these degenerate days; our grandmothers to be sure—but it's folly to look back.

We have been saying, Lucy, that 'tis the strangest thing in the world people should quarrel about religion, since we undoubtedly all mean the same thing; all good minds in every religion aim at pleasing the Supreme Being; the means we take differ according to the country where we are born, and the prejudices we imbibe from education; a consideration which ought to inspire us with kindness and indulgence to each other.

If we examine each other's sentiments with candour, we shall find much less difference in essentials than we imagine:

> "Since all agree to own, at least to mean,
> One great, one good, one general Lord of all."

There is, I think, a very pretty Sunday reflexion for you, Lucy.

You must know, I am extremely religious; and for this amongst other reasons, that I think infidelity a vice peculiarly contrary to the native softness of woman: it is bold, daring, masculine; and I should almost doubt the sex of an unbeliever in petticoats.

Women are religious as they are virtuous, less from principles founded on reasoning and argument, than from elegance of mind, delicacy of moral taste, and a certain quick perception of the beautiful and becoming in everything.

This instinct, however, for such it is, is worth all the tedious reasonings of the men; which is a point I flatter myself you will not dispute with me.

Monday, Jan. 5

This is the first day I have ventured in an open carriole; we have been running a race on the snow, your brother and I against Emily and Fitzgerald: we conquered from Fitzgerald's complaisance to Emily. I shall like it mightily, well wrapt up: I set off with a crape over my face to keep off the cold, but in three minutes it was a cake of solid ice, from my breath which froze upon it; yet this is called a mild day, and the sun shines in all his glory.

Silleri, Thursday, Jan. 8, midnight

We are just come from the general's assembly; much company, and we danced till this minute; for I believe we have not been more, coming these four miles.

Fitzgerald is the very pink of courtesy; he never uses his covered carriole himself, but devotes it entirely to the ladies; it stands at the general's door in waiting on Thursdays: if any lady comes out before her carriole arrives, the servants call out mechanically, "Captain Fitzgerald's carriole here, for a lady." The Colonel is equally gallant, but I generally lay an embargo on his: they have each of them an extremely pretty one for themselves, or to drive a fair lady a morning's airing, when she will allow them the honour, and the weather is mild enough to permit it.

Bon soir! I am sleepy.

Yours,

A. FERMOR

TO JOHN TEMPLE, ESQ; PALL MALL

LETTER 51   QUEBEC, JAN. 9: You mistake me extremely, Jack, as you generally do: I have by no means forsworn marriage: on the contrary, though happiness is not so often found there as I wish it was, yet I am convinced it is to be found no where else; and, poor as I am, I should not hesitate about trying the experiment myself to-morrow, if I could meet with a woman to my taste, unappropriated, whose ideas of the state agreed with mine, which I allow are something out of the common road: but I must be certain those ideas are her own, therefore they must arise spontaneously, and not in complaisance to mine; for which reason, if I could, I would endeavour to lead my mistress into the subject, and know her sentiments on the manner of living in that state before I discovered my own.

I must also be well convinced of her tenderness before I make a declaration of mine: she must not distinguish me because I flatter her, but because she thinks I have merit; those fancied passions, where gratified vanity assumes the form of love, will not satisfy my heart: the eyes, the air, the voice of the woman I love, a thousand little indiscretions dear to the heart, must convince me I am beloved, before I confess I love.

Though sensible of the advantages of fortune, I can be happy without it: if I should ever be rich enough to live in the world, no one will enjoy it with greater gust; if not, I can with great spirit, provided I find such a companion as I wish, retire from it to love, content, and a cottage: by which I mean to the life of a little country gentleman.

You ask me my opinion of the winter here. If you can bear a degree of cold, of which Europeans can form no idea, it is far from being unpleasant; we have settled frost, and an eternal blue sky. Travelling in this country in winter is particularly agreeable: the carriages are easy, and go on the ice with an amazing velocity, though drawn only by one horse.

The continual plain of snow would be extremely fatiguing both to the eye and imagination, were not both relieved, not only by the woods in prospect, but by the tall branches of pines with which the road is marked out on each side, and which form a verdant avenue agreeably contrasted with the dazzling whiteness of the snow, on which, when the sun shines, it is almost impossible to look steadily even for a moment.

Were it not for this method of marking out the roads, it would be impossible to find the way from one village to another.

The eternal sameness however of this avenue is tiresome when you go far in one road.

I have passed the last two months in the most agreeable manner possible, in a little society of persons I extremely love: I feel myself so attached to this little circle of friends, that I have no pleasure in any other company, and think all the time absolutely lost that politeness forces me to spend any where else. I extremely dread our party's being dissolved, and wish the winter to last for ever, for I am afraid the spring will divide us.

Adieu! and believe me,

Yours,

Ed. Rivers

TO MISS RIVERS, CLARGES STREET

LETTER 52 SILLERI, JAN. 9: I begin not to disrelish the winter here; now I am used to the cold, I don't feel it so much: as there is no business done here in the winter, 'tis the season of general dissipation; amusement is the study of every body, and the pains people take to please themselves contribute to the general pleasure: upon the whole, I am not sure it is not a pleasanter winter than that of England.

Both our houses and our carriages are uncommonly warm; the clear serene sky, the dry pure air, the little parties of dancing and cards, the good tables we all keep, the driving about on the ice, the abundance of people we see there, for every body has a carriole, the variety of objects new to an European, keep the spirits in a continual agreeable hurry, that is difficult to describe, but very pleasant to feel.

Sir George (would you believe it?) has written Emily a very warm letter; tender, sentimental, and almost impatient;

Mrs Melmoth's dictating, I will answer for it; not at all in his own composed agreeable style. He talks of coming down in a few days: I have a strong notion he is coming, after his long tedious two years' siege, to endeavour to take us by storm at last; he certainly prepares for a *coup de main*. He is right, all women hate a regular attack.

Adieu for the present.

Monday, Jan. 12

We sup at your brother's to-night, with all the *beau monde* of Quebec: we shall be superbly entertained, I know. I am malicious enough to wish Sir George may arrive during the entertainment, because I have an idea it will mortify him; though I scarce know why I think so. Adieu!

Yours,

A. FERMOR

TO MISS RIVERS, CLARGES STREET

LETTER 53 JAN. 13, ELEVEN O'CLOCK: We passed a most agreeable evening with your brother, though a large company, which is seldom the case: a most admirable supper, excellent wine, an elegant dessert of preserved fruits, and every body in spirits and good humour.

The Colonel was the soul of our entertainment: amongst his other virtues, he has the companionable and convivial ones to an immense degree, which I never had an opportunity of discovering so clearly before. He seemed charmed beyond words to see us all so happy: we staid till four o'clock in the morning, yet all complained to-day we came away too soon.

I need not tell you we had fiddles, for there is no entertainment in Canada without them: never was such a race of dancers.

One o'clock

The dear man is come, and with an equipage which puts the Empress of Russia's traineau to shame. America never beheld any thing so brilliant:

> "*All other carrioles, at sight of this,*
> "*Hide their diminish'd heads.*"

Your brother's and Fitzgerald's will never dare to appear now; they sink into nothing.

Seven in the evening

Emily has been in tears in her chamber; 'tis a letter of Mrs Melmoth's which has had this agreeable effect: some wise advice, I suppose. Lord! how I hate people that give advice! don't you, Lucy?

I don't like this lover's coming; he is almost as bad as a husband: I am afraid he will derange our little coterie; and we have been so happy, I can't bear it.

Good night, my dear.

Yours,

A. FERMOR

TO MISS RIVERS, CLARGES STREET

LETTER 54 SILLERI, JAN. 14: We have passed a mighty stupid day; Sir George is civil, attentive, and dull; Emily pensive, thoughtful, and silent; and my little self as peevish as an old maid: nobody comes near us, not even your brother, because we are supposed to be settling preliminaries; for you must know Sir George has graciously condescended to change his mind, and will marry her, if she pleases, without waiting for his mother's letter, which resolution he has communicated to twenty people at Quebec in his way hither; he is really extremely obliging. I suppose the Melmoths have spirited him up to this.

One o'clock

Emily is strangely reserved to me; she avoids seeing me alone, and when it happens talks of the weather; papa is however in her confidence: he is as strong an advocate for this milky baronet as Mrs Melmoth.

Ten at night

All is over, Lucy; that is to say, all is fixed: they are to be married on Monday next at the Recollects' church, and to set off immediately for Montreal: my father has been telling me the whole plan of operations: we go up with them, stay a fortnight, then all come down, and stay away till summer, when the happy pair embark in the first ship for England.

Emily is really what one would call a prudent sort of

woman, I did not think it had been in her: she is certainly right, there is danger in delay; she has a thousand proverbs on her side; I thought what all her fine sentiments would come to; she should at least have waited for mamma's consent; this hurry is not quite consistent with that extreme delicacy on which she piques herself; it looks exceedingly as if she was afraid of losing him.

I don't love her half so well as I did three days ago; I hate discreet young ladies that marry and settle; give me an agreeable fellow and a knapsack.

My poor Rivers! what will become of him when we are gone? he has neglected every body for us.

As she loves the pleasures of conversation, she will be amazingly happy in her choice;

"*With such a companion to spend the long day!*"

He is to be sure a most entertaining creature.

Adieu! I have no patience.

Yours,

A. FERMOR

After all, I am a little droll; I am angry with Emily for concluding an advantageous match with a man she does not absolutely dislike, which all good mammas say is sufficient; and this only because it breaks in on a little circle of friends, in whose society I have been happy. O! self! self! I would have her hazard losing a fine fortune and a coach and six, that I may continue my coterie two or three months longer.

Adieu! I will write again as soon as we are married. My next will, I suppose, be from Montreal. I die to see your brother and my little Fitzgerald; this man gives me the vapours. Heavens! Lucy, what a difference there is in men!

TO MISS RIVERS, CLARGES STREET

LETTER 55 SILLERI, JAN. 16: So, my dear, we went on too fast, it seems: Sir George was so obliging as to settle all without waiting for Emily's consent; not having supposed her refusal to be in the chapter of possibilities: after having communicated their plan of operations to me as an affair settled, papa was dispatched, as Sir George's ambassador, to inform Emily of his gracious intentions in her favour.

She received him with proper dignity, and like a girl of true spirit told him, that as the delay was originally from Sir George, she should insist on observing the conditions very exactly, and was determined to wait till spring, whatever might be the contents of Mrs Clayton's expected letter; reserving to herself also the privilege of refusing him even then, if upon mature deliberation she should think proper so to do.

She has further insisted, that till that time he shall leave Silleri; take up his abode at Quebec, unless, which she thinks most adviseable, he should return to Montreal for the winter; and never attempt seeing her without witnesses, as their present situation is particularly delicate, and that whilst it continues they can have nothing to say to each other which their common friends may not with propriety hear: all she can be prevailed on to consent to in his favour, is to allow him *en attendant* to visit here like any other gentleman.

I wish she would send him back to Montreal, for I see plainly he will spoil all our little parties.

Emily is a fine girl, Lucy, and I am friends with her again; so, my dear, I shall revive my coterie, and be happy two or three months longer. I have sent to ask my two sweet fellows at Quebec to dine here: I really long to see them; I shall let them into the present state of affairs here, for they both despise Sir George as much as I do; the creature looks amazingly foolish, and I enjoy his humiliation not a little; such an animal to set up for being beloved indeed! O to be sure!

Emily has sent for me to her apartment. Adieu for a moment.

Eleven o'clock

She has shewn me Mrs Melmoth's letter on the subject of concluding the marriage immediately: it is in the true spirit of family impertinence. She writes with the kind discreet insolence of a relation; and Emily has answered her with the genuine spirit of an independent Englishwoman, who is so happy as to be her own mistress, and who is therefore determined to think for herself.

She has refused going to Montreal at all this winter; and has hinted, though not impolitely, that she wants no guardian of her conduct but herself; adding a compliment to my ladyship's discretion so very civil, it is impossible for me to repeat it with decency.

O Heavens! your brother and Fitzgerald! I fly. The

dear creatures! my life has been absolute vegetation since they absented themselves.

Adieu! my dear,

Your faithful

A. FERMOR

TO MISS RIVERS, CLARGES STREET

LETTER 56 SILLERI, JAN. 24: We have the same parties and amusements we used to have, my dear, but there is by no means the same spirit in them; constraint and dullness seem to have taken the place of that sweet vivacity and confidence which made our little society so pleasing: this odious man has infected us all; he seems rather a spy on our pleasures than a partaker of them; he is more an antidote to joy than a tall maiden aunt.

I wish he would go; I say spontaneously every time I see him, without considering I am impolite, "La! Sir George, when do you go to Montreal?" He reddens, and gives me a peevish answer; and I then, and not before, recollect how very impertinent the question is.

But pray, my dear, because he has no taste for social companionable life, has he therefore a right to damp the spirit of it in those that have? I intend to consult some learned casuist on this head.

He takes amazing pains to please in his way, is curled, powdered, perfumed, and exhibits every day in a new suit of embroidery; but with all this, has the mortification to see your brother please more in a plain coat. I am lazy. Adieu!

Yours, ever and ever,

A. FERMOR

TO JOHN TEMPLE, ESQ; PALL MALL

LETTER 57 JAN. 25: So you intend, my dear Jack, to marry when you are quite tired of a life of gallantry: the lady will be much obliged to you for a heart, the refuse of half the prostitutes in town; a heart, the best feelings of which will be entirely obliterated; a heart hardened by a long commerce with the most unworthy of the sex; and which will bring disgust, suspicion, coldness, and depravity of taste, to the bosom of sensibility and innocence.

For my own part, though fond of women to the greatest degree, I have had, considering my profession and complexion, very few intrigues. I have always had an idea I should some time or other marry, and have been unwilling to bring to a state in which I hoped for happiness from mutual affection, a heart worn out by a course of gallantries: to a contrary conduct is owing most of our unhappy marriages; the woman brings with her all her flock of tenderness, truth, and affection; the man's is exhausted before they meet: she finds the generous delicate tenderness of her soul, not only unreturned, but unobserved; she fancies some other woman the object of his affection, she is unhappy, she pines in secret; he observes her discontent, accuses her of caprice; and her portion is wretchedness for life.

If I did not ardently wish your happiness, I should not thus repeatedly combat a prejudice, which, as you have sensibility, will infallibly make the greater part of your life a scene of insipidity and regret.

You are right, Jack, as to the savages; the only way to civilize them is to *feminize* their women; but the task is rather difficult: at present their manners differ in nothing from those of the men; they even add to the ferocity of the latter.

You desire to know the state of my heart; excuse me, Jack; you know nothing of love; and we who do, never disclose its mysteries to the prophane: besides, I always choose a female for the confidante of my sentiments; I hate even to speak of love to one of my own sex.

Adieu! I am going to a party with half a dozen ladies, and have not another minute to spare.

Yours,

Ed. Rivers

TO MISS RIVERS, CLARGES STREET

LETTER 58 JAN. 28: I every hour, my dear, grow more in love with French manners; there is something charming in being young and sprightly all one's life: it would appear absurd in England to hear, what I have just heard, a fat virtuous lady of seventy toast *Love and Opportunity* to a young fellow: but 'tis nothing here: they dance too to the last gasp; I have seen the daughter, mother, and grand-daughter, in the same French country dance.

They are perfectly right; and I honour them for their good sense and spirit, in determining to make life agreeable as long as they can.

A propos to age, I am resolved to go home, Lucy; I have found three grey hairs this morning; they tell me 'tis common; this vile climate is at war with beauty, makes one's hair grey, and one's hands red. I won't stay absolutely.

Do you know there is a very pretty fellow here, Lucy, Captain Howard, who has taken a fancy to make people believe he and I are on good terms? He affects to sit by me, to dance with me, to whisper nothing to me, to bow with an air of mystery, and to shew me all the little attentions of a lover in public, though he never yet said a civil thing to me when we were alone.

I was standing with him this morning near the brow of the hill, leaning against a tree in the sunshine, and looking down the precipice below, when I said something of the lover's leap, and in play, as you will suppose, made a step forwards: we had been talking of indifferent things, his air was till then indolence itself; but on this little motion of mine, though there was not the least danger, he with the utmost seeming eagerness catched hold of me as if alarmed at the very idea, and with the most passionate air protested his life depended on mine, and that he would not live an hour after me. I looked at him with astonishment, not being able to comprehend the meaning of this sudden flight, when turning my head, I saw a gentleman and lady close behind us, whom he had observed though I had not. They were retiring: "Pray approach, my dear Madam," said I; "we have no secrets, this declaration was intended for you to hear; we were talking of the weather before you came."

He affected to smile, though I saw he was mortified; but as his smile shewed the finest teeth imaginable I forgave him: he is really very handsome, and 'tis pity he has this foolish quality of preferring the shadow to the substance.

I shall, however, desire him to flirt elsewhere, as this *badinage*, however innocent, may hurt my character, and give pain to my little Fitzgerald: I believe I begin to love this fellow, because I begin to be delicate on the subject of flirtations, and feel my spirit of coquetry decline every day.

Mrs Clayton has wrote, my dear; and, has at last con-descended to allow Emily the honour of being her daughter-in-law, in consideration of her son's happiness, and of engagements entered into with her own consent; though she very prudently observes that what was a proper match for Captain Clayton is by no means so for Sir George; and talks something of an offer of a citizen's daughter with fifty thousand pounds, and the promise of an Irish title. She has, however, observed that indiscreet en-gagements are better broke than kept.

Sir George has shewn the letter, a very indelicate one in my opinion, to my father and me; and has talked a great deal of nonsense on the subject. He wants to shew it to Emily, and I advise him to it, because I know the effect it will have. I see plainly he wishes to make a great merit of keeping his engage-ment, if he does keep it: he hinted a little fear of breaking her heart; and I am convinced if he thought she could survive his infidelity, all his tenderness and constancy would cede to filial duty and a coronet.

After much deliberation, Sir George has determined to write to Emily, inclose his mother's letter, and call in the after-noon to enjoy the triumph of his generosity in keeping his en-gagements, when it is in his power to do so much better: 'tis a pretty plan, and I encourage him in it; my father, who wishes the match, shrugs his shoulders, and frowns at me; but the little man is fixed as fate in his resolve, and is writing at this moment in my father's apartment. I long to see his letter; I dare say it will be a curiosity: 'tis short however, for he is coming out of the room already.

Adieu! my father calls for this letter; it is to go in one of his to New York, and the person who takes it waits for it at the door.

Ever yours,

A. Fermor

LETTER 59   Dear Madam, I send you the inclosed from my mother: I thought it necessary you should see it, though not even a mother's wishes shall ever influence me to break those engagements which I have had the happiness of entering into with the most charming of women, and which a man of honour ought to hold sacred.

I do not think happiness entirely dependent on rank or fortune, and have only to wish my mother's sentiments on this subject more agreeable to my own, as there is nothing I so much wish as to oblige her: at all events, however, depend on my fulfilling those promises, which ought to be the more binding, as they were made at a time when our situations were more equal.

I am happy in an opportunity of convincing you and the world that interest and ambition have no power over my heart, when put in competition with what I owe to my engagements; being with the greatest truth,

My dearest Madam,

Yours, etc.

G. CLAYTON

You will do me the honour to name the day to make me happy.

TO SIR GEORGE CLAYTON, AT QUEBEC

LETTER 60   Dear Sir, I have read Mrs Clayton's letter with attention; and am of her opinion, that indiscreet engagements are better broke than kept.

I have the less reason to take ill your breaking the kind of engagement between us at the desire of your family, as I entered into it at first entirely in compliance with mine. I have ever had the sincerest esteem and friendship for you, but never that romantic love which hurries us to forget all but itself: I have therefore no reason to expect in you the imprudent disinterestedness that passion occasions.

A fuller explanation is necessary on this subject than it is possible to enter into in a letter: if you will favour us with your company this afternoon at Silleri, we may explain our sentiments more clearly to each other: be assured, I never will prevent your complying in every instance with the wishes of so kind and prudent a mother.

I am, dear Sir,

Your affectionate friend

and obedient servant,

EMILY MONTAGUE

LETTER 61 I have been with Emily, who has been reading Mrs Clayton's letter; I saw joy sparkle in her eyes as she went on, her little heart seemed to flutter with transport; I see two things very clearly, one of which is, that she never loved this little insipid Baronet; the other I leave your sagacity to find out. All the spirit of her countenance is returned: she walks in air; her cheeks have the blush of pleasure; I never saw so astonishing a change. I never felt more joy from the acquisition of a new lover, than she seems to find in the prospect of losing an old one.

She has written to Sir George, and in a style that I know will hurt him; for though I believe he wishes her to give him up, yet his vanity would desire it should cost her very dear; and appear the effort of disinterested love, and romantic generosity, not what it really is, the effect of the most tranquil and perfect indifference.

By the way, a disinterested mistress is, according to my ideas, a mistress who *fancies* she loves: we may talk what we please, at a distance, of sacrificing the dear man to his interest, and promoting his happiness by destroying our own; but when it comes to the point, I am rather inclined to believe all women are of my way of thinking; and let me die if I would give up a man I loved to the first duchess in Christendom: 'tis all mighty well in theory; but for the practical part, let who will believe it for Bell.

Indeed when a woman finds her lover inclined to change, 'tis good to make a virtue of necessity, and give the thing a sentimental turn, which gratifies his vanity, and does not wound one's own.

Adieu! I see Sir George and his fine carriole; I must run, and tell Emily.

Ever yours,

A. Fermor

LETTER 62 JAN. 28: Yes, my Lucy, your brother tenderly regrets the absence of a sister endeared to him much more by her amiable qualities than by blood; who would be the object of his esteem and admiration, if she was not that of his fraternal tenderness; who has all the blooming graces, simplicity, and innocence of nineteen, with the accomplishments and understanding of five and twenty; who joins the strength of mind so often confined to our sex, to the softness, delicacy, and vivacity of her own; who, in short, is all that is estimable and lovely; and who, except one, is the most charming of her sex: you will forgive the exception, Lucy, perhaps no man but a brother would make it.

My sweet Emily appears every day more amiable; she is now in the full tyranny of her charms, at the age when the mind is improved, and the person in its perfection. I every day see in her more indifference to her lover, a circumstance which gives me a pleasure which perhaps it ought not: there is a selfishness in it, for which I am afraid I ought to blush.

You judge perfectly well, my dear, in checking the natural vivacity of your temper, however pleasing it is to all who converse with you: coquetry is dangerous to Englishwomen, because they have sensibility; it is more suited to the French, who are naturally something of the salamander kind.

I have this moment a note from Bell Fermor, that she must see me this instant. I hope my Emily is well: Heaven preserve the most perfect of all its works!

Adieu! my dear girl.

Your affectionate

ED. RIVERS

TO MISS RIVERS, CLARGES STREET

LETTER **63** FEB. 1: We have passed three or four droll days, my dear. Emily persists in resolving to break with Sir George; he thinks it decent to combat her resolution, lest he should lose the praise of generosity: he is also piqued to see her give him up with such perfect composure, though I am convinced he will not be sorry upon the whole to be given up; he has, from the first receipt of the letter, plainly wished her to resign him, but hoped for a few faintings and tears, as a sacrifice to his vanity on the occasion.

My father is setting every engine at work to make things up again, supposing Emily to have determined from pique, not from the real feelings of her heart; he is frighted to death lest I should counter-work him, and so jealous of my advising her to continue a conduct he so much disapproves, that he won't leave us a moment together; he even observes carefully that each goes into her respective apartment when we retire to bed.

This jealousy has started an idea which I think will amuse us, and which I shall take the first opportunity of communicating to Emily; 'tis to write each other at night our sentiments on whatever passes in the day: if she approves the plan, I will send you the letters, which will save me a great deal of trouble in telling you all our *petites histoires*.

This scheme will have another advantage; we shall be a thousand times more sincere and open to each other by letter than face to face; I have long seen by her eyes that the little fool has twenty things to say to me, but has not courage; now letters you know, my dear,

Excuse the blush, and pour out all the heart.

Besides, it will be so romantic and pretty, almost as agreeable as a love affair: I long to begin the correspondence.

Adieu!

Yours

A. FERMOR

TO MISS RIVERS, CLARGES STREET

LETTER 64 QUEBEC, FEB. 5: I have but a moment, my Lucy, to tell you, my divine Emily has broke with her lover, who this morning took an eternal leave of her, and set out for Montreal in his way to New York, whence he proposes to embark for England.

My sensations on this occasion are not to be described: I admire that amiable delicacy which has influenced her to give up every advantage of rank and fortune which could tempt the heart of woman, rather than unite herself to a man for whom she felt the least degree of indifference; and this, without regarding the censures of her family, or of the world, by whom, what they will call her imprudence, will never be forgiven: a woman who is capable of acting so nobly, is worthy of being loved, of being adored, by every man who has a soul to distinguish her perfections.

If I was a vain man, I might perhaps fancy her regard for me had some share in determining her conduct, but I am convinced of the contrary; 'tis the native delicacy of her soul alone, incapable of forming an union in which the heart has no share, which, independent of any other consideration, has been the cause of a resolution so worthy of herself.

That she has the tenderest affection for me, I cannot doubt one moment; her attention is too flattering to be unobserved; but 'tis that kind of affection in which the mind alone is concerned. I never gave her the most distant hint that I loved her: in her situation, it would have been even an outrage to have done so. She knows the narrowness of my circumstances, and how near impossible it is for me to marry; she therefore could not have an idea—no, my dear girl, 'tis not to love, but to true delicacy, that she has sacrificed avarice and ambition; and she is a thousand times the more estimable from this circumstance.

I am interrupted. You shall hear from me in a few days. Adieu!

Your affectionate
Ed. Rivers

TO MISS RIVERS, CLARGES STREET

LETTER **65** SILLERI, FEB. 10: I have mentioned my plan to Emily, who is charmed with it; 'tis a pretty evening amusement for two solitary girls in the country.

Behold the first fruits of our correspondence.

"To Miss Fermor

"It is not to you, my dear girl, I need vindicate my conduct in regard to Sir George; you have from the first approved it; you have even advised it. If I have been to blame, 'tis in having too long delayed an explanation on a point of such importance to us both. I have been long on the borders of a precipice, without courage to retire from so dangerous a situation: overborne by my family, I have been near marrying a man for whom I have not the least tenderness, and whose conversation is even now tedious to me.

"My dear friend, we were not formed for each other: our minds have not the least resemblance. Have you not observed, that, when I have timidly hazarded my ideas on the delicacy necessary to keep love alive in marriage, and the difficulty of preserving the heart of the object beloved in so intimate an union, he has indolently assented, with a coldness not to be described, to sentiments which it is plain from his manner he did not understand; whilst another, not interested in the conversation, has, by his countenance, by the fire of his eyes, by looks more eloquent than all language, shewed his soul was of intelligence with mine!

"A strong sense of the force of engagements entered into with my consent, though not the effect of my free, unbiassed choice, and the fear of making Sir George, by whom I supposed myself beloved, unhappy, have thus long prevented my resolving to break with him for ever; and though I could not bring myself to marry him, I found myself at the same time incapable of assuming sufficient resolution to tell him so, 'till his mother's letter gave me so happy an occasion.

"There is no saying what transport I feel in being freed from the insupportable yoke of this engagement, which has long sat heavy on my heart, and suspended the natural chearfulness of my temper.

"Yes, my dear, your Emily has been wretched, without daring to confess it even to you: I was ashamed of owning I had entered into such engagements with a man whom I had never loved, though I had for a short time mistaken esteem for a greater degree of affection than my heart ever really knew. How fatal, my dear Bell, is this mistake to half our sex, and how happy am I to have discovered mine in time.

"I have scarce yet asked myself what I intend; but I think it will be most prudent to return to England in the first ship, and retire to a relation of my mother's in the country, where I can live with decency on my little fortune.

"Whatever is my fate, no situation can be equally unhappy with that of being wife to a man for whom I have not even the slightest friendship or esteem, for whose conversation I have not the least taste, and who, if I know him, would for ever think me under an obligation to him for marrying me.

"I have the pleasure to see I give no pain to his heart by a step which has relieved mine from misery: his feelings are those of wounded vanity, not of love.

"Adieu! Your

"EMILY MONTAGUE"

I have no patience with relations, Lucy; this sweet girl has been two years wretched under the bondage her uncle's avarice (for he foresaw Sir George's acquisition, though she did not) prepared for her. Parents should choose our company, but never even pretend to direct our choice; if they take care we converse with men of honour only, 'tis impossible we can choose amiss: a conformity of taste and sentiment alone can make marriage happy, and of that none but the parties concerned can judge.

By the way, I think long engagements, even between persons who love, extremely unfavourable to happiness: it is certainly right to be long enough acquainted to know something of each other's temper; but 'tis bad to let the first fire burn out before we come together; and when we have once resolved, I have no notion of delaying a moment.

If I should ever consent to marry Fitzgerald, and he should not fly for a licence before I had finished the sentence, I would dismiss him if there was not another lover to be had in Canada.

Adieu!

Your faithful

A. Fermor

My Emily is now free as air; a sweet little bird escaped from the gilded cage. Are you not glad of it, Lucy? I am amazingly.

TO MISS RIVERS, CLARGES STREET

LETTER 66 QUEBEC, FEB. 11: Would one think it possible, Lucy, that Sir George should console himself for the loss of all that is lovely in woman, by the sordid prospect of acquiring, by an interested marriage, a little more of that wealth of which he has already much more than he can either enjoy or become? By what wretched motives are half mankind influenced in the most important action of their lives!

The vulgar of every rank expect happiness where it is not to be found, in the ideal advantages of splendour and dissipation; those who dare to think, those minds who partake of the celestial fire, seek it in the real, solid pleasures of nature and soft affection.

I have seen my lovely Emily since I wrote to you; I shall not see her again for some days; I do not intend at present to make my visits to Silleri so frequent as I have done lately, lest the world, ever studious to blame, should misconstrue her conduct on this very delicate occasion. I am even afraid to shew my usual attention to her when present, lest she herself should think I presume on the politeness she has ever shewn me, and see her breaking with Sir George in a false light: the greater I think her obliging partiality to me, the more guarded I ought to be in my behaviour to her; her situation has some resemblance to widowhood, and she has equal decorums to observe.

I cannot however help encouraging a pleasing hope that I am not absolutely indifferent to her; her lovely eyes have a softness when they meet mine, to which words cannot do justice: she talks less to me than to others, but it is in a tone of voice which penetrates my soul; and when I speak, her attention is most flattering, though of a nature not to be seen by common observers; without seeming to distinguish me from the crowd who strive to engage her esteem and friendship, she has a manner of addressing me which the heart alone can feel; she contrives to prevent my appearing to give her any preference to the rest of her sex, yet I have seen her blush at my civility to another.

She has at least a friendship for me, which alone would make the happiness of my life; and which I would prefer to the love of the most charming woman imagination could form, sensible as I am to the sweetest of all passions: this friendship, however, time and assiduity may ripen into love; at least I should be most unhappy if I did not think so.

I love her with a tenderness of which few of my sex are capable: you have often told me, and you were right, that my heart has all the sensibility of woman.

A mail is arrived, by which I hope to hear from you; I must hurry to the post-office; you shall hear again in few days.

Adieu!

Your affectionate

ED. RIVERS

TO COLONEL RIVERS, AT QUEBEC

LETTER 67   LONDON, DEC. 1: You need be in no pain, my dear brother, on Mr Temple's account, my heart is in no danger from a man of his present character: his person and manner are certainly extremely pleasing; his understanding, and I believe his principles, are worthy of your friendship; an encomium which, let me observe, is from me a very high one: he will be admired every where, but to be beloved, he wants, or at least appears to me to want, the most endearing of all qualities, that genuine tenderness of soul, that almost feminine sensibility, which, with all your firmness of mind and spirit, you possess beyond any man I ever yet met with.

If your friend wishes to please me, which I almost fancy he does, he must endeavour to resemble you; 'tis rather hard upon me, I think, that the only man I perfectly approve, and whose disposition is formed to make me happy, should be my brother: I beg you will find out somebody very like yourself for your sister, for you have really made me saucy.

I pity you heartily, and wish above all things to hear of Emily's marriage, for your present situation must be extremely unpleasant.

But, my dear brother, as you were so very wise about Temple, allow me to ask you whether it is quite consistent with prudence to throw yourself in the way of a woman so formed to inspire you with tenderness, and whom it is so impossible you can ever hope to possess: is not this acting a little like a foolish girl, who plays round the flame which she knows will consume her?

My mother is well, but will never be happy till your return to England; I often find her in tears over your letters: I will say no more on a subject which I know will give you pain. I hope however to hear you have given up all thoughts of settling in America: it would be a better plan to turn farmer in Rutlandshire; we could double the estate by living upon it, and I am sure I should make the prettiest milk-maid in the country.

I am serious, and think we could live very superbly all together in the country; consider it well, my dear Ned, for I cannot bear to see my mother so unhappy as your absence makes her. I hear her on the stairs; I must hurry away my letter, for I don't choose she should know I write to you on this subject.

Adieu!

Your affectionate
Lucy Rivers

Say every thing for me to Bell Fermor; and in your own manner to your Emily, in whose friendship I promise myself great happiness.

LETTER 68   MONTREAL, FEB. 10: Never any astonishment equalled mine, my dear Emily, at hearing you had broke an engagement of years, so much to your advantage as to fortune, and with a man of so very unexceptionable a character as Sir George, without any other apparent cause than a slight indelicacy in a letter of his mother's, for which candour and affection would have found a thousand excuses. I will not allow myself to suppose, what is however publicly said here, that you have sacrificed prudence, decorum, and I had almost said honour, to an imprudent inclination for a man, to whom there is the strongest reason to believe you are indifferent, and who is even said to have an attachment to another: I mean Colonel Rivers, who, though a man of worth, is in a situation which makes it impossible for him to think of you, were you even as dear to him as the world says he is to you.

I am too unhappy to say more on this subject, but expect from our past friendship a very sincere answer to two questions; whether love for Colonel Rivers was the real motive for the indiscreet step you have taken? and whether, if it was, you have the excuse of knowing he loves you? I should be glad to know what are your views, if you have any. I am,

My dear Emily,
        Your affectionate friend,

E. MELMOTH

LETTER 69   SILLERI, FEB. 19: My dear Madam, I am too sensible of the rights of friendship, to refuse answering your questions; which I shall do in as few words as possible. I have not the least reason to suppose myself beloved by Colonel Rivers; nor, if I know my heart, do I *love him* in that sense of the word your question supposes; I think him the best, the most amiable of mankind; and my extreme affection for him, though I believe that affection only a very lively friendship, first awakened me to a sense of the indelicacy and impropriety of marrying Sir George.

To enter into so sacred an engagement as marriage with

one man, with a stronger affection for another, of how calm and innocent a nature soever that affection may be, is a degree of baseness of which my heart is incapable.

When I first agreed to marry Sir George, I had no superior esteem for any other man; I thought highly of him, and wanted courage to resist the pressing solicitations of my uncle, to whom I had a thousand obligations. I even almost persuaded myself I loved him, nor did I find my mistake till I saw Colonel Rivers, in whose conversations I had so very lively a pleasure as soon convinced me of my mistake; I therefore resolved to break with Sir George, and nothing but the fear of giving him pain prevented my doing it sooner: his behaviour on the receipt of his mother's letter removed that fear, and set me free in my own opinion, and I hope will in yours, from engagements which were equally in the way of my happiness, and his ambition. If he is sincere, he will tell you my refusal of him made him happy, though he chooses to affect a chagrin which he does not feel.

I have no view but that of returning to England in the spring, and fixing with a relation in the country.

If Colonel Rivers has an attachment, I hope it is to one worthy of him; for my own part, I never entertained the remotest thought of him in any light but that of the most sincere and tender of friends. I am, Madam, with great esteem,

Your affectionate friend
and obedient servant,
EMILY MONTAGUE

TO MISS RIVERS, CLARGES STREET

LETTER 70 SILLERI, FEB. 27: There are two parties at Quebec in regard to Emily: the prudent mammas abuse her for losing a good match, and suppose it to proceed from her partiality to your brother, to the imprudence of which they give no quarter; whilst the misses admire her generosity and spirit, in sacrificing all for love; so impossible it is to please every body. However, she has, in my opinion, done the wisest thing in the world; that is, she has pleased herself.

As to her inclination for your brother, I am of their opinion, that she loves him without being quite clear in the point herself: she has not yet confessed the fact even to me; but she has speaking eyes, Lucy, and I think I can interpret their language.

Whether he sees it or not I cannot tell; I rather think he does, because he has been less here, and more guarded in his manner when here, than before this matrimonial affair was put an end to, which is natural enough on that supposition, because he knows the impertinence of Quebec, and is both prudent and delicate to a great degree.

He comes, however, and we are pretty good company, only a little more reserved on both sides; which is, in my opinion, a little symptomatic.

La! here's papa come up to write at my bureau; I dare say, it's only to pry into what I am about; but excuse me, my dear Sir, for that Adieu! *jusqu'au demain, ma très chère.*

Yours,

A. FERMOR

TO MISS RIVERS, CLARGES STREET

LETTER 71 QUEBEC, FEB. 20: Every hour, my Lucy, convinces me more clearly there is no happiness for me without this lovely woman; her turn of mind is so correspondent to my own, that we seem to have but one soul: the first moment I saw her the idea struck me that we had been friends in some pre-existent state, and were only renewing our acquaintance here; when she speaks, my heart vibrates to the sound, and owns every thought she expresses a native there.

The same dear affections, the same tender sensibility, the most precious gift of Heaven, inform our minds, and make us peculiarly capable of exquisite happiness or misery.

The passions, my Lucy, are common to all; but the affections, the lively sweet affections, the only sources of true pleasure, are the portion only of a chosen few.

Uncertain at present of the nature of her sentiments, I am determined to develop them clearly before I discover mine: if she loves as I do, even a perpetual exile here will be pleasing. The remotest wood in Canada with her would be no longer a desert wild; it would be the habitation of the Graces.

But I forget your letter, my dear girl; I am hurt beyond words at what you tell me of my mother; and would instantly return to England, did not my fondness for this charming woman detain me here: you are both too good in wishing to retire with me to the country; will your tenderness lead you a step farther, my Lucy? It would be too much to hope to see you here; and yet, if I marry Emily, it will be impossible for me to think of returning to England.

There is a man whom I should prefer of all men I ever saw for you; but he is already attached to your friend Bell Fermor, who is very inattentive to her own happiness, if she refuses him: I am very happy in finding you think of Temple as I wish you should.

You are so very civil, Lucy, in regard to me, I am afraid of becoming vain from your praises.

Take care, my dear, you don't spoil me by this excess of civility, for my only merit is that of not being a coxcomb.

I have a heaviness of heart, which has never left me since I read your letter: I am shocked at the idea of giving pain to the best parent that ever existed; yet have less hope than ever of seeing England, without giving up the tender friend, the dear companion, the adored mistress; in short the very woman I have all my life been in search of: I am also hurt that I cannot place this object of all my wishes in a station equal to that she has rejected, and I begin to think rejected for me.

I never before repined at seeing the gifts of fortune lavished on the unworthy.

Adieu, my dear! I will write again when I can write more cheerfully.

Your affectionate

ED. RIVERS

TO THE EARL OF ——

LETTER 72 SILLERI, FEB. 20: My Lord, Your Lordship does me great honour in supposing me capable of giving any satisfactory account of a country in which I have spent only a few months.

As a proof, however, of my zeal, and the very strong desire I have to merit the esteem you honour me with, I shall communicate from time to time the little I have observed, and may observe, as well as what I hear from good authority, with that lively pleasure with which I have ever obeyed every command of your Lordship's.

The French, in the first settling this colony, seem to have had an eye only to the conquest of ours: their whole system of policy seems to have been military, not commercial; or only so far commercial as was necessary to supply the wants, and by so doing to gain the friendship, of the savages, in order to make use of them against us.

The lands are held on military tenure: every peasant is a soldier, every seigneur an officer, and both serve without pay whenever called upon; this service is, except a very small quit-rent by way of acknowledgment, all they pay for their lands: the seigneur holds of the crown, the peasant of the seigneur, who is at once his lord and commander.

The peasants are in general tall and robust, notwithstanding their excessive indolence; they love war, and hate labour; are brave, hardy, alert in the field, but lazy and inactive at home; in which they resemble the savages, whose manners they seem strongly to have imbibed. The government appears to have encouraged a military spirit all over the colony; though ignorant and stupid to a great degree, these peasants have a strong sense of honour; and though they serve, as I have said, without pay, are never so happy as when called to the field.

They are excessively vain, and not only look on the French as the only civilized nation in the world, but on themselves as the flower of the French nation: they had, I am told, a great aversion to the regular troops which came from France in the late war, and a contempt equal to that aversion; they however had an affection and esteem for the late Marquis De Montcalm, which almost rose to idolatry; and I have even at this distance of time seen many of them in tears at the mention of his name: an honest tribute to the memory of a commander equally brave and humane; for whom his enemies wept even on the day when their own hero fell.

I am called upon for this letter, and have only time to assure your Lordship of my respect, and of the pleasure I always receive from your commands. I have the honour to be,

My Lord,
　　　Your Lordship's, &c.

　　　　　　　　　　　　　　WILLIAM FERMOR

LETTER 73 FEB. 24, ELEVEN AT NIGHT: I have indeed, my dear, a pleasure in his conversation, to which words cannot do justice: love itself is less tender and lively than my friendship for Rivers; from the first moment I saw him, I lost all taste for other conversation; even yours, amiable as you are, borrows its most prevailing charm from the pleasure of hearing you talk of him.

When I call my tenderness for him friendship, I do not mean either to paint myself as an enemy to tenderer sentiments, or him as one whom it is easy to see without feeling them: all I mean is, that, as our situations make it impossible for us to think of each other except as friends, I have endeavoured—I hope with success—to see him in no other light: it is not in his power to marry without fortune, and mine is a trifle: had I worlds, they should be his, but, I am neither so selfish as to desire, nor so romantic as to expect, that he should descend from the rank of life he has been bred in, and live lost to the world with me.

As to the impertinence of two or three women, I hear of it with perfect indifference: my dear Rivers esteems me, he approves my conduct, and all else is below my care: the applause of worlds would give me less pleasure than one smile of approbation from him.

I am astonished your father should know me so little, as to suppose me capable of being influenced even by you: when I determined to refuse Sir George, it was from the feelings of my own heart alone; the first moment I saw Colonel Rivers convinced me my heart had till then been a stranger to true tenderness: from that moment my life has been one continued struggle between my reason, which shewed me the folly as well as indecency of marrying one man when I so infinitely preferred another, and a false point of honour and mistaken compassion: from which painful state, a concurrence of favourable accidents has at length happily relieved me, and left me free to act as becomes me.

Of this, my dear, be assured, that, though I have not the least idea of ever marrying Colonel Rivers, yet, whilst my sentiments for him continue what they are, I will never marry any other man.

Adieu! Your

EMILY MONTAGUE

LETTER 74 FEB. 25, EIGHT O'CLOCK, JUST UP: My dear, you deceive yourself: you love Colonel Rivers; you love him even with all the tenderness of romance: read over again the latter part of your letter; I know friendship, and of what it is capable; but I fear the sacrifices it makes are of a different nature.

Examine your heart, my Emily, and tell me the result of that examination. It is of the utmost consequence to you to be clear as to the nature of your affection for Rivers.

Adieu! Yours,

A. FERMOR

LETTER 75 Yes, my dear Bell, you know me better than I know myself; your Emily loves— But tell me, and with that clear sincerity which is the cement of our friendship; has not your own heart discovered to you the secret of mine? do you not also love this most amiable of mankind? Yes, you do, and I am lost: it is not in woman to see him without love; there are a thousand charms in his conversation, in his look, nay in the very sound of his voice, to which it is impossible for a soul like yours to be insensible.

I have observed you a thousand times listening to him with that air of softness and complacency— Believe me, my dear, I am not angry with you for loving him; he is formed to charm the heart of woman: I have not the least right to complain of you; you knew nothing of my passion for him; you even regarded me almost as the wife of another. But tell me, though my heart dies within me at the question, is your tenderness mutual? does he love you? I have observed a coldness in his manner lately, which now alarms me—My heart is torn in pieces. Must I receive this wound from the two persons on earth most dear to me? Indeed, my dear, this is more than your Emily can bear. Tell me only whether you love: I will not ask more— Is there on earth a man who can please where he appears?

LETTER 76 You have discovered me, my sweet Emily: I love—not quite so dyingly as you do; but I love; will you forgive me when I add that I am beloved? It is unnecessary to add the name of him I love, as you have so kindly appropriated the whole sex to Colonel Rivers.

However, to shew you it is possible you may be mistaken, 'tis the little Fitz I love, who, in my eye, is ten times more agreeable than even your nonpareil of a Colonel; I know you will think me a shocking wretch for this depravity of taste; but so it is.

Upon my word, I am half inclined to be angry with you for not being in love with Fitzgerald; a tall Irishman, with good eyes, has as clear a title to make conquests as other people.

Yes, my dear, *there is a man on earth*, and even in the little town of Quebec, *who can please where he appears*. Surely, child, if there was but one man on earth who could please, you would not be so unreasonable as to engross him all to yourself.

For my part, though I like Fitzgerald extremely, I by no means insist that every other woman shall.

Go, you are a foolish girl, and don't know what you would be at. Rivers is a very handsome agreeable fellow; but *it is in woman* to see him without dying for love, of which behold your little Bell an example. Adieu! be wiser, and believe me.

Ever yours,

A. Fermor

Will you go this morning to Montmorenci on the ice, and dine on the island of Orleans? dare you trust yourself in a covered carriole with the dear man? Don't answer this, because I am certain you can say nothing on the subject, which will not be very foolish.

TO MISS FERMOR

LETTER 77 I am glad you do not see Colonel Rivers with my eyes; yet it seems to me very strange; I am almost piqued at your giving another the preference. I will say no more, it being, as you observe, impossible to avoid being absurd on such a subject.

I will go to Montmorenci; and, to shew my courage, will venture in a covered carriole with Colonel Rivers, though I should rather wish your father for my cavalier at present.

Yours,

EMILY MONTAGUE

TO MISS MONTAGUE

LETTER 78 You are right, my dear: 'tis more prudent to go with my father. I love prudence; and will therefore send for Mademoiselle Clairaut to be Rivers's belle.

A. FERMOR

TO MISS FERMOR

LETTER 79 You are a provoking chit, and I will go with Rivers. Your father may attend Madame Villiers, who you know will naturally take it ill if she is not of our party. We can ask Mademoiselle Clairaut another time.

Adieu! Your

EMILY MONTAGUE

TO MISS RIVERS, CLARGES STREET

LETTER 80 SILLERI, FEB. 25: Those who have heard no more of a Canadian winter than what regards the intenseness of its cold, must suppose it a very joyless season: 'tis, I assure you, quite otherwise; there are indeed some days here of the severity of which those who were never out of England can form no conception; but those days seldom exceed a dozen in a whole winter; nor do they come in succession, but at intermediate periods, as the winds set in from the North-West; which, coming some hundred leagues, from frozen lakes and rivers, over woods and mountains covered with snow, would be insupportable, were it not for the furs with which the country abounds, in such variety and plenty as to be within the reach of all its inhabitants.

Thus defended, the British belles set the winter of Canada at defiance; and the season of which you seem to entertain such terrible ideas, is that of the utmost chearfulness and festivity.

But what particularly pleases me is, there is no place where women are of such importance: not one of the sex, who has the least share of attractions, is without a levee of beaux interceding for the honour of attending her on some party, of which every day produces three or four.

I am just returned from one of the most agreeable jaunts imagination can paint, to the island of Orleans, by the falls of Montmorenci; the latter is almost nine miles distant, across the great bason of Quebec; but as we are obliged to reach it in winter by the waving line, our direct road being intercepted by the inequalities of the ice, it is now perhaps a third more. You will possibly suppose a ride of this kind must want one of the greatest essentials to entertainment, that of variety, and imagine it only one dull whirl over an unvaried plain of snow: on the contrary, my dear, we pass hills and mountains of ice in the trifling space of these few miles. The bason of Quebec is formed by the conflux of the rivers St Charles and Montmorenci with the great river St Lawrence, the rapidity of whose flood-tide, as these rivers are gradually seized by the frost, breaks up the ice, and drives it back in heaps, till it forms ridges of transparent rock to an height that is astonishing, and of a strength which bids defiance to the utmost rage of the most furiously rushing tide.

This circumstance makes this little journey more pleasing than you can possibly conceive: the serene blue sky above, the dazzling brightness of the sun, and the colours from the refraction of its rays on the transparent part of these ridges of ice, the winding course these oblige you to make, the sudden disappearing of a train of fifteen or twenty carrioles, as these ridges intervene, which again discover themselves on your rising to the top of the frozen mount, the tremendous appearance both of the ascent and descent, which however are not attended with the least danger; all together give a grandeur and variety to the scene, which almost rise to enchantment.

Your dull foggy climate affords nothing that can give you the least idea of our frost-pieces in Canada; nor can you form any notion of our amusements, of the agreeableness of a covered carriole, with a sprightly fellow, rendered more sprightly by the keen air and romantic scene about him; to say nothing of the fair lady at his side.

Even an overturning has nothing alarming in it; you are laid gently down on a soft bed of snow, without the least danger of any kind; and an accident of this sort only gives a pretty fellow occasion to vary the style of his civilities, and shew a greater degree of attention.

But it is almost time to come to Montmorenci; to avoid, however, fatiguing you or myself. I shall refer the rest of our tour to another letter, which will probably accompany this: my meaning is, that two moderate letters are vastly better than one long one; in which sentiment I know you agree with.

Yours,

A. Fermor

TO MISS RIVERS, CLARGES STREET

LETTER 81 SILLERI, FEB. 25, AFTERNOON: So, my dear, as I was saying, this same ride to Montmorenci—where was I, Lucy? I forget—O, I believe pretty near the mouth of the bay, embosomed in which lies the lovely cascade of which I am to give you a winter description, and which I only slightly mentioned when I gave you an account of the rivers by which it is supplied.

The road, about a mile before you reach this bay, is a regular glassy level, without any of those intervening hills of ice which I have mentioned, hills, which with the ideas, though false ones, of danger and difficulty, give those of beauty and magnificence too.

As you gradually approach the bay, you are struck with an awe, which increases every moment, as you come nearer, from the grandeur of a scene, which is one of the noblest works of nature: the beauty, the proportion, the solemnity, the wild magnificence of which, surpassing every possible effect of art, impress one strongly with the idea of its Divine Almighty Architect.

The rock on the east side, which is first in view as you approach, is a smooth and almost perpendicular precipice, of the same height as the fall; the top, which a little over-hangs, is beautifully covered with pines, firs, and ever-greens of various kinds, whose verdant lustre is rendered at this season more shining and lovely by the surrounding snow, as well as by that which is sprinkled irregularly on their branches, and glitters half melted in the sun-beams: a thousand smaller shrubs are scattered on the side of the ascent, and, having their roots in almost imperceptible clefts of the rock, seem to those below to grow in air.

The west side is equally lofty, but more sloping, which from that circumstance, affords soil all the way, upon shelving inequalities of the rock, at little distances, for the growth of trees and shrubs, by which it is almost entirely hid.

The most pleasing view of this miracle of nature is certainly in summer, and in the early part of it, when every tree is in foliage and full verdure, every shrub in flower; and when the river, swelled with a waste of waters from the mountains from which it derives its source, pours down in a tumultuous torrent, that equally charms and astonishes the beholder.

The winter scene has, notwithstanding, its beauties, though of a different kind, more resembling the stillness and inactivity of the season.

The river being on its sides bound up in frost, and its channel rendered narrower than in the summer, affords a less body of water to supply the cascade; and the fall, though very steep, yet not being exactly perpendicular, masses of ice are formed, on different shelving projections of the rock, in a great variety of forms and proportions.

The torrent, which before rushed with such impetuosity down the deep descent in one vast sheet of water, now descends in some parts with a slow and majestic pace; in others seems almost suspended in mid air; and in others, bursting through the obstacles which interrupt its course, pours down with re-doubled fury into the foaming bason below, from whence a spray arises, which, freezing in its ascent, becomes on each side a wide and irregular frozen breast-work; and in front, the spray being there much greater, a lofty and magnificent pyramid of solid ice.

I have not told you half the grandeur, half the beauty, half the lovely wildness of this scene: if you would know what it is, you must take no information but that of your own eyes, which I pronounce strangers to the loveliest work of creation till they have seen the river and fall of Montmorenci.

In short, my dear, I am Montmorenci-mad.

I can hardly descend to tell you, we passed the ice from

thence to Orleans, and dined out of doors on six feet of snow, in the charming enlivening warmth of the sun, though in the month of February, at a time when you in England scarce feel his beams.

Fitzgerald made violent love to me all the way, and I never felt myself listen with such complacency.

Adieu!

Adieu! I have wrote two immense letters. Write oftener; you are lazy, yet expect me to be an absolute slave in the scribbling way.

Your faithful

A. FERMOR

Do you know your brother has admirable ideas? He contrived to lose his way on our return, and kept Emily ten minutes behind the rest of the company. I am apt to fancy there was something like a declaration, for she blushed.

"Celestial rosy red,"

when he led her into the dining-room at Silleri.

Once more, Adieu!

TO MISS RIVERS, CLARGES STREET

LETTER 82 MARCH 1: I was mistaken, my dear; not a word of love between your brother and Emily, as she positively assures me; something very tender has passed, I am convinced, notwithstanding, for she blushes more than ever when he approaches, and there is a certain softness in his voice when he addresses her, which cannot escape a person of my penetration.

Do you know, my dear Lucy, that there is a little impertinent girl here, a Mademoiselle Clairaut, who, on the meer merit of features and complexion, sets up for being as handsome as Emily and me?

If beauty, as I will take the liberty to assert, is given us for the purpose of pleasing, she who pleases most, that is to say, she who excites the most passion, is to all intents and purposes the most beautiful woman; and, in this case, I am inclined to believe your little Bell stands pretty high on the roll of beauty; the men's *eyes* may perhaps *say* she is handsome, but their *hearts feel* that I am so.

There is, in general, nothing so insipid, so uninteresting, as a Beauty; which those men experience to their cost, who choose from vanity, not inclination. I remember Sir Charles Herbert, a Captain in the same regiment with my father, who determined to marry Miss Raymond before he saw her, merely because he had been told she was a celebrated beauty, though she was never known to have inspired a real passion: he saw her not with his own eyes but those of the public, took her charms on trust; and, till he was her husband, never found out she was not his taste; a secret, however, of some little importance to his happiness.

I have, however, known some Beauties who had a right to please; that is, who had a mixture of that invisible charm, that nameless grace which by no means depends on beauty, and which strikes the heart in a moment; but my first aversion is your *fine women*; don't you think a *fine woman* a detestable creature, Lucy? I do; they are vastly well to *fill* public places: but as to the heart—Heavens, my dear! yet there are men, I suppose, to be found, who have a taste for the great sublime in beauty.

Men are vastly foolish, my dear; very few of them have spirit to think for themselves; there are a thousand Sir Charles Herberts: I have seen some of them weak enough to decline marrying the woman on earth most pleasing to themselves, because not thought handsome by the generality of their companions.

Women are above this folly, and therefore chuse much oftener from affection than men. We are a thousand times wiser, Lucy, than these important beings, these mighty lords,

"Who strut and fret their hour upon the stage;"

and, instead of playing the part in life which nature dictates to their reason and their hearts, act a borrowed one at the will of others.

I had rather even judge ill, than not judge for myself.
Adieu! yours ever,

A. FERMOR

LETTER 83 QUEBEC, MARCH 4: After debating with myself some days, I am determined to pursue Emily; but before I make a declaration, will go to see some ungranted lands at the back of Madame Des Roches's estate; which, lying on a very fine river, and so near the St Lawrence, may I think be cultivated at less expence than those above Lake Champlain, though in a much inferior climate: if I make my settlement here, I will purchase the estate Madame Des Roches has to sell, which will open me a road to the river St Lawrence, and consequently treble the value of my lands.

I love, I adore this charming woman; but I will not suffer my tenderness for her to make her unhappy, or to lower her station in life: if I can by my present plan, secure her what will in this country be a degree of affluence, I will endeavour to change her friendship for me into a tenderer and more lively affection; if she loves, I know by my own heart, that Canada will be no longer a place of exile; if I have flattered myself, and she has only a friendship for me, I will return immediately to England, and retire with you and my mother to our little estate in the country.

You will perhaps say, why not make Emily of our party? I am almost ashamed to speak plain; but so weak are we, and so guided by the prejudices we fancy we despise, that I cannot bear my Emily, after refusing a coach and six, should live without an equipage suitable at least to her birth, and the manner in which she has always lived when in England.

I know this is folly, that it is a despicable pride; but it is a folly, a pride, I cannot conquer.

There are moments when I am above all this childish prejudice, but it returns upon me in spite of myself.

Will you come to us, my Lucy? Tell my mother, I will build her a rustic palace, and settle a little principality on you both.

I make this a private excursion, because I don't chuse any body should even guess at my views. I shall set out in the evening, and make a circuit to cross the river above the town.

I shall not even take leave at Silleri, as I propose being back in four days, and I know your friend Bell will be inquisitive about my journey.

Adieu!
Your affectionate
ED. RIVERS

LETTER 84 SILLERI, MARCH 6: Your brother is gone nobody knows whither, and without calling upon us before he set off; we are piqued, I assure you, my dear, and with some little reason.

Four o'clock

Very strange news, Lucy; they say Colonel Rivers is gone to marry Madame Des Roches, a lady at whose house he was some time in autumn; if this is true, I forswear the whole sex: his manner of stealing off is certainly very odd, and she is rich and agreeable; but, if he does not love Emily, he has been excessively cruel in shewing an attention which has deceived her into a passion for him. I cannot believe it possible: not that he has ever told her he loved her; but a man of honour will not tell an untruth even with his eyes, and his have spoke a very unequivocal language.

I never saw anything like her confusion, when she was told he was gone to visit Madame Des Roches; but, when it was hinted with what design, I was obliged to take her out of the room, or she would have discovered all the fondness of her soul. I really thought she would have fainted as I led her out.

Eight o'clock

I have sent away all the men, and drank tea in Emily's apartment; she has scarce spoke to me; I am miserable for her; she has a paleness which alarms me, the tears steal every moment into her lovely eyes. Can Rivers act so unworthy a part? Her tenderness cannot have been unobserved by him; it was too visible to every body.

9th, Ten o'clock

Not a line from your brother yet; only a confirmation of his being with Madame Des Roches, having been seen there by some Canadians who are come up this morning: I am not quite pleased, though I do not believe the report; he might have told us surely where he was going.

I pity Emily beyond words; she says nothing, but there is a dumb eloquence in her countenance which is not to be described.

Twelve o'clock

I have been an hour alone with the dear little girl, who has, from a hint I dropt on purpose, taken courage to speak to me on this very interesting subject; she says, *she shall be most unhappy if this report is true, though without the least right to complain of Colonel Rivers, who never even hinted a word of any affection for her more tender than friendship; that if her vanity, her self-love, or her tenderness, have deceived her, she ought only to blame herself.* She added, *that she wished him to marry Madame Des Roches, if she could make him happy*; but when she said this, an involuntary tear seemed to contradict the generosity of her sentiments.

I beg your pardon, my dear, but my esteem for your brother is greatly lessened; I cannot help fearing there is something in the report, and that this is what Mrs Melmoth meant when she mentioned his having an attachment.

I shall begin to hate the whole sex, Lucy, if I find your brother unworthy and shall give Fitzgerald his dismission immediately.

I am afraid Mrs Melmoth knows men better than we foolish girls do: she said, he attached himself to Emily merely from vanity, and I begin to believe she was right: how cruel is this conduct! The man who from vanity, or perhaps only to amuse an idle hour, can appear to be attached where he is not, and by that means seduce the heart of a deserving woman, or indeed of any woman, falls in my opinion very little short in baseness of him who practises a greater degree of seduction.

What right has he to make the most amiable of women wretched? a woman who would have deserved him had he been monarch of the universal world! I might add, who has sacrificed ease and affluence to her tenderness for him?

You will excuse my warmth on such an occasion; however, as it may give you pain, I will say no more.

Adieu!

Your faithful

A. FERMOR

TO MISS RIVERS, CLARGES STREET

LETTER 85 KAMARASKAS, MARCH 12: I have met with something, my dear Lucy, which has given me infinite uneasiness; Madame Des Roches, from my extreme zeal to serve her in an affair wherein she has been hardly used, from my second visit, and a certain involuntary attention, and softness of manner, I have to all women, has supposed me in love with her, and with a frankness I cannot but admire, and a delicacy not to be described, has let me know I am far from being indifferent to her.

I was at first extremely embarrassed; but when I had reflected a moment, I considered that the ladies, tho' another may be the object, always regard with a kind of complacency a man who *loves*, as one who acknowledges the power of the sex, whereas an indifferent is a kind of rebel to their empire; I considered also that the confession of a prior inclination saves the most delicate vanity from being wounded; and therefore determined to make her the confidante of my tenderness for Emily; leaving her an opening to suppose that, if my heart had been disengaged, it could not have escaped her attractions.

I did this with all possible precaution, and with every softening that friendship and politeness could suggest; she was shocked at my confession, but soon recovered herself enough to tell me she was highly flattered by this proof of my confidence and esteem; that she believed me a man to have only the more respect for a woman who by owning her partiality had told me she considered me not only as the most amiable, but the most noble of my sex; that she had heard, no love was so tender as that which was the child of friendship; but that of this she was convinced, that no friendship was so tender as that which was the child of love; that she offered me this tender, this lively friendship, and would for the future find her happiness in the consideration of mine.

Do you know, my dear, that since this confession, I feel a kind of tenderness for her, to which I cannot give a name? It is not love; for I love, I idolize another: but it is softer and more pleasing, as well as more animated, than friendship.

You cannot conceive what pleasure I find in her conversation; she has admirable understanding, a feeling heart, and a mixture of softness and spirit in her manner, which is peculiarly pleasing to men. My Emily will love her; I must bring them acquainted: she promises to come to Quebec in May; I shall be happy to shew her every attention when there.

I have seen the lands, and am pleased with them: I believe this will be my residence, if Emily, as I cannot avoid hoping, will make me happy; I shall declare myself as soon as I return, but must continue here a few days longer: I shall not be less pleased with this situation for its being so near Madame Des

Roches, in whom Emily will find a friend worthy of her esteem, and an entertaining lively companion.

Adieu, my dear Lucy
Your affectionate

ED. RIVERS

I have fixed on the loveliest spot on earth, on which to build a house for my mother: do I not expect too much in fancying she will follow me hither?

LETTER 86 SILLERI, MARCH 13: Still with Madame Des Roches; appearances are rather against him, you must own, Lucy: but I will not say all I think to you. Poor Emily! we dispute continually, for she will persist in defending his conduct; she says, he has a right to marry whoever he pleases; that her loving him is no tie upon his honour, especially as he does not even know of this preference; that she ought only to blame the weakness of her own heart, which has betrayed her into a false belief that their tenderness was mutual: this is pretty talking, but he has done every thing to convince her of his feeling the strongest passion for her, except making a formal declaration.

She talks of returning to England the moment the river is open: indeed, if your brother marries, it is the only step left her to take. I almost wish now she had married Sir George: she would have had all the *douceurs* of marriage; and as to love, I begin to think men are incapable of feeling it: some of them can indeed talk well on the subject; but self-interest and vanity are the real passions of their souls. I detest the whole sex.

Adieu!

A. FERMOR

LETTER 87   SILLERI, MARCH 13: My Lord:
I generally distrust my own opinion when it differs from
your Lordship's; but in this instance I am most certainly in
the right: allow me to say, nothing can be more ill-judged
than your Lordship's design of retiring into a small circle, from
that world of which you have so long been one of the most
brilliant ornaments. What you say of the disagreeableness of
age, is by no means applicable to your Lordship; nothing is in
this respect so fallible as the parish register. Why should any
man retire from society whilst he is capable of contributing to
the pleasures of it? Wit, vivacity, good-nature, and politeness,
give an eternal youth, as stupidity and moroseness a premature
old age. Without a thousandth part of your Lordship's shining
qualities, I think myself much younger than half the boys about
me merely because I have more good-nature, and a stronger
desire of pleasing.

My daughter is much honoured by your Lordship's enquiries: she is Bell Fermor still; but is addressed by a gentleman who is extremely agreeable to me, and I believe not less
so to her; I however know too well the free spirit of woman, of
which she has her full share, to let Bell know I approve her
choice; I am even in doubt whether it would not be good policy
to seem to dislike the match, in order to secure her consent:
there is something very pleasing to a young girl, in opposing
the will of her father.

To speak truth, I am a little out of humour with her at
present, for having contributed, and I believe entirely from a
spirit of opposition to me, to break a match on which I had
extremely set my heart; the lady was the niece of my particular
friend, and one of the most lovely and deserving women I ever
knew: the gentleman very worthy, with an agreeable, indeed a
handsome person, and a fortune which with those who know
the world, would have compensated for the want of most other
advantages.

The fair lady, after an engagement of two years, took a
whim that there was no happiness in marriage without being
madly in love, and that her passion was not sufficiently romantic; in which piece of folly my rebel encouraged her, and the
affair broke off in a manner which has brought on her the im-
putation of having given way to an idle prepossession in favour
of another.

Your Lordship will excuse my talking on a subject very

near my heart, though uninteresting to you; I have too often experienced your Lordship's indulgence to doubt it on this occasion: your good-natured philosophy will tell you, much fewer people talk or write to amuse or inform their friends, than to give way to the feelings of their own hearts, or indulge the governing passion of the moment.

In my next, I will endeavour in the best manner I can, to obey your Lordship's commands in regard to the political and religious state of Canada: I will make a point of getting the best information possible; what I have yet seen, has been only the surface.

I have the honour to be,
My Lord,
Your Lordship's &c.

WILLIAM FERMOR

TO MISS RIVERS, CLARGES STREET

LETTER 88 SILLERI, MARCH 16, MONDAY: Your brother is come back; and has been here: he came after dinner yesterday. My Emily is more than woman; I am proud of her behaviour: he entered with his usual impatient air; she received him with a dignity which astonished me, and disconcerted him: there was a cool dispassionate indifference in her whole manner, which I saw cut his vanity to the quick, and for which he was by no means prepared.

On such an occasion I should have flirted violently with some other man, and have shewed plainly I was piqued: she judged much better; I have only to wish it may last. He is the veriest coquet in nature; for, after all, I am convinced he loves Emily.

He stayed a very little time, and has not been here this morning; he may pout if he pleases, but I flatter myself we shall hold out the longest.

Nine o'clock

He came to dine; we kept up our state all dinner time; he begged a moment's conversation, which we refused, but with a timid air that makes me begin to fear we shall beat a parley; he is this moment gone, and Emily retired to her apartment on pretence of indisposition: I am afraid she is a foolish girl.

Half hour after six

It will not do, Lucy: I found her in tears at the window, following Rivers's carriole with her eyes: she turned to me with such a look—in short, my dear,

"The weak, the fond, the fool, the coward woman"

has prevailed over all her resolution: her love is only the more violent for having been a moment restrained; she is not equal to the task she has undertaken; her resentment was concealed tenderness, and has retaken its first form.

I am sorry to find there is not one wise woman in the world but myself.

Past ten

I have been with her again: she seemed a little calmer; I commended her spirit; she disavowed it; was peevish with me, angry with herself; said she had acted in a manner unworthy her character; accused herself of caprice, artifice, and cruelty; said she ought to have seen him, if not alone, yet with me only: that it was natural he should be surprized at a reception so inconsistent with true friendship, and therefore that he should wish an explanation: that *her* Rivers (and why not Madame Des Roches's Rivers?) was incapable of acting otherwise than as became the best and most tender of mankind, and that therefore she ought not to have suffered a whisper injurious to his honour: that I had meant well, but had, by depriving her of Rivers's friendship, which she had lost by her haughty behaviour, destroyed all the happiness of her life.

To be sure, your poor Bell is always to blame: but if ever I intermeddle between lovers again, Lucy—

I am sure she was ten times more angry with him than I was, but this it is to be too warm in the interest of our friends.

Adieu! till to-morrow,

Yours

A. FERMOR

I can only say, that if Fitzgerald had visited a handsome rich French widow, and staid with her ten days *tête-à-tête* in the country, without my permission—

O Heavens! here is *mon cher père*: I must hide my letter.

Bon soir

LETTER 89   QUEBEC, MARCH 6: I cannot account, my dear, for what has happened to me. I left Madame Des Roches's full of the warm impatience of love, and flew to my Emily at Silleri: I was received with a disdainful coldness which I did not think had been in her nature, and which has shocked me beyond all expression.

I went again to-day, and met with the same reception; I even saw my presence was painful to her, therefore shortened my visit, and, if I have resolution to persevere, will not go again till invited by Captain Fermor in form.

I could bear anything but to lose her affection; my whole heart was set upon her: I had every reason to believe myself dear to her. Can caprice find a place in that bosom which is the abode of every virtue?

I must have been misrepresented to her, or surely this could not have happened: I will wait to-morrow, and if I hear nothing will write her, and ask an explanation by letter; she refused me a verbal one to-day, though I begged to speak with her only for a moment.

Tuesday

I have been asked on a little riding-party, and, as I cannot go to Silleri, have accepted it: it will amuse my present anxiety.

I am to drive Mademoiselle Clairaut, a very pretty French lady: this is however of no consequence, for my eyes see nothing lovely but Emily.

Adieu!

Your affectionate

ED. RIVERS

LETTER 90   SILLERI, WEDNESDAY MORNING: Poor Emily is to meet with perpetual mortification: we have been carrioling with Fitzgerald and my father: and, coming back, met your brother driving Mademoiselle Clairaut: Emily trembled, turned pale, and scarce returned Rivers's bow; I never saw a poor little girl so in love; she is amazingly altered within the last fortnight.

Two o'clock

A letter from Mrs Melmoth: I send you a copy of it with this.

Adieu!

Yours,

A. FERMOR

TO MISS MONTAGUE, AT SILLERI

LETTER 91 MONTREAL, MARCH 19: If you are not absolutely resolved on destruction, my dear Emily, it is yet in your power to retrieve the false step you have made.

Sir George, whose good-nature is in this instance almost without example, has been prevailed on by Mr Melmoth to consent I should write to you before he leaves Montreal, and again offer you his hand, though rejected in a manner so very mortifying both to vanity and love.

He gives you a fortnight to consider his offer, at the end of which if you refuse him he sets out for England over the lakes.

Be assured, the man for whom it is too plain you have acted this imprudent part, is so far from returning your affection, that he is at this moment addressing another; I mean Madame Des Roches, a near relation of whose assured me that there was an attachment between them: indeed it is impossible he could have thought of a woman whose fortune is as small as his own. Men, Miss Montague, are not the romantic beings you seem to suppose them; you will not find many Sir George Claytons.

I beg as early an answer as is consistent with the attention so important a proposal requires, as a compliment to a passion so generous and disinterested as that of Sir George.

I am, my dear Emily,

Your affectionate friend,

E. MELMOTH

LETTER **92**   SILLERI, MARCH 19: I am sorry, my dear Madam, you should know so little of my heart, as to suppose it possible I could have broke my engagements with Sir George from any motive but the full conviction of my wanting that tender affection for him, and that lively taste for his conversation, which alone could have insured either his felicity or my own; happy is it for both that I discovered this before it was too late: it was a very unpleasing circumstance, even under an intention only of marrying him, to find my friendship stronger for another; what then would it have been under the most sacred of all engagements, that of marriage? What wretchedness would have been the portion of both, had timidity, decorum, or false honour, carried me, with this partiality in my heart, to fulfill those views, entered into from compliance to my family, and continued from a false idea of propriety, and weak fear of the censures of the world?

The same reason therefore still subsisting, nay being every moment stronger, from a fuller conviction of the merit of him my heart prefers, in spite of me, to Sir George, our union is more impossible than ever.

I am however obliged to you, and Major Melmoth, for your zeal to serve me, though you must permit me to call it a mistaken one; and to Sir George, for a concession, which I own I should not have made in his situation, and which I can only suppose the effect of Major Melmoth's persuasions, which he might suppose were known to me, and an imagination that my sentiments for him were changed: assure him of my esteem, tho' love is not in my power.

As Colonel Rivers never gave me the remotest reason to suppose him more than my friend, I have not the least right to disapprove of his marrying: on the contrary, as his friend, I *ought* to wish a connexion which I am told is greatly to his advantage.

To prevent all future importunity, painful to me, and, all circumstances considered, degrading to Sir George, whose honour is very dear to me, though I am obliged to refuse him that hand which he surely cannot wish to receive without my heart, I am compelled to say, that, without an idea of ever being united to Colonel Rivers, I will never marry any other man.

Were I never again to behold him, were he even the husband of another, my tenderness, a tenderness as innocent as it is lively, would never cease: nor would I give up the refined delight of loving him, independently of any hope of being beloved, for any advantage in the power of fortune to bestow.

These being my sentiments, sentiments which no time can alter, they cannot be too soon known to Sir George: I would not one hour keep him in suspence in a point, which this step seems to say is of consequence to his happiness.

Tell him, I entreat him to forget me, and to come into views which will make his mother, and I have no doubt himself, happier than a marriage with a woman whose chief merit is that very sincerity of heart which obliges her to refuse him.

I am, Madam,
Your affectionate, etc.

EMILY MONTAGUE

TO MISS RIVERS, CLARGES STREET

LETTER **93**   SILLERI, THURSDAY: Your brother dines here to-day, by my father's invitation; I am afraid it will be but an aukward party.

Emily is at this moment an exceeding fine model for a statue of tender melancholy.

Her anger is gone; not a trace remaining; 'tis sorrow, but the most beautiful sorrow I ever beheld: she is all grief for having offended the dear man.

I am out of patience with this look; it is so flattering to him, I could beat her for it: I cannot bear his vanity should be so gratified.

I wanted her to treat him with a saucy, unconcerned, flippant air; but her whole appearance is gentle, tender, I had almost said supplicating: I am ashamed of the folly of my own sex: O, that I could to-day inspire her with a little of my spirit! she is a poor tame household dove, and there is no making any thing of her.

Eleven o'clock

"For my shepherd is kind, and my heart is at ease."

What fools women are, Lucy! He took her hand, expressed concern for her health, softened the tone of his voice, looked a

138

few civil things with those expressive lying eyes of his, and without one word of explanation all was forgot in a moment.

Good night! Yours,

A. FERMOR

Heavens! the fellow is here, has followed me to my dressing-room; was ever anything so confident? These modest men have ten times the assurance of your impudent fellows. I believe absolutely he is going to make love to me: 'tis a critical hour, Lucy; and to rob one's friend of a lover is really a temptation.

Twelve o'clock

The dear man is gone, and has made all up: he insisted on my explaining the reasons of the cold reception he had met with: which you know was impossible, without betraying the secret of poor Emily's foolish heart.

I however contrived to let him know we were a little piqued at his going without seeing us, and that we were something inclined to be jealous of his *friendship* for Madame Des Roches.

He made a pretty decent defence; and, though I don't absolutely acquit him of coquetry, yet upon the whole I think I forgive him.

He loves Emily, which is great merit with me: I am only sorry they are two such poor devils, it is next to impossible they should ever come together.

I think I am not angry now; as to Emily, her eyes dance with pleasure; she has not the same countenance as in the morning; this love is the finest cosmetick in the world.

After all, he is a charming fellow, and his eyes, Lucy— Heaven be praised, he never pointed their fire at me!

Adieu! I will try to sleep.

Yours,

A. FERMOR

TO MISS RIVERS, CLARGES STREET

LETTER 94   QUEBEC, MARCH 20: The coldness of which I complained, my dear Lucy, in regard to Emily, was the most flattering circumstance which could have happened: I will not say it was the effect of jealousy, but it certainly was of a delicacy of affection which extremely resembles it.

Never did she appear so lovely as yesterday; never did she display such variety of loveliness: there was a something in her look, when I first addressed her on entering the room, touching beyond all words, a certain inexpressible melting languor, a dying softness, which it was not in man to see unmoved: what then must a lover have felt?

I had the pleasure, after having been in the room a few moments, to see this charming languor change to a joy which animated her whole form, and of which I was so happy as to believe myself the cause: my eyes had told her all that passed in my heart; hers had shewed me plainly they understood their language. We were standing at a window at some little distance from the rest of the company, when I took an opportunity of hinting my concern at having, though without knowing it, offended her: She blushed, she looked down, she again raised her lovely eyes, they met mine, she sighed; I took her hand, she withdrew it, but not in anger; a smile, like that of the poet's Hebe, told me I was forgiven.

There is no describing what then passed in my soul: with what difficulty did I restrain my transports! never before did I really know love: what I had hitherto felt even for her, was cold to that enchanting, that impassioned moment.

She is a thousand times dearer to me than life: my Lucy, I cannot live without her.

I contrived, before I left Silleri, to speak to Bell Fermor on the subject of Emily's reception of me; she did not fully explain herself, but she convinced me hatred had no part in her resentment.

I am going again this afternoon: every hour not passed with her is lost.

I will seek a favourable occasion of telling her the whole happiness of my life depends on her tenderness.

Before I write again, my fate will possibly be determined: with every reason to hope, the timidity inseparable from love makes me dread a full explanation of my sentiments: if her native softness should have deceived me—but I will not study to be unhappy.

Adieu!

Your affectionate

ED. RIVERS

LETTER 95 SILLERI, MARCH 20: I have been telling Fitzgerald I am jealous of his prodigious attention to Emily, whose *cecisbeo* he has been the last ten days: the simpleton took me seriously, and began to vindicate himself, by explaining the nature of his regard for her, pleading her late indisposition as an excuse for shewing her some extraordinary civilities.

I let him harangue ten minutes, then stops me him short, puts on my poetical face, and repeats,

> "When sweet Emily complains,
> "I have sense of all her pains;
> "But for little Bella, I
> "Do not only grieve, but die."

He smiled, kissed my hand, praised my amazing penetration and was going to take this opportunity of saying a thousand civil things, when my divine Rivers appeared on the side of the hill; I flew to meet him, and left my love to finish the conversation alone.

Twelve o'clock

I am the happiest of all possible women; Fitzgerald is in the sullens about your brother; surely there is no pleasure in nature equal to that of plaguing a fellow who really loves one, especially if he has as much merit as Fitzgerald, for otherwise he would not be worth tormenting. He had better not pout with me: I believe I know who will be tired first.

Eight in the evening

I have passed a most delicious day: Fitzgerald took it into his wise head to endeavour to make me jealous of a little pert Frenchwoman, the wife of a Croix de St Louis, who I know he despises; I then thought myself at full liberty to play off all my airs, which I did with ineffable success, and have sent him home in a humour to hang himself. Your brother stays the evening, so does a very handsome fellow I have been flirting with all the day: Fitz was engaged here too, but I told him it was impossible for him not to attend Madame La Brosse to Quebec; he looked at me with a spite in his countenance which charmed me to the soul, and handed the fair lady to his carriole.

I'll teach him to coquet, Lucy; let him take his Madame La Brosse: indeed, as her husband is at Montreal, I don't see how he can avoid pursuing his conquest: I am delighted, because I know she is his aversion.

Emily calls me to cards. Adieu! my dear little Lucy.

Yours,

A. FERMOR

TO COLONEL RIVERS, AT QUEBEC

LETTER **96** PALL MALL, JANUARY 3: I have but a moment, my dear Ned, to tell you, that without so much as asking your leave, and in spite of all your wise admonitions, your lovely sister has this morning consented to make me the happiest of mankind: to-morrow gives me all that is excellent and charming in woman.

You are to look on my writing this letter as the strongest proof I ever did, or ever can give you of my friendship. I must love you with no common affection to remember at this moment that there is such a man in being: perhaps you owe this recollection only to your being brother to the loveliest woman nature ever formed; whose charms in a month have done more towards my conversion than seven years of your preaching would have done. I am going back to Clarges Street. Adieu!

Yours, etc.

JOHN TEMPLE

TO COLONEL RIVERS, AT QUEBEC

LETTER **97** CLARGES STREET, JANUARY 3: I am afraid you knew very little of the sex, my dear brother, when you cautioned me so strongly against loving Mr Temple: I should perhaps, with all his merit, have never thought of him but for that caution.

There is something very interesting to female curiosity in the idea of these very formidable men, whom no woman can see without danger; we gaze on the terrible creature at a distance, see nothing in him so very alarming; he approaches, our little hearts palpitate with fear, he is gentle, attentive, respectful; we are surprized at this respect, we are sure the world wrongs the dear civil creature; he flatters, we are pleased with his flattery; our little hearts still palpitate—but not with fear.

In short, my dear brother, if you wish to serve a friend with us, describe him as the most dangerous of his sex; the very idea that he is so, makes us think resistance vain, and we throw down our defensive arms in absolute despair.

I am not sure this is the reason of my discovering Mr Temple to be the most amiable of men; but of this I am certain, that I love him with the most lively affection, and that I am convinced, notwithstanding all you have said, that he deserves all my tenderness.

Indeed, my dear prudent brother, you men fancy yourselves extremely wise and penetrating, but you don't know each other half as well as we know you: I shall make Temple in a few weeks as tame a domestic animal as you can possibly be, even with your Emily.

I hope you won't be very angry with me for accepting an agreeable fellow, and a coach and six: if you are, I can only say, that finding the dear man steal every day upon my heart, and recollecting how very dangerous a creature he was,

"I held it both safest and best
"To marry, for fear you should chide."

Adieu!
Your affectionate, etc.
LUCY RIVERS

Please to observe, mamma was on Mr Temple's side, and that I only take him from obedience to her commands. He has behaved like an angel to her; but I leave himself to explain how: she has promised to live with us. We are going a party to Richmond, and only wait for Mr Temple.

With all my pertness, I tremble at the idea that tomorrow will determine the happiness or misery of my life.

Adieu! my dearest brother.

LETTER **98** QUEBEC, MARCH 21: Were I convinced of your conversion, my dear Jack, I should be the happiest man breathing in the thought of your marrying my sister; but I tremble lest this resolution should be the effect of passion merely, and not of that settled esteem and tender confidence without which mutual repentance will be the necessary consequence of your connexion.

Lucy is one of the most beautiful women I ever knew, but she has merits of a much superior kind; her understanding and her heart are equally lovely: she has also a sensibility which exceedingly alarms me for her, as I know it is next to impossible that even her charms can fix a heart so long accustomed to change.

Do I not guess too truly, my dear Temple, when I suppose the charming mistress is the only object you have in view; and that the tender amiable friend, the pleasing companion, the faithful confidante, is forgot?

I will not however anticipate evils: if any merit has power to fix you, Lucy's cannot fail of doing it.

I expect with impatience a further account of an event in which my happiness is so extremely interested.

If she is yours, may you know her value, and you cannot fail of being happy: I only fear from your long habit of improper attachments; naturally, I know not a heart filled with nobler sentiments than yours, nor is there on earth a man for whom I have equal esteem. Adieu!

Your affectionate
ED. RIVERS

LETTER **99** QUEBEC, MARCH 23: I have received your second letter, my dear Temple, with the account of your marriage.

Nothing could make me so happy as an event which unites a sister I idolize to the friend on earth most dear to me, did I not tremble for your future happiness, from my perfect knowledge of both.

I know the sensibility of Lucy's temper and that she loves you: I know also the difficulty of weaning the heart from such a habit of inconstancy as you have unhappily acquired.

Virtues like Lucy's will for ever command your esteem and friendship; but in marriage it is equally necessary to keep love alive: her beauty, her gaiety, her delicacy, will do much; but it is also necessary, my dearest Temple, that you keep a guard on your heart, accustomed to liberty, to give way to every light impression.

I need not tell you, who have experienced the truth of what I say, that happiness is not to be found in a life of intrigue; there is no real pleasure in the possession of beauty without the heart; with it, the fears, the anxieties, a man not absolutely destitute of humanity must feel for the honour of her who ventures more than life for him, must extremely counterbalance his transports.

Of all the situations this world affords, a marriage of choice gives the fairest prospect of happiness; without love, life would be a tasteless void; an unconnected human being is the most wretched of all creatures: by love I would be understood to mean that tender lively friendship, that mixed sensation, which the libertine never felt; and with which I flatter myself my amiable sister cannot fail of inspiring a heart naturally virtuous, however at present warped by a foolish compliance with the world.

I hope, my dear Temple, to see you recover your taste for those pleasures peculiarly fitted to our natures; to see you enjoy the pure delights of peaceful domestic life, the calm social evening hour, the circle of friends, the prattling offspring, and the tender impassioned smile of real love.

Your generosity is no more than I expected from your character; and to convince you of my perfect esteem, I so far accept it, as to draw out the money in the funds, which I intended for my sister: it will make my settlement here turn to greater advantage, and I allow you the pleasure of convincing Lucy of the perfect disinterestedness of your affection: it would be a trifle to you, and will make me happy.

But I am more delicate in regard to my mother, and will never consent to resume the estate I have settled on her: I esteem you above all mankind, but will not let *her* be dependent even on you: I consent she visit you as often as she pleases, but insist on her continuing her house in town, and living in every respect as she has been accustomed.

As to Lucy's own little fortune, as it is not worth your receiving, suppose she lays it out in jewels? I love to see beauty adorned; and two thousand pounds, added to what you have given her, will set her on a footing in this respect with a nabobess.

Your marriage, my dear Temple, removes the strongest objection to mine; the money I have in the funds, which whilst Lucy was unmarried I never would have taken, enables me to fix to great advantage here. I have now only to try whether Emily's friendship for me is sufficiently strong to give up all hopes of a return to England.

I shall make an immediate trial: you shall know the event in a few days. If she refuses me, I bid adieu to all my schemes, and embark in the first ship.

Give my kindest tenderest wishes to my mother and sister. My dear Temple, only know the value of the treasure you possess, and you must be happy. Adieu!

Your affectionate

ED. RIVERS

TO THE EARL OF ——

LETTER **100** SILLERI, MARCH 24: My Lord: Nothing can be more just than your Lordship's observation; and I am the more pleased with it, as it coincides with what I had the honour of saying to you in my last, in regard to the impropriety, the cruelty, I had almost said the injustice, of your intention of deserting that world of which you are at once the ornament and example.

Good people, as your Lordship observes, are generally too retired and abstracted to let their example be of much service to the world: whereas the bad, on the contrary, are conspicuous to all; they stand forth, they appear on the fore ground of the picture, and force themselves into observation.

'Tis to that circumstance, I am persuaded, we may attribute that dangerous and too common mistake, that vice is natural to the human heart, and virtuous characters the creatures of fancy; a mistake of the most fatal tendency, as it tends to harden our hearts, and destroy that mutual confidence so necessary to keep the bands of society from loosening, and without which man is the most ferocious of all beasts of prey.

Would all those whose virtues like your Lordship's are adorned by politeness and knowledge of the world, mix more in society, we should soon see vice hide her head: would all the good appear in full view, they would, I am convinced, be found infinitely the majority.

Virtue is too lovely to be hid in cells, the world is her scene of action: she is soft, gentle, indulgent; let her appear then in her own form, and she must charm: let politeness be for ever her attendant, that politeness which can give graces even to vice itself, which makes superiority easy, removes the sense of inferiority, and adds to every one's enjoyment both of himself and others.

I am interrupted, and must postpone till to-morrow what I have further to say to your Lordship. I have the honour to be, my Lord,

Your Lordship's, etc.

W. FERMOR

TO MRS TEMPLE, PALL MALL

LETTER **101** SILLERI, MARCH 25: Your brother, my dear Lucy, has made me happy in communicating to me the account he has received of your marriage. I know Temple; he is, besides being very handsome, a fine, sprightly, agreeable fellow, and is particularly formed to keep a woman's mind in that kind of play, that gentle agitation, which will for ever secure her affection.

He has in my opinion just as much coquetry as is necessary to prevent marriage from degenerating into that sleepy kind of existence, which to minds of the awakened turn of yours and mine would be insupportable.

He has also a fine fortune, which I hold to be a pretty enough ingredient in marriage.

In short, he is just such a man, upon the whole, as I should have chose for myself.

Make my congratulations to the dear man, and tell him, if he is not the happiest man in the world, he will forfeit all his pretensions to taste; and if he does not make you the happiest woman, he forfeits all title to my favour, as well as to the favour of the whole sex.

I meant to say something civil; but, to tell you the truth, I am not *en train*; I am excessively out of humour: Fitzgerald has not been here of several days, but spends his whole time in gallanting Madame La Brosse, a woman to whom he knows I have an aversion, and who has nothing but a tolerable complexion and a modest assurance to recommend her.

I certainly gave him some provocation, but this is too much: however, 'tis very well; I don't think I shall break my heart, though my vanity is a little piqued. I may perhaps live to take my revenge.

I am hurt, because I began really to like the creature; a secret however to which he is happily a stranger. I shall see him to-morrow at the governor's, and suppose he will be in his penitentials: I have some doubt whether I shall let him dance with me; yet it would look so particular to refuse him, that I believe I shall do him the honour.

Adieu!

Your affectionate

A. Fermor

26th, Thursday, 11 at night

No, Lucy, if I forgive him this, I have lost all free spirit of woman; he had the insolence to dance with Madame La Brosse to-night at the governor's. I never will forgive him. There are men perhaps quite his equals!—but 'tis no matter—I do him too much honour to be piqued—yet on the footing we were —I could not have believed—

Adieu!

I was so certain he would have danced with me, that I refused Colonel H——, one of the most agreeable men in the place, and therefore could not dance at all. Nothing hurt me so much as the impertinent looks of the women; I could cry for vexation.

Would your brother have behaved thus to Emily? But why do I name other men with your brother! do you know he and Emily had the good-nature to refuse to dance, that my sitting still might be less taken notice of? We all played at cards, and Rivers contrived to be my party, by which he would have won Emily's heart if he had not had it before.

Good night.

LETTER 102   QUEBEC, MARCH 2: I have been twice at Silleri with the intention of declaring my passion, and explaining my situation to Emily; but have been prevented by company, which made it impossible for me to find the opportunity I wished.

Had I found that opportunity, I am not sure I should have made use of it; a degree of timidity is inseparable from true tenderness; and I am afraid of declaring myself a lover, lest, if not beloved, I should lose the happiness I at present possess in visiting her as her friend: I cannot give up the dear delight I find in seeing her, in hearing her voice, in tracing and admiring every sentiment of that lovely unaffected generous mind as it rises.

In short, my Lucy, I cannot live without her esteem and friendship; and though her eyes, her attention to me, her whole manner, encourage me in the hope of being beloved, yet the possibility of my being mistaken makes me dread an explanation by which I hazard losing the lively pleasure I find in her friendship.

This timidity however must be conquered; 'tis pardonable to feel it, but not to give way to it. I have ordered my carriole, and am determined to make my attack this very morning like a man of courage and a soldier.

Adieu!

Your affectionate

ED. RIVERS

A letter from Bell Fermor, to whom I wrote this morning on the subject:

"To COLONEL RIVERS, *at Quebec*

Silleri, Friday morning

"*You are a foolish creature, and know nothing of women. Dine at Silleri, and we will air after dinner; 'tis a glorious day, and if you are timid in a covered carriole, I give you up.*

"*Adieu!*

"*Yours,*
"A. FERMOR"

LETTER 103 She is an angel, my dear Lucy, and no words can do her justice: I am the happiest of mankind; I painted my passion with all the moving eloquence of undissembled love; she heard me with the most flattering attention; she said little but her looks, her air, her tone of voice, her blushes, her very silence—how could I ever doubt her tenderness? have not those lovely eyes a thousand times betrayed the dear secret of her heart?

My Lucy, we were formed for each other; our souls are of intelligence; every thought, every idea—from the first moment I beheld her—I have a thousand things to say, but the tumult of my joy—she has given me leave to write to her; what has she not said in that permission?

I cannot go to bed; I will go and walk an hour on the battery; 'tis the loveliest night I ever beheld, even in Canada: the day is scarce brighter.

One in the morning

I have had the sweetest walk imaginable: the moon shines with a splendour I never saw before; a thousand streaming meteors add to her brightness; I have stood gazing on the lovely planet, and delighting myself with the idea that 'tis the same moon that lights my Emily.

Good night, my Lucy! I love you beyond all expression; I always loved you tenderly, but there is a softness about my heart to-night—this lovely woman—

I know not what I would say, but till this night I could never be said to live.

Adieu! Your affectionate

ED. RIVERS

LETTER 104 QUEBEC, MARCH 28: I had this morning a short billet from her dear hand, entreating me to make up a quarrel between Bell Fermor and her lover: your friend has been indiscreet; her spirit of coquetry is eternally carrying her wrong; but in my opinion Fitzgerald has been at least equally to blame.

His behaviour at the governor's on Thursday night was inexcusable, as it exposed her to the sneers of a whole circle of her own sex, many of them jealous of her perfections.

A lover should overlook little caprices where the heart is good and amiable like Bell's: I should think myself particularly obliged to bring this affair to an amicable conclusion, even if Emily had not desired it, as I was originally the innocent cause of their quarrel. In my opinion he ought to beg her pardon; and, as a friend tenderly interested for both, I have a right to tell him I think so: he loves her, and I know must suffer greatly, though a foolish pride prevents his acknowledging it.

My great fear is, that an idle resentment may engage him in an intrigue with the lady in question, who is a woman of gallantry, and whom he may find very troublesome hereafter. It is much easier to commence an affair of this kind than to break it off; and a man, though his heart was disengaged, should be always on his guard against any thing like an attachment where his affections are not really interested: meer passion or meer vanity will support an affair *en passant*; but, where the least degree of constancy and attention are expected, the heart must feel, or the lover is subjecting himself to a slavery as irksome as a marriage without inclination.

Temple will tell you I speak like an oracle; for I have often seen him led by vanity into this very disagreeable situation: I hope I am not too late to save Fitzgerald from it.

Six in the evening

All goes well: his proud heart is come down, he has begged her pardon, and is forgiven; you have no idea how civil both are to me, for having persuaded them to do what each of them has longed to do from the first moment: I love to advise, when I am sure the heart of the person advised is on my side. Both were to blame, but I always love to save the ladies from any thing mortifying to the dignity of their characters; a little pride in love becomes them, but not us; and 'tis always our part to submit on these occasions.

I never saw two happier people than they are at present, as I have a little preserved decorum on both sides, and taken the whole trouble of the reconciliation on myself. Bell knows nothing of my having applied to Fitzgerald, nor he that I did it at Emily's request: my conversation with him on this subject seemed accidental. I was obliged to leave them, having business in town; but my lovely Emily thanked me by a smile which would overpay a thousand such little services.

I am to spend to-morrow at Silleri: how long shall I think this evening?

Adieu! my tenderest wishes attend you all!

Your affectionate

ED. RIVERS

LETTER 105 SILLERI, MARCH 27, EVENING: Fitzgerald has been here, and has begged my pardon; he declares he had no thought of displeasing me at the governor's, but from my behaviour was afraid of importuning me if he addressed me as usual.

I thought who would come to first; for my part, if he had stayed away for ever, I would not have suffered papa to invite him to Silleri: it was easy to see his neglect was all pique; it would have been extraordinary indeed if such a woman as Madame La Brosse could have rivalled me: I am something younger; and, if either my glass or the men are to be believed, as handsome: *entre nous*, there is some little difference; if she was not so very fair, she would be absolutely ugly: and these very fair women, you know, Lucy, are always insipid; she is the taste of no man breathing, though eternally making advances to every man; without spirit, fire, understanding, vivacity, or any quality capable of making amends for the mediocrity of her charms.

Her insolence in attempting to attach Fitzgerald is intolerable, especially when the whole province knows him to be my lover: there is no expressing to what a degree I hate her.

The next time we meet I hope to return her impertinence on Thursday night at the governor's. I will never forgive Fitzgerald if he takes the least notice of her.

Emily has read my letter; and says she did not think I had so much of the woman in me; insists on my being civil to Madame La Brosse, but if I am, Lucy—

These Frenchwomen are not to be supported; they fancy vanity and assurance are to make up for the want of every other virtue; forgetting that delicacy, softness, sensibility, tenderness, are attractions to which they are strangers: some of them here are however tolerably handsome, and have a degree of liveliness which makes them not quite insupportable.

You will call all this spite, as Emily does, so I will say no more: only that, in order to shew her how very easy it is to be civil to a rival, I wish for the pleasure of seeing another French lady, that I could mention, at Quebec.

Good night, my dear! tell Temple, I am every thing but in love with him.

Your faithful

A. Fermor

I will however own, I encouraged Fitzgerald by a kind look. I was so pleased at his return, that I could not keep up the farce of disdain I had projected: in love affairs, I am afraid, we are all fools alike.

LETTER 106   SATURDAY NOON: Come to my dressing-room, my dear; I have a thousand things to say to you: I want to talk of my Rivers, to tell you all the weakness of my soul.

No, my dear, I cannot love him more, a passion like mine will not admit addition; from the first moment I saw him my whole soul was his: I knew not that I was dear to him; but true genuine love is self-existent, and does not depend on being beloved: I should have loved him even had he been attached to another.

This declaration has made me the happiest of my sex; but it has not increased, it could not increase, my tenderness: with what softness, what diffidence, what respect, what delicacy, was this declaration made! my dear friend, he is a god, and my ardent affection for him is fully justified.

I love him—no words can speak how much I love him.

My passion for him is the first and shall be the last of my life: my bosom never heaved a sigh but for my Rivers.

Will you pardon the folly of a heart which till now was ashamed to own its feelings, and of which you are even now the only confidante?

I find all the world so insipid, nothing amuses me one

moment; in short, I have no pleasure but in Rivers's conversation, nor do I count the hours of his absence in my existence.

I know all this will be called folly, but it is folly which makes all the happiness of my life.

You love, my dear Bell; and therefore will pardon the weakness of your

EMILY

TO MISS MONTAGUE

LETTER 107 SATURDAY: Yes, my dear, I love, at least I think so; but, thanks to my stars, not in the manner you do.

I prefer Fitzgerald to all the rest of his sex; but *I count the hours of his absence in my existence*; and contrive sometimes to pass them pleasantly enough, if any other agreeable man is in the way: in short, I relish flattery and attention from others, tho' I infinitely prefer them from him.

I certainly love him, for I was jealous of Madame La Brosse; but in general, I am not alarmed when I see him flirt a little with others. Perhaps my vanity was as much wounded as my love, with regard to Madame La Brosse.

I find love is quite a different plant in different soils; it is an exotic, and grows faintly, with us coquets; but in its native climate with you people of sensibility and sentiment.

Adieu! I will attend you in a quarter of an hour.

Yours,

A. FERMOR

TO MISS FERMOR

LETTER 108 Not alarmed, my dear, at his attention to others? believe me, you know nothing of love.

I think every woman who beholds my Rivers a rival; I imagine I see in every female countenance a passion tender and lively as my own; I turn pale, my heart dies within me, if I observe his eyes a moment fixed on any other woman; I tremble at the possibility of his changing; I cannot support the idea that the time may come when I may be less dear to my Rivers than at present. Do you believe it possible, my dearest Bell, for any heart, not prepossessed, to be insensible one moment to my Rivers?

He is formed to charm the soul of woman; his delicacy, his sensibility, the mind that speaks through those eloquent eyes; the thousand graces of his air, the sound of his voice—my dear, I never heard him speak without feeling a softness of which it is impossible to convey an idea.

But I am wrong to encourage a tenderness which is already too great; I will think less of him; I will not talk of him; do not speak of him to me, my dear Bell: talk to me of Fitzgerald; there is no danger of your passion becoming too violent.

I wish you loved more tenderly, my dearest; you would then be more indulgent to my weakness: I am ashamed of owning it even to you.

Ashamed, did I say? no, I rather glory in loving the most amiable, the most angelic of mankind.

Speak of him to me for ever; I abhor all conversation of which he is not the subject. I am interrupted. Adieu!

Your faithful

EMILY

My dearest, I tremble; he is at the door; how shall I meet him without betraying all the weakness of my heart? come to me this moment, I will not go down without you. Your father is come to fetch me? follow me, I entreat: I cannot see him alone; my heart is too much softened at this moment. He must not know to what excess he is loved.

TO MRS TEMPLE, PALL MALL

LETTER 109 QUEBEC, MARCH 28: I am at present, my dear Lucy, extremely embarrassed; Madame Des Roches is at Quebec: it is impossible for me not to be more than polite to her; yet my Emily has all my heart, and demands all my attention; there is but one way of seeing them both as often as I wish; 'tis to bring them as often as possible together: I wish extremely that Emily would visit her, but 'tis a point of the utmost delicacy to manage.

Will it not on reflection be cruel to Madame Des Roches? I know her generosity of mind, but I also know the weakness of the human heart: can she see with pleasure a beloved rival?

My Lucy, I never so much wanted your advice: I will consult Bell Fermor, who knows every thought of my Emily's heart.

Eleven o'clock

I have visited Madame Des Roches at her relation's; she received me with a pleasure which was too visible not to be observed by all present: she blushed, her voice faltered when she addressed me; her eyes had a softness which seemed to reproach my insensibility; I was shocked at the idea of having inspired her with a tenderness not in my power to return; I was afraid of increasing that tenderness; I scarce dared to meet her looks.

I felt a criminal in the presence of this amiable woman; for both our sakes, I must see her seldom; yet what an appearance will any neglect have, after the attention she has shewed me, and the friendship she has expressed for me to all the world?

I know not what to determine. I am going to Silleri. Adieu till my return.

Eight o'clock

I have entreated Emily to admit Madame Des Roches among the number of her friends, and have asked her to visit her to-morrow morning: she changed colour at my request, but promised to go.

I almost repent of what I have done: I am to attend Emily and Bell Fermor to Madame Des Roches in the morning: I am afraid I shall introduce them with a bad grace. Adieu!

Your affectionate

ED. RIVERS

TO MISS FERMOR

LETTER 110 SUNDAY MORNING: Could you have believed he would have expected such a proof of my desire to oblige him? but what can he ask that his Emily will refuse? I will see this *friend* of his, this Madame Des Roches; I will even

156

love her, if it is in woman to be so disinterested. She loves him; he sees her; they say she is amiable; I could have wished her visit to Quebec had been delayed.

But he comes; he looks up; his eyes seem to thank me for this excess of complaisance: what is there I would not do to give him pleasure?

Do you think her so very pleasing, my dear Bell? she has fine eyes, but have they not more fire than softness? There was a vivacity in her manner which hurt me extremely: could she have behaved with such unconcern, had she loved as I do?

Do you think it possible, Lucy, for a Frenchwoman to love? is not vanity the ruling passion of their hearts?

May not Rivers be deceived in supposing her so much attached to him? was there not some degree of affectation in her particular attention to me? I cannot help thinking her artful.

Perhaps I am prejudiced: she may be amiable, but I will own she does not please me.

Rivers begged me to have a friendship for her; I am afraid this is more than is in my power: friendship, like love, is the child of sympathy, not of constraint.

Adieu! Yours,

EMILY MONTAGUE

TO MISS MONTAGUE

LETTER 111 MONDAY: The inclosed, my dear, is as much to you as to me, perhaps more; I pardon the lady for thinking you the handsomest. Is not this the strongest proof I could give of my friendship? perhaps I should have been piqued, however, had the preference been given by a man; but I can with great tranquillity allow you to be the women's beauty.

Dictate an answer to your little Bell, who waits your commands at her bureau.

Adieu!

"To Miss FERMOR, *at Silleri*

Monday

"*You and your lovely friend obliged me beyond words, my dear Bell, by your visit of yesterday: Madame Des Roches is charmed with you both: you will not be displeased when I tell*

you she gives Emily the preference; she says she is beautiful as
an angel; that she should think the man insensible, who could
see her without love; that she is touchant, *to use her own word,*
beyond any thing she ever beheld.

"*She however does justice to your charms, though*
Emily's seem to affect her most. She even allows you to be per-
haps more the taste of men in general.

"*She intends paying her respects to you and Emily this*
afternoon; and has sent to desire me to conduct her. As it is so
far, I would wish to find you at home.

"*Yours,*

Ed. Rivers"

TO MISS FERMOR

LETTER 112 Always Madame Des Roches! but let
her come: indeed, my dear, she is artful; she gains upon him
by this appearance of generosity; I cannot return it, I do not
love her; yet I will receive her with politeness.

He is to drive her too; but 'tis no matter; if the tenderest
affection can secure his heart, I have nothing to fear: Loving
him as I do, it is impossible not to be apprehensive: indeed,
my dear, he knows not how I love him.

Adieu!

Your Emily

TO MISS FERMOR

LETTER 113 MONDAY EVENING: Surely I am
the weakest of my weak sex; I am ashamed to tell you all my
feelings: I cannot conquer my dislike to Madame Des Roches:
she said a thousand obliging things to me, she praised my
Rivers; I made no answer, I even felt tears ready to start; what
must she think of me? there is a meanness in my jealousy of her,
which I cannot forgive myself.

I cannot account for her attention to me, it is not
natural; she behaved to me not only with politeness, but with

the appearance of affection; she seemed to feel and pity my confusion. She is either the most artful, or the most noble of women.

Adieu!

Your

EMILY

TO MRS TEMPLE, PALL MALL

LETTER 114 SILLERI, MARCH 29: We are going to dine at a farm-house in the country, where we are to meet other company, and have a ball: the snow begins a little to soften, from the warmth of the sun, which is greater than in England in May. Our winter parties are almost at an end.

My father drives Madame Des Roches, who is of our party, and your brother Emily; I hope the little fool will be easy now, Lucy; she is very humble, to be jealous of one, who though really very pleasing, is neither so young nor so handsome as herself; and who professes to wish only for Rivers's friendship.

But I have no right to say a word on this subject, after having been so extremely hurt at Fitzgerald's attention to such a woman as Madame La Brosse; an attention too which was so plainly meant to pique me.

We are all, I am afraid, a little absurd in these affairs, and therefore ought to have some degree of indulgence for others.

Emily and I, however, differ in our ideas of love: it is the business of her life, the amusement of mine; 'tis the food of her hours, the seasoning of mine.

Or, in other words, she loves like a foolish woman, I like a sensible man: for men, you know, compared to women, love in about the proportion of one to twenty.

'Tis a mighty wrong thing, after all, Lucy, that parents will educate creatures so differently who are to live with and for each other.

Every possible means is used, even from infancy, to soften the minds of women, and to harden those of men; the contrary endeavour might be of use, for the men creatures are unfeeling enough by nature, and we are born too tremblingly alive to love, and indeed to every soft affection.

Your brother is almost the only one of his sex I know, who has the tenderness of woman with the spirit and firmness of man; a circumstance which strikes every woman who converses with him, and which contributes to make him the favourite he is amongst us. Foolish women who cannot distinguish characters may possibly give the preference to a coxcomb; but I will venture to say, no woman of sense was ever much acquainted with Colonel Rivers without feeling for him an affection of some kind or other.

A propos to women, the estimable part of us are divided into two classes only, the tender and the lively.

The former, at the head of which I place Emily, are infinitely more capable of happiness; but, to counterbalance this advantage, they are also capable of misery in the same degree. We of the other class, who feel less keenly, are perhaps upon the whole as happy, at least I would fain think so.

For example, if Emily and I marry our present lovers, she will certainly be more exquisitely happy than I shall; but if they should change their minds, or any accident prevent our coming together, I am inclined to fancy my situation would be much the most agreeable.

I should pout a month, and then look about for another lover; whilst the tender Emily would

> *"Sit like patience on a monument,"*

and pine herself into a consumption.

Adieu! They wait for me.

Yours,

A. FERMOR

Tuesday, midnight

We have had a very agreeable day, Lucy, a pretty enough kind of a ball and every body in good humour; I danced with Fitzgerald, whom I never knew so agreeable.

Happy love is gay, I find; Emily is all sprightliness, your brother's eyes have never left her a moment, and her blushes seemed to shew her sense of the distinction; I never knew her look so handsome as this day.

Do you know I felt for Madame Des Roches? Emily was excessively complaisant to her: she returned her civility, but I could perceive a kind of constraint in her manner, very different from the ease of her behaviour when we saw her before: she felt the attention of Rivers to Emily very strongly: in short, the ladies seemed to have changed characters for the day.

We supped with your brother on our return, and from his windows, which look on the river St Charles, had the pleasure of observing one of the most beautiful objects imaginable, which I never remember to have seen before this evening.

You are to observe the winter method of fishing here, is to break openings like small fish ponds on the ice, to which the fish coming for air, are taken in prodigious quantities on the surface.

To shelter themselves from the excessive cold of the night, the fishermen build small houses of ice on the river, which are arranged in a semicircular form, and which, from the blazing fires within, have a brilliant transparency and vivid lustre, not easy either to imagine or to describe: the starry semicircle looks like an immense crescent of diamonds, on which the sun darts his meridian rays.

Absolutely, Lucy, you see nothing in Europe: you are cultivated, you have the tame beauties of art, but to see nature in her lovely wild luxuriance, you must visit your brother when he is prince of the Kamaraskas.

Adieu!

Your faithful

A. FERMOR

The variety, as well of grand objects, as of amusements, in this country, confirms me in an opinion I have always had, that Providence had made the conveniences and inconveniences of life nearly equal everywhere.

We have pleasures here even in winter peculiar to the climate, which counterbalance the evils we suffer from its rigour.

Good night, my dear Lucy!

TO MRS TEMPLE, PALL MALL

LETTER 115 QUEBEC, APRIL 2: I have this moment, my dear, a letter from Montreal, describing some lands on Lake Champlain, which my friend thinks much better worth my taking than those near the Kamaraskas: he presses me to come up immediately to see them, as the ice on the rivers will in a few days be dangerous to travel on.

I am strongly inclined to go, and for this reason; I am convinced my wish of bringing about a friendship between Emily and Madame Des Roches, the strongest reason I had for fixing at the Kamaraskas, was an imprudent one: gratitude and (if the expression is not impertinent) compassion give me a softness in my behaviour to the latter, which a superficial observer would take for love, and which her own tenderness may cause even her to misconstrue; a circumstance which must retard her resolution of changing the affection with which she has honoured me, into friendship.

I am also delicate in my love, and cannot bear to have it one moment supposed, my heart can know a wish but for my Emily.

Shall I say more? The blush on Emily's cheek on her first seeing Madame Des Roches convinced me of my indiscretion, and that vanity alone carried me to desire to bring together two women whose affection for me is from their extreme merit so very flattering.

I shall certainly now fix in Canada; I can no longer doubt of Emily's tenderness, tho' she refuses me her hand, from motives which make her a thousand times more dear to me, but which I flatter myself love will over-rule.

I am setting off in an hour for Montreal, and shall call at Silleri to take Emily's commands.

Seven in the evening, Des Chambeaux

I asked her advice as to fixing the place of my settlement; she said much against my staying in America at all; but, if I was determined, recommended Lake Champlain rather than the Kamaraskas, on account of climate. Bell smiled; and a blush, which I perfectly understood, overspread the lovely cheek of my sweet Emily. Nothing could be more flattering than this circumstance; had she seen Madame Des Roches with a calm indifference, had she not been alarmed at the idea of fixing near her, I should have doubted of the degree of her affection; a little apprehension is inseparable from real love.

My courage has been to-day extremely put to the proof: had I staid three days longer, it would have been impossible to have continued my journey.

The ice cracks under us at every step the horses set, a rather unpleasant circumstance on a river twenty fathom deep: I should not have attempted the journey had I been aware of this particular. I hope no man meets inevitable danger with more spirit, but no man is less fond of seeking it where it is honourably to be avoided.

I am going to sup with the seigneur of the village, who is, I am told, married to one of the handsomest women in the province.

Adieu! my dear! I shall write to you from Montreal.
Your affectionate

ED. RIVERS

LETTER 116 MONTREAL, APRIL 3: I am arrived, my dear, after a very disagreeable and dangerous journey; I was obliged to leave the river soon after I left Des Chambeaux, and to pursue my way on the land over melting snow, into which the horses' feet sunk half a yard every step.

An officer from New York has given me a letter from you, which came thither by private ship: I am happy to hear of your health, and that Temple's affection for you seems rather to increase than lessen since your marriage.

You ask me, my dear Lucy, how to preserve this affection, on the continuance of which, you justly say, your whole happiness depends.

The question is perhaps the most delicate and important which respects human life; the caprice, the inconstancy, the injustice of men, makes the task of women in marriage infinitely difficult.

Prudence and virtue will certainly secure esteem; but unfortunately, esteem alone will not make a happy marriage; passion must also be kept alive, which the continual presence of the object beloved is apt to make subside into that apathy, so insupportable to sensible minds.

The higher your rank, and the less your manner of life separates you from each other, the more danger there will be of this indifference.

The poor whose necessary avocations divide them all day, and whose sensibility is blunted by the coarseness of their education, are in no danger of being weary of each other; and, unless naturally vicious, you will see them generally happy in marriage, whereas even the virtuous, in more affluent situations, are not secure from this unhappy cessation of tenderness.

When I received your letter, I was reading Madame De Maintenon's advice to the Duchess of Burgundy, on this subject. I will transcribe so much of it as relates to *the woman*, leaving her advice to *the princess* to those whom it may concern.

"*Do not hope for perfect happiness; there is no such thing in this sublunary state.*

"*Your sex is the more exposed to suffer, because it is always in dependence: be neither angry nor ashamed of this dependence on a husband, nor of any of those which are in the order of Providence.*

"*Let your husband be your best friend and your only confidant.*

"Do not hope that your union will procure you perfect peace: the best marriages are those where with softness and patience they bear by turns with each other; there are none without some contradiction and disagreement.

"Do not expect the same degree of friendship that you feel: men are in general less tender than women; and you will be unhappy if you are too delicate in friendship.

"Beg of God to guard your heart from jealousy: do not hope to bring back a husband by complaints, ill-humour, and reproaches. The only means which promise success, are patience and softness: impatience sours and alienates hearts: softness leads them back to their duty.

"In sacrificing your own will, pretend to no right over that of a husband: men are more attached to theirs than women, because educated with less constraint.

"They are naturally tyrannical; they will have pleasures and liberty, yet insist that woman renounce both: do not examine whether their rights are well founded; let it suffice to you, that they are established; they are masters, we have only to suffer and obey with a good grace."

Thus far Madame De Maintenon, who must be allowed to have known the heart of man, since, after having been above twenty years a widow, she enflamed, even to the degree of bringing him to marry her, that of a great monarch, younger than herself, surrounded by Beauties, habituated to flattery, in the plenitude of power, and covered with glory; and retained him in her chains to the last moments of his life.

Do not, however, my dear, be alarmed at the picture she has drawn of marriage; nor fancy with her, that women are only born to suffer and to obey.

That we are generally tyrannical, I am obliged to own; but such of us as know how to be happy, willingly give up the harsh title of Master, for the more tender and endearing one of Friend: Men of sense abhor those customs which treat your sex as if created merely for the happiness of the other; a supposition injurious to the Deity, though flattering to our tyranny and self-love; and wish only to bind you in the soft chains of affection.

Equality is the soul of friendship: marriage, to give delight, must join two minds, not devote a slave to the will of an imperious lord; whatever conveys the idea of subjection necessarily destroys that of love, of which I am so convinced, that I have always wished the word OBEY expunged from the marriage ceremony.

If you will permit me to add my sentiments to those of a lady so learned in the art of pleasing; I would wish you to study the taste of your husband, and endeavour to acquire a relish for those pleasures which appear most to affect him; let him find amusement at home, but never be peevish at his going abroad; he will return to you with the higher gust for your conversation: have separate apartments, since your fortune makes it not inconvenient; be always elegant, but not too expensive, in your dress; retain your present exquisite delicacy of every kind; receive his friends with good-breeding and complacency; contrive such little parties of pleasure as you know are agreeable to him, and with the most agreeable people you can select: be lively even to playfulness in your general turn of conversation with him; but, at the same time, spare no pains so to improve your understanding, which is an excellent one, as to be no less capable of being the companion of his graver hours: be ignorant of nothing which it becomes your sex to know, but avoid all affectation of knowledge: let your economy be exact, but without appearing otherwise than by the effect.

Do not imitate those of your sex who by ill-temper make a husband pay dear for their fidelity; let virtue in you be dressed in smiles; and be assured that chearfulness is the native garb of innocence.

In one word, my dear, do not lose the mistress in the wife, but let your behaviour to him as a husband be such as you would have thought most proper to attract him as a lover: have always the idea of pleasing before you, and you cannot fail to please.

Having lectured you, my dear Lucy, I must say a word to Temple: a great variety of rules have been given for the conduct of women in marriage; scarce any for that of men; as if it was not essential to domestic happiness, that the man should preserve the heart of her with whom he is to spend his life; or as if bestowing happiness were not worth a man's attention, so he possessed it: if, however, it is possible to feel true happiness without giving it.

You, my dear Temple, have too just an idea of pleasure to think in this manner: you would be beloved; it has been the pursuit of your life, though never really attained perhaps before. You at present possess a heart full of sensibility, a heart capable of loving with ardour, and from the same cause as capable of being estranged by neglect: give your whole attention to preserving this invaluable treasure; observe every rule I have given to her, if you would be happy; and believe me, the heart of woman is not less delicate than tender; their sensibility is more keen, they feel more strongly than we do, their tenderness is more easily wounded, and their hearts are more difficult to recover if once lost.

At the same time, they are both by nature and education more constant, and scarce ever change the object of their affections but from ill-treatment: for which reason there is some excuse for a custom which appears cruel, that of throwing contempt on the husband for the ill-conduct of the wife.

Above all things, retain the politeness and attention of a lover; and avoid that careless manner which wounds the vanity of human nature, a passion given us, as were all passions, for the wisest ends, and which never quits us but with life.

There is a certain attentive tenderness, difficult to be described, which the manly of our sex feel, and which is peculiarly pleasing to woman: 'tis also a very delightful sensation to ourselves, as well as productive of the happiest consequences: regarding them as creatures placed by Providence under our protection, and depending on us for their happiness, is the strongest possible tie of affection to a well-turned mind.

If I did not know Lucy perfectly I should perhaps hesitate in the next advice I am going to give you; which is, to make her the confidante, and the *only* confidante, of your gallantries, if you are so unhappy as to be inadvertently betrayed into any: her heart will possibly be at first a little wounded by the confession, but this proof of perfect esteem will increase her friendship for you; she will regard your error with compassion and indulgence, and lead you gently back by her endearing tenderness to honour and herself.

Of all tasks I detest that of giving advice: you are therefore under infinite obligation to me for this letter.

Be assured of my tenderest affection; and believe me.

Yours, etc.

ED. RIVERS

TO THE EARL OF ——

LETTER 117 SILLERI, APRIL 8: Nothing can be more true, my Lord, than that poverty is ever the inseparable companion of indolence.

I see proofs of it every moment before me; with a soil fruitful beyond all belief, the Canadians are poor on lands which are their own property, and for which they pay only a trifling quit-rent to their seigneurs.

This indolence appears in every thing: you scarce see the meanest peasant walking; even on horseback appears to them a fatigue insupportable; you see them lolling at ease, like their lazy lords, in carrioles and calashes, according to the season; a boy to guide the horse on a seat in the front of the carriage, too lazy even to take the trouble of driving themselves, their hands in winter folded in an immense muff, though perhaps their families are in want of bread to eat at home.

The winter is passed in a mixture of festivity and inaction; dancing and feasting in their gayer hours; in their graver smoking, and drinking brandy, by the side of a warm stove: and when obliged to cultivate the ground in spring to procure the means of subsistence, you see them just turn the turf once lightly over, and, without manuring the ground, or even breaking the clods of earth, throw in the seed in the same careless manner, and leave the event to chance, without troubling themselves further till it is fit to reap.

I must, however, observe, as some alleviation, that there is something in the climate which strongly inclines both the body and mind, but rather the latter, to indolence: the heat of the summer, though pleasing, enervates the very soul, and gives a certain lassitude unfavourable to industry; and the winter, at its extreme, binds up and chills all the active faculties of the soul.

Add to this, that the general spirit of amusement, so universal here in winter, and so necessary to prevent the ill-effects of the season, gives a habit of dissipation and pleasure, which makes labour doubly irksome at its return.

Their religion, to which they are extremely bigoted, is another great bar, as well to industry as population: their numerous festivals inure them to idleness; their religious houses rob the state of many subjects who might be highly useful at present, and at the same time retard the increase of the colony.

Sloth and superstition equally counter-work providence, and render the bounty of Heaven of no effect.

I am surprized the French, who generally make their religion subservient to the purposes of policy, do not discourage convents, and lessen the number of festivals, in the colonies, where both are so peculiarly pernicious.

It is to this circumstance one may in great measure attribute the superior increase of the British American settlements compared to those of France: a religion which encourages idleness, and makes a virtue of celibacy, is particularly unfavourable to colonization.

However religious prejudice may have been suffered to

counter-work policy under a French government, it is scarce to be doubted that this cause of the poverty of Canada will by degrees be removed; that these people, slaves at present to ignorance and superstition, will in time be enlightened by a more liberal education, and gently led by reason to a religion which is not only preferable, as being that of the country to which they are now annexed, but which is so much more calculated to make them happy and prosperous as a people.

Till that time, till their prejudices subside, it is equally just, humane, and wise, to leave them the free right of worshipping the Deity in the manner which they have been early taught to believe the best, and to which they are consequently attached.

It would be unjust to deprive them of any of the rights of citizens on account of religion, in America, where every other sect of dissenters are equally capable of employ with those of the established church; nay where, from whatever cause, the church of England is on a footing in many colonies little better than a toleration.

It is undoubtedly, in a political light, an object of consequence everywhere, that the national religion, whatever it is, should be as universal as possible, agreement in religious worship being the strongest tie to unity and obedience: had all prudent means been used to lessen the number of dissenters in our colonies, I cannot avoid believing, from what I observe and hear, that we should have found in them a spirit of rational loyalty and true freedom, instead of that factious one from which so much is to be apprehended.

It seems consonant to reason, that the religion of every country should have a relation to, and coherence with, the civil constitution: the Romish religion is best adapted to a despotic government, the presbyterian to a republican, and that of the church of England to a limited monarchy like ours.

As therefore the civil government of America is on the same plan with that of the mother country, it were to be wished the religious establishment was also the same, especially in those colonies where the people are generally of the national church; though with the fullest liberty of conscience to dissenters of all denominations.

I would be clearly understood, my Lord; from all I have observed here, I am convinced, nothing would so much contribute to diffuse a spirit of order, and rational obedience, in the colonies, as the appointment, under proper restrictions, of bishops: I am equally convinced that nothing would so much strengthen the hands of government, or give such pleasure to the well-affected in the colonies, who are by much the most numerous, as such an appointment, however clamoured against by a few abettors of sedition.

I am called upon for this letter, and must remit to another time what I wished to say more to your Lordship in regard to this country.

I have the honour to be,
My Lord, etc.

WM. FERMOR

TO MRS MELMOTH, AT MONTREAL

LETTER 118 SILLERI, APRIL 8: I am indeed, Madam, this inconsistent creature. I have at once refused to marry Colonel Rivers, and owned to him all the tenderness of my soul.

Do not however think me mad, or suppose my refusal the effect of an unmeaning childish affection of disinterestedness: I can form to myself no idea of happiness equal to that of spending my life with Rivers, the best, the most tender, the most amiable of mankind; nor can I support the idea of his marrying any other woman: I would therefore marry him to-morrow were it possible without ruining him, without dooming him to a perpetual exile, and obstructing those views of honest ambition at home, which become his birth, his connexions, his talents, his time of life; and with which, as his friend, it is my duty to inspire him.

His affection for me at present blinds him, he sees no object but me in the whole universe; but shall I take advantage of that inebriation of tenderness, to seduce him into a measure inconsistent with his real happiness and interest? He must return to England, must pursue fortune in that world for which he was formed: shall his Emily retard him in the glorious race? shall she not rather encourage him in every laudable attempt? shall she suffer him to hide that shining merit in the uncultivated wilds of Canada, the seat of barbarism and ignorance, which entitles him to hope a happy fate in the dear land of arts and arms?

I entreat you to do all you can to discourage his design. Remind him that his sister's marriage has in some degree removed the cause of his coming hither; that he can have now no motive for fixing here, but his tenderness for me; that I shall be justly blamed by all who love him for keeping him here. Tell him I will not marry him in Canada; that his stay makes the best mother in the world wretched; that he owes his return to himself, nay to his Emily, whose whole heart is set on seeing him in a situation worthy of him: though without ambition as to myself, I am proud, I am ambitious for him; if he loves me, he will gratify that pride, that ambition; and leave Canada to those whose duty confines them here, or whose interest it is to remain unseen. Let him not once think of me in his determination: I am content to be beloved, and will leave all else to time. You cannot so much oblige or serve me, as by persuading Colonel Rivers to return to England.

Believe me, my dear Madam,
Your affectionate

EMILY MONTAGUE

TO MRS TEMPLE, PALL MALL

LETTER 119 SILLERI, APRIL 9: Your brother, my dear, is gone to Montreal to look out for a settlement, and Emily to spend a fortnight at Quebec, with a lady she knew in England, who is lately arrived from thence by New York.

I am lost without my friend, though my lover endeavours in some degree to supply her place; he lays close siege; I know not how long I shall be able to hold out: this fine weather is exceedingly in his favour; the winter freezes up all the avenues to the heart; but this sprightly April sun thaws them again amazingly. I was the cruellest creature breathing whilst the chilly season lasted, but can answer for nothing now the sprightly May is approaching.

I can see papa is vastly in Fitzgerald's interest; but he knows our sex well enough to keep this to himself.

I shall however, for decency's sake, ask his opinion on the affair as soon as I have taken my resolution; which is the very time at which all the world ask advice of their friends.

A letter from Emily, which I must answer: she is extremely absurd, which your tender lovers always are.

Adieu! yours,

A. FERMOR

Sir George Clayton had left Montreal some days before your brother arrived there; I was pleased to hear it, because, with all your brother's good sense, and concern for Emily's honour, and Sir George's natural coldness of temper, a quarrel between them would have been rather difficult to have been avoided.

TO MISS FERMOR

LETTER **120** QUEBEC, THURSDAY MORNING:
Do you think, my dear, that Madame Des Roches has heard from Rivers? I wish you would ask her this afternoon at the governor's: I am anxious to know, but ashamed to enquire.

Not, my dear, that I have the weakness to be jealous; but I shall think his letter to me a higher compliment, if I know he writes to nobody else. I extremely approve his friendship for Madame Des Roches; she is very amiable, and certainly deserves it: but you know, Bell, it would be cruel to encourage an affection, which she must conquer, or be unhappy: if she did not love him, there would be nothing wrong in his writing to her; but, as she does, it would be doing her the greatest injury possible: 'tis as much on her account as my own I am thus anxious.

Did you ever read so tender, yet so lively a letter as Rivers's to me? he is alike in all: there is in his letters, as in his conversation,

> "All that can softly win, or gaily charm
> "The heart of woman."

Even strangers listen to him with an involuntary attention, and hear him with a pleasure for which they scarce know how to account.

He charms even without intending it, and in spite of himself; but when he wishes to please, when he addresses the woman he loves, when his eyes speak the soft language of his heart, when your Emily reads in them the dear confession of his tenderness, when that melodious voice utters the sentiments of the noblest mind that ever animated a human form— My dearest, the eloquence of angels cannot paint my Rivers as he is.

I am almost inclined not to go to the governor's to-night; I am determined not to dance till Rivers returns, and I know there are too many who will be ready to make observations on my refusal: I think I will stay at home, and write to him against Monday's post: I have a thousand things to say, and you know we are continually interrupted at Quebec; I shall have this evening to myself, as all the world will be at the governor's.

Adieu, your faithful

EMILY MONTAGUE

TO MISS MONTAGUE, AT QUEBEC

LETTER 121   SILLERI, THURSDAY MORN-
ING: I dare say, my dear, Madame Des Roches has not heard from Rivers; but suppose she had. If he loves you, of what consequence is it to whom he writes? I would not for the world any friend of yours should ask her such a question.

I shall call upon you at six o'clock, and shall expect to find you determined to go to the governor's this evening, and to dance: Fitzgerald begs the honour of being your partner.

Believe me, Emily, these kind of unmeaning sacrifices are childish; your heart is new to love, and you have all the romance of a girl: Rivers would, on your account, be hurt to hear you had refused to dance in his absence, though he might be flattered to know you had for a moment entertained such an idea.

I pardon you for having the romantic fancies of seventeen, provided you correct them with the good sense of four and twenty.

Adieu! I have engaged myself to Colonel H——, on the presumption that you are too polite to refuse to dance with Fitzgerald, and too prudent to refuse to dance at all.

Your affectionate

A. FERMOR

TO MISS FERMOR, AT SILLERI

LETTER 122 How unjust have I been in my hatred of Madame Des Roches! she spent yesterday with us, and after dinner desired to converse with me an hour in my apartment, where she opened to me all her heart on the subject of her love for Rivers.

She is the noblest and most amiable of women, and I have been in regard to her the most capricious and unjust: my hatred of her was unworthy my character; I blush to own the meanness of my sentiments, whilst I admire the generosity of hers.

Why, my dear, should I have hated her? she was unhappy, and deserved rather my compassion: I had deprived her of all hope of being beloved, it was too much to wish to deprive her also of his conversation. I knew myself the only object of Rivers's love; why then should I have envied her his friendship? she had the strongest reason to hate me, but I should have loved and pitied her.

Can there be a misfortune equal to that of loving Rivers without hope of a return? Yet she has not only borne this misfortune without complaint, but has been the confidante of his passion for another; he owned to her all his tenderness for me, and drew a picture of me, which, she told me, ought, had she listened to reason, to have destroyed even the shadow of hope: but that love, ever ready to flatter and deceive, had betrayed her into the weakness of supposing it possible I might refuse him, and that gratitude might, in that case, touch his heart with tenderness for one who loved him with the most pure and disinterested affection; that her journey to Quebec had removed the veil love had placed between her and truth; that she was now convinced the faint hope she had encouraged was madness, and that our souls were formed for each other.

She owned she still loved him with the most lively affection; yet assured me, since she was not allowed to make the most amiable of mankind happy herself, she wished him to be so with the woman on earth she thought most worthy of him.

She added, that she had on first seeing me, though she thought me worthy his heart, felt an impulse of dislike which she was ashamed to own, even now that reason and reflexion had conquered so unworthy a sentiment; that Rivers's complaisance had a little dissipated her chagrin, and enabled her to behave to me in the manner she did: that she had, however, almost hated me at the ball in the country: that the tenderness in Rivers's eyes that day whenever they met mine, and his comparative inattention to her, had wounded her to the soul.

That this preference had, however, been salutary, though painful; since it had determined her to conquer a passion, which could only make her life wretched if it continued; that, as the first step to this conquest, she had resolved to see him no more: that she would return to her house the moment she could cross the river with safety; and conjured me, for her sake, to persuade him to give up all thoughts of a settlement near her; that she could not answer for her own heart if she continued to see him; that she believed in love there was no safety but in flight.

That his absence had given her time to think coolly; and that she now saw so strongly the amiableness of my character, and was so convinced of my perfect tenderness for him, that she should hate herself were she capable of wishing to interrupt our happiness.

That she hoped I would pardon her retaining a tender remembrance of a man who, had he never seen me, might have returned her affection; that she thought so highly of my heart, as to believe I could not hate a woman who esteemed me, and who solicited my friendship, though a happy rival.

I was touched, even to tears, at her behaviour: we embraced; and, if I know my own weak foolish heart, I love her.

She talks of leaving Quebec before Rivers's return; she said, her coming was an imprudence which only love could excuse; and that she had no motive for her journey but the desire of seeing him, which was so lively as to hurry her into an indiscretion of which she was afraid the world took but too much notice. What openness, what sincerity, what generosity, was there in all she said!

How superior, my dear, is her character to mine! I blush for myself on the comparison; I am shocked to see how much she soars above me: how is it possible Rivers should not have preferred her to me? Yet this is the woman I fancied incapable of any passion but vanity.

I am sure, my dear Bell, I am not naturally envious of the merit of others; but my excess of love for Rivers makes me apprehensive of every woman who can possibly rival me in his tenderness.

I was hurt at Madame Des Roches's uncommon merit; I saw with pain the amiable qualities of her mind; I could scarce even allow her person to be pleasing: but this injustice is not that of my natural temper, but of love.

She is certainly right, my dear, to see him no more; I applaud, I admire her resolution: do you think, however, she would pursue it if she loved as I do? She has perhaps loved before, and her heart has lost something of its native trembling sensibility.

I wish my heart felt her merit as strongly as my reason: I esteem, I admire, I even love her at present; but I am convinced Rivers's return while she continues here would weaken these sentiments of affection: the least appearance of preference, even for a moment, would make me relapse into my former weakness. I adore, I idolize her character; but I cannot sincerely wish to cultivate her friendship.

Let me see you this afternoon at Quebec; I am told the roads will not be passable for carrioles above three days longer: let me therefore see you as often as I can before we are absolutely shut from each other.

Adieu! my dear!

Your faithful

EMILY MONTAGUE

TO THE EARL OF ———

LETTER 123 SILLERI, APRIL 14: England, however populous, is undoubtedly, my Lord, too small to afford very large supplies of people to her colonies: and her people are also too useful, and of too much value, to be suffered to emigrate, if they can be prevented, whilst there is sufficient employment for them at home.

It is not only our interest to have colonies; they are not only necessary to our commerce, and our greatest and surest sources of wealth, but our very being as a powerful commercial nation depends on them: it is therefore an object of all others most worthy our attention, that they should be as flourishing and populous as possible.

It is however equally our interest to support them at as little expence of our own inhabitants as possible: I therefore look on the acquisition of such a number of subjects as we found in Canada, to be a much superior advantage to that of gaining ten times the immense tract of land ceded to us, if uncultivated and destitute of inhabitants.

But it is not only contrary to our interest to spare many of our own people as settlers in America; it must also be considered, that, if we could spare them, the English are the worst settlers on new lands in the universe.

Their attachment to their native country, especially amongst the lower ranks of people, is so very strong, that few of the honest and industrious can be prevailed on to leave it; those therefore who go, are generally the dissolute and the idle, who are of no use any where.

The English are also, though industrious, active, and enterprizing, ill-fitted to bear the hardships, and submit to the wants, which inevitably attend an infant settlement even on the most fruitful lands.

The Germans, on the contrary, with the same useful qualities, have a patience, a perseverance, and abstinence, which peculiarly fit them for the cultivation of new countries; too great encouragement therefore cannot be given to them to settle in our colonies: they make better settlers than our own people; and at the same time their numbers are an acquisition of real strength where they fix, without weakening the mother country.

It is long since the populousness of Europe has been the cause of her sending out colonies: a better policy prevails; mankind are enlightened; we are now convinced, both by reason and experience, that no industrious people can be too populous.

The northern swarms were compelled to leave their respective countries, not because those countries were unable to support them, but because they were too idle to cultivate the ground: they were a ferocious, ignorant, barbarous people, averse to labour, attached to war, and, like our American savages, believing every employment not relative to this favourite object, beneath the dignity of man.

Their emigrations therefore were less owing to their populousness, than to their want of industry, and barbarous contempt of agriculture and every useful art.

It is with pain I am compelled to say, the late spirit of encouraging the monopoly of farms, which, from a narrow, short-sighted policy, prevails amongst our landed men at home, and the alarming growth of celibacy amongst the peasantry, which is its necessary consequence, to say nothing of the same ruinous increase of celibacy in higher ranks, threatens us with such a decrease of population, as will probably equal that caused by the ravages of those scourges of Heaven, the sword, the famine, and the pestilence.

If this selfish policy continues to extend itself, we shall in a few years be so far from being able to send emigrants to America, that we shall be reduced to solicit their return, and that of their posterity, to prevent England's becoming in its turn an uncultivated desert.

But to return to Canada; this large acquisition of people is an invaluable treasure, if managed, as I doubt not it will be, to the best advantage; if they are won by the gentle arts of persuasion, and the gradual progress of knowledge, to adopt so much of our manners as tends to make them happier in themselves, and more useful members of the society to which they belong: if with our language, which they should by every means be induced to learn, they acquire the mild genius of our religion and laws, and that spirit of industry, enterprize, and commerce, to which we owe all our greatness.

Amongst the various causes which concur to render France more populous than England, notwithstanding the disadvantage of a less gentle government, and a religion so very unfavourable to the increase of mankind, the cultivation of vineyards may be reckoned a principal one; as it employs a much greater number of hands than even agriculture itself, which has however infinite advantages in this respect above pasturage, the certain cause of a want of people wherever it prevails above its due proportion.

Our climate denies us the advantages arising from the culture of vines, as well as many others which nature has accorded to France; a consideration which should awaken us from the lethargy into which the avarice of individuals has plunged us, and set us in earnest on improving every advantage we enjoy, in order to secure us by our native strength from so formidable a rival.

The want of bread to eat, from the late false and cruel policy of laying small farms into great ones, and the general discouragement of tillage which is its consequence, is in my opinion much less to be apprehended than the want of people to eat it.

In every country where the inhabitants are at once numerous and industrious, there will always be a proportionable cultivation.

This evil is so very destructive and alarming, that, if the great have not virtue enough to remedy it, it is to be hoped it will in time, like most great evils, cure itself.

Your Lordship enquires into the nature of this climate in respect to health. The air being uncommonly pure and serene, it is favourable to life beyond any I ever knew: the people live generally to a very advanced age; and are remarkably free from diseases of every kind, except consumptions, to which the younger part of the inhabitants are a good deal subject.

It is however a circumstance one cannot help observing, that they begin to look old much sooner than the people in Europe; on which my daughter observes, that it is not very pleasant for women to come to reside in a country where people have a short youth, and a long old age.

The diseases of cold countries are in general owing to

want of perspiration; for which reason exercise, and even dissipation, are here the best medicines.

The Indians therefore shewed their good sense in advising the French, on their first arrival, to use dancing, mirth, chearfulness, and content, as the best remedies against the inconveniences of the climate.

I have already swelled this letter to such a length, that I must postpone to another time my account of the peculiar natural productions of Canada; only observing, that one would imagine Heaven intended a social intercourse between the most distant nations, by giving them productions of the earth so very different each from the other, and each more than sufficient for itself, that the exchange might be the means of spreading the bond of society and brotherhood over the whole globe.

In my opinion, the man who conveys, and causes to grow, in any country, a grain, a fruit, or even a flower, it never possessed before, deserves more praise than a thousand heroes: he is a benefactor, he is in some degree a creator.

I have the honour to be,
My Lord,

WM. FERMOR

TO MISS MONTAGUE, AT QUEBEC

LETTER 124 MONTREAL, APRIL 14: Is it possible, my dear Emily, you can, after all I have said, persist in endeavouring to dissuade me from a design on which my whole happiness depends, and which I flattered myself was equally essential to yours? I forgave, I even admired, your first scruple; I thought it generosity: but I have answered it; and if you had loved as I do, you would never again have named so unpleasing a subject.

Does your own heart tell you mine will call a settlement here, with you, an exile? Examine yourself well, and tell me whether your aversion to staying in Canada is not stronger than your tenderness for your Rivers.

I am hurt beyond all words at the earnestness with which you press Mrs Melmoth to dissuade me from staying in this country: you press with warmth my return to England, though it would put an eternal bar between us: you give reasons which, though the understanding may approve, the heart abhors: can ambition come in competition with tenderness? you fancy yourself generous, when you are only indifferent. Insensible girl! you know nothing of love.

Write to me instantly, and tell me every emotion of your soul, for I tremble at the idea that your affection is less lively than mine.

Adieu! I am wretched till I hear from you. Is is possible, my Emily, you can have ceased to love him, who, as you yourself own, sees no other object than you in the universe?

Adieu! Yours,

Ed. Rivers

You know not the heart of your Rivers, if you suppose it capable of any ambition but that dear one of being beloved by you.

What have you said, my dear Emily? *You will not marry me in Canada.* You have passed a hard sentence on me: you know my fortune will not allow me to marry you in England.

●

TO COLONEL RIVERS, AT QUEBEC

LETTER 125 QUEBEC, APRIL 17: How different, my Rivers, is your last letter from all your Emily has ever yet received from you! What have I done to deserve such suspicions? How unjust are your sex in all their connexions with ours!

Do I not know love? and does this reproach come from the man on whom my heart dotes, the man, whom to make happy, I would with transport cease to live? can you one moment doubt your Emily's tenderness? have not her eyes, her air, her look, her indiscretion, a thousand times told you, in spite of herself, the dear secret of her heart, long before she was conscious of the tenderness of yours?

Did I think only of myself, I could live with you in a desert; all places, all situations are equally charming to me, with you: without you, the whole world affords nothing which could give a moment's pleasure to your Emily.

Let me but see those eyes in which the tenderest love is painted, let me but hear that enchanting voice, I am insensible to all else, I know nothing of what passes around me; all that has no relation to you passes away like a morning dream, the impression of which is effaced in a moment: my tenderness for you fills my whole soul, and leaves no room for any other idea. Rank, fortune, my native country, my friends, all are nothing in the balance with my Rivers.

For your own sake, I once more entreat you to return to England: I will follow you; I will swear never to marry another; I will see you, I will allow you to continue the tender inclination which unites us. Fortune may there be more favourable to our wishes than we now hope; may join us without destroying the peace of the best of parents.

But if you persist, if you will sacrifice every consideration to your tenderness— My Rivers, I have no will but yours.

TO MISS FERMOR, AT SILLERI

LETTER 126 LONDON, FEB. 17: My dear Bell, Lucy, being deprived of the pleasure of writing to you, as she intended, by Lady Anne Melville's dining with her, desires me to make her apologies.

Allow me to say something for myself, and to share my joy with one who will, I am sure, so very sincerely sympathize with me in it.

I could not have believed, my dear Bell, it had been so very easy a thing to be constant: I declare, but don't mention this, lest I should be laughed at, I have never felt the least inclination for any other woman, since I married your lovely friend.

I now see a circle of Beauties with the same indifference as a bed of snowdrops: no charms affect me but hers; the whole creation to me contains no other woman.

I find her every day, every hour, more lovely; there is in my Lucy a mixture of modesty, delicacy, vivacity, innocence, and blushing sensibility, which add a thousand unspeakable graces to the most beautiful person the hand of nature ever formed.

There is no describing her enchanting smile, the smile of unaffected, artless tenderness. How shall I paint to you the sweet involuntary glow of pleasure, the kindling fire of her eyes, when I approach; or those thousand little dear attentions of which love alone knows the value?

I never, my dear girl, knew happiness till now; my

tenderness is absolutely a species of idolatry; you cannot think what a slave this lovely girl has made me.

As a proof of this, the little tyrant insists on my omitting a thousand civil things I had to say to you, and attending her and Lady Anne immediately to the opera; she bids me however tell you, she loves you *passing the love of woman*, at least of handsome women, who are not generally celebrated for their candour and good-will to each other.

Adieu, my dearest Bell!

Yours,

J. TEMPLE

TO JOHN TEMPLE, ESQ; PALL MALL

LETTER 127 SILLERI, APRIL 18: Indeed?

"Is this that haughty, gallant, gay Lothario,
"That dear perfidious—"

Absolutely, my dear Temple, the sex ought never to forgive Lucy for daring to monopolize so very charming a fellow. I had some thoughts of a little *badinage* with you myself, if I should return soon to England; but I now give up the very idea.

One thing I will, however, venture to say, that love Lucy as much as you please, you will never love her half so well as she deserves; which, let me tell you, is a great deal for one woman, especially, as you well observe, one handsome woman, to say of another.

I am, however, not quite clear your idea is just: *cattism*, if I may be allowed the expression, seeming more likely to be the vice of those who are conscious of wanting themselves the dear power of pleasing.

Handsome women ought to be, what I profess myself, who am however only pretty, too vain to be envious; and yet we see, I am afraid, too often, some little sparks of this mean passion between rival Beauties.

Impartially speaking, I believe the best-natured women, and the most free from envy, are those who, without being very handsome, have that *je ne sçai quoi*, those nameless graces, which please even without beauty; and who therefore, finding more attention paid to them by men than their looking-glass tells them they have a right to expect, are for that reason in constant good humour with themselves, and of course with every body else: whereas Beauties, claiming universal empire, are at war with all who dispute their rights; that is, with half the sex.

I am very good-natured myself; but it is perhaps, because, though a pretty woman, I am more agreeable than handsome, and have an infinity of the *je ne sçai quoi*.

A propos, my dear Temple, I am so pleased with what Montesquieu says on this subject, that I find it is not in my nature to resist translating and inserting it; you cannot then say I have sent you a letter in which there is nothing worth reading.

I beg you will read this to the misses, for which you cannot fail of their thanks, and for this reason: there are perhaps a dozen women in the world who do not think themselves handsome, but I will venture to say, not one who does not think herself agreeable, and that she has this nameless charm, this so much talked of *I know not what*, which is so much better than beauty. But to my Montesquieu:

"There is sometimes, both in persons and things, an invisible charm, a natural grace, which we cannot define, and which we are therefore obliged to call the je ne sçai quoi.

"It seems to me that this is an effect principally founded on surprise.

"We are touched that a person pleases us more than she seemed at first to have a right to do; and we are agreeably surprized that she should have known how to conquer those defects which our eyes shewed us, but which our hearts no longer believe: 'tis for this reason that women, who are not handsome, have often graces or agreeablenesses; and that beautiful ones very seldom have.

For a beautiful person does generally the very contrary of what we expected; she appears to us by degrees less amiable, and, after having surprized us pleasingly, she surprizes us in a contrary manner; but the agreeable impression is old, the disagreeable one new: 'tis also seldom that Beauties inspire violent passions, which are almost always reserved for those who have graces, that is to say, agreeablenesses, which we did not expect, and which we had no reason to expect.

"Magnificent habits have seldom grace, which the dresses of shepherdesses often have.

"We admire the majesty of the draperies of Paul Veronese; but we are touched with the simplicity of Raphael, and the exactness of Correggio.

182

"*Paul Veronese promises much, and pays all he promises; Raphael and Correggio promise little, and pay much, which pleases us more.*

"*These graces, these agreeablenesses, are found oftener in the mind than in the countenance: the charms of a beautiful countenance are seldom hidden, they appear at first view; but the mind does not shew itself except by degrees, when it pleases, and as much as it pleases; it can conceal itself in order to appear, and give that species of surprize to which those graces, of which I speak, owe their existence.*

"*This grace, this agreeableness, is less in the countenance than in the manner; the manner changes every instant, and can therefore every moment give us the pleasure of surprize: in one word, a woman can be handsome but in one way, but she may be agreeable in a hundred thousand.*"

I like this doctrine of Montesquieu's extremely, because it gives every woman her chance, and because it ranks me above a thousand handsomer women, in the dear power of inspiring passion.

Cruel creature! why did you give me the idea of flowers? I now envy you your foggy climate: the earth with you is at this moment covered with a thousand lovely children of the spring; with us, it is an universal plain of snow.

Our beaux are terribly at a loss for similes: you have lillies of the valley for comparisons; we nothing but what with the idea of whiteness gives that of coldness too.

This is all the quarrel I have with Canada: the summer is delicious, the winter pleasant with all its severities; but alas! the smiling spring is not here; we pass from winter to summer in an instant, and lose the sprightly season of the Loves.

A letter from the God of my idolatry—I must answer it instantly.

Adieu! Yours, etc.

A. Fermor

TO CAPTAIN FITZGERALD

LETTER 128 Yes, I give permission; you may come this afternoon: there is something amusing enough in your dear nonsense; and, as my father will be at Quebec, I shall want amusement.

It will also furnish a little chat for the misses at Quebec; a *tête-à-tête* with a tall Irishman is a subject which cannot escape their sagacity.

Adieu! Yours,

A. F.

TO MRS TEMPLE, PALL MALL

LETTER **129** SILLERI, APRIL 20: After my immense letter to your love, my dear, you must not expect me to say much to your fair ladyship.

I am glad to find you manage Temple so admirably; the wisest, the wildest, the gravest, and the gayest, are equally our slaves, when we have proper ideas of petticoat politics.

I intend to compose a code of laws for the government of husbands, and get it translated into all the modern languages; which I apprehend will be of infinite benefit to the world.

Do you know I am a greater fool than I imagined? You may remember I was always extremely fond of sweet waters. I left them off lately, upon an idea, though a mistaken one, that Fitzgerald did not like them: I yesterday heard him say the contrary; and, without thinking of it, went mechanically to my dressing-room, and put lavender water on my handkerchief.

This is, I am afraid, rather a strong symptom of my being absurd; however, I find it pleasant to be so, and therefore give way to it.

It is divinely warm to-day, though the snow is still on the ground; it is melting fast however, which makes it impossible for me to get to Quebec. I shall be confined for at least a week, and Emily not with me: I die for amusement. Fitzgerald ventures still at the hazard of his own neck and his horses' legs; for the latter of which animals I have so much compassion, that I have ordered both to stay at home a few days, which days I shall devote to study and contemplation, and little pert chit-chats with papa, who is ten times more fretful at being kept within doors than I am: I intend to win a little fortune of him at piquet before the world breaks in upon our solitude. Adieu! I am idle, but always

Your faithful

A. FERMOR

LETTER 130 SILLERI, APRIL 20: 'Tis indeed, my Lord, an advantage for which we cannot be too thankful to the Supreme Being, to be born in a country whose religion and laws are such, as would have been the objects of our wishes, had we been born in any other.

Our religion, I would be understood to mean Christianity in general, carries internal conviction by the excellency of its moral precepts, and its tendency to make mankind happy; and the peculiar mode of it established in England breathes beyond all others the mild spirit of the Gospel, and that charity which embraces all mankind as brothers.

It is equally free from enthusiasm and superstition; its outward form is decent and respectful, without affected ostentation; and what shews its excellence above all others is, that every other church allows it to be the best, except itself: and it is an established rule, that he has an undoubted right to the first rank of merit, to whom every man allows the second.

As to our government, it would be impertinent to praise it; all mankind allow it to be the master-piece of human wisdom.

It has the advantage of every other form, with as little of their inconveniences as the imperfection attendant on all human inventions will admit: it has the monarchic quickness of execution and stability, the aristocratic diffusive strength and wisdom of counsel, the democratic freedom and equal distribution of property.

When I mention equal distribution of property, I would not be understood to mean such an equality as never existed, nor can exist but in idea; but that general, that comparative equality, which leaves to every man the absolute and safe possession of the fruits of his labours; which softens offensive distinctions, and curbs pride, by leaving every order of men in some degree dependent on the other; and admits of those gentle and almost imperceptible gradations, which the poet so well calls,

"*Th' according music of a well-mix'd state.*"

The prince is here a centre of union; an advantage, the want of which makes a democracy, which is so beautiful in theory, the very worst of all possible governments, except absolute monarchy, in practice.

I am called upon, my Lord, to go to the citadel, to see the going away of the ice; an object so new to me, that I cannot resist the curiosity I have to see it, though my going thither is attended with infinite difficulty.

Bell insists on accompanying me: I am afraid for her, but she will not be refused.

At our return, I will have the honour of writing to your Lordship, by the gentleman who carries this to New York.

I have the honour to be, my Lord.

Your Lordship's, etc.

WM. FERMOR

TO THE EARL OF ——

LETTER 131   SILLERI, APRIL 20, EVENING:
We are returned, my Lord, from having seen an object as beautiful and magnificent in itself, as pleasing from the idea it gives of renewing once more our intercourse with Europe.

Before I saw the breaking up of the vast body of ice, which forms what is here called *the bridge*, from Quebec to Point Levi, I imagined there could be nothing in it worth attention; that the ice would pass away, or dissolve gradually, day after day, as the influence of the sun, and warmth of the air and earth increased; and that we should see the river open, without having observed by what degrees it became so.

But I found *the great river*, as the savages with much propriety call it, maintain its dignity in this instance as in all others, and assert its superiority over those petty streams which we honour with the names of rivers in England. Sublimity is the characteristic of this western world; the loftiness of the mountains, the grandeur of the lakes and rivers, the majesty of the rocks shaded with a picturesque variety of beautiful trees and shrubs, and crowned with the noblest of the offspring of the forest, which form the banks of the latter, are as much beyond the power of fancy as that of description: a landscape-painter might here expand his imagination, and find ideas which he will seek in vain in our comparatively little world.

The object of which I am speaking has all the American magnificence.

The ice before the town, or, to speak in the Canadian style, *the bridge*, being of a thickness not less than five feet, a league in length, and more than a mile broad, resists for a long time the rapid tide that attempts to force it from the banks.

We are prepared by many previous circumstances to expect something extraordinary in this event, if I may so call it: every increase of heat in the weather for near a month before the ice leaves the banks; every warm day gives you terror for those you see venturing to pass it in carrioles; yet one frosty night makes it again so strong, that even the ladies, and the timid amongst them, still venture themselves over in parties of pleasure; though greatly alarmed at their return, if a few hours of uncommon warmth intervene.

But, during the last fortnight, the alarm grows indeed a very serious one: the eye can distinguish, even at a considerable distance, that the ice is softened and detached from the banks; and you dread every step being death to those who have still the temerity to pass it, which they will continue always to do till one or more pay their rashness with their lives.

From the time the ice is no longer a bridge on which you see crowds driving with such vivacity on business or pleasure, every one is looking eagerly for its breaking away, to remove the bar to the continually wished and expected event, of the arrival of ships from that world from whence we have seemed so long in a manner excluded.

The hour is come; I have been with a crowd of both sexes, and all ranks, hailing the propitious moment: our situation, on the top of Cape Diamond, gave us a prospect some leagues above and below the town; above Cape Diamond the river was open, it was so below Point Levi, the rapidity of the current having forced a passage for the water under the transparent bridge, which for more than a league continued firm.

We stood waiting with all the eagerness of expectation; the tide came rushing with an amazing impetuosity; the bridge seemed to shake, yet resisted the force of the waters; the tide recoiled, it made a pause, it stood still, it returned with redoubled fury, the immense mass of ice gave way.

A vast plain appeared in motion; it advanced with solemn and majestic pace: the points of land on the banks of the river for a few moments stopped its progress; but the immense weight of so prodigious a body, carried along by a rapid current, bore down all opposition with a force irresistible.

There is no describing how beautiful the opening river appears, every moment gaining on the sight, till, in a time less than can possibly be imagined, the ice passing Point Levi, is hid in one moment by the projecting land, and all is once more a clear plain before you; giving at once the pleasing, but unconnected, ideas of that direct intercourse with Europe from which we have been so many months excluded, and of the earth's again

187

opening her fertile bosom, to feast our eyes and imagination with her various verdant and flowery productions.

I am afraid I have conveyed a very inadequate idea of the scene which has just passed before me; it however struck me so strongly, that it was impossible for me not to attempt it.

If my painting has the least resemblance to the original, your Lordship will agree with me, that the very vicissitudes of season here partake of the sublimity which so strongly characterizes the country.

The changes of season in England, being slow and gradual, are but faintly felt; but being here sudden, instant, violent, afford to the mind, with the lively pleasure arising from meer change, the very high additional one of its being accompanied with grandeur. I have the honour to be,

My Lord,
Your Lordship's, etc.

WILLIAM FERMOR

TO MRS TEMPLE, PALL MALL

LETTER 132 APRIL 22: Certainly, my dear, you are so far right; a nun may be in many respects a less unhappy being than some women who continue in the world; her situation is, I allow, paradise to that of a married woman, of sensibility and honour, who dislikes her husband.

The cruelty therefore of some parents here, who sacrifice their children to avarice, in forcing or seducing them into convents, would appear more striking, if we did not see too many in England guilty of the same inhumanity, though in a different manner, by marrying them against their inclination.

Your letter reminds me of what a French married lady here said to me on this very subject: I was exclaiming violently against convents; and particularly urging, what I thought unanswerable, the extreme hardship of one circumstance; that, however unhappy the state was found on trial, there was no retreat; that it was *for life*.

Madame De—— turned quick, "And is not marriage for life?"

"True, Madam; and, what is worse, without a year of probation. I confess the force of your argument."

I have never dared since to mention convents before Madame De——.

Between you and I, Lucy, it is a little unreasonable that people will come together entirely upon sordid principles, and then wonder they are not happy: in delicate minds, love is seldom the consequence of marriage.

It is not absolutely certain that a marriage of which love is the foundation will be happy; but it is infallible, I believe, that no other can be so to souls capable of tenderness.

Half the world, you will please to observe, have no souls; at least none but of the vegetable and animal kinds: to this species of beings, love and sentiment are entirely unnecessary; they were made to travel through life in a state of mind neither quite awake nor asleep; and it is perfectly equal to them in what company they take the journey.

You and I, my dear, are something *awakened*; therefore it is necessary we should love where we marry, and for this reason: our souls, being of the active kind, can never be totally at rest; therefore, if we were not to love our husbands, we should be in dreadful danger of loving somebody else.

For my part, whatever tall maiden aunts and cousins may say of the indecency of a young woman's distinguishing one man from another, and of love coming after marriage; I think marrying, in that expectation, on sober prudent principles, a man one dislikes, the most deliberate and shameful degree of vice of which the human mind is capable.

I cannot help observing here, that the great aim of modern education seems to be, to eradicate the best impulses of the human heart, love, friendship, compassion, benevolence; to destroy the social, and increase the selfish principle. Parents wisely attempt to root out those affections which should only be directed to proper objects, and which Heaven gave us as the means of happiness; not considering that the success of such an attempt is doubtful; and that, if they succeed, they take from life all its sweetness, and reduce it to a dull inactive round of tasteless days, scarcely raised above vegetation.

If my ideas of things are right, the human mind is naturally virtuous; the business of education is therefore less to give us good impressions, which we have from nature, than to guard us against bad ones, which are generally acquired.

And so ends my sermon.

Adieu! my dear!

Your faithful

A. Fermor

A letter from your brother; I believe the dear creature is out of his wits: Emily has consented to marry him, and one would imagine by his joy that nobody was ever married before.

He is going to Lake Champlain, to fix on his seat of empire, or rather Emily's; for I see she will be the reigning queen, and he only her majesty's consort.

I am going to Quebec; two or three dry days have made the roads passable for summer carriages: Fitzgerald is come to fetch me. Adieu!

Eight o'clock

I am come back, have seen Emily, who is the happiest woman existing; she has heard from your brother, and in such terms—his letter breathes the very soul of tenderness. I wish they were richer. I don't half relish their settling in Canada; but, rather than not live together, I believe they would consent to be set ashore on a desert island. Good night.

TO THE EARL OF ——

LETTER **133** SILLERI, APRIL 25: The pleasure the mind finds in travelling, has undoubtedly, my Lord, its source in that love of novelty, that delight in acquiring new ideas, which is interwoven in its very frame, which shews itself on every occasion from infancy to age, which is the first passion of the human mind, and the last.

There is nothing the mind of man abhors so much as a state of rest: the great secret of happiness is to keep the soul in continual action, without those violent exertions, which wear out its powers, and dull its capacity of enjoyment; it should have exercise, not labour.

Vice may justly be called the fever of the soul, inaction its lethargy; passion, under the guidance of virtue, its health.

I have the pleasure to see my daughter's coquetry giving place to a tender affection for a very worthy man, who seems formed to make her happy: his fortune is easy; he is a gentleman, and a man of worth and honour, and, what perhaps inclines me to be more partial to him, of my own profession.

I mention the last circumstance in order to introduce a

request, that your Lordship would have the goodness to employ that interest for him in the purchase of a majority, which you have so generously offered to me; I am determined, as there is no prospect of real duty, to quit the army, and retire to that quiet which is so pleasing at my time of life: I am privately in treaty with a gentleman for my company, and propose returning to England in the first ship, to give in my resignation: in this point, as well as that of serving Mr Fitzgerald, I shall without scruple call upon your Lordship's friendship.

I have settled every thing with Fitzgerald, but without saying a word to Bell; and he is to seduce her into matrimony as soon as he can, without my appearing at all interested in the affair: he is to ask my consent in form, though we have already settled every preliminary.

All this, as well as my intention of quitting the army, is yet a secret to my daughter.

But to the questions your Lordship does me the honour to ask me in regard to the Americans, I mean those of our old colonies: they appear to me, from all I have heard and seen of them, a rough, ignorant, positive, very selfish, yet hospitable people.

Strongly attached to their own opinions, but still more so to their interests, in regard to which they have inconceivable sagacity and address; but in all other respects I think naturally inferior to the Europeans; as education does so much, it is however difficult to ascertain this.

I am rather of opinion they would not have refused submission to the stamp act, or disputed the power of the legislature at home, had not their minds been first embittered by what touched their interests so nearly, the restraints laid on their trade with the French and Spanish settlements, a trade by which England was an immense gainer; and by which only a few enormously rich West India planters were hurt.

Every advantage you give the North Americans in trade centers at last in the mother country, they are the bees, who roam abroad for that honey which enriches the paternal hive.

Taxing them immediately after their trade is restrained, seems like drying up the source, and expecting the stream to flow.

Yet too much care cannot be taken to support the majesty of government, and assert the dominion of the parent country.

A good mother will consult the interest and happiness

of her children, but will never suffer her authority to be disputed.

An equal mixture of mildness and spirit cannot fail of bringing these mistaken people, misled by a few of violent temper and ambitious views, into a just sense of their duty.

I have the honour to be

My Lord, etc.

WILLIAM FERMOR

TO MRS TEMPLE, PALL MALL

LETTER 134 MAY 5: I have got my Emily again, to my great joy; I am nobody without her. As the roads are already very good, we walk and ride perpetually, and amuse ourselves as well as we can, *en attendant* your brother, who is gone a settlement hunting.

The quickness of vegetation in this country is astonishing; though the hills are still covered with snow, and though it even continues in spots in the vallies, the latter with the trees and shrubs in the woods are already in beautiful verdure; and the earth every where putting forth flowers in a wild and lovely variety and profusion.

'Tis amazingly pleasing to see the strawberries and wild pansies peeping their little foolish heads from beneath the snow.

Emily and I are prodigiously fond after having been separated; it is a divine relief to us both, to have again the delight of talking of our lovers to each other: we have been a month divided; and neither of us have had the consolation of a friend to be foolish to.

Fitzgerald dines with us: he comes.

Adieu! yours,

A. FERMOR

LETTER **135** SILLERI, MAY 5: My Lord, I have been conversing, if the expression is not improper when I have not had an opportunity of speaking a syllable, more than two hours with a French officer, who has declaimed the whole time with the most astonishing volubility, without uttering one word which could either entertain or instruct his hearers; and even without starting any thing that deserved the name of a thought.

People who have no ideas out of the common road are, I believe, generally the greatest talkers, because all their thoughts are low enough for common conversation; whereas those of more elevated understandings have ideas which they cannot easily communicate except to persons of equal capacity with themselves.

This might be brought as an argument of the inferiority of women's understanding to ours, as they are generally greater talkers, if we did not consider the limited and trifling educations we give them; men, amongst other advantages, have that of acquiring a greater variety as well as sublimity of ideas.

Women who have conversed much with men are undoubtedly in general the most pleasing companions; but this only shews of what they are capable when properly educated since they improve so greatly by that accidental and limited opportunity of acquiring knowledge.

Indeed the two sexes are equal gainers, by conversing with each other: there is a mutual desire of pleasing, in a mixed conversation, restrained by politeness, which sets every amiable quality in a stronger light.

Bred in ignorance from one age to another, women can learn little of their own sex.

I have often thought this the reason why officers' daughters are in general more agreeable than other women in an equal rank of life.

I am almost tempted to bring Bell as an instance; but I know the blindness and partiality of nature, and therefore check what paternal tenderness would dictate.

I am shocked at what your Lordship tells me of Miss H———. I know her imprudent, I believe her virtuous: a great flow of spirits has been ever hurrying her into indiscretions; but allow me to say, my Lord, it is particularly hard to fix the character by our conduct, at a time of life when we are not competent judges of our own actions; and when the hurry and vivacity of youth carries us to commit a thousand follies and indiscretions, for which we blush when the empire of reason begins.

Inexperience and openness of temper betray us in early life into improper connexions; and the very constancy, and nobleness of nature, which characterize the best hearts, continue the delusion.

I know Miss H—— perfectly; and am convinced, if her father will treat her as a friend, and with the indulgent tenderness of affection endeavour to wean her from a choice so very unworthy of her, he will infallibly succeed; but if he treats her with harshness, she is lost for ever.

He is too stern in his behaviour, too rigid in his morals: it is the interest of virtue to be represented as she is, lovely, smiling, and ever walking hand in hand with pleasure: we were formed to be happy, and to contribute to the happiness of our fellow-creatures; there are no real virtues but the social ones.

'Tis the enemy of human kind who has thrown around us the gloom of superstition, and taught that austerity and voluntary misery is virtue.

If moralists would indeed improve human nature, they should endeavour to expand, not to contract the heart; they should build their system on the passions and affections. the only foundations of the nobler virtues.

From the partial representations of narrow-minded bigots, who paint the Deity from their own gloomy conceptions, the young are too often frighted from the paths of virtue; despairing of ideal perfections, they give up all virtue as unattainable, and start aside from the road which they falsely suppose strewed with thorns.

I have studied the heart with some attention; and am convinced every parent, who will take the pains to gain his children's friendship, will for ever be the guide and arbiter of their conduct: I speak from a happy experience.

Notwithstanding all my daughter says in gaiety of heart, she would sooner even relinquish the man she loves, than offend a father in whom she has always found the tenderest and most faithful of friends. I am interrupted, and have only time to say, I have the honour to be,

My Lord, etc.

WM. FERMOR

LETTER 136   SILLERI, MAY 13: Madame Des Roches has just left us; she returns to-day to the Kamaraskas: she came to take leave of us, and shewed a concern at parting from Emily, which really affected me. She is a most amiable woman; yet I think my sweet friend is not sorry for her return: she loves her, but yet cannot absolutely forget she has been her rival, and is as well satisfied that she leaves Quebec before your brother's arrival.

The weather is lovely; the earth is in all its verdure, the trees in foliage, and no snow but on the sides of the mountains; we are looking eagerly out for ships from dear England: I expect by them volumes of letters from my Lucy. We expect your brother in a week: in short, we are all hope and expectation; our hearts beat at every rap of the door, supposing it brings intelligence of a ship, or of the dear man.

Fitzgerald takes such amazing pains to please me, that I begin to think it is pity so much attention should be thrown away; and am half inclined, from meer compassion, to follow the example you have so heroically set me.

Absolutely, Lucy, it requires amazing resolution to marry.

Adieu! yours,

A. FERMOR

TO COLONEL RIVERS, AT MONTREAL

LETTER 137   SILLERI, MAY 14: I am returned, my Rivers, to my sweet friend, and have again the dear delight of talking of you without restraint; she bears with, she indulges me in, all my weakness; if that name ought to be given to a tenderness of which the object is the most exalted and worthy of his sex.

It was impossible I should not have loved you; the soul that spoke in those eloquent eyes told me, the first moment we met, our hearts were formed for each other; I saw in that amiable countenance a sensibility similar to my own, but which I had till then sought in vain: I saw there those benevolent smiles, which are the marks, and the emanations of virtue; those thousand graces which ever accompany a mind conscious of its own dignity, and satisfied with itself; in short, that mental beauty which is the express image of the Deity.

What defence had I against you, my Rivers, since your merit was such that my reason approved the weakness of my heart?

We have lost Madame Des Roches; we were both in tears at parting; we embraced, I pressed her to my bosom: I love her, my dear Rivers; I have an affection for her which I scarce know how to describe. I saw her every day, I found infinite pleasure in being with her; she talked of you, she praised you, and my heart was soothed; I however found it impossible to mention your name to her; a reserve for which I cannot account; I found pleasure in looking at her from the idea that she was dear to you, that she felt for you the tenderest friendship: do you know I think she has some resemblance of you? there is something in her smile, which gives me an idea of you.

Shall I, however, own all my folly? I never found this pleasure in seeing her when you were present: on the contrary, your attention to her gave me pain: I was jealous of every look; I even saw her amiable qualities with a degree of envy, which checked the pleasure I should otherwise have found in her conversation.

There is always, I fear, some injustice mixed with love, at least with love so ardent and tender as mine.

You, my Rivers, will however pardon that injustice which is a proof of my excess of tenderness.

Madame Des Roches has promised to write to me: indeed I will love her; I will conquer this little remain of jealousy, and do justice to the most gentle and amiable of women.

Why should I dislike her for seeing you with my eyes, for having a soul whose feelings resemble my own?

I have observed her voice is softened, and trembles like mine, when she names you.

My Rivers, you were formed to charm the heart of woman; there is more pleasure in loving you, even without the hope of a return, than in the adoration of all your sex: I pity every woman who is so insensible as to see you without tenderness. This is the only fault I ever found in Bell Fermor; she has the most lively friendship for you, but she has seen you without love. Of what materials must her heart be composed?

No other man can inspire the same sentiments with my Rivers; no other man can deserve them: the delight of loving you appears to me so superior to all other pleasures, that, of all human beings, if I was not Emily Montague, I would be Madame Des Roches.

I blush for what I have written; yet why blush for having a soul to distinguish perfection, or why conceal the real feelings of my heart?

I will never hide a thought from you; you shall be at once the confidant and the dear object of my tenderness.

In what words — my Rivers, you rule every emotion of my heart; dispose as you please of your Emily: yet, if you allow her to form a wish in opposition to yours, indulge her in the transport of returning you to your friends: let her receive you from the hands of a mother, whose happiness you ought to prefer even to hers.

Why will you talk of the mediocrity of your fortune? have you not enough for every real want? much less, with you, would make your Emily blest: what have the trappings of life to do with happiness? 'tis only sacrificing pride to love and filial tenderness; the worst of human passions to the best.

I have a thousand things to say, but am forced to steal this moment to write to you: we have some French ladies here, who are eternally coming to my apartment.

They are at the door. Adieu!

Yours,

EMILY MONTAGUE

TO THE EARL OF ——

LETTER **138** SILLERI, MAY 12: It were indeed, my Lord, to be wished that we had here schools, at the expence of the public, to teach English to the rising generation: nothing is a stronger tie of brotherhood and affection, a greater cement of union, than speaking one common language.

The want of attention to this circumstance has, I am told, had the worst effects possible in the province of New York, where the people, especially at a distance from the capital, continuing to speak Dutch, retain their affection for their ancient masters, and still look on their English fellow-subjects as strangers and intruders.

The Canadians are the more easily to be won to this, or whatever else their own, or the general good requires, as their noblesse have the strongest attachment to a court, and that favour is the great object of their ambition: were English made by degrees the court language, it would soon be universally spoke.

Of the three great springs of the human heart, interest, pleasure, vanity, the last appears to me much the strongest in the Canadians; and I am convinced the most forcible tie their noblesse have to France, is their unwillingness to part with their croix de St Louis: might not therefore some order of the same kind be instituted for Canada, and given to all who have the croix, on their sending back the ensigns they now wear, which are inconsistent with their allegiance as British subjects?

Might not such an order be contrived, to be given at the discretion of the governor, as well to the Canadian gentlemen who merited most of the government, as to the English officers of a certain rank, and such other English as purchased estates, and settled in the country? and, to give it additional lustre, the governor, for the time being, be always head of the order?

'Tis possible something of the same kind all over America might be also of service; the passions of mankind are nearly the same every where: at least I never yet saw the soil or climate, where vanity did not grow; and till all mankind become philosophers, it is by their passions they must be governed.

The common people, by whom I mean the peasantry, have been great gainers here by the change of masters; their property is more secure, their independence greater, their profits much more than doubled: it is not them therefore whom it is necessary to gain.

The noblesse, on the contrary, have been in a great degree undone: they have lost their employs, their rank, their consideration, and many of them their fortunes.

It is therefore equally consonant to good policy and to humanity that they should be considered, and in the way most acceptable to them; the rich conciliated by little honorary distinctions, those who are otherwise by sharing in all lucrative employs; and all of them by bearing a part in the legislature of their country.

The great objects here seem to be to heal those wounds, which past unhappy disputes have left still in some degree open; to unite the French and English, the civil and military, in one firm body; to raise a revenue, to encourage agriculture, and especially the growth of hemp and flax; and find a staple, for the improvement of a commerce, which at present labours under a thousand disadvantages.

But I shall say little on this or any political subject relating to Canada, for a reason which, whilst I am in this colony, it would look like flattery to give: let it suffice to say; that, humanly speaking, it is impossible that the inhabitants of this province should be otherwise than happy.

> I have the honour to be,
> > My Lord, etc.
> > > WILLIAM FERMOR

TO MRS TEMPLE, PALL MALL

LETTER 139 SILLERI, MAY 20: I confess the fact, my dear; I am, thanks to papa, amazingly learned, and all that, for a young lady of twenty-two: yet you will allow I am not the worse; no creature breathing would ever find it out: envy itself must confess, I talk of lace and blond like another christian woman.

I have been thinking, Lucy, as indeed my ideas are generally a little pindaric, how entertaining and improving would be the history of the human heart, if people spoke all the truth, and painted themselves as they really are; that is to say, if all the world were as sincere and honest as I am; for, upon my word, I have such a contempt for hypocrisy, that upon the whole, I have always appeared to have fewer good qualities than I really have.

I am afraid we should find in the best characters, if we withdrew the veil, a mixture of errors and inconsistencies, which would greatly lessen our veneration.

Papa has been reading me a wise lecture, this morning, on playing the fool: I reminded him, that I was now arrived at years of *indiscretion*; that every body must have their day; and that those who did not play the fool young, ran a hazard of doing it when it would not half so well become them.

A propos to playing the fool, I am strongly inclined to believe I shall marry.

Fitzgerald is so astonishingly pressing— Besides, some how or other, I don't feel happy without him: the creature has something of a magnetic virtue; I find myself generally, without knowing it, on the same side the room with him, and often in the next chair; and lay a thousand little schemes to be of the same party at cards.

I write pretty sentiments in my pocket-book, and carve

his name on trees when nobody sees me: did you think it possible I could be such an idiot?

I am as absurd as even the gentle love-sick Emily.

I am thinking, my dear, how happy it is, since most human beings differ so extremely one from another, that Heaven has given us the same variety in our tastes.

Your brother is a divine fellow, and yet there is a sauciness about Fitzgerald which pleases me better; as he has told me a thousand times, he thinks me infinitely more agreeable than Emily.

Adieu! I am going to Quebec.

Yours,

A. FERMOR

TO MRS TEMPLE, PALL MALL

LETTER 140 MAY 20, EVENING: *Io triumphe!* A ship from England! You can have no idea of the universal transport at the sight; the whole town was on the beach, eagerly gazing at the charming stranger, who danced gaily on the waves, as if conscious of the pleasure she inspired.

If our joy is so great, who preserve a correspondence with Europe, through our other colonies, during the winter, what must that of the French have been, who were absolutely shut up six months from the rest of the world?

I can scarce conceive a higher delight than they must have felt at being thus restored to a communication with mankind.

The letters are not delivered; our servant stays for them at the post-office; we expect him every moment: if I have not volumes from you, I shall be very angry.

He comes. Adieu! I have not patience to wait their being brought up stairs.

Yours,

A. FERMOR

They are here; six letters from you; I shall give three of them to Emily to read, whilst I read the rest: you are very good, Lucy, and I will never call you lazy again.

LETTER **141** PALL MALL, APRIL 8: Whilst I was sealing my letter, I received yours of the 1st of February.

I am excessively alarmed, my dear, at the account it gives me of Miss Montague's having broke with her lover, and of my brother's extreme affection for her.

I did not dare to let my mother see that letter, as I am convinced the very idea of a marriage which must for ever separate her from a son she loves to idolatry, would be fatal to her; she is altered since his leaving England more than you can imagine; she is grown pale and thin, her vivacity has entirely left her. Even my marriage scarce seemed to give her pleasure; yet such is her delicacy, her ardour for his happiness, she will not suffer me to say this to him, lest it should constrain him, and prevent his making himself happy in his own way. I often find her in tears in her apartment; she affects a smile when she sees me, but it is a smile which cannot deceive one who knows her whole soul as I do. In short, I am convinced she will not live long unless my brother returns. She never names him without being softened to a degree not to be expressed.

Amiable and lovely as you represent this charming woman, and great as the sacrifice is she has made to my brother, it seems almost cruelty to wish to break this attachment to her; yet, situated as they are, what can be the consequence of their indulging their tenderness at present, but ruin to both?

At all events, however, my dear, I entreat, I conjure you, to press my brother's immediate return to England; I am convinced, my mother's life depends on seeing him.

I have often been tempted to write to Miss Montague, to use her influence with him even against herself.

If she loves him, she will have his true happiness at heart; she will consider what a mind like his must hereafter suffer, should his fondness for her be fatal to the best of mothers; she will urge, she will oblige him to return, and make this step the condition of preserving her tenderness.

Read this letter to her; and tell her, it is to her affection for my brother, to her generosity, I trust for the life of a parent who is dearer to me than my existence.

Tell her my heart is hers, that I will receive her as my guardian angel, that we will never part, that we will be friends, that we will be sisters, that I will omit nothing possible to make her happy with my brother in England, and that I have very rational hopes it may be in time accomplished; but that, if she marries him in Canada, and suffers him to pursue his present design, she plants a dagger in the bosom of her who gave him life.

I scarce know what I would say, my dear Bell; but I am wretched; I have no hope but in you. Yet if Emily is all you represent her—

I am obliged to break off: my mother is here; she must not see this letter.

Adieu! your affectionate

LUCY TEMPLE

TO MRS TEMPLE, PALL MALL

LETTER 142 SILLERI, MAY 21: Your letter of the 8th of April, my dear, was first read by Emily, being one of the three I gave her for that purpose, as I before mentioned.

She went through it, and melting into tears, left the room without speaking a word: she has been writing this morning, and I fancy to you, for she enquired when the mail set out for England, and seemed pleased to hear it went to-day.

I am excessively shocked at your account of Mrs Rivers: assure her, in my name, of your brother's immediate return; I know both him and Emily too well to believe they will sacrifice her to their own happiness: there is nothing, on the contrary, they will not suffer rather than even afflict her.

Do not, however, encourage an idea of ever breaking an attachment like theirs: an attachment founded less in passion than in the tenderest friendship, in a similarity of character, and a sympathy the most perfect the world ever saw.

Let it be your business, my Lucy, to endeavour to make them happy, and to remove the bars which prevent their union in England; and depend on seeing them there the very moment their coming is possible.

From what I know of your brother, I suppose he will insist on marrying Emily before he leaves Quebec; but, after your letter, which I shall send him, you may look on his return as infallible.

I send all yours and Temple's letters for your brother to-day: you may expect to hear from him by the same mail with this.

I have only to say, I am,

A. FERMOR

LETTER 143 LONDON, APRIL 3: My own happiness, my dear Rivers, in a marriage of love, makes me extremely unwilling to prevent your giving way to a tenderness, which promises you the same felicity, with so amiable a woman as both you and Bell Fermor represent Miss Montague to be.

But, my dear Ned, I cannot, without betraying your friendship, and hazarding all the quiet of your future days, dispense with myself from telling you, though I have her express commands to the contrary, that the peace, perhaps the life, of your excellent mother, depends on your giving up all thoughts of a settlement in America, and returning immediately to England.

I know the present state of your affairs will not allow you to marry this charming woman here, without descending from the situation you have ever held, and which you have a right from your birth to hold, in the world.

Would you allow me to gratify my friendship for you, and shew, at the same time, your perfect esteem for me, by commanding, what our long affection gives you a right to, such a part of my fortune as I could easily spare without the least inconvenience to myself, we might all be happy, and you might make your Emily so: but you have already convinced me, by your refusal of a former request of this kind, that your esteem for me is much less warm than mine for you; and that you do not think I merit the delight of making you happy.

I will therefore say no more on this subject till we meet, than that I have no doubt this letter will bring you immediately to us.

If the tenderness you express for Miss Montague is yet conquerable, it will surely be better for both it should be conquered, as fortune has been so much less kind to each of you than nature; but if your hearts are immoveably fixed on each other, if your love is of the kind which despises every other consideration, return to the bosom of friendship, and depend on our finding some way to make you happy.

If you persist in refusing to share my fortune, you can have no objection to my using all my interest, for a friend and brother so deservedly dear to me, and in whose happiness I shall ever find my own.

Allow me now to speak of myself; I mean of my dearer self, your amiable sister, for whom my tenderness, instead of decreasing, grows every moment stronger.

Yes, my friend, my sweet Lucy is every hour more an angel: her desire of being beloved, renders her a thousand times more lovely; a countenance animated by true tenderness will always charm beyond all the dead uninformed features the hand of nature ever framed; love embellishes the whole form, gives spirit and softness to the eyes, the most vivid bloom to the complexion, dignity to the air, grace to every motion, and throws round beauty almost the rays of divinity.

In one word, my Lucy was always more lovely than any other woman; she is now more lovely than even her former self.

You, my Rivers, will forgive the overflowings of my fondness, because you know the merit of its object.

Adieu! We die to embrace you!

Your faithful

J. TEMPLE

TO MRS TEMPLE, PALL MALL

LETTER 144   SILLERI, MAY 21: Your letter, Madam, to Miss Fermor, which, by an accident, was first read by me, has removed the veil which love had placed before mine eyes, and shewed me, in one moment, the folly of all those dear hopes I had indulged.

You do me but justice in believing me incapable of suffering your brother to sacrifice the peace, much less the life, of an amiable mother, to my happiness: I have no doubt of his returning to England the moment he receives your letters; but, knowing his tenderness, I will not expose him to a struggle on this occasion: I will myself, unknown to him, as he is fortunately absent, embark in a ship which has wintered here, and will leave Quebec in ten days.

Your invitation is very obliging; but a moment's reflection will convince you of the extreme impropriety of my accepting it.

Assure Mrs Rivers, that her son will not lose a moment, that he will probably be with her as soon as this letter; assure her also, that the woman who has kept him from her, can never forgive herself for what she suffers.

I am too much afflicted to say more than that

I am, Madam,

EMILY MONTAGUE

LETTER 145 MONTREAL, MAY 20: It is with a pleasure no words can express I tell my sweet Emily, I have fixed on a situation which promises every advantage we can wish as to profit, and which has every beauty that nature can give.

The land is rich, and the wood will more than pay the expence of clearing it; there is a settlement within a few leagues, on which there is an extreme agreeable family: a number of Acadians have applied to me to be received as settlers: in short, my dear angel, all seems to smile on our design.

I have spent some days at the house of a German officer, lately in our service, who is engaged in the same design, but a little advanced in it. I have seen him increasing every hour his little domain, by clearing the lands; he has built a pretty house in a beautiful rustic style: I have seen his pleasing labours with inconceivable delight. I already fancy my own settlement advancing in beauty: I paint to myself my Emily adorning those lovely shades: I see her, like the mother of mankind, admiring a new creation which smiles around her: we appear, to my idea, like the first pair in paradise.

I hope to be with you the 1st of June: will you allow me to set down the 2d as the day which is to assure to me a life of happiness?

My Acadians, your new subjects, are waiting in the next room to speak with me.

All good angels guard my Emily!
Adieu! Your

ED. RIVERS

LETTER 146 SILLERI, MAY 24: Emily has wrote to you, and appears more composed; she does not however tell me what she has resolved; she has only mentioned a design of spending a week at Quebec. I suppose she will take no resolution till your brother comes down: he cannot be here in less than ten days.

She has heard from him, and he has fixed on a settlement: depend however on his return to England, even if it is not to stay. I wish he could prevail on Mrs Rivers to accompany him back. The advantages of his design are too great to lose: the voyage is nothing; the climate healthy beyond all conception.

I fancy he will marry as soon as he comes down from Montreal, set off in the first ship for England, leave Emily with me, and return to us next year: at least, this is the plan my heart has formed.

I wish Mrs Rivers had borne his absence better; her impatience to see him has broken in on all our schemes; Emily and I had in fancy formed a little Eden on Lake Champlain: Fitzgerald had promised me to apply for lands near them; we should have been so happy in our little new world of friendship.

There is nothing certain in this vile state of existence: I could philosophize extremely well this morning.

All our little plans of amusement too for this summer are now at an end; your brother was the soul of all our parties. This is a trifle, but my mind to-day seeks for every subject of chagrin.

Let but my Emily be happy, and I will not complain, even if I lose her: I have a thousand fears, a thousand uneasy reflections: if you knew her merit, you would not wish to break the attachment.

My sweet Emily is going this morning to Quebec; I have promised to accompany her, and she now waits for me.

I cannot write: I have a heaviness about my heart, which has never left me since I read your letter. 'Tis the only disagreeable one I ever received from my dear Lucy: I am not sure I love you so well as before I saw this letter. There is something unfeeling in the style of it, which I did not expect from you.

Adieu! Your faithful

A. Fermor

TO MRS TEMPLE, PALL MALL

LETTER **147** SILLERI, MAY 25: I am unhappy beyond all words; my sweet Emily is gone to England; the ship sailed this morning: I am just returned from the beach, after conducting her on board.

I used every art, every persuasion, in the power of friendship, to prevent her going till your brother came down; but all I said was in vain. She told me, she knew too well her own weakness to hazard seeing him; that she also knew his tenderness, and was resolved to spare him the struggle between his affection and his duty; that she was determined never to marry him but with the consent of his mother; that their meeting at Quebec, situated as they were, could only be the source of unhappiness to both; that her heart doted on him, but that she would never be the cause of his acting in a manner unworthy his character: that she would see his family the moment she got to London, and then retire to the house of a relation in Berkshire, where she would wait for his arrival.

That she had given you her promise, which nothing should make her break, to embark in the first ship for England.

She expressed no fears for herself as to the voyage, but trembled at the idea of her Rivers's danger.

She sat down several times yesterday to write to him, but her tears prevented her: she at last assumed courage enough to tell him her design; but it was in such terms as convinced me she could not have pursued it, had he been here.

She went to the ship with an appearance of calmness that astonished me; but the moment she entered, all her resolution forsook her: she retired with me to her room, where she gave way to all the agony of her soul.

The word was given to sail; I was summoned away; she rose hastily, she pressed me to her bosom. "Tell him," said she, "his Emily"—she could say no more.

Never in my life did I feel any sorrow equal to this separation. Love her, my Lucy; you can never have half the tenderness for her she merits.

She stood on the deck till the ship turned Point Levi, her eyes fixed passionately on our boat.

Twelve o'clock

I have this moment a letter from your brother to Emily, which she directed me to open, and send to her; I inclose it to you, as the safest way of conveyance: there is one in it from Temple to him, on the same subject with yours to me.

Adieu! I will write again when my mind is more composed.

Yours,

A. FERMOR

LETTER 148 MONTREAL, MAY 28: It was my wish, my hope, my noblest ambition, my dear Emily, to see you in a situation worthy of you; my sanguine temper flattered me with the idea of seeing this wish accomplished in Canada, though fortune denied it me in England.

The letter which I inclose has put an end to those fond delusive hopes: I must return immediately to England; did not my own heart dictate this step. I know too well the goodness of yours, to expect the continuance of your esteem, were I capable of purchasing happiness, even the happiness of calling you mine, at the expence of my mother's life, or even of her quiet.

I must now submit to see my Emily in an humbler situation; to see her want those pleasures, those advantages, those honours, which fortune gives, and which she has no nobly sacrificed to true delicacy of mind, and, if I do not flatter myself, to her generous and disinterested affection for me.

Be assured, my dearest angel, the inconveniences attendant on a narrow fortune, the only one I have to offer, shall be softened by all which the most lively esteem, the most perfect friendship, the tenderest love, can inspire; by that attention, that unwearied solicitude to please, of which the heart alone knows the value.

Fortune has no power over minds like ours; we possess a treasure to which all she has to give is nothing, the dear exquisite delight of loving, and of being beloved.

Awake to all the finer feelings of tender esteem and elegant desire, we have every real good in each other.

I shall hurry down, the moment I have settled my affairs here; and hope soon to have the transport of presenting the most charming of friends, of mistresses, allow me to add, of wives, to a mother whom I love and revere beyond words, and to whom she will soon be dearer than myself.

My going to England will detain me at Montreal a few days longer than I intended; a delay I can very ill-support.

Adieu! my Emily! no language can express my tenderness or my impatience.

Your faithful

ED. RIVERS

LETTER 149 MONTREAL, MAY 28: I cannot enough, my dear Temple, thank you for your last, though it destroys my air-built scheme of happiness.

Could I have supposed my mother would thus severely have felt my absence, I had never left England; to make her easier, was my only motive for that step.

I with pleasure sacrifice my design of settling here to her peace of mind; no consideration, however, shall ever make me give up that of marrying the best and most charming of women.

I could have wished to have had a fortune worthy of her; this was my wish, not that of my Emily; she will with equal pleasure share with me poverty or riches: I hope her consent to marry me before I leave Canada. I know the advantages of affluence, my dear Temple, and am too reasonable to despise them; I would only avoid rating them above their worth.

Riches undoubtedly purchase a variety of pleasures which are not otherwise to be obtained; they give power, they give honours, they give consequence; but if, to enjoy these subordinate goods, we must give up those which are more essential, more real, more suited to our natures, I can never hesitate one moment to determine between them.

I know nothing fortune has to bestow, which can equal the transport of being dear to the most amiable, most lovely of womankind.

The stream of life, my dear Temple, stagnates without the gentle gale of love; till I knew my Emily, till the dear moment which assured me of her tenderness, I could scarce be said to live.

Adieu!
Your affectionate

ED. RIVERS

LETTER 150 SILLERI, JUNE 1: I can write, I can talk, of nothing but Emily; I never knew how much I loved her till she was gone: I run eagerly to every place where we have been together; every spot reminds me of her; I remember a thousand conversations, endeared by confidence and affection: a tender tear starts in spite of me: our walks, our airings, our pleasing little parties, all rush at once on my memory: I see the same lovely scenes around me, but they have lost half their power of pleasing.

I visit every grove, every thicket, that she loved; I have a redoubled fondness for every object in which she took pleasure.

Fitzgerald indulges me in this enthusiasm of friendship; he leads me to every place which can recall my Emily's idea; he speaks of her with a warmth which shews the sensibility and goodness of his own heart; he endeavours to soothe me by the most endearing attention.

What infinite pleasure, my dear Lucy, there is in being truly beloved! Fond as I have ever been of general admiration, that of all mankind is nothing to the least mark of Fitzgerald's tenderness.

Adieu! it will be some days before I can send this letter.

June 4

The governor gives a ball in honour of the day; I am dressing to go, but without my sweet companion: every hour I feel more sensibly her absence.

5th

We had last night, during the ball, the most dreadful storm I ever heard; it seemed to shake the whole habitable globe.

Heaven preserve my Emily from its fury! I have a thousand fears on her account.

Twelve o'clock

Your brother is arrived; he has been here about an hour: he flew to Silleri, without going at all to Quebec; he enquired for Emily; he would not believe she was gone.

There is no expressing how much he was shocked when convinced she had taken this voyage without him; he would have followed her in an open boat, in hopes of overtaking her at Coudre, if my father had not detained him almost by force, and at last convinced him of the impossibility of overtaking her, as the winds, having been constantly fair, must before this have carried them out of the river.

He has sent his servant to Quebec, with orders to take passage for him in the first ship that sails; his impatience is not to be described.

He came down in the hope of marrying her here, and conducting her himself to England; he forms to himself a thousand dangers to her, which he fondly fancies his presence could have averted: in short, he has all the unreasonableness of a man in love.

I propose sending this, and a large packet more, by your brother, unless some unexpected opportunity offers before.

Adieu! my dear!

Yours,

A. FERMOR

LETTER 151 6TH: Your brother has taken his passage in a very fine ship, which will sail the 10th; you may expect him every hour after you receive this; which I send, with what I wrote yesterday, by a small vessel which sails a week sooner than was intended.

Rivers persuades Fitzgerald to apply for the lands which he had fixed upon on Lake Champlain, as he has no thoughts of ever returning hither.

I will prevent this, however, if I have any influence: I cannot think with patience of continuing in America, when my two amiable friends have left it; I had no motive for wishing a settlement here, but to form a little society of friends, of which they made the principal part.

Besides, the spirit of emulation would have kept up my courage, and given fire and brilliancy to my fancy.

Emily and I should have been trying who had the most lively genius at creation; who could have produced the fairest flowers; who have formed the woods and rocks into the most beautiful arbours, vistoes, grottoes; have taught the streams to flow in the most pleasing meanders; have brought into view the greatest number and variety of those lovely little falls of water with which this fairy land abounds; and shewed nature in the fairest form.

In short, we should have been continually endeavouring, following the luxuriancy of female imagination, to render more charming the sweet abodes of love and friendship; whilst our heroes, changing their swords into plough-shares, and engaged in more substantial, more profitable labours, were clearing land, raising cattle and corn, and doing every thing becoming good farmers; or, to express it more poetically,

"*Taming the genius of the stubborn plain,*
"*Almost as quickly as they conquer'd Spain*":

By which I would be understood to mean the Havannah, where, vanity apart, I am told both of them did their duty, and a little more, if a man can in such a case be said to do more.

In one word, they would have been studying the useful, to support us; we the agreeable, to please and amuse them; which I take to be assigning to the two sexes the employments for which nature intended them, notwithstanding the vile example of the savages to the contrary.

There are now no farmeresses in Canada worth my contending with; therefore the whole pleasure of the thing would be at an end, even on the supposition that friendship had not been the soul of our design.

Say every thing for me to Temple and Mrs Rivers; and to my dearest Emily, if arrived.

Adieu! your faithful

A. FERMOR

TO THE EARL OF ——

LETTER 152 SILLERI, JUNE 6, 1767: It is very true, my Lord, that the Jesuit missionaries still continue in the Indian villages in Canada; and I am afraid it is no less true, that they use every art to instill into those people an aversion to the English; at least I have been told this by the Indians themselves, who seem equally surprized and piqued that we do not send missionaries amongst them.

Their ideas of Christianity are extremely circumscribed, and they give no preference to one mode of our faith above another; they regard a missionary of any nation as a kind father, who comes to instruct them in the best way of worshipping the Deity, whom they suppose more propitious to the Europeans than to themselves; and as an ambassador from the prince whose subject he is: they therefore think it a mark of honour, and a proof of esteem, to receive missionaries; and to our remissness, and the French wise attention on this head, is owing the extreme attachment the greater part of the savage nations have ever had to the latter.

The French missionaries, by studying their language, their manners, their tempers, their dispositions; by conforming to their way of life, and using every art to gain their esteem, have acquired an influence over them which is scarce to be conceived; nor would it be difficult for ours to do the same, were they judiciously chose, and properly encouraged.

I believe I have said, that there is a striking resemblance between the manners of the Canadians and the savages; I should have explained it, by adding, that this resemblance has been brought about, not by the French having won the savages to receive European manners, but by the very contrary; the peasants having acquired the savage indolence in peace, their activity and ferocity in war; their fondness for field sports, their hatred of labour; their love of a wandering life, and of liberty; in the latter of which they have been in some degree indulged, the laws here being much milder, and more favourable to the people, than in France.

Many of the officers also, and those of rank in the colony troops, have been adopted into the savage tribes; and there is stronger evidence than, for the honour of humanity, I would wish there was, that some of them have led the death dance at the execution of English captives, have even partook the horrid repast, and imitated them in all their cruelties; cruelties, which, to the eternal disgrace, not only of our holy religion, but even of our nature, these poor people, whose ignorance is their excuse, have been instigated to, both by the French and English colonies, who, with a fury truly diabolical, have offered rewards to those who brought in the scalps of their enemies. Rousseau has taken great pains to prove that the most uncultivated nations are the most virtuous: I have all due respect for this philosopher, of whose writings I am an enthusiastic admirer; but I have a still greater respect for truth, which I believe is not in this instance on his side.

There is little reason to boast of the virtues of a people, who are such brutal slaves to their appetites as to be unable to avoid drinking brandy to an excess scarce to be conceived, whenever it falls in their way, though eternally lamenting the murders and other atrocious crimes of which they are so perpetually guilty when under its influence.

It is unjust to say we have corrupted them, that we have taught them a vice to which we are ourselves not addicted; both French and English are in general sober: we have indeed given them the means of intoxication, which they had not before their intercourse with us; but he must be indeed fond of praising them, who makes a virtue of their having been sober, when water was the only liquor with which they were acquainted.

From all that I have observed, and heard of these people, it appears to me an undoubted fact, that the most civilized Indian nations are the most virtuous; a fact which makes directly against Rousseau's ideal system.

Indeed all systems make against, instead of leading to, the discovery of truth.

Père Lafitau has, for this reason, in his very learned comparison of the manners of the savages with those of the first ages, given a very imperfect account of Indian manners; he is even so candid as to own, he tells you nothing but what makes for the system he is endeavouring to establish.

My wish, on the contrary, is not to make truth subservient to any favourite sentiment or idea, any child of my fancy; but to discover it, whether agreeable or not to my own opinion.

My accounts may therefore be false or imperfect from mistake or misinformation, but will never be designedly warped from truth.

That the savages have virtues, candour must own; but only a love of paradox can make any man assert they have more than polished nations.

Your Lordship asks me what is the general moral character of the Canadians; they are simple and hospitable, yet extremely attentive to interest, where it does not interfere with that laziness which is their governing passion.

They are rather devout than virtuous; have religion without morality, and a sense of honour without very strict honesty.

Indeed I believe wherever superstition reigns, the moral sense is greatly weakened; the strongest inducement to the practice of morality is removed, when people are brought to believe that a few outward ceremonies will compensate for the want of virtue.

I myself heard a man, who had raised a large fortune by very indirect means, confess his life had been contrary to every precept of the Gospel; but that he hoped the pardon of Heaven for all his sins, as he intended to devote one of his daughters to a conventual life as an expiation.

This way of being virtuous by proxy, is certainly very easy and convenient to such sinners as have children to sacrifice.

By Colonel Rivers, who leaves us in a few days, I intend myself the honour of addressing your Lordship again.

I have the honour to be

Your Lordship's, etc.

WM. FERMOR

TO THE EARL OF ——

LETTER 153 SILLERI, JUNE 9: Your Lordship will receive this from the hands of one of the most worthy and amiable men I ever knew, Colonel Rivers, whom I am particularly happy in having the honour to introduce to your Lordship, as I know your delicacy in the choice of friends, and that there are so few who have your perfect esteem and confidence, that the acquaintance of one who merits both, at his time of life, will be regarded, even by your Lordship, as an acquisition.

'Tis to him I shall say the advantage I procure him, by making him known to a nobleman, who, with the wisdom and experience of age, has all the warmth of heart, the generosity, the noble confidence, the enthusiasm, the fire, and vivacity of youth.

Your Lordship's idea, in regard to Protestant convents here, on the footing of that we visited together at Hamburgh, is extremely well worth the consideration of those whom it may concern; especially if the Romish ones are abolished, as will most probably be the case.

The noblesse have numerous families, and, if there are no convents, will be at a loss where to educate their daughters, as well as where to dispose of those who do not marry in a reasonable time: the convenience they find in both respects from these houses, is one strong motive to them to continue in their ancient religion.

As I would however prevent the more useful, by which I mean the lower, part of the sex from entering into this state, I would wish only the daughters of the seigneurs to have the privilege of becoming nuns: they should be obliged, on taking the vow, to prove their noblesse for at least three generations; which would secure them respect, and, at the same time, prevent their becoming too numerous.

They should take the vow of obedience, but not of celibacy: and reserve the power, as at Hamburgh, of going out to marry, though on no other consideration.

215

Your Lordship may remember, every nun at Hamburgh has a right of marrying, except the Abbess; and that, on your Lordship's telling the lady who then presided, and who was young and very handsome, you thought this a hardship, she answered with great spirit, "O, my Lord, you know it is in my power to resign."

I refer your Lordship to Colonel Rivers for that farther information in regard to this colony, which he is much more able to give you than I am, having visited every part of Canada in the design of settling in it.

I have the honour to be,

My Lord, etc.

WM. FERMOR

Your Lordship's mention of nuns has brought to my memory a little anecdote on this subject, which I will tell you.

I was, a few mornings ago, visiting a French lady, whose very handsome daughter, of almost sixteen, told me, she was going into a convent. I enquired which she had made choice of: she said, "The General Hospital."

"I am glad, Mademoiselle, you have not chose the Ursulines; the rules are so very severe, you would have found them hard to conform to."

"As to the rules, Sir, I have no objection to their severity; but the habit of the General Hospital——"

I smiled.

"Is so very light——"

"And so becoming, Mademoiselle."

She smiled in her turn, and I left her fully convinced of the sincerity of her vocation, and the great propriety and humanity of suffering young creatures to choose a kind of life so repugnant to human nature, at an age when they are such excellent judges of what will make them happy.

TO MRS TEMPLE, PALL MALL

LETTER 154 SILLERI, JUNE 9: I send this by your brother, who sails to-morrow.

Time, I hope, will reconcile me to his and Emily's absence; but at present I cannot think of losing them without a dejection of mind which takes from me the very idea of pleasure.

I conjure you, my dear Lucy, to do every thing possible to facilitate their union; and remember, that to your request, and to Mrs Rivers's tranquillity, they have sacrificed every prospect they had of happiness.

I would say more; but my spirits are so affected, I am incapable of writing.

Love my sweet Emily, and let her not repent the generosity of her conduct.

Adieu!
Your affectionate

A. FERMOR

TO MRS TEMPLE, PALL MALL

LETTER 155 SILLERI, JUNE 10, EVENING: My poor Rivers! I think I felt more from his going than even from Emily's: whilst he was here, I seemed not quite to have lost her: I now feel doubly the loss of both.

He begged me to shew attention to Madame Des Roches, who he assured me merited my tenderest friendship; he wrote to her, and has left the letter open in my care: it is to thank her, in the most affectionate terms, for her politeness and friendship, as well to himself as to his Emily; and to offer her his best services in England in regard to her estate, part of which some people here have very ungenerously applied for a grant of, on pretence of its not being all settled according to the original conditions.

He owned to me, he felt some regret at leaving this amiable woman in Canada, and at the idea of never seeing her more.

I love him for this sensibility; and for his delicate attention to one whose disinterested affection for him most certainly deserves it.

Fitzgerald is below, he does all possible to console me for the loss of my friends; but indeed, Lucy, I feel their absence most severely.

I have an opportunity of sending your brother's letter to Madame Des Roches, which I must not lose, as they are not very frequent: 'tis by a French gentleman who is now with my father.

Adieu! Your faithful

A. FERMOR

Twelve at night

We have been talking of your brother; I have been saying, there is nothing I so much admire in him as that tenderness of soul, and almost female sensibility, which is so uncommon in a sex, whose whole education tends to harden their hearts.

Fitzgerald admires his spirit, his understanding, his generosity, his courage, the warmth of his friendship.

My father has knowledge of the world; not that indiscriminate suspicion of mankind which is falsely so called; but that clearness of mental sight, and discerning faculty, which can distinguish virtue as well as vice, wherever it resides.

"I also love in him," said my father, "that noble sincerity, that integrity of character, which is the foundation of all the virtues."

"And yet, my dear papa, you would have had Emily prefer to him, that *white curd of asses milk*, Sir George Clayton, whose highest claim to virtue is the constitutional absence of vice, and who never knew what it was to feel for the sorrows of another."

"You mistake, Bell: such a preference was impossible; but she was engaged to Sir George; and he had also a fine fortune. Now, in these degenerate days, my dear, people must eat; we have lost all taste for the airy food of romances, when ladies rode behind their enamoured knights, dined luxuriously on a banquet of haws, and quenched their thirst at the first stream."

"But, my dear papa——"

"But, my dear Bell——"

I saw the sweet old man look angry, so chose to drop the subject; but I do aver, now he is out of sight, that haws and a pillion, with such a noble fellow as your brother, are preferable to ortolans and a coach and six, with such a piece of still life and insipidity as Sir George.

Good night! my dear Lucy.

TO MRS TEMPLE, PALL MALL

LETTER 156   SILLERI, JUNE 17: I have this moment received a packet of letters from my dear Lucy; I shall only say, in answer to what makes the greatest part of them, that in a fortnight I hope you will have the pleasure of seeing your brother, who did not hesitate one moment in giving up to Mrs Rivers's peace of mind, all his pleasing prospects here, and the happiness of being united to the woman he loved.

You will not, I hope, my dear, forget his having made such a sacrifice: but I think too highly of you to say more on this subject. You will receive Emily as a friend, as a sister, who merits all your esteem and tenderness, and who has lost all the advantages of fortune, and incurred the censure of the world, by her disinterested attachment to your brother.

I am extremely sorry, but not surprized, at what you tell me of poor Lady H——. I knew her intimately; she was sacrificed at eighteen, by the avarice and ambition of her parents, to age, disease, ill-nature, and a coronet; and her death is the natural consequence of her regret: she had a soul formed for friendship; she found it not at home; her elegance of mind, and native probity, prevented her seeking it abroad; she died a melancholy victim to the tyranny of her friends, the tenderness of her heart, and her delicate sense of honour.

If her father has any of the feelings of humanity left, what must he not suffer on this occasion?

It is a painful consideration, my dear, that the happiness or misery of our lives are generally determined before we are proper judges of either.

Restrained by custom, and the ridiculous prejudices of the world, we go with the crowd, and it is late in life before we dare to think.

How happy are you and I, Lucy, in having parents, who, far from forcing our inclinations, have not even endeavoured to betray us into choosing from sordid motives! They have not laboured to fill our young hearts with vanity or avarice; they have left us those virtues, those amiable qualities, we received from nature. They have painted to us the charms of friendship, and not taught us to value riches above their real price.

My father, indeed, checks a certain excess of romance which there is in my temper; but, at the same time, he never encouraged my receiving the addresses of any man who had only the gifts of fortune to recommend him; he even advised me, when very young, against marrying an officer in his regiment, of a large fortune, but an unworthy character.

If I have any knowledge of the human heart, it will be my own fault if I am not happy with Fitzgerald.

I am only afraid, that when we are married and begin to settle into a calm, my volatile disposition will carry me back to coquetry: my passion for admiration is naturally strong, and has been increased by indulgence; for without vanity I have been extremely the taste or the men.

I have a kind of an idea it won't be long before I try the strength of my resolution, for I heard papa and Fitzgerald in high consultation this morning.

Do you know, that, having nobody to love but Fitzgerald, I am ten times more enamoured of the dear creature than ever? My love is now like the rays of the sun collected.

He is so much here, I wonder I don't grow tired of him; but somehow he has the art of varying himself beyond any man I ever knew: it was that agreeable variety of character that first struck me; I considered that with him I should have all the sex in one; he says the same of me; and indeed, it must be owned we have both an infinity of agreeable caprice, which in love affairs is worth all the merit in the world.

Have you never observed, Lucy, that the same person is seldom greatly the object of both love and friendship?

Those virtues which command esteem do not often inspire passion.

Friendship seeks the more real, more solid virtues; integrity, constancy, and a steady uniformity of character: love, on the contrary, admires it knows not what; creates itself the idol it worships; finds charms even in defects; is pleased with follies, with inconsistency, with caprice: to say all in one line,

"Love is a child, and like a child he plays."

The moment Emily arrives, I entreat that one of you will write to me: no words can speak my impatience: I am equally anxious to hear of my dear Rivers. Heaven send them prosperous gales!

Adieu!

Your faithful

A. FERMOR

TO MRS TEMPLE, PALL MALL

LETTER 157   SILLERI, JUNE 30: You are extremely mistaken, my dear, in your idea of the society here; I had rather live at Quebec, take it for all in all, than in any town in England, except London; the manner of living here is uncommonly agreeable; the scenes about us are lovely, and the mode of amusements makes us taste those scenes in full perfection.

Whilst your brother and Emily were here, I had not a wish to leave Canada; but their going has left a void in my heart, which will not easily be filled up: I have loved Emily almost from childhood, and there is a peculiar tenderness in those friendships, which

"*Grow with our growth, and strengthen with our strength.*"

There was also something romantic and agreeable in finding her here, and unexpectedly, after we had been separated by Colonel Montague's having left the regiment in which my father served.

In short, every thing concurred to make us dear to each other, and therefore to give a greater poignancy to the pain of parting a second time.

As to your brother, I love him so much, that a man who had less candour and generosity than Fitzgerald, would be almost angry at my very lively friendship.

I have this moment a letter from Madame Des Roches; she laments the loss of our two amiable friends; begs me to assure them both of her eternal remembrance: says, she congratulates Emily on possessing the heart of the man on earth most worthy of being beloved; that she cannot form an idea of any human felicity equal to that of the woman, the business of whose life it is to make Colonel Rivers happy. That, Heaven having denied her that happiness, she will never marry, nor enter into an engagement, which would make it criminal in her to remember him with tenderness; that it is, however, she believes, best for her he has left the country, for that it is impossible she should ever have seen him with indifference.

It is perhaps as prudent not to mention these circumstances either to your brother or Emily; I thought of sending her letter to them, but there is a certain fire in her style, mixed with tenderness, when she speaks of Rivers, which would only have given them both regret, by making them see the excess of her affection for him; her expressions are much stronger than those in which I have given you the sense of them.

I intend to be very intimate with her, because she loves my dear Rivers; she loves Emily too, at least she fancies she does, but I am a little doubtful as to the friendships between rivals: at this distance, however, I dare say, they will always continue on the best terms possible, and I would have Emily write to her.

Do you know she has desired me to contrive to get her a picture of your brother, without his knowing it? I am not determined whether I shall indulge her in this fancy or not; if I do, I must employ you as my agent. It is madness in her to desire it; but, as there is a pleasure in being mad, I am not sure my morality will let me refuse her, since pleasures are not very thick sown in this world.

Adieu!

Your affectionate

A. FERMOR

TO MRS TEMPLE, PALL MALL

LETTER 158 SILLERI, JULY 10: By this time, my dear Lucy, I hope you are happy with your brother and my sweet Emily: I am all impatience to know this from yourselves; but it will be five or six weeks, perhaps much more, before I can have that satisfaction.

As to me—to be plain, my dear, I can hold no longer; I have been married this fortnight. My father wanted to keep it a secret, for some very foolish reasons; but it is not in my nature; I hate secrets, they are only fit for politicians, and people whose thoughts and actions will not bear the light.

For my part, I am convinced the general loquacity of human kind, and our inability to keep secrets without a natural kind of uneasiness, were meant by Providence to guard against our laying deep schemes of treachery against each other.

I remember a very sensible man, who perfectly knew the world, used to say, there was no such thing in nature as a secret; a maxim as true, at least I believe so, as it is salutary, and which I would advise all good mammas, aunts, and governesses, to impress strongly on the minds of young ladies.

So, as I was saying, *violà Madame Fitzgerald!*

This is, however, yet a secret here; but, according to my present doctrine, and following the nature of things, it cannot long continue so.

You never saw so polite a husband, but I suppose they are all so the first fortnight, especially when married in so interesting and romantic a manner; I am very fond of the fancy of being thus married *as it were*; but I have a notion I shall blunder it out very soon: we were married on a party to Three Rivers, nobody with us but papa and Madame Villiers, who have not yet published the mystery. I hear some misses at Quebec are scandalous about Fitzgerald's being so much here; I will leave them in doubt a little, I think, merely to gratify their love of scandal; every body should be amused in their way.

Adieu! Yours,

A. FITZGERALD

Pray let Emily be married; everybody marries but poor little Emily.

TO THE EARL OF ——

LETTER **159** SILLERI, JULY 10: I have the pleasure to tell your Lordship I have married my daughter to a gentleman with whom I have reason to hope she will be happy.

He is the second son of an Irish baronet of good fortune, and has himself about five hundred pounds a year, independent of his commission; he is a man of an excellent sense, and of honour, and has a very lively tenderness for my daughter.

It will, I am afraid, be some time before I can leave this country, as I choose to take my daughter and Mr Fitzgerald with me, in order to the latter's soliciting a majority, in which pursuit I shall without scruple tax your Lordship's friendship to the utmost.

I am extremely happy at this event, as Bell's volatile temper made me sometimes afraid of her choosing inconsiderately: their marriage is not yet declared, for some family reasons, not worth particularizing to your Lordship.

As soon as leave of absence comes from New York, for me and Mr Fitzgerald, we shall settle things for taking leave of Canada, which I however assure your Lordship I shall do with some reluctance.

The climate is all the year agreeable and healthy, in summer divine; a man at my time of life cannot leave this chearing, enlivening sun without reluctance; the heat is very like that of Italy or the South of France, without that oppressive closeness which generally attends our hot weather in England.

The manner of life here is chearful; we make the most

of our fine summers, by the pleasantest country parties you can imagine. Here are some very estimable persons, and the spirit of urbanity begins to diffuse itself from the centre; in short, I shall leave Canada at the very time when one would wish to come to it.

It is astonishing, in a small community like this, how much depends on the personal character of him who governs.

I am obliged to break off abruptly, the person who takes this to England being going immediately on board.

I have the honour to be,

My Lord,

Your Lordship's, etc.

WM. FERMOR

TO JOHN TEMPLE, ESQ; PALL MALL

LETTER 160 SILLERI, JULY 13: I agree with you, my dear Temple, that nothing can be more pleasing than an *awakened* Englishwoman; of which you and my *caro sposo* have, I flatter myself, the happy experience; and wish with you that the character was more common: but I must own, and I am sorry to own it, that my fair countrywomen and fellow-citizens (I speak of the nation in general, and not of the capital) have an unbecoming kind of reserve, which prevents their being the agreeable companions, and amiable wives, which nature meant them.

From a fear, and I think a prudish one, of being thought too attentive to please your sex, they have acquired a certain distant manner to men, which borders on ill-breeding; they take great pains to veil, under an affected appearance of disdain, that winning sensibility of heart, that delicate tenderness, which renders them doubly lovely.

They are even afraid to own their friendships, if not according to the square and rule; are doubtful whether a modest woman may own she loves even her husband; and seem to think affections were given them for no purpose but to hide.

Upon the whole, with at least as good a native right to charm as any women on the face of the globe, the English have found the happy secret of pleasing less.

Is my Emily arrived? I can say nothing else.

I am the happiest woman in the creation: papa has just told me, we are to go home in six or seven weeks.

Not but this is a divine country, and our farm a terrestrial paradise; but we have lived in it almost a year, and one grows tired of every thing in time, you know, Temple.

I shall see my Emily, and flirt with Rivers; to say nothing of you and my little Lucy.

Adieu! I am grown very lazy since I married; for the future, I shall make Fitzgerald write all my letters, except billet-doux, in which I think I excel him.

Yours,

A. FITZGERALD

TO MISS FERMOR, AT SILLERI

LETTER **161** DOVER, JULY 8: I am this moment arrived, my dear Bell, after a very agreeable passage, and am setting out immediately for London, from whence I shall write to you the moment I have seen Mrs Rivers; I will own to you I tremble at the idea of this interview, yet am resolved to see her, and open all my soul to her in regard to her son; after which, I shall leave her the mistress of my destiny; for, ardently as I love him, I will never marry him but with her approbation.

I have a thousand anxious fears for my Rivers's safety: may Heaven protect him from the dangers his Emily has escaped!

I have but a moment to write, a ship being under way which is bound to Quebec; a gentleman, who is just going off in a boat to the ship, takes the care of this.

May every happiness attend my dear girl! Say every thing affectionate for me to Captain Fermor and Mr Fitzgerald.

Adieu! Yours,

EMILY MONTAGUE

LETTER 162 LONDON, JULY 19: I got to town last night, my dear, and am at a friend's, from whence I have this morning sent to Mrs Rivers; I every moment expect her answer; my anxiety of mind is not to be expressed; my heart sinks; I almost dread the return of my messenger.

If the affections, my dear friend, give us the highest happiness of which we are capable, they are also the source of our keenest misery; what I feel at this instant, is not to be described: I have been near resolving to go into the country without seeing or sending to Mrs Rivers. If she should receive me with coldness—why should I have exposed myself to the chance of such a reception? It would have been better to have waited for Rivers's arrival; I have been too precipitate; my warmth of temper has misled me: what had I to do to seek his family? I would give the world to retract my message, though it was only to let her know I was arrived; that her son was well, and that she might every hour expect him in England.

There is a rap at the door: I tremble I know not why; the servant comes up, he announces Mr and Mrs Temple: my heart beats, they are at the door.

One o'clock

They are gone, and return for me in an hour; they insist on my dining with them, and tell me Mrs Rivers is impatient to see me. Nothing was ever so polite, so delicate, so affectionate, as the behaviour of both; they saw my confusion, and did every thing to remove it: they enquired after Rivers, but without the least hint of the dear interest I take in him: they spoke of the happiness of knowing me: they asked my friendship, in a manner the most flattering that can be imagined. How strongly does Mrs Temple, my dear, resemble her amiable brother! her eyes have the same sensibility, the same pleasing expression; I think I scarce ever saw so charming a woman; I love her already; I feel a tenderness for her, which is inconceivable; I caught myself two or three times looking at her, with an attention for which I blushed.

I believe, there was something very foolish in my behaviour; but they had the good-breeding and humanity not to seem to observe it.

I had almost forgot to tell you, they said every thing obliging and affectionate of you and Captain Fermor.

My mind is in a state not to be described; I feel joy, I

feel anxiety, I feel doubt, I feel a timidity I cannot conquer at the thought of seeing Mrs Rivers.

I have to dress; therefore must finish this when I return.

Twelve at night

I am come back, my dearest Bell; I have gone through the scene I so much dreaded, and am astonished I should ever think of it but with pleasure. How much did I injure this most amiable of women! Her reception of me was that of a tender parent, who had found a long-lost child; she kissed me, she pressed me to her bosom; her tears flowed in abundance; she called me her daughter, her other Lucy: she asked me a thousand questions of her son; she would know all that concerned him, however minute: how he looked, whether he talked much of her, what were his amusements; whether he was as handsome as when he left England.

I answered her with some hesitation, but with a pleasure that animated my whole soul; I believe, I never appeared to such advantage as this day.

You will not ascribe it to an unmeaning vanity, when I tell you, I never took such pains to please; I even gave a particular attention to my dress, that I might, as much as possible, justify my Rivers's tenderness: I never was vain for myself; but I am so for him: I am indifferent to admiration as Emily Montague; but as the object of his love, I would be admired by all the world; I wish to be the first of my sex in all that is amiable and lovely, that I might make a sacrifice worthy of my Rivers, in shewing to all his friends, that he only can inspire me with tenderness, that I live for him alone.

Mrs Rivers pressed me extremely to pass a month with her: my heart yielded too easily to her request; but I had courage to resist my own wishes, as well as her solicitations; and shall set out in three days for Berkshire: I have, however, promised to go with them to-morrow, on a party to Richmond, which Mr Temple was so obliging as to propose on my account.

Late as the season is, there is one more ship going to Quebec, which sails to-morrow.

You shall hear from me again in a few days by the packet.

Adieu! my dearest friend!
Your faithful
EMILY MONTAGUE

Surely it will not be long before Rivers arrives; you, my dear Bell, will judge what must be my anxiety till that moment.

LETTER **163**   DOVER, JULY 24, ELEVEN

o'clock: I am arrived, my dear friend, after a passage agreeable in itself; but which my fears for Emily made infinitely anxious and painful; every wind that blew, I trembled for her; I formed to myself ideal dangers on her account, which reason had not power to dissipate.

We had a very tumultuous head-sea a great part of the voyage, though the wind was fair; a certain sign there had been stormy weather, with a contrary wind. I fancied my Emily exposed to those storms; there is no expressing what I suffered from this circumstance.

On entering the Channel of England, we saw an empty boat, and some pieces of a wreck floating; I fancied it part of the ship which conveyed my lovely Emily; a sudden chillness seized my whole frame, my heart died within me at the sight: I had scarce courage, when I landed, to enquire whether she was arrived.

I asked the question with a trembling voice, and had the transport to find the ship had passed by, and to hear the person of my Emily described amongst the passengers who landed; it was not easy to mistake her.

I hope to see her this evening: what do I not feel from that dear hope!

Chance gives me an opportunity of forwarding this by New York; I write whilst my chaise is getting ready.

Adieu! Yours,

ED. RIVERS

I shall write to my dear little Bell as soon as I get to town. There is no describing what I felt at first seeing the coast of England: I saw the white cliffs with a transport mixed with veneration; a transport, which, however, was checked by my fears for the dearer part of myself.

My chaise is at the door.

Adieu!

Your faithful, etc.

ED. RIVERS

LETTER **164** ROCHESTER, JULY 24: I am obliged to wait ten minues for a Canadian gentleman who is with me, and has some letters to deliver here: how painful is this delay! But I cannot leave a stranger alone on the road, though I lose so many minutes with my charming Emily.

To soften this moment as much as possible, I will begin a letter to my dear Bell: our sweet Emily is safe; I wrote to Captain Fermor this morning.

My heart is gay beyond words: my fellow-traveller is astonished at the beauty and riches of England, from what he has seen of Kent: for my part, I point out every fine prospect, and am so proud of my country, that my whole soul seems to be dilated; for which perhaps there are other reasons. The day is fine, the numerous herds and flocks on the side of the hills, the neatness of the houses, of the people, the appearance of plenty; all exhibit a scene which must strike one who has been used only to the wild graces of nature.

Canada has beauties; but they are of another kind.

This unreasonable man; he has no mistress to see in London; he is not expected by the most amiable of mothers, by a family he loves as I do mine.

I will order another chaise, and leave my servant to attend him.

He comes. Adieu! my dear little Bell! at this moment a gentleman is come into the inn, who is going to embark at Dover for New York; I will send this by him. Once more adieu!

LETTER **165** CLARGES STREET, JULY 25: I am the only person here, my dear Bell, enough composed to tell you Rivers is arrived in town. He stopped in his post-chaise, at the end of the street, and sent for me, that I might prepare my mother to see him, and prevent a surprize which might have hurried her spirits too much.

I came back, and told her I had seen a gentleman who had left him at Dover, and that he would soon be here; he followed me in a few minutes.

I am not painter enough to describe their meeting; tho'
prepared, it was with difficulty we kept my mother from faint-
ing; she pressed him in her arms, she attempted to speak, her
voice faltered, tears stole softly down her cheeks: nor was
Rivers less affected, though in a different manner; I never saw
him look so handsome; the manly tenderness, the filial respect,
the lively joy, that were expressed in his countenance, gave him
a look to which it is impossible to do justice: he hinted going
down to Berkshire to-night; but my mother seemed so hurt at
the proposal, that he wrote to Emily, and told her his reason
for deferring it till to-morrow, when we are all to go in my
coach, and hope to bring her back with us to town.

You judge rightly, my dear Bell, that they were formed
for each other; never were two minds so familiar; we must contrive some method of making them happy: nothing but a too
great delicacy in Rivers prevents their being so to-morrow; were
our situations changed, I should not hesitate a moment to let
him make me so.

Lucy has sent for me. Adieu!
Believe me,
Your faithful and devoted,

J. TEMPLE

LETTER **166** PALL MALL, JULY 29: I am the happiest of human beings: my Rivers is arrived, he is well, he loves
me; I am dear to his family; I see him without restraint; I am
every hour more convinced of the excess of his affection: his
attention to me is inconceivable; his eyes every moment tell me,
I am dearer to him than life.

I am to be for some time on a visit to his sister; he is
at Mrs Rivers's, but we are always together: we go down next
week to Mr Temple's, in Rutland; they only stayed in town,
expecting Rivers's arrival. His seat is within six miles of Rivers's
little paternal estate, which he settled on his mother when he
left England; she presses him to resume it, but he peremptorily
refuses; he insists on her continuing her house in town, and
being perfectly independent, and mistress of herself.

I love him a thousand times more for this tenderness to
her; though it disappoints my dear hope of being his. Did I

think it possible, my dear Bell, he could have risen higher in my esteem?

If we are never united, if we always live as at present, his tenderness will still make the delight of my life; to see him, to hear that voice, to be his friend, the confidante of all his purposes, of all his designs, to hear the sentiments of that generous, that exalted soul—I would not give up this delight, to be empress of the world.

My ideas of affection are perhaps uncommon; but they are not the less just, nor the less in nature.

A blind man may as well judge of colours as the mass of mankind of the sentiments of a truly-enamoured heart.

The sensual and the cold will equally condemn my affection as romantic; few minds, my dear Bell, are capable of love; they feel passion, they feel esteem; they even feel that mixture of both which is the best counterfeit of love; but of that vivifying fire, that lively tenderness which hurries us out of ourselves, they know nothing: that tenderness which makes us forget ourselves, when the interest, the happiness, the honour, of him we love is concerned; that tenderness which renders the beloved object all that we see in the creation.

Yes, my Rivers, I live, I breathe, I exist, for you alone: be happy, and your Emily is so.

My dear friend, you know love, and will therefore bear with all the impertinence of a tender heart.

I hope you have by this time made Fitzgerald happy; he deserves you, amiable as you are, and you cannot too soon convince him of your affection: you sometimes play cruelly with his tenderness: I have been astonished to see you torment a heart which adores you.

I am interrupted.

Adieu! my dear Bell.

Your affectionate

EMILY MONTAGUE

TO CAPTAIN FERMOR, AT SILLERI

LETTER 167 CLARGES STREET, AUG. 1: Lord —— not being in town, I went to his villa at Richmond, to deliver your letter.

I cannot enough, my dear Sir, thank you for this introduction; I passed part of the day at Richmond, and never was more pleasingly entertained.

His politeness, his learning, his knowledge of the world, however amiable, are in character at his season of life; but his vivacity is astonishing.

What fire, what spirit, there is in his conversation! I hardly thought myself a young man near him. What must he have been at five-and-twenty?

He desired me to tell you, all his interest should be employed for Fitzgerald, and that he wished you to come to England as soon as possible.

We are just setting off for Temple's house in Rutland.

Adieu!

Your affectionate

ED. RIVERS

TO CAPTAIN FERMOR, AT SILLERI

LETTER 168 TEMPLE-HOUSE, AUG. 4: I enjoy, my dear friend, in one of the pleasantest houses, and most agreeable situations imaginable, the society of the four persons in the world most dear to me; I am in all respects as much at home as if master of the family, without the cares attending that station; my wishes, my desires, are prevented by Temple's attention and friendship, and my mother and sister's amiable anxiety to oblige me; I find an unspeakable softness in seeing my lovely Emily every moment, in seeing her adored by my family, in seeing her without restraint, in being in the same house, in living in that easy converse which is born from friendship alone: yet I am not happy.

It is that we lose the present happiness in the pursuit of greater: I look forward with impatience to that moment which will make Emily mine; and the difficulties, which I see on every side arising, embitter hours which would otherwise be exquisitely happy.

The narrowness of my fortune, which I see in a much stronger light in this land of luxury, and the apparent impossibility of placing the most charming of women in the station my heart wishes, give me anxieties which my reason cannot conquer.

I cannot live without her, I flatter myself our union is in some degree necessary to her happiness; yet I dread bringing her into distresses, which I am doubly obliged to protect her from, because she would with transport meet them all, from tenderness to me.

I have nothing which I can call my own, but my half-pay, and four thousand pounds: I have lived amongst the first company in England; all my connexions have been rather suited to my birth than fortune. My mother presses me to resume my estate, and let her live with us alternately; but against this I am firmly determined; she shall have her own house, and never change her manner of living.

Temple would share his estate with me, if I would allow him; but I am too fond of independence to accept favours of this kind even from him.

I have formed a thousand schemes; and as often found them abortive; I go to-morrow to see our little estate, with my mother; it is a private party of our own, and nobody is in the secret; I will there talk over every thing with her.

My mind is at present in a state of confusion not to be expressed; I must determine on something; it is improper Emily should continue long with my sister in her present situation; yet I cannot live without seeing her.

I have never asked about Emily's fortune; but I know it is a small one; perhaps two thousand pounds; I am pretty certain, not more.

We can live on little, but we must live in some degree on a genteel footing: I cannot let Emily, who refused a coach and six for me, pay visits on foot; I will be content with a post-chaise, but cannot with less; I have a little, a very little pride, for my Emily.

I wish it were possible to prevail on my mother to return with us to Canada: I could then reconcile my duty and happiness, which at present seem almost incompatible.

Emily appears perfectly happy, and to look no further than to the situation in which we now are; she seems content with being my friend only, without thinking of a nearer connexion; I am rather piqued at a composure which has the air of indifference: why should not her impatience equal mine?

The coach is at the door, and my mother waits for me.

Every happiness attend my friend, and all connected with him! in which number I hope I may, by this time, include Fitzgerald.

Adieu!

Your affectionate

ED. RIVERS

LETTER **169** AUG. 6: I have been taking an exact survey of the house and estate with my mother, in order to determine on some future plan of life.

'Tis inconceivable what I felt on returning to a place so dear to me, and which I had not seen for many years; I ran hastily from one room to another; I traversed the garden with inexpressible eagerness: my eye devoured every object; there was not a tree, not a bush, which did not revive some pleasing, some soft idea.

I felt, to borrow a very pathetic expression of Thomson's,

"A thousand little tendernesses throb,"

on revisiting those dear scenes of infant happiness; which were increased by having with me that estimable, that affectionate mother, to whose indulgence all my happiness had been owing.

But to return to the purpose of our visit: the house is what most people would think too large for the estate, even had I a right to call it all my own; this is, however, a fault, if it is one, which I can easily forgive.

There is furniture enough in it for my family, including my mother; it is unfashionable, but some of it very good: and I think Emily has tenderness enough for me to live with me in a house, the furniture of which is not perfectly in taste.

In short, I know her much above having the slightest wish of vanity, where it comes in competition with love.

We can, as to the house, live here commodiously enough; and our only present consideration is, on what we are to live: a consideration, however, which as lovers, I believe in strictness we ought to be much above!

My mother again solicits me to resume this estate; and has proposed my making over to her my half-pay instead of it, though of much less value, which, with her own two hundred pounds a year, will, she says, enable her to continue her house in town, a point I am determined never to suffer her to give up; because she loves London; and because I insist on her having her own house to go to, if she should ever chance to be displeased with ours.

I am inclined to like this proposal: Temple and I will make a calculation; and, if we find it will answer every necessary purpose to my mother, I owe it to Emily to accept it.

I endeavour to persuade myself, that I am obliging my

mother, by giving her an opportunity of shewing her generosity, and of making me happy: I have been in spirits ever since she mentioned it.

I have already projected a million of improvements; have taught new streams to flow, planted ideal groves, and walked, fancy-led, in shades of my own raising.

The situation of the house is enchanting; and with all my passion for the savage luxuriance of America, I begin to find my taste return for the more mild and regular charms of my native country.

We have no Chaudières, no Montmorencis, none of those magnificent scenes on which the Canadians have a right to pride themselves; but we excel them in the lovely, the smiling; in enamelled meadows, in waving corn-fields, in gardens the boast of Europe; in every elegant art which adorns and softens human life; in all the riches and beauty which cultivation can give.

I begin to think I may be blest in the possession of my Emily, without betraying her into a state of want; we may, I begin to flatter myself, live with decency, in retirement; and, in my opinion, there are a thousand charms in retirement with those we love.

Upon the whole, I believe we shall be able to live, taking the word *live* in the sense of lovers, not of the *beau monde*, who will never allow a little country squire of four hundred pounds a year to *live*.

Time may do more for us; at least, I am of an age and temper to encourage hope.

All here are perfectly yours.

Adieu! my dear friend,

Your affectionate

ED. RIVERS

TO MRS TEMPLE, PALL MALL

LETTER 170 SILLERI, AUG. 6: The leave of absence for my father and Fitzgerald being come some weeks sooner than we expected, we propose leaving Canada in five or six days.

I am delighted with the idea of revisiting dear England, and seeing friends whom I so tenderly love: yet I feel a regret, which I had no idea I should have felt, at leaving the scenes of a thousand past pleasures; the murmuring rivulets to which Emily and I have sat listening, the sweet woods where I have walked with my little circle of friends: I have even a strong attachment to the scenes themselves, which are infinitely lovely, and speak the inimitable hand of nature which formed them: I want to transport this fairy ground to England.

I sigh when I pass any particularly charming spot; I feel a tenderness beyond what inanimate objects seem to merit.

I must pay one more visit to the naiads of Montmorenci.

Eleven at night

I am just come from the general's assembly; where, I should have told you, I was this day fortnight announced *Madame Fitzgerald*, to the great mortification of two or three cats, who had very sagaciously determined, that Fitzgerald had too much understanding ever to think of such a flirting, coquetish creature as a wife.

I was grave at the assembly to-night, in spite of all the pains I took to be otherwise: I was hurt at the idea it would probably be *the last* at which I should be; I felt a kind of concern at parting, not only with the few I loved, but with those who had till to-night been indifferent to me.

There is something affecting in the idea of *the last time* of seeing even those persons or places, for which we have no particular affection.

I go to-morrow to take leave of the nuns, at the Ursuline convent; I suppose I shall carry this melancholy idea with me there, and be hurt at seeing them too *for the last time*.

I pay visits every day amongst the peasants, who are very fond of me. I talk to them of their farms, give money to their children, and teach their wives to be good huswives: I am the idol of the country people five miles round, who declare me the most amiable, most generous woman in the world, and think it a thousand pities I should be damned.

Adieu! Say every thing for me to my sweet friends, if arrived.

7th, Eleven o'clock

I have this moment a large packet of letters for Emily from Mrs Melmoth, which I intend to take the care of myself, as I hope to be in England almost as soon as this.

Good morrow!

Yours ever, etc.

A. FITZGERALD

I am just come from visiting the nuns; they expressed great concern at my leaving Canada, and promised me their prayers on my voyage; for which proof of affection, though a good protestant, I thanked them very sincerely.

I wished exceedingly to have brought some of them away with me; my nun, as they call the amiable girl I saw take the veil, paid me the flattering tribute of a tear at parting; her fine eyes had a concern in them, which affected me extremely.

I was not less pleased with the affection the late superior, my good old country woman, expressed for me, and her regret at seeing me *for the last time*.

Surely there is no pleasure on earth equal to that of being beloved! I did not think I had been such a favourite in Canada: it is almost a pity to leave it; perhaps nobody may love me in England.

Yes, I believe Fitzgerald will; and I have a pretty party enough of friends in your family.

Adieu! I shall write a line the day we embark, by another ship, which may possibly arrive before us.

TO MRS TEMPLE, PALL MALL

LETTER 171 SILLERI, AUG. 11: We embark to-morrow, and hope to see you in less than a month, if this fine wind continues.

I am just come from Montmorenci, where I have been paying my devotions to the tutelary deities of the place *for the last time*.

I had only Fitzgerald with me; we visited every grotto on the lovely banks, where we dined; kissed every flower, raised a votive altar on the little island, poured a libation of wine to the river goddess; and, in short, did every thing which it became good heathens to do.

We stayed till day-light began to decline, which, with the idea of the *last time*, threw round us a certain melancholy solemnity; a solemnity which

"*Deepen'd the murmur of the falling floods,*
"*And breath'd a browner horror on the woods.*"

I have twenty things to do, and but a moment to do them in. Adieu!

I am called down; it is to Madame Des Roches: she is very obliging to come thus far to see me.

12th

We go on board at one; Madame Des Roches goes down with us as far as her estate, where her boat is to fetch her on shore. She has made me a present of a pair of extreme pretty bracelets; has sent your brother an elegant sword-knot, and Emily a very beautiful cross of diamonds.

I don't believe she would be sorry if we were to run away with her to England: I protest I am half inclined; it is pity such a woman should be hid all her life in the woods of Canada: besides, one might convert her you know; and, on a religious principle, a little deviation from rules is allowable.

Your brother is an admirable missionary amongst un-believing ladies: I really think I shall carry her off; if it is only for the good of her soul.

I have but one objection; if Fitzgerald should take a fancy to prefer the tender to the lively, I should be in some danger: there is something very seducing in her eyes, I assure you.

TO MRS TEMPLE, PALL MALL

LETTER 172 KAMARASKAS, AUG. 14: By Madame Des Roches, who is going on shore, I write two or three lines, to tell you we have got thus far, and have a fair wind; she will send it immediately to Quebec, to be put on board any ship going, that you may have the greater variety of chances to hear of me.

There is a French lady on board, whose superstition bids fair to amuse us; she has thrown half her little ornaments over-board for a wind, and has promised I know not how many votive offerings of the same kind to St Joseph, the patron of Canada, if we get safe to land; on which I shall only observe, that there is nothing so like ancient absurdity as modern: she has classical authority for this manner of playing the fool; Horace, when afraid on a voyage, having, if my memory quotes fair, vowed

> *"His dank and dropping weeds*
> *"To the stern god of sea."*

The boat is ready, and Madame Des Roches going; I am very unwilling to part with her; and her present concern at leaving me would be very flattering, if I did not think the remembrance of your brother had the greatest share in it.

She has wrote four or five letters to him, since she came on board, very tender ones I fancy, and destroyed them; she has at last wrote a meer complimentary kind of card, only thanking him for his offers of service; yet I see it gives her pleasure to write even this, however cold and formal; because addressed to him: she asked me, if I thought there was any impropriety in her writing to him, and whether it would not be better to address herself to Emily. I smiled at her simplicity, and she finished her letter; she blushed and looked down when she gave it me.

She is less like a sprightly French widow than a foolish English girl, who loves for the first time.

But I suppose, when the heart is really touched, the feelings of all nations have a pretty near resemblance: it is only that the French ladies are generally more coquets, and less inclined to the romantic style of love, than the English; and we are, therefore, surprized when we find in them this trembling sensibility.

There are exceptions, however, to all rules; and your little Bell seems, in point of love, to have changed countries with Madame Des Roches.

The gale increases, it flutters in the sails; my fair friend is summoned; the captain chides our delay.

Adieu! *ma chère Madame Des Roches*. I embrace her; I feel the force of its being *for the last time*. I am afraid she feels it yet more strongly than I do: in parting with the last of his friends, she seems to part with her Rivers for ever.

One look more at the wild graces of nature I leave behind.

Adieu! Canada! Adieu! sweet abode of the wood-nymphs! never shall I cease to remember with delight the place where I have passed so many happy hours.

Heaven preserve my dear Lucy, and give prosperous gales to her friends!

Your faithful

A. Fitzgerald

LETTER 173 ISLE OF BIC, AUG. 16: You are little obliged to me, my dear, for writing to you on ship-board; one of the greatest miseries here being the want of employment: I therefore write for my own amusement, not yours.

We have some French ladies on board, but they do not resemble Madame Des Roches. I am weary of them already, though we have been so few days together.

The wind is contrary, and we are at anchor under this island; Fitzgerald has proposed going to dine on shore: it looks excessively pretty from the ship.

Seven in the Evening

We are returned from Bic, after passing a very agreeable day.

We dined on the grass, at a little distance from the shore, under the shelter of a very fine wood, whose form, the trees rising above each other in the same regular confusion, brought the dear shades of Silleri to our remembrance.

We walked after dinner, and picked rasberries, in the wood; and in our ramble came unexpectedly to the middle of a visto, which, whilst some ships of war lay here, the sailors had cut through the island.

From this situation, being a rising ground, we could see directly through the avenue to both shores: the view of each was wildly majestic; the river comes finely in, whichever way you turn your sight; but to the south, which is more sheltered, the water just trembling to the breeze, our ship which had put all her streamers out, and to which the tide gave a gentle motion, with a few scattered houses, faintly seen amongst the trees at a distance, terminated the prospect, in a manner which was enchanting.

I die to build a house on this island; it is pity such a sweet spot should be uninhabited: I should like excessively to be Queen of Bic.

Fitzgerald has carved my name on a maple, near the shore; a pretty piece of gallantry in a husband, you will allow: perhaps he means it as taking possession for me of the island.

We are going to cards. Adieu! for the present.

Aug. 18

'Tis one of the loveliest days I ever saw: we are fishing under the Magdalen islands; the weather is perfectly calm, the sea just dimpled, the sun-beams dance on the waves, the fish are playing on the surface of the water: the island is at a proper distance to form an agreeable point of view; and upon the whole the scene is divine.

There is one house on the island, which, at a distance, seems so beautifully situated, that I have lost all desire of fixing at Bic: I want to land, and go to the house for milk, but there is no good landing-place on this side; the island seems here to be fenced in by a regular wall of rock.

A breeze springs up; our fishing is at an end for the present: I am afraid we shall not pass many days so agreeably as we have done this. I feel horror at the idea of so soon losing sight of land, and launching on the *vast* Atlantic.

Adieu! Yours,

A. FITZGERALD

TO MRS TEMPLE, PALL MALL

LETTER 174 AUG. 26, AT SEA: We have just fallen in with a ship from New York to London, and, as it is a calm, the master of it is come aboard; whilst he is drinking a bottle of very fine Madeira, which Fitzgerald has tempted him with on purpose to give me this opportunity, as it is possible he may arrive first, I will write a line, to tell my dear Lucy we are all well, and hope soon to have the happiness of telling her so in person; I also send what I scribbled before we lost sight of land; for I have had no spirits to write or do any thing since.

There is inexpressible pleasure in meeting a ship at sea, and renewing our commerce with the human kind, after having been so absolutely separated from them. I feel strongly at this moment the inconstancy of the species: we naturally grow tired of the company on board our own ship, and fancy the people in every one we meet more agreeable.

For my part, this spirit is so powerful in me, that I would gladly, if I could have prevailed on my father and Fitzgerald, have gone on board with this man, and pursued our voyage in the New York ship. I have felt the same thing on land in a coach, on seeing another pass.

We have had a very unpleasant passage hitherto, and weather to fright a better sailor than your friend: it is to me astonishing, that there are men found, and those men of fortune too, who can fix on a sea life as a profession.

How strong must be the love of gain, to tempt us to embrace a life of danger, pain, and misery; to give up all the beauties of nature and of art, all the charms of society, and separate ourselves from mankind, to amass wealth, which the very profession takes away all possibility of enjoying!

Even glory is a poor reward for a life passed at sea.

I had rather be a peasant on a sunny bank, with peace, safety, obscurity, bread, and a little garden of roses, than lord high admiral of the British fleet.

Setting aside the variety of dangers at sea, the time passed there is a total suspension of one's existence: I speak of the best part of our time there, for at least a third of every voyage is positive misery.

I abhor the sea, and am peevish with every creature about me.

If there were no other evil attending this vile life, only think of being cooped up weeks together in such a space, and with the same eternal set of people.

If cards had not a little relieved me, I should have died of meer vexation before I had finished half the voyage.

What would I not give to see the dear white cliffs of Albion!

Adieu! I have not time to say more.

Your affectionate

A. FITZGERALD

TO MRS TEMPLE, PALL MALL

LETTER 175 DOVER, SEPT. 8: We are this instant landed, my dear, and shall be in town to-morrow.

My father stops one day on the road, to introduce Mr Fitzgerald to a relation of ours, who lives a few miles from Canterbury.

I am wild with joy at setting foot once more on dry land.

I am not less happy to have traced your brother and Emily, by my enquiries here, for we left Quebec too soon to have advice there of their arrival.

Adieu! If in town, you shall see us the moment we get

there; if in the country, write immediately, to the care of the agent.

Let me know where to find Emily, whom I die to see: is she still Emily Montague?

Adieu!

Your affectionate

A. FITZGERALD

LETTER **176** TEMPLE-HOUSE, SEPT. II: Your letter, my dear Bell, was sent by this post to the country.

It is unnecessary to tell you the pleasure it gives us all to hear of your safe arrival.

All our argosies have now landed their treasures: you will believe us to have been more anxious about friends so dear to us, than the merchant for his gold and spices; we have suffered the greater anxiety, by the circumstance of your having returned at different times.

I flatter myself, the future will pay us for the past.

You may now, my dear Bell, revive your coterie, with the addition of some friends who love you very sincerely.

Emily (still Emily Montague) is with a relation in Berkshire, settling some affairs previous to her marriage with my brother, to which we flatter ourselves there will be no further objections.

I assure you, I begin to be a little jealous of this Emily of yours; she rivals me extremely with my mother, and indeed with every body else.

We all come to town next week, when you will make us very unhappy if you do not become one of our family in Pall Mall, and return with us for a few months to the country.

My brother is at his little estate, six miles from hence, where he is making some alterations, for the reception of Emily; he is fitting up her apartment in a style equally simple and elegant, which, however, you must not tell her, because she is to be surprized: her dressing-room, and a little adjoining closet of books, will be enchanting: yet the expence of all he has done is a meer trifle.

I am the only person in the secret; and have been with him this morning to see it: there is a gay, smiling air in the

243

whole apartment, which pleases me infinitely; you will suppose he does not forget jars of flowers, because you know how much they are Emily's taste: he has forgot no ornament which he knew was agreeable to her.

Happily for his fortune, her pleasures are not of the expensive kind; he would ruin himself if they were.

He has bespoke a very handsome post-chaise, which is also a secret to Emily, who insists on not having one.

Their income will be about five hundred pounds a year: it is not much; yet, with their dispositions, I think it will make them happy.

My brother will write to Mr Fitzgerald next post: say every thing affectionate for us to him and Captain Fermor.

Adieu! Yours,

LUCY TEMPLE

TO CAPTAIN FITZGERALD

LETTER 177 BELLFIELD, SEPT. 13: I congratulate you, my dear friend, on your safe arrival, and on your marriage.

You have got the start of me in happiness; I love you, however, too sincerely to envy you.

Emily has promised me her hand, as soon as some little family affairs are settled, which I flatter myself will not take above another week.

When she gave me this promise, she begged me to allow her to return to Berkshire till our marriage took place; I felt the propriety of this step, and therefore would not oppose it: she pleaded having some business also to settle with her relation there.

My mother has given back the deed of settlement of my estate, and accepted of an assignment on my half-pay: she is greatly a loser; but she insisted on making me happy, with such an air of tenderness, that I could not deny her that satisfaction.

I shall keep some land in my own hands, and farm; which will enable me to have a post-chaise for Emily, and my mother, who will be a good deal with us; and a constant decent table for a friend.

Emily is to superintend the dairy and garden; she has

a passion for flowers, with which I am extremely pleased, as it will be to her a continual source of pleasure.

I feel such delight in the idea of making her happy that I think nothing a trifle which can be in the least degree pleasing to her.

I could even wish to invent new pleasures for her gratification.

I hope to be happy; and to make the loveliest of womankind so, because my notions of the state, into which I am entering, are I hope just, and free from that romantic turn so destructive to happiness.

I have, once in my life, had an attachment nearly resembling marriage, to a widow of rank, with whom I was acquainted abroad; and with whom I almost secluded myself from the world near a twelve-month, when she died of a fever, a stroke I was long before I recovered.

I loved her with tenderness; but that love, compared to what I feel for Emily, was as a grain of sand to the globe of earth, or the weight of a feather to the universe.

A marriage where not only esteem, but passion is kept awake, is, I am convinced, the most perfect state of sublunary happiness: but it requires great care to keep this tender plant alive; especially, I blush to say it, on our side.

Women are naturally more constant, education improves this happy disposition: the husband who has the politeness, the attention, and delicacy of a lover, will always be beloved.

The same is generally, but not always, true on the other side: I have sometimes seen the most amiable, the most delicate of the sex, fail in keeping the affection of their husbands.

I am well aware, my friend, that we are not to expect here a life of continual rapture: in the happiest marriage there is danger of some languid moments: to avoid these, shall be my study; and I am certain they are to be avoided.

The inebriation, the tumult of passion, will undoubtedly grow less after marriage, that is, after peaceable possession; hopes and fears alone keep it in its first violent state; but, though it subsides, it gives place to a tenderness still more pleasing, to a soft, and, if you will allow the expression, a voluptuous tranquillity: the pleasure does not cease, does not even lessen; it only changes its nature.

My sister tells me, she flatters herself, you will give a few months to hers and Mr Temple's friendship; I will not give up the claim I have to the same favour.

My little farm will induce only friends to visit us; and

it is not less pleasing to me for that circumstance: one of the misfortunes of a very exalted station, is the slavery it subjects us to in regard to the ceremonial world.

Upon the whole, I believe, the most agreeable, as well as most free of all situations, to be that of a little country gentleman, who lives upon his income, and knows enough of the world not to envy his richer neighbours.

Let me hear from you, my dear Fitzgerald, and tell me, if, little as I am, I can be any way of the least use to you.

You will see Emily before I do; she is more lovely, more enchanting, than ever.

Mrs Fitzgerald will make me happy if she can invent any commands for me.

Adieu! Believe me,

Your faithful, etc.

ED. RIVERS

TO COLONEL RIVERS, AT BELLFIELD, RUTLAND

LETTER 178 LONDON, SEPT. 15: Every mark of your friendship, my dear Rivers, must be particularly pleasing to one who knows your worth as I do: I have, therefore, to thank you as well for your letter, as for those obliging offers of service, which I shall make no scruple of accepting, if I have occasion for them.

I rejoice in the prospect of your being as happy as myself: nothing can be more just than your ideas of marriage; I mean, of a marriage founded on inclination: all that you describe, I am so happy as to experience.

I never loved my sweet girl so tenderly as since she has been mine; my heart acknowledges the obligation of her having trusted the future happiness or misery of her life in my hands. She is every hour more dear to me; I value as I ought those thousand little attentions, by which a new softness is every moment given to our affection.

I do not indeed feel the same tumultuous emotion at seeing her; but I feel a sensation equally delightful: a joy more tranquil, but not less lively.

I will own to you, that I had strong prejudices against marriage, which nothing but love could have conquered; the idea of an indissoluble union deterred me from thinking of a serious engagement: I attached myself to the most seducing, most attractive of women, without thinking the pleasure I found in seeing her of any consequence: I thought her lovely, but never suspected I loved; I thought the delight I tasted in hearing her, merely the effects of those charms which all the world found in her conversation; my vanity was gratified by the flattering preference she gave me to the rest of my sex; I fancied this all, and imagined I could cease seeing the little syren whenever I pleased.

I was, however, mistaken; love stole upon me imperceptibly, and *en badinant*; I was enslaved, when I only thought myself amused.

We have not yet seen Miss Montague; we go down on Friday to Berkshire, Bell having some letters for her, which she was desired to deliver herself.

I will write to you again the moment I have seen her.

The invitation Mr and Mrs Temple have been so obliging as to give us, is too pleasing to ourselves not to be accepted; we also expect with impatience the time of visiting you at your farm.

   Adieu!

    Your affectionate

       J. FITZGERALD

TO CAPTAIN FITZGERALD

LETTER **179** STAMFORD, SEPT. 16, EVENING: Being here on some business, my dear friend, I receive your letter in time to answer it to-night.

We hope to be in town this day seven-night; and I flatter myself, my dearest Emily will not delay my happiness many days longer: I grudge you the pleasure of seeing her on Friday.

I triumph greatly in your having been seduced into matrimony, because I never knew a man more of a turn to make an agreeable husband; it was the idea that occurred to me the first moment I saw you.

Do you know, my dear Fitzgerald, that, if your little syren had not anticipated my purpose, I had designs upon you for my sister?

Through that careless, inattentive look of yours, I saw

so much right sense, and so affectionate a heart, that I wished nothing so much as that she might have attached you; and had laid a scheme to bring you acquainted, hoping the rest from the merit so conspicuous in you both.

Both are, however, so happily disposed of elsewhere, that I have no reason to regret my scheme did not succeed.

There is something in your person, as well as manner, which I am convinced must be particularly pleasing to women; with an extremely agreeable form, you have a certain manly, spirited air, which promises them a protector; a look of understanding, which is the indication of a pleasing companion; a sensibility of countenance, which speaks a friend and a lover; to which I ought to add, an affectionate, constant attention to women, and a polite indifference to men, which above all things flatters the vanity of the sex.

Of all men breathing, I should have been most afraid of you as a rival; Mrs Fitzgerald has told me, you have said the same thing of me.

Happily, however, our tastes were different; the two amiable objects of our tenderness were perhaps equally lovely; but it is not the meer form, it is the character that strikes: the fire, the spirit, the vivacity, the awakened manner, of Miss Fermor won you; whilst my heart was captivated by that bewitching languor, that seducing softness, that melting sensibility, in the air of my sweet Emily, which is, at least to me, more touching than all the sprightliness in the world.

There is in true sensibility of soul, such a resistless charm, that we are even affected by that of which we are not ourselves the object: we feel a degree of emotion at being witness to the affection which another inspires.

'Tis late, and my horses are at the door.

Adieu!

Your faithful

ED. RIVERS

TO MISS MONTAGUE, ROSE-HILL, BERKSHIRE

LETTER 180 TEMPLE-HOUSE, SEPT. 16: I have but a moment, my dearest Emily, to tell you Heaven favours your tenderness: it removes every anxiety from two of the worthiest and most gentle of human hearts.

You and my brother have both lamented to me the painful necessity you were under, of reducing my mother to a less income than that to which she had been accustomed.

An unexpected event has restored to her more than what her tenderness for my brother had deprived her of.

A relation abroad, who owed everything to her father's friendship, has sent her, as an acknowledgment of that friendship, a deed of gift, settling on her four hundred pounds a year for life.

My brother is at Stamford, and is yet unacquainted with this agreeable event.

You will hear from him next post.

Adieu! my dear Emily!

Your affectionate

L. TEMPLE

TO COLONEL RIVERS, AT BELLFIELD, RUTLAND

LETTER 181 ROSE-HILL, SEPT. 17: Can you in earnest ask such a question? can you suppose I ever felt the least degree of love for Sir George? No, my Rivers, never did your Emily feel tenderness till she saw the loveliest, the most amiable of his sex, till those eyes spoke the sentiments of a soul every idea of which was familiar to her own.

Yes, my Rivers, our souls have the most perfect resemblance: I never heard you speak without finding the feeling of my own heart developed; your conversation conveyed your Emily's ideas, but clothed in the language of angels.

I thought well of Sir George; I saw him as the man destined to be my husband; I fancied he loved me, and that gratitude obliged me to a return; carried away by the ardour of my friends for this marriage, I rather suffered than approved his addresses; I had not courage to resist the torrent, I therefore gave way to it; I loved no other, I fancied my want of affection a native coldness of temper. I felt a languid esteem, which I endeavoured to flatter myself was love; but the moment I saw you, the delusion vanished.

Your eyes, my Rivers, in one moment convinced me I had a heart; you staid some weeks with us in the country: with what transport do I recollect those pleasing moments! how did my heart beat whenever you approached me! what charms did

I find in your conversation! I heard you talk with a delight of which I was not mistress. I fancied every woman who saw you, felt the same emotions: my tenderness increased imperceptibly without my perceiving the consequence of my indulging the dear pleasure of seeing you.

I found I loved, yet was doubtful of your sentiments; my heart, however, flattered me yours was equally affected; my situation prevented an explanation; but love has a thousand ways of making himself understood.

How dear to me were those soft, those delicate attentions, which told me all you felt for me, without communicating it to others!

Do you remember that day, my Rivers, when, sitting in the little hawthorn grove, near the borders of the river, the rest of the company, of which Sir George was one, ran to look at a ship that was passing: I would have followed; you asked me to stay, by a look which it was impossible to mistake; nothing could be more imprudent than my stay, yet I had not resolution to refuse what I saw gave you pleasure: I staid; you pressed my hand, you regarded me with a look of unutterable love.

My Rivers, from that dear moment your Emily vowed never to be another's: she vowed not to sacrifice all the happiness of her life to a romantic parade of fidelity to a man whom she had been betrayed into receiving as a lover; she resolved, if necessary, to own to him the tenderness with which you had inspired her, to entreat from his esteem, from his compassion, a release from engagements which made her wretched.

My heart burns with the love of virtue, I am tremblingly alive to fame: what bitterness then must have been my portion had I first seen you when the wife of another!

Such is the powerful sympathy that unites us, that I fear, that virtue, that strong sense of honour and fame, so powerful in minds most turned to tenderness, would only have served to make more poignant the pangs of hopeless, despairing love.

How blest am I, that we met before my situation made it a crime to love you! I shudder at the idea how wretched I might have been, had I seen you a few months later.

I am just returned from a visit at a few miles distance. I find a letter from my dear Bell, that she will be here to-morrow; how do I long to see her, to talk to her of my Rivers!

I am interrupted.

Adieu! Yours,

EMILY MONTAGUE

LETTER 182 ROSE-HILL, SEPT. 18, MORNING:
I have this moment, my dear Mrs Temple's letter: she will
imagine my transport at the happy event she mentions; my dear
Rivers has, in some degree, sacrificed even filial affection to his
tenderness for me; the consciousness of this has ever cast a damp
on the pleasure I should otherwise have felt, at the prospect of
spending my life with the most excellent of mankind: I shall
now be his, without the painful reflection of having lessened the
enjoyments of the best parent that ever existed.

I should be blest indeed, my amiable friend, if I did not
suffer from my too anxious tenderness; I dread the possibility
of my becoming in time less dear to your brother; I love him
to such excess that I could not survive the loss of his affection.

There is no distress, no want, I could not bear with
delight for him; but if I lose his heart, I lose all for which life is
worth keeping.

Could I bear to see those looks of ardent love converted
into the cold glances of indifference!

You will, my dearest friend, pity a heart, whose too
great sensibility wounds itself: why should I fear? was ever
tenderness equal to that of my Rivers? can a heart like his
change from caprice? It shall be the business of my life to merit
his tenderness.

I will not give way to fears which injure him, and,
indulged, would destroy all my happiness.

I expect Mr and Mrs Fitzgerald every moment. Adieu!
Your affectionate

EMILY MONTAGUE

TO CAPTAIN FITZGERALD

LETTER 183 BELLFIELD, SEPT. 17: You say
true, my dear Fitzgerald: friendship, like love, is more the
child of sympathy than of reason; though inspired by qualities
very opposite to those which give love, it strikes like that in a
moment: like that, it is free as air, and, when constrained, loses
all its spirit.

In both, from some nameless cause, at least some cause

to us incomprehensible, the affections take fire the instant two persons, whose minds are in unison, observe each other, which, however, they may often meet without doing.

It is therefore as impossible for others to point out subjects of our friendship as love; our choice must be uninfluenced, if we wish to find happiness in either.

Cold, lifeless esteem may grow from a long tasteless acquaintance; but real affection makes a sudden and lively impression.

This impression is improved, is strengthened by time, and a more intimate knowledge of the merit of the person who makes it; but it is, it must be, spontaneous, or be nothing.

I felt this sympathy powerfully in regard to yourself; I had the strongest partiality for you before I knew how very worthy you were of my esteem.

Your countenance and manner made an impression on me, which inclined me to take your virtues upon trust.

It is not always safe to depend on these preventive feelings; but in general the face is a pretty faithful index of the mind.

I propose being in town in four or five days.

Twelve o'clock

My mother has this moment a second letter from her relation, who is coming home, and proposes a marriage between me and his daughter, to whom he will give twenty thousand pounds now, and the rest of his fortune at his death.

As Emily's fault, if love can allow her one, is an excess of romantic generosity, the fault of most uncorrupted female minds, I am very anxious to marry her before she knows of this proposal, lest she should think it a proof of tenderness to aim at making me wretched, in order to make me rich.

I therefore entreat you and Mrs Fitzgerald to stay at Rose-hill, and prevent her coming to town, till she is mine past the power of retreat.

Our relation may have mentioned his design to persons less prudent than our little party; and she may hear of it, if she is in London.

But, independently of my fear of her spirit of romance, I feel that it would be an indelicacy to let her know of this proposal at present, and look like attempting to make a merit of my refusal.

It is not to you, my dear friend, I need say the gifts of fortune are nothing to me without her for whose sake alone I

sight; but when you appeared, my heart beat, I blushed, I turned pale by turns, my eyes assumed a new softness, I trembled, and every pulse confessed the master of my soul.

My friends are come: I am called down. Adieu! Be assured your Emily never breathed a sigh but for her Rivers!

Adieu! Yours,

EMILY MONTAGUE

TO COLONEL RIVERS, BELLFIELD, RUTLAND

LETTER 186 LONDON, SEPT. 18: I have this moment your letter; we are setting out in ten minutes for Rose-hill, where I will finish this, and hope to give you a pleasing account of your Emily.

You are certainly right in keeping this proposal secret at present; depend on our silence; I could, however, wish you the fortune, were it possible to have it without the lady.

Were I to praise your delicacy on this occasion, I should injure you; it was not in your power to act differently; you are only consistent with yourself.

I am pleased with your idea of a situation: a house embosomed in the grove, where all the view is what the eye can take in, speaks a happy master, content at home; a wide-extended prospect, one who is looking abroad for happiness.

I love the country: the taste for rural scenes is the taste born with us. After seeking pleasure in vain amongst the works of art, we are forced to come back to the point from whence we set out, and find our enjoyment in the lovely simplicity of nature.

Rose-hill, Evening

I am afraid Emily knows your secret; she has been in tears almost ever since we came; the servant is going to the post-office, and I have but a moment to tell you we will stay here till your arrival, which you will hasten as much as possible.

Adieu!

Your affectionate

J. FITZGERALD

255

LETTER **187** ROSE-HILL, SEPT. 18: If I was not certain of your esteem and friendship, my dear Rivers, I should tremble at the request I am going to make you.

It is to suspend our marriage for some time, and not ask me the reason of this delay.

Be assured of my tenderness; be assured my whole soul is yours, that you are dearer to me than life, that I love you as never woman loved; that I live, I breathe but for you; that I would die to make you happy.

In what words shall I convey to the most beloved of his sex, the ardent tenderness of my soul, how convince him of what I suffer from being forced to make a request so contrary to the dictates of my heart?

He cannot, will not doubt his Emily's affection: I cannot support the idea that it is possible he should for one instant. What I suffer at this moment is inexpressible.

My heart is too much agitated to say more.

I will write again in a few days.

I know not what I would say; but indeed, my Rivers, I love you; you yourself can scarce form an idea to what excess!

Adieu! Your faithful

EMILY MONTAGUE

LETTER **188** BELLFIELD, SEPT. 20: No, Emily, you never loved; I have been long hurt by your tranquillity in regard to our marriage; your too scrupulous attention to decorum in leaving my sister's house might have alarmed me, if love had not placed a bandage before my eyes.

Cruel girl! I repeat it; you never loved; I have your friendship, but you know nothing of that ardent passion, that dear enthusiasm, which makes us indifferent to all but itself: your love is from the imagination, not the heart.

The very professions of tenderness in your last, are a proof of your consciousness of indifference; you repeat too often that you love me; you say too much; that anxiety to persuade me of your affection, shews too plainly you are sensible I have reason to doubt it.

You have placed me on the rack; a thousand fears, a thousand doubts, succeed each other in my soul. Has some happier man—

No, my Emily, distracted as I am, I will not be unjust: I do not suspect you of inconstancy; 'tis of your coldness only I complain: you never felt the lively impatience of love; or you would not condemn a man, whom you at least esteem, to suffer longer its unutterable tortures.

If there is a real cause for this delay, why conceal it from me? have I not a right to know what so nearly interests me? but what cause? are you not mistress of yourself?

My Emily, you blush to own to me the insensibility of your heart: you once fancied you loved; you are ashamed to say you were mistaken.

You cannot surely have been influenced by any motive relative to our fortune; no idle tale can have made you retract a promise, which rendered me the happiest of mankind: if I have your heart, I am richer than an oriental monarch.

Short as life is, my dearest girl, is it of consequence what part we play in it? is wealth at all essential to happiness?

The tender affections are the only sources of true pleasure; the highest, the most respectable titles, in the eye of reason, are the tender ones of friend, of husband, and of father: it is from the dear soft ties of social love your Rivers expects his felicity.

You have but one way, my dear Emily, to convince me of your tenderness: I shall set off for Rose-hill in twelve hours; you must give me your hand the moment I arrive, or confess your Rivers was never dear to you.

Write, and send a servant instantly to meet me at my mother's house in town: I cannot support the torment of suspense.

There is not on earth so wretched a being as I am at this moment; I never knew till now to what excess I loved: you must be mine, my Emily, or I must cease to live.

LETTER 189 BELLFIELD, SEPT. 20: All I feared has certainly happened; Emily has undoubtedly heard of this proposal, and, from a parade of generosity, a generosity, however, inconsistent with love, wishes to postpone our marriage till my relation arrives.

I am hurt beyond words, at the manner in which she has wrote to me on this subject; I have, in regard to Sir George, experienced that these are not the sentiments of a heart truly enamoured.

I therefore fear this romantic step is the effect of a coldness of which I thought her incapable; and that her affection is only a more lively degree of friendship, with which, I will own to you, my heart will not be satisfied.

I would engross, I would employ, I would absorb, every faculty of that lovely mind.

I have too long suffered prudence to delay my happiness: I cannot longer live without her: if she loves me, I shall on Tuesday call her mine.

Adieu! I shall be with you almost as soon as this letter.
Your affectionate
ED. RIVERS

LETTER 190 ROSE-HILL, SEPT. 21: Is it then possible? can my Rivers doubt his Emily's tenderness!

Do I only esteem you, my Rivers? can my eyes have so ill-explained the feelings of my heart?

You accuse me of not sharing your impatience: do you then allow nothing to the modesty, the blushing delicacy of my sex?

Could you see into my soul, you would cease to call me cold and insensible.

Can you forget, my Rivers, those moments, when, doubtful of the sentiments of your heart, mine every instant betrayed its weakness? when every look spoke the resistless fondness of my soul! when, lost in the delight of seeing you, I forgot I was almost the wife of another?

But I will say no more; my Rivers tells me I have already said too much: he is displeased with his Emily's tenderness; he complains, that I tell him too often I love him.

You say I can give but one certain proof of my affection.

I will give you that proof: I will be yours whenever you please, though ruin should be the consequence to both; I despise every other consideration, when my Rivers's happiness is at stake: is there any request he is capable of making, which his Emily will refuse?

You are the arbiter of my fate: I have no will but yours; yet I entreat you to believe no common cause could have made me hazard giving a moment's pain to that dear bosom: you will one time know to what excess I have loved you.

Were the empire of the world or your affection offered me, I should not hesitate one moment on the choice, even were I certain never to see you more.

I cannot form an idea of happiness equal to that of being beloved by the most amiable of mankind.

Judge then, if I would lightly wish to defer an event, which is to give me the transport of passing my life in the dear employment of making him happy.

I only entreat that you will decline asking me, till I judge proper to tell you, why I first begged our marriage might be deferred: let it be till then forgot I ever made such a request.

You will not, my dear Rivers, refuse this proof of complaisance to her who too plainly shews she can refuse you nothing.

Adieu! Yours,

EMILY MONTAGUE

TO MISS MONTAGUE, ROSE-HILL, BERKSHIRE

LETTER 191 CLARGES STREET, SEPT. 21, TWO O'CLOCK: Can you, my angel, forgive my insolent impatience, and attribute it to the true cause, excess of love?

Could I be such a monster as to blame my sweet Emily's dear expressions of tenderness? I hate myself for being capable of writing such a letter.

Be assured, I will strictly comply with all she desires: what condition is there on which I would not make the loveliest of women mine?

I will follow the servant in two hours; I shall be at Rose-hill by eight o'clock.

Adieu! my dearest Emily!

Your faithful

ED. RIVERS

LETTER 192 SEPT. 21, NINE AT NIGHT: The loveliest of women has consented to make me happy: she remonstrated, she doubted; but her tenderness conquered all her reluctance. To-morrow I shall call her mine.

We shall set out immediately for your house, where we hope to be the next day to dinner: you will therefore postpone your journey to town a week, at the end of which we intend going to Bellfield. Captain Fermor and Mrs Fitzgerald accompany us down. Emily's relation, Mrs H——, has business which prevents her; and Fitzgerald is obliged to stay another month in town, to transact the affair of his majority.

Never did Emily look so lovely as this evening: there is a sweet confusion, mixed with tenderness, in her whole look and manner, which is charming beyond all expression.

Adieu! I have not a moment to spare: even this absence from her is treason to love. Say every thing for me to my mother and Lucy.

Yours,

ED. RIVERS

LETTER 193 ROSE-HILL, SEPT. 22, TEN O'CLOCK: She is mine, my dear Temple; and I am happy almost above mortality.

I cannot paint to you her loveliness; the grace, the dignity, the mild majesty of her air, is formed by a smile like that of angels: her eyes have a tender sweetness, her cheeks a blush of refined affection, which must be seen to be imagined.

I envy Captain Fermor the happiness of being in the same chaise with her; I shall be very bad company to Bell, who insists on my being her *cecisbeo* for the journey.

Adieu! The chaises are at the door.

Your affectionate

ED. RIVERS

TO CAPTAIN FITZGERALD

LETTER **194** TEMPLE-HOUSE, SEPT. 29: I regret your not being with us, more than I can express.

I would have every friend I love a witness of my happiness.

I thought my tenderness for Emily as great as man could feel, yet find it every moment increase; every moment she is more dear to my soul.

The angel delicacy of that lovely mind is inconceivable; had she no other charm, I should adore her: what a lustre does modesty throw round beauty!

We remove to-morrow to Bellfield: I am impatient to see my sweet girl in her little empire: I am tired of the continual crowd in which we live at Temple's: I would not pass the life he does for all his fortune: I sigh for the power of spending my time as I please, for the dear shades of retirement and friendship.

How little do mankind know their own happiness! every pleasure worth a wish is in the power of almost all mankind.

Blind to true joy, ever engaged in a wild pursuit of what is always in our power, anxious for that wealth which we falsely imagine necessary to our enjoyments, we suffer our best hours to pass tastelessly away; we neglect the pleasures which are suited to our natures; and, intent on ideal schemes of establishments at which we never arrive, let the dear hours of social delight escape us.

Hasten to us, my dear Fitzgerald: we want only you, to fill our little circle of friends.

Your affectionate

ED. RIVERS

LETTER 195 BELLFIELD, OCT. 3: What delight is there in obliging those we love!

My heart dilated with joy at seeing Emily pleased with the little embellishments of her apartment, which I had made as gay and smiling as the morn; it looked, indeed, as if the hand of love had adorned it: she has a dressing-room and closet of books, into which I shall never intrude; there is a pleasure in having some place which we can say is peculiarly our own, some *sanctum sanctorum*, whither we can retire even from those most dear to us.

This is a pleasure in which I have been indulged almost from infancy, and therefore one of the first I thought of procuring for my sweet Emily.

I told her I should, however, sometimes expect to be amongst her guests in this little retirement.

Her look, her tender smile, the speaking glance of grateful love, gave me a transport, which only minds turned to affection can conceive. I never, my dear Fitzgerald, was happy before: the attachment I once mentioned was pleasing; but I felt a regret, at knowing the object of my tenderness had forfeited the good opinion of the world, which embittered all my happiness.

She possessed my esteem, because I knew her heart; but I wanted to see her esteemed by others.

With Emily I enjoy this pleasure in its utmost extent: she is the adoration of all who see her; she is equally admired, esteemed, respected.

She seems to value the admiration she excites, only as it appears to gratify the pride of her lover; what transport, when all eyes are fixed on her, to see her searching around for mine, and attentive to no other object, as if insensible to all other approbation!

I enjoy the pleasures of friendship as well as those of love: were you here, my dear Fitzgerald, we should be the happiest groupe on the globe; but all Bell's sprightliness cannot preserve her from an air of chagrin in your absence.

Come as soon as possible, my dear friend, and leave us nothing to wish for.

Adieu!

Your affectionate

ED. RIVERS

LETTER **196** LONDON, OCT. 8: You are very cruel, my dear Rivers, to tantalize me with your pictures of happiness.

Notwithstanding this spite, I am sorry I must break in on your groupe of friends; but it is absolutely necessary for Bell and my father to return immediately to town, in order to settle some family business, previous to my purchase of the majority.

Indeed, I am not very fond of letting Bell stay long amongst you; for she gives me such an account of your attention and complaisance to Mrs Rivers, that I am afraid she will think me a careless fellow when we meet again.

You seem in the high road, not only to spoil your own wife, but mine too; which it is certainly my affair to prevent.

Say every thing for me to the ladies of your family.

Adieu! Your affectionate

J. FITZGERALD

LETTER **197** BELLFIELD, SEPT. 10: You are a malicious fellow, Fitzgerald, and I am half inclined to keep the sweet Bell by force; take all the men away if you please, but I cannot bear the loss of a woman, especially of such a woman.

If I was not more a lover than a husband, I am not sure I should not wish to take my revenge.

To make me happy, you must place me in a circle of females, all as pleasing as those now with me, and turn every male creature out of the house.

I am a most intolerable monopolizer of the sex; in short, I have very little relish for any conversation but theirs: I love their sweet prattle beyond all the sense and learning in the world.

Not that I would insinuate they have less understanding than we, or are less capable of learning, or even that it less becomes them.

On the contrary, all such knowledge as tends to adorn

263

and soften human life and manners, is, in my opinion, peculiarly becoming in women.

You don't deserve a longer letter.
Adieu! Yours,

ED. RIVERS

LETTER 198 BELLFIELD, OCT. 12: I am very conscious, my dear Bell, of not meriting the praises my Rivers lavishes on me, yet the pleasure I receive from them is not the less lively for that consideration; on the contrary, the less I deserve these praises, the more flattering they are to me, as the stronger proofs of his love; of that love which gives ideal charms, which adorns, which embellishes its object.

I had rather be lovely in his eyes, than in those of all mankind; or, to speak more exactly, if I continue to please him, the admiration of all the world is indifferent to me: it is for his sake alone I wish for beauty, to justify the dear preference he has given me.

How pleasing are these sweet shades! were they less so, my Rivers's presence would give them every charm: every object has appeared to me more lovely since the dear moment when I first saw him; I seem to have acquired a new existence from his tenderness.

You say true, my dear Bell: Heaven doubtless formed us to be happy even in this world; and we obey its dictates in being so, when we can without encroaching on the happiness of others.

This lesson is, I think, plain from the book Providence has spread before us: the whole universe smiles, the earth is clothed in lively colours, the animals are playful, the birds sing: in being chearful with innocence, we seem to conform to the order of nature, and the will of that beneficent Power to whom we owe our being.

If the Supreme Creator had meant us to be gloomy, he would, it seems to me, have clothed the earth in black, not in that lively green, which is the livery of chearfulness and joy.

I am called away.
Adieu! my dearest Bell.
Your faithful

EMILY RIVERS

LETTER 199 BELLFIELD, OCT. 14: You flatter me most agreeably, my dear Fitzgerald, by praising Emily; I want you to see her again; she is every hour more charming: I am astonished any man can behold her without love.

Yet, lovely as she is, her beauty is her least merit; the finest understanding, the most pleasing kind of knowledge, tenderness, sensibility, modesty, and truth, adorn her almost with rays of divinity.

She has, beyond all I ever saw in either sex, the polish of the world, without having lost that sweet simplicity of manner, that unaffected innocence, and integrity of heart, which are so very apt to evaporate in a crowd.

I ride out often alone, in order to have the pleasure of returning to her: these little absences give new spirit to our tenderness. Every care forsakes me at the sight of this temple of real love; my sweet Emily meets me with smiles; her eyes brighten when I approach; she receives my friends with the most lively pleasure, because they are my friends; I almost envy them her attention, though given for my sake.

Elegant in her dress and house, she is all transport when any little ornament of either pleases me; but what charms me most, is her tenderness for my mother, in whose heart she rivals both me and Lucy.

My happiness, my friend, is beyond every idea I had formed; were I a little richer, I should not have a wish remaining.

Do not, however, imagine this wish takes from my felicity.

I have enough for myself, I have even enough for Emily; love makes us indifferent to the parade of life.

But I have not enough to entertain my friends as I wish, nor to enjoy the god-like pleasure of beneficence.

We shall be obliged, in order to support the little appearance necessary to our connexions, to give an attention rather too strict to our affairs; even this, however, our affection for each other will make easy to us.

My whole soul is so taken up with this charming woman, I am afraid I shall become tedious even to you; I must learn to restrain my tenderness, and write on common subjects.

I am more and more pleased with the way of life I have chose; and, were my fortune ever so large, would pass the greatest part of the year in the country: I would only enlarge my house, and fill it with friends.

My situation is a very fine one, though not like the magnificent scenes to which we have been accustomed in Canada: the house stands on the sunny side of a hill, at the foot of which, the garden intervening, runs a little trout stream, which to the right seems to be lost in an island of oziers, and over which is a rustic bridge into a very beautiful meadow, where at present graze a numerous flock of sheep.

Emily is planning a thousand embellishments for the garden, and will next year make it a wilderness of sweets, a paradise worthy its lovely inhabitant: she is already forming walks and flowery arbours in the wood, and giving the whole scene every charm which taste, at little expence, can bestow.

I, on my side, am selecting spots for plantations of trees; and mean, like a good citizen, to serve at once myself and the public, by raising oaks, which may hereafter bear the British thunder to distant lands.

I believe we country gentlemen, whilst we have spirit to keep ourselves independent, are the best citizens, as well as subjects, in the world.

Happy ourselves, we wish not to destroy the tranquillity of others; intent on cares equally useful and pleasing, with no views but to improve our fortunes by means equally profitable to ourselves and to our country, we form no schemes of dishonest ambition; and therefore disturb no government to serve our private designs.

It is the profuse, the vicious, the profligate, the needy, who are the Clodios and Catilines of this world.

That love of order, of moral harmony, so natural to virtuous minds, to minds at ease, is the strongest tie of rational obedience.

The man who feels himself prosperous and happy, will not easily be persuaded by factious declamation that he is undone.

Convinced of the excellency of our constitution, in which liberty and prerogative are balanced with the steadiest hand, he will not endeavour to remove the boundaries which secure both: he will not endeavour to root it up, whilst he is pretending to give it nourishment: he will not strive to cut down the lovely and venerable tree under whose shade he enjoys security and peace.

In short, and I am sure you will here be of my opinion, the man who has competence, virtue, true liberty, and the woman he loves, will chearfully obey the laws which secure him these blessings, and the prince under whose mild sway he enjoys them.

      Adieu!

Your faithful

ED. RIVERS

TO CAPTAIN FITZGERALD

LETTER **200**   OCT. 17: I every hour see more strongly, my dear Fitzgerald, the wisdom, as to our own happiness, of not letting our hearts be worn out by a multitude of intrigues before marriage.

Temple loves my sister, he is happy with her; but his happiness is by no means of the same kind with yours and mine; she is beautiful, and he thinks her so; she is amiable, and he esteems her; he prefers her to all other women, but he feels nothing of that trembling delicacy of sentiment, that quick sensibility, which gives to love its most exquisite pleasures, and which I would not give up for the wealth of worlds.

His affection is meer passion, and therefore subject to change; ours is that heartfelt tenderness, which time renders every moment more pleasing.

The tumult of desire is the fever of the soul; its health, that delicious tranquillity where the heart is gently moved, not violently agitated; that tranquillity which is only to be found where friendship is the basis of love, and where we are happy without injuring the object beloved: in other words, in a marriage of choice.

In the voyage of life, passion is the tempest, love the gentle gale.

Dissipation, and a continual round of amusements at home, will probably secure my sister all of Temple's heart which remains; but his love would grow languid in that state of retirement, which would have a thousand charms for minds like ours.

I will own to you, I have fears for Lucy's happiness.

But let us drop so painful a subject.

      Adieu!

Your affectionate

ED. RIVERS

LETTER 201 OCT. 19: Nothing, my dear Rivers, shews the value of friendship more than the envy it excites.

The world will sooner pardon us any advantage, even wealth, genius, or beauty, than that of having a faithful friend; every selfish bosom swells with envy at the sight of those social connexions, which are the cordials of life, and of which our narrow prejudices alone prevent our enjoyment.

Those who have neither hearts to feel this generous affection, nor merit to deserve it, hate all who are in this respect happier· than themselves; they look on a friend as an invaluable blessing, and a blessing out of their reach; and abhor all who possess the treasure for which they sigh in vain.

For my own part, I had rather be the dupe of a thousand false professions of friendship, than, for fear of being deceived, give up the pursuit.

Dupes are happy at least for a time; but the cold, narrow, suspicious heart never knows the glow of social pleasure.

In the same proportion as we lose our confidence in the virtues of others, we lose our proper happiness.

The observation of this mean jealousy, so humiliating to human nature, has influenced Lord Halifax, in his Advice to a Daughter, the school of art, prudery, and selfish morals, to caution her against all friendships, or, as he calls them, *dearnesses*, as what will make the world envy and hate her.

After my sweet Bell's tenderness, I know no pleasure equal to your friendship; nor would I give it up for the revenue of an eastern monarch.

I esteem Temple, I love his conversation; he is gay and amusing; but I shall never have for him the affection I feel for you.

I think you are too apprehensive in regard to your sister's happiness: he loves her, and there is a certain variety in her manner, a kind of agreeable caprice, that I think will secure the heart of a man of his turn, much more than her merit, or even the loveliness of her person.

She is handsome, exquisitely so; handsomer than Bell, and, if you will allow me to say so, than Emily.

I mean, that she is so in the eye of a painter; for in that of a lover his mistress is the only beautiful object on earth.

I allow your sister to be very lovely, but I think Bell more desirable a thousand times; and, rationally speaking, she who has, *as to me*, the art of inspiring the most tenderness is, *as to me*, to all intents and purposes the most beautiful woman.

In which faith I chuse to live and die.

I have an idea, Rivers, that you and I shall continue to be happy: a real sympathy, a lively taste, mixed with esteem, led us to marry; the delicacy, tenderness, and virtue, of the two most charming of women, promise to keep our love alive.

We have both strong affections: both love the conversation of women; and neither of our hearts are depraved by ill-chosen connexions with the sex.

I am broke in upon, and must bid you adieu!

Your affectionate

J. FITZGERALD

Bell is writing to you. I shall be jealous.

TO COLONEL RIVERS, BELLFIELD, RUTLAND

LETTER 202 LONDON, OCT. 19: I die to come to Bellfield again, my dear Rivers; I have a passion for your little wood; it is a mighty pretty wood for an English wood, but nothing to your Montmorencis; the dear little Silleri too—

But to return to the shades of Bellfield: your little wood is charming indeed; not to particularize detached pieces of your scenery, the *tout ensemble* is very inviting; observe, however, I have no notion of paradise without an Adam, and therefore shall bring Fitzgerald with me next time.

What could induce you, with this sweet little retreat, to cross that vile ocean to Canada? I am astonished at the madness of mankind, who can expose themselves to pain, misery, and danger; and range the world from motives of avarice and ambition, when the rural cot, the fanning gale, the clear stream, and flowery bank, offer such delicious enjoyments at home.

You men are horrid, rapacious animals, with your spirit of enterprize, and your nonsense: ever wanting more land than you can cultivate, and more money than you can spend.

That eternal pursuit of gain, that rage of accumulation, in which you are educated, corrupts your hearts, and robs you of half the pleasures of life.

269

I should not, however, make so free with the sex, if you and my *caro sposo* were not exceptions.

You two have really something of the sensibility and generosity of women.

Do you know, Rivers, I have a fancy you and Fitzgerald will always be happy husbands? this is something owing to yourselves, and something to us; you have both that manly tenderness, and true generosity, which inclines you to love creatures who have paid you the compliment of making their happiness or misery depend entirely on you, and partly to the little circumstance of your being married to two of the most agreeable women breathing.

To speak *en philosophe*, my dear Rivers, you are not to be told, that the fire of love, like any other fire, is equally put out by too much or too little fuel.

Now Emily and I, without vanity, besides our being handsome and amazingly sensible, to say nothing of our pleasing kind of sensibility, have a certain just idea of causes and effects, with a natural blushing reserve, and bridal delicacy, which I am apt to flatter myself——

Do you understand me, Rivers? I am not quite clear I understand myself.

All that I would insinuate is, that Emily and I are, take us for all in all, the two most charming women in the world, and that, whoever leaves us, must change immensely for the worse.

I believe Lucy equally pleasing, but I think her charms have not so good a subject to work upon.

Temple is a handsome fellow, and loves her; but he has not the tenderness of heart that I so much admire in two certain youths of my acquaintance.

He is rich indeed; but who cares?

Certainly, my dear Rivers, nothing can be more absurd, or more destructive to happiness, than the very wrong turn we give our children's imaginations about marriage.

If miss and master are good, she is promised a rich husband, and a coach and six, and he a wife with a monstrous great fortune.

Most of these fine promises must fail; and where they do not, the poor things have only the consolation of finding, when too late to retreat, that the objects to which all their wishes were pointed have really nothing to do with happiness.

Is there a nabobess on earth half as happy as the two foolish little girls about whom I have been writing, though

270

married to such poor devils as you and Fitzgerald? *Certainement* no.

And so ends my sermon.

Adieu!

Your most obedient,

A. FITZGERALD

LETTER 203 BELLFIELD, OCT. 21: You ridicule my enthusiasm, my dear Temple, without considering there is no exertion of the human mind, no effort of the understanding, imagination, or heart, without a spark of this divine fire.

Without enthusiasm, genius, virtue, pleasure, even love itself, languishes; all that refines, adorns, softens, exalts, ennobles life, has its source in this animating principle.

I glory in being an enthusiast in every thing; but in nothing so much as in my tenderness for this charming woman.

I am a perfect Quixote in love, and would storm enchanted castles, and fight giants, for my Emily.

Coldness of temper damps every spring that moves the human heart; it is equally an enemy to pleasure, riches, fame, to all which is worth living for.

I thank you for your wishes that I was rich, but am by no means anxious myself on the subject.

You sons of fortune, who possess your thousands a year, and find them too little for your desires, desires which grow from that very abundance, imagine every man miserable who wants them; in which you are greatly mistaken.

Every real pleasure is within the reach of my little fortune, and I am very indifferent about those which borrow their charms, not from nature, but from fashion and caprice.

My house is indeed less than yours; but it is finely situated, and large enough for my fortune: that part of it which belongs peculiarly to my Emily is elegant.

I have an equipage, not for parade but use; and the loveliest of women prefers it with me to all that luxury and magnificence could bestow with another.

The flowers in my garden bloom as fair, the peach glows as deep, as in yours: does a flower blush more lovely, or smell more sweet; a peach look more tempting than its fellows,

I select it for my Emily, who receives it with delight, as the tender tribute of love.

In some respects, we are the more happy for being less rich: the little avocations, which our mediocrity of fortune makes necessary to both, are the best preventives of that languor, from being too constantly together, which is all that love founded on taste and friendship has to fear.

Had I my choice, I should wish for a very small addition only to my income, and that for the sake of others, not myself.

I love pleasure, and think it our duty to make life as agreeable as is consistent with what we owe to others; but a true pleasurable philosopher seeks his enjoyments where they are really to be found; not in the gratifications of a childish pride, but of those affections which are born with us, and which are the only rational sources of enjoyment.

When I am walking in these delicious shades with Emily; when I see those lovely eyes, softened with artless fondness, and hear the music of that voice; when a thousand trifles, unobserved but by the prying sight of love, betray all the dear sensations of that bosom, where truth and delicate tenderness have fixed their seat, I know not the Epicurean of whom I do not deserve to be the envy.

Does your fortune, my dear Temple, make you more than happy? if not, why so very earnestly wish an addition to mine? believe me, there is nothing about which I am more indifferent. I am ten times more anxious to get the finest collection of flowers in the world for my Emily.

You observe justly, that there is nothing so insipid as women who have conversed with women only; let me add, nor so brutal as men who have lived only amongst men.

The desire of pleasing on each side, in an intercourse enlivened by taste, and governed by delicacy and honour, calls forth all the graces of the person and understanding, all the amiable sentiments of the heart: it also gives good-breeding, ease, and a certain awakened manner, which is not to be acquired but in mixed conversation.

Remember, you and my dear Lucy dine with us to-morrow; it is to be a little family party, to indulge my mother in the delight of seeing her children about her, without interruption: I have saved all my best fruit for this day; we are to drink tea and sup in Emily's apartment.

Adieu! Your affectionate

ED. RIVERS

I will to-morrow shew you better grapes than any you have at Temple-house: you rich men fancy nobody has any thing good but yourselves; but I hope next year to shew you that you are mistaken in a thousand instances. I will have such roses and jessamines, such bowers of intermingled sweets —— you shall see what astonishing things Emily's taste and my industry can do.

TO MRS FITZGERALD

LETTER 204 BELLFIELD, OCT. 22: Finish your business, my dear girl, and let us see you again at Bellfield. I need not tell you the pleasure Mr Fitzgerald's accompanying you will give us.

I die to see you, my dear Bell; it is not enough to be happy, unless I have somebody to tell every moment that I am so: I want a confidante of my tenderness, a friend like my Bell, indulgent to all my follies, to talk to of the loveliest and most beloved of mankind. I want to tell you a thousand little instances of that ardent, that refined affection, which makes all the happiness of my life! I want to paint the flattering attention, the delicate fondness of that dear lover, who is only the more so for being a husband.

You are the only woman on earth to whom I can, without the appearance of insult, talk of my Rivers, because you are the only one I ever knew as happy as myself.

Fitzgerald, in the tenderness and delicacy of his mind, resembles strongly——

I am interrupted: Adieu! for a moment.

It was my Rivers, he brought me a bouquet; I opened the door, supposing it was my mother; conscious of what I had been writing, I was confused at seeing him; he smiled, and guessing the reason of my embarrassment, "I must leave you, Emily; you are writing, and, by your blushes, I know you have been talking of your lover."

I should have told you, he insists on never seeing the letters I write, and gives this reason for it: That he should be a great loser by seeing them, as it would restrain my pen when I talk of him.

I believe, I am very foolish in my tenderness; but you will forgive me.

273

Rivers yesterday was throwing flowers at me and Lucy, in play, as we were walking in the garden; I catched a wall-flower, and, by an involuntary impulse, kissed it, and placed it in my bosom.

He observed me, and his look of pleasure and affection is impossible to be described. What exquisite pleasure there is in these agreeable follies!

He is the sweetest trifler in the world, my dear Bell: but in what does he not excel all mankind!

As the season of autumnal flowers is almost over, he is sending for all those which blow early in the spring: he prevents every wish his Emily can form.

Did you ever, my dear, see so fine an autumn as this? you will, perhaps, smile when I say, I never saw one so pleasing; such a season is more lovely than even the spring: I want you down before this agreeable weather is all over.

I am going to air with my mother; my Rivers attends us on horseback; you cannot think how amiable his attention is to both.

Adieu! my dear; my mother has sent to let me know she is ready.

Your affectionate

EMILY RIVERS

TO CAPTAIN FITZGERALD

LETTER 205 BELLFIELD, OCT. 24: Some author has said, "The happiness of the next world, to the virtuous, will consist in enjoying the society of minds like their own."

Why then should we not do our best to possess as much as possible of this happiness here?

You will see this is a preface to a very earnest request to see Captain Fermor and the lovely Bell immediately at our farm: take notice, I will not admit even business as an excuse much longer.

I am just come from a walk in the wood behind the house, with my mother and Emily; I want you to see it before it loses all its charms; in another fortnight, its present variegated foliage will be literally *humbled in the dust*.

There is something very pleasing in this season, if it did not give us the idea of the winter, which is approaching too fast.

The dryness of the air, the soft western breeze, the tremulous motion of the falling leaves, the rustling of those already fallen under our feet, their variety of lively colours, give a certain spirit and agreeable fluctuation to the scene, which is unspeakably pleasing.

By the way, we people of warm imaginations have vast advantages over others; we scorn to be confined to present scenes, or to give attention to such trifling objects as times and seasons.

I already anticipate the spring; see the woodbines and wild roses bloom in my grove, and almost catch the gale of perfume.

Twelve o'clock

I have this moment received your letter.

I am sorry for what you tell me of Miss H——; whose want of art has led her into indiscretions.

'Tis too common to see the most innocent, nay, even the most laudable actions censured by the world; as we cannot, however, eradicate the prejudices of others, it is wisdom to yield to them in things which are indifferent.

One ought to conform to, and respect the customs, as well as the laws and religion of our country, where they are not contrary to virtue, and to that moral sense which Heaven has imprinted on our souls; where they are contrary, every generous mind will despise them.

I agree with you, my dear friend, that two persons who love, not only *seem*, but really are, handsomer to each other than to the rest of the world.

When we look at those we ardently love, a new softness steals unperceived into the eyes, the countenance is more animated, and the whole form has that air of tender languor which has such charms for sensible minds.

To prove the truth of this, my Emily approaches, fair as the rising morn, led by the hand of the Graces; she sees her lover, and every charm is redoubled; an involuntary smile, a blush of pleasure, speak a passion, which is the pride of my soul.

Even her voice, melodious as it is by nature, is softened when she addresses her happy Rivers.

She comes to ask my attendance on her and my mother; they are going to pay a morning visit a few miles off.

Adieu! tell the little Bell I kiss her hand.

Your affectionate

ED. RIVERS

LETTER 206 THREE O'CLOCK: We are returned, and have met with an adventure, which I must tell you.

About six miles from home, at the entrance of a small village, as I was riding very fast, a little before the chaise, a boy about four years old, beautiful as a Cupid, came out of a cottage on the right-hand, and, running cross the road, fell almost under my horse's feet.

I threw myself off in a moment; and snatching up the child, who was, however, unhurt, carried him to the house.

I was met at the door by a young woman, plainly drest; but of a form uncommonly elegant; she had seen the child fall, and her terror for him was plainly marked in her countenance; she received him from me, pressed him to her bosom, and, without speaking, melted into tears.

My mother and Emily had by this time reached the cottage; the humanity of both was too much interested to let them pass: they alighted, came into the house, and enquired about the child, with an air of tenderness which was not lost on the young person, whom we supposed his mother.

She appeared about two-and-twenty, was handsome, with an air of the world, which the plainness of her dress could not hide; her countenance was pensive, with a mixture of sensibility which instantly prejudiced us all in her favour; her look seemed to say, she was unhappy, and that she deserved to be otherwise.

Her manner was respectful, but easy and unconstrained; polite, without being servile; and she acknowledged the interest we all seemed to take in what related to her, in a manner that convinced us she deserved it.

Though every thing about us, the extreme neatness, the elegant simplicity of her house and little garden, her own person, that of the child, both perfectly genteel, her politeness, her air of the world, in a cottage like that of the meanest labourer, tended to excite the most lively curiosity; neither good-breeding, humanity, nor the respect due to those who appear unfortunate, would allow us to make any enquiries: we left the place full of this adventure, convinced of the merit, as well as unhappiness, of its fair inhabitant, and resolved to find out, if possible, whether her misfortunes were of a kind to be alleviated, and within our little power to alleviate.

I will own to you, my dear Fitzgerald, I at that moment felt the smallness of my fortune: and I believe Emily had the same sensations, though her delicacy prevented her naming them to me, who have made her poor.

We can talk of nothing but the stranger; and Emily is determined to call on her again to-morrow, on pretence of enquiring after the health of the child.

I tremble lest her story, for she certainly has one, should be such as, however it may entitle her to compassion, may make it impossible for Emily to shew it in the manner she seems to wish.

Adieu!

Your faithful

ED. RIVERS

TO CAPTAIN FITZGERALD

LETTER 207 BELLFIELD, OCT. 24: We have been again at the cottage; and are more convinced than ever, that this amiable girl is not in the station in which she was born; we staid two hours, and varied the conversation in a manner which, in spite of her extreme modesty, made it impossible for her to avoid shewing she had been educated with uncommon care: her style is correct and elegant; her sentiments noble, yet unaffected; we talked of books, she said little on the subject; but that little shewed a taste which astonished us.

Anxious as we are to know her true situation, in order, if she merits it, to endeavour to serve her, yet delicacy made it impossible for us to give the least hint of a curiosity which might make her suppose we entertained ideas to her prejudice.

She seemed greatly affected with the humane concern Emily expressed for the child's danger yesterday, as well as with the polite and even affectionate manner in which she appeared to interest herself in all which related to her; Emily made her general offers of service with a timid kind of softness in her air, which seemed to speak rather a person asking a favour than wishing to confer an obligation.

She thanked my sweet Emily with a look of surprize and gratitude to which it is not easy to do justice; there was, however, an embarrassment in her countenance at those offers, which a little alarms me; she absolutely declined coming to Bellfield: I know not what to think.

Emily, who has taken a strong prejudice in her favour

will answer for her conduct with her life; but I will own to you, I am not without my doubts.

When I consider the inhuman arts of the abandoned part of one sex, and the romantic generosity and too unguarded confidence, of the most amiable ot the other; when I reflect that where women love, they love without reserve; that they fondly imagine the man who is dear to them possessed of every virtue; that their very integrity of mind prevents their suspicions; when I think of her present retirement, so apparently ill-suited to her education; when I see her beauty, her elegance of person, with that tender and melancholy air, so strongly expressive of the most exquisite sensibility; when, in short, I see the child, and I observe her fondness for him, I have fears for her, which I cannot conquer.

I am as firmly convinced as Emily of the goodness of her heart; but I am not so certain that even that very goodness may not have been, from an unhappy concurrence of circumstances, her misfortune.

We have company to dine.

Adieu! till the evening.

Ten at night

About three hours ago, Emily received the inclosed, from our fair cottager.

Adieu!

Your affectionate

ED. RIVERS

"To Mrs Rivers

"Madam,

"Though I have every reason to wish the melancholy event which brought me here, might continue unknown; yet your generous concern for a stranger, who had no recommendation to your notice but her appearing unhappy, and whose suspicious situation would have injured her in a mind less noble than yours, has determined me to lay before you a story, which it was my resolution to conceal for ever.

"I saw, Madam, in your countenance, when you honoured me by calling at my house this morning, and I saw with an admiration no words can speak, the amiable struggle between the desire of knowing the nature of my distress in order to soften it, and the delicacy which forbad your enquiries, lest they should wound my sensibility and self-love.

"To such a heart I run no hazard in relating what in

the world would, perhaps, draw on me a thousand reproaches; reproaches, however, I flatter myself, undeserved.

"You have had the politeness to say, there is something in my appearance which speaks my birth above my present situation: in this, Madam, I am so happy as not to deceive your generous partiality.

"My father, who was an officer of family and merit, had the misfortune to lose my mother whilst I was an infant.

"He had the goodness to take on himself the care of directing my education, and to have me taught whatever he thought becoming my sex, though at an expence much too great for his income.

"As he had little more than his commission, his parental tenderness got so far the better of his love for his profession, that, when I was about fifteen, he determined on quitting the army, in order to provide better for me; but, whilst he was in treaty for this purpose, a fever carried him off in a few days, and left me to the world, with little more than five hundred pounds, which, however, was, by his will, immediately in my power.

"I felt too strongly the loss of this excellent parent to attend to any other consideration; and, before I was enough myself to think what I was to do for a subsistence, a friend of my own age, whom I tenderly loved, who was just returning from school to her father's, in the north of England, insisted on my accompanying her, and spending some time with her in the country.

"I found in my dear Sophia, all the consolation my grief could receive; and, at her pressing solicitation, and that of her father, who saw his daughter's happiness depended on having me with her, I continued there three years, blest in the calm delights of friendship, and those blameless pleasures, with which we should be too happy, if the heart could content itself, when a young baronet, whose form was as lovely as his soul was dark, came to interrupt our felicity.

"My Sophia, at a ball, had the misfortune to attract his notice; she was rather handsome, though without regular features; her form was elegant and feminine, and she had an air of youth, of softness, of sensibility, of blushing innocence, which seemed intended to inspire delicate passions alone, and which would have disarmed any mind less depraved than that of the man, who only admired to destroy.

"She was the rose-bud yet impervious to the sun.

"Her heart was tender, but had never met an object which seemed worthy of it; her sentiments were disinterested, and romantic to excess.

279

"Her father was, at that time, in Holland, whither the death of a relation, who had left him a small estate, had called him: we were alone, unprotected, delivered up to the unhappy inexperience of youth, mistresses of our own conduct; myself, the eldest of the two, but just eighteen, when my Sophia's ill-fate conducted Sir Charles Verville to the ball where she first saw him.

"He danced with her, and endeavoured to recommend himself by all those little unmeaning, but flattering attentions, by which our credulous sex are so often misled; his manner was tender, yet timid, modest, respectful; his eyes were continually fixed on her, but when he met hers, artfully cast down, as if afraid of offending.

"He asked permission to enquire after her health the next day; he came, he was enchanting, polite, lively, soft, insinuating, adorned with every outward grace which could embellish virtue, or hide vice from view; to see and to love him was almost the same thing.

"He entreated leave to continue his visits, which he found no difficulty in obtaining: during two months, not a day passed without our seeing him; his behaviour was such as would scarce have alarmed the most suspicious heart; what then could be expected of us, young, sincere, totally ignorant of the world, and strongly prejudiced in favour of a man, whose conversation spoke his soul the abode of every virtue?

"Blushing I must own, nothing but the apparent preference he gave to my lovely friend, could have saved my heart from being a prey to the same tenderness which ruined her.

"He addressed her with all the specious arts which vice could invent to seduce innocence; his respect, his esteem, seemed equal to his passion; he talked of honour, of the delight of an union where the tender affections alone were consulted; wished for her father's return, to ask her of him in marriage; pretended to count impatiently the hours of his absence, which delayed his happiness: he even prevailed on her to write her father an account of his addresses.

"New to love, my Sophia's young heart too easily gave way to the soft impression; she loved, she idolized this most base of mankind; she would have thought it a kind of sacrilege to have had any will in opposition to his.

"After some months of unremitted assiduity, her father being expected in a few days, he dropped a hint, as if by accident, that he wished his fortune less, that he might be the more certain he was loved for himself alone; he blamed himself for this delicacy, but charged it on excess of love; vowed he would rather die than injure her, yet wished to be convinced her fondness was without reserve.

"Generous, disinterested, eager to prove the excess and sincerity of her passion, she fell into the snare; she agreed to go off with him, and live some time in a retirement where she was to see only himself, after which he engaged to marry her publicly.

"He pretended ecstasies at this proof of affection, yet hesitated to accept it; and, by piquing the generosity of her soul, which knew no guile, and therefore suspected none, led her to insist on devoting herself to wretchedness.

"In order, however, that this step might be as little known as possible, as he pretended the utmost concern for that honour he was contriving to destroy, it was agreed between them, that he should go immediately to London, and that she should follow him, under pretence of a visit to a relation at some distance; the greatest difficulty was, how to hide this design from me.

"She had never before concealed a thought from her beloved Fanny; nor could he now have prevailed on her to deceive me, had he not artfully persuaded her I was myself in love with him; and that, therefore, it would be cruel, as well as imprudent, to trust me with the secret.

"Nothing shews so strongly the power of love, in absorbing every faculty of the soul, as my dear Sophia's being prevailed on to use art with the friend most dear to her on earth.

"By an unworthy piece of deceit, I was sent to a relation for some weeks; and the next day Sophia followed her infamous lover, leaving letters for me and her father, calculated to persuade us, they were privately married.

"My distress, and that of the unhappy parent, may more easily be conceived than described; severe by nature, he cast her from his heart and fortune for ever, and settled his estate on a nephew, then at the university.

"As to me, grief and tenderness were the only sensations I felt: I went to town, and took every private method to discover her retreat, but in vain; till near a year after, when, being in London, with a friend of my mother's, a servant, who had lived with my Sophia, saw me in the street, and knew me: by her means, I discovered that she was in distress, abandoned by her lover, in that moment when his tenderness was most necessary.

"I flew to her, and found her in a miserable apartment, in which nothing but an extreme neatness would have made me suppose she had ever seen happier days: the servant who brought me to her attended her.

"She was in bed, pale, emaciated; the lovely babe you saw with me in her arms.

"Though prepared for my visit, she was unable to bear the shock of seeing me; I ran to her, she raised herself in the bed, and, throwing her feeble arms round my neck, could only say, 'My Fanny, is this possible!' and fainted away.

"Our cares having recovered her, she endeavoured to compose herself; her eyes were fixed tenderly on me, she pressed my hand between hers, the tears stole silently down her cheeks; she looked at her child, then at me; she would have spoke, but the feelings of her heart were too strong for expression.

"I begged her to be calm, and promised to spend the day with her; I did not yet dare, lest the emotion should be too much for her weak state, to tell her we would part no more.

"I took a room in the house, and determined to give all my attention to the restoration of her health; after which, I hoped to contrive to make my little fortune, with industry, support us both.

"I sat up with her that night; she got a little rest, she seemed better in the morning; she told me the particulars I have already related; she, however, endeavoured to soften the cruel behaviour of the wretch, whose name I could not hear without horror.

"She had in the afternoon a little fever; I sent for a physician, he thought her in danger; what did not my heart feel from this information? she grew worse, I never left her one moment.

"The next morning she called me to her; she took my hand, and looking at me with a tenderness no language can describe,

"'My dear, my only friend,' said she. 'I am dying; you are come to receive the last breath of your unhappy Sophia: I wish with ardour for my father's blessing and forgiveness, but dare not ask them.

"'The weakness of my heart has undone me; I am lost, abandoned by him on whom my soul doted; by him, for whom I would have sacrificed a thousand lives; he has left me with my babe to perish, yet I still love him with unabated fondness: the pang of losing him sinks me to the grave!'

"Her speech here failed her for a time; but recovering, she proceeded,

"'Hard as this request may seem, and to whatever

miseries it may expose my angel friend, I adjure you not to desert my child; save him from the wretchedness that threatens him; let him find in you a mother not less tender, but more virtuous, than his own.

" 'I know, my Fanny, I undo you by this cruel confidence; but who else will have mercy on this innocent?'

"Unable to answer, my heart torn with unutterable anguish, I snatched the lovely babe to my bosom, I kissed him, I bathed him with my tears.

"She understood me, a gleam of pleasure brightened her dying eyes, the child was still pressed to my heart, she gazed on us both with a look of wild affection; then, clasping her hands together, and breathing a fervent prayer to Heaven, sunk down, and expired without a groan——

"To you, Madam, I need not say the rest.

"The eloquence of angels could not paint my distress; I saw the friend of my soul, the best and most gentle of her sex, a breathless corse before me; her heart broke by the ingratitude of the man she loved, her honour the sport of fools, her guiltless child a sharer in her shame.

"And all this ruin brought on by a sensibility of which the best minds alone are susceptible, by that noble integrity of soul which made it impossible for her to suspect another.

"Distracted with grief, I kissed my Sophia's pale lips, talked to her lifeless form; I promised to protect the sweet babe, who smiled on me, and with his little hand pressed mine, as if sensible of what I said.

"As soon as my grief was enough calmed to render me capable of any thing, I wrote an account of Sophia's death to her father, who had the inhumanity to refuse to see her child.

"I disdained an application to her murderer; and retiring to this place, where I was, and resolved to continue, unknown, determined to devote my life to the sweet infant, and to support him by an industry which I did not doubt Heaven would prosper.

"The faithful girl who had attended Sophia, begged to continue with me; we work for the milleners in the neighbouring towns, and, with a little pittance I have, keep above want.

"I know the consequence of what I have undertaken; I know I give up the world and all hopes of happiness to myself: yet will I not desert this friendless little innocent, nor betray the confidence of my expiring friend, whose last moments were soothed with the hope of his finding a parent's care in me.

"You have had the goodness to wish to serve me. Sir

283

Charles Verville is dead: a fever, the consequence of his un-governed intemperance, carried him off suddenly: his brother Sir William has a worthy character; if Colonel Rivers, by his general acquaintance with the great world, can represent this story to him, it possibly may procure my little Charles happier prospects than my poverty can give him.

"Your goodness, Madam, makes it unnecessary to be more explicit: to be unhappy, and not to have merited it, is a sufficient claim to your protection.

"You are above the low prejudices of common minds; you will pity the wretched victim of her own unsuspecting heart, you will abhor the memory of her savage undoer, you will ap-prove my complying with her dying request, though in contra-diction to the selfish maxims of the world: you will, if in your power, endeavour to serve my little prattler.

"'Till I had explained my situation, I could not think of accepting the honour you allowed me to hope for, of enquir-ing after your health at Bellfield; if the step I have taken meets with your approbation, I shall be most happy to thank you and Colonel Rivers for your attention to one, whom you would before have been justified in supposing unworthy of it.

"I am, Madam, with the most perfect respect and gratitude,

"Your obliged
"and obedient servant,

"F. WILLIAMS"

Your own heart, my dear Fitzgerald, will tell you what were our reflections on reading the inclosed: Emily, whose gentle heart feels for the weaknesses as well as misfortunes of others, will to-morrow fetch this heroic girl and her little ward, to spend a week at Bellfield; and we will then consider what is to be done for them.

You know Sir William Verville; go to him from me with the inclosed letter, he is a man of honour, and will, I am certain, provide for the poor babe, who, had not his father been a monster of unfeeling inhumanity, would have inherited the estate and title Sir William now enjoys.

Is not the midnight murderer, my dear friend, white as snow to this vile seducer? this betrayer of unsuspecting, trust-ing, innocence? what transport is it to me to reflect, that not one bosom ever heaved a sigh of remorse of which I was the cause!

I grieve for the poor victim of a tenderness, amiable in

284

itself, though productive of such dreadful consequences when not under the guidance of reason.

It ought to be a double tie on the honour of men, that the woman who truly loves gives up her will without reserve to the object of her affection.

Virtuous less from reasoning and fixed principle, than from elegance, and a lovely delicacy of mind; naturally tender, even to excess; carried away by a romance of sentiment; the helpless sex are too easily seduced, by engaging their confidence, and piquing their generosity.

I cannot write; my heart is softened to a degree which makes me incapable of any thing.

Do not neglect one moment going to Sir William Verville.

Adieu!

Your affectionate

Ed. Rivers

TO COLONEL RIVERS

LETTER 208 OCT. 28: The story you have told me has equally shocked and astonished me: my sweet Bell has dropped a pitying tear on poor Sophia's grave.

Thank Heaven! we meet with few minds like that of Sir Charles Verville; such a degree of savage insensibility is unnatural.

The human heart is created weak, not wicked: avid of pleasure and of gain; but with a mixture of benevolence, which prevents our seeking either to the destruction of others.

Nothing can be more false than that we are naturally inclined to evil: we are indeed naturally inclined to gratify the selfish passions of every kind; but those passions are not evil in themselves, they only become so from excess.

The malevolent passions are not inherent in our nature. They are only to be acquired by degrees, and generally are born from chagrin and disappointment; a wicked character is a depraved one.

What must this unhappy girl have suffered! no misery can equal the struggles of a virtuous mind wishing to act in a manner becoming its own dignity, yet carried by passions to do otherwise.

I have been at Sir William Verville's, who is at Bath; I will write, and inclose the letter to him this evening; you shall have his answer the moment I receive it.

We are going to dine at Richmond with Lord H——.

Adieu! my dear Rivers; Bell complains you have never answered her letter: I own, I thought you a man of more gallantry than to neglect a lady.

> Adieu!
>
> Your faithful
>
> J. FITZGERALD

TO CAPTAIN FITZGERALD

LETTER 209   BELLFIELD, OCT. 30: I am very impatient, my dear friend, till you hear from Sir William, though I have no doubt of his acting as he ought: our cottagers shall not leave us till their fate is determined; I have not told Miss Williams the step I have taken.

Emily is more and more pleased with this amiable girl: I wish extremely to be able to keep her here; as an agreeable companion of her own age and sex, whose ideas are similar, and who, from being in the same season of life, sees things in the same point of view, is all that is wanting to Emily's happiness.

'Tis impossible to mention similarity of ideas, without observing how exactly ours coincide; in all my acquaintance with mankind, I never yet met a mind so nearly resembling my own; a tie of affection much stronger than all your merit would be without that similarity.

I agree with you, that mankind are born virtuous, and that it is education and example which make them otherwise.

The believing other men knaves is not only the way to make them so, but is also an infallible method of becoming such ourselves.

A false and ill-judged method of instruction, by which we imbibe prejudices instead of truths, makes us regard the human race as beasts of prey; not as brothers, united by one common bond, and promoting the general interest by pursuing our own particular one.

There is nothing of which I am more convinced than that,

"True self-love and social are the same":

That those passions which make the happiness of individuals, tend directly to the general good of the species.

The beneficent Author of nature has made public and private happiness the same; man has in vain endeavoured to divide them; but in the endeavour he has almost destroyed both.

'Tis with pain I say, that the business of legislation in most countries seems to have been to counter-work this wise order of Providence, which has ordained, that we shall make others happy in being so ourselves.

This is in nothing so glaring as in the point on which not only the happiness, but the virtue of almost the whole human race is concerned: I mean marriage; the restraints on which, in almost every country, not only tend to encourage celibacy, and a destructive libertinism the consequence of it, to give fresh strength to domestic tyranny, and subject the generous affections of uncorrupted youth to the guidance of those in whom every motive to action but avarice is dead; to condemn the blameless victims of duty to a life of indifference, of disgust, and possibly of guilt; but, by opposing the very spirit of our constitution, throwing property into a few hands, and favouring that excessive inequality, which renders one part of the species wretched, without adding to the happiness of the other; to destroy at once the domestic felicity of individuals, contradict the will of the Supreme Being, as clearly wrote in the book of nature, and sap the very foundations of the most perfect form of government on earth.

A pretty long-winded period this: Bell would call it true Ciceronian, and quote

"——Rivers for a period of a mile."

But to proceed. The only equality to which parents in general attend, is that of fortune; whereas a resemblance in age, in temper, in personal attractions, in birth, in education, understanding, and sentiment, are the only foundations of that lively taste, that tender friendship, without which no union deserves the sacred name of marriage.

Timid, compliant youth may be forced into the arms of age and disease; a lord may invite a citizen's daughter he despises to his bed, to repair a shattered fortune; and she may accept him, allured by the rays of a coronet: but such conjunctions are only a more shameful species of prostitution.

Men who marry from interested motives are inexcusable; but the very modesty of women makes against their happiness in this point, by giving them a kind of bashful fear of objecting to such persons as their parents recommend as proper objects of their tenderness.

I am prevented by company from saying all I intended.
Adieu! Your faithful

ED. RIVERS

LETTER 210   TEMPLE-HOUSE, NOV. 1: You wrong me excessively, my dear Rivers, in accusing me of a natural levity in love and friendship.

As to the latter, my frequent changes which I freely acknowledge, have not been owing to any inconstancy, but to precipitation and want of caution in contracting them.

My general fault has been the folly of chusing my friends for some striking and agreeable accomplishment, instead of giving to solid merit the preference which most certainly is its due.

My inconstancy in love has been merely from vanity.

There is something so flattering in the general favour of women that it requires great firmness of mind to resist that kind of gallantry which indulges it, though absolutely destructive to real happiness.

I blush to say, that when I first married I have more than once been in danger, from the mere boyish desire of conquest, notwithstanding my adoration for your lovely sister: such is the force of habit, for I must have been infinitely a loser by changing.

I am now perfectly safe; my vanity has taken another turn: I pique myself on keeping the heart of the loveliest woman that ever existed, as a nobler conquest than attracting the notice of a hundred coquets, who would be equally flattered by the attention of any other man, at least any other man who had the good fortune to be as fashionable.

Every thing conspires to keep me in the road of domestic happiness: the manner of life I am engaged in, your friendship, your example, and society; and the very fear I am in of losing your esteem.

That I have the seeds of constancy in my nature, I call

on you and your lovely sister to witness; I have been *your* friend from almost infancy, and am every hour more *her* lover.

She is my friend, my companion, as well as mistress; her wit, her sprightliness, her pleasing kind of knowledge, fill with delight those hours which are so tedious with a fool, however lovely.

With my Lucy, possession can never cure the wounded heart.

Her modesty, her angel purity of mind and person, render her literally,

> *"My ever-new delight."*

She has convinced me, that if beauty is the mother, delicacy is the nurse of love.

Venus has lent her cestus, and shares with her the attendance of the Graces.

My vagrant passions, like the rays of the sun collected in a burning glass, are now united in one point.

Lucy is here. Adieu! I must not let her know her power.

You spend to-morrow with us; we have a little ball, and are to have a masquerade next week.

Lucy wants to consult Emily on her dress; you and I are not to be in the secret: we have wrote to ask the Fitzgeralds to the masquerade; I will send Lucy's post-coach for them the day before, or perhaps fetch them myself.

Adieu!

Your affectionate

J. TEMPLE

TO CAPTAIN FITZGERALD

LETTER **211** BELLFIELD, NOV. 1: I have this moment a letter from Temple which has set my heart at rest: he writes like a lover, yet owns his past danger, with a frankness which speaks more strongly than any professions could do, the real present state of his heart.

My anxiety for my sister has a little broke in on my own happiness; in England, where the married women are in general the most virtuous in the world, it is of infinite consequence they should love their husbands, and be beloved by

289

them; in countries where gallantry is more permitted, it is less necessary.

Temple will make her happy whilst she preserves his heart; but, if she loses it, every thing is to be feared from the vivacity of his nature, which can never support one moment a life of indifference.

He has that warmth of temper which is the natural soil of the virtues; but which is unhappily, at the same time, most apt to produce indiscretions.

Tame, cold, dispassionate minds resemble barren lands; warm, animated ones, rich ground, which, if properly cultivated, yields the noblest fruit; but, if neglected, from its luxuriance is most productive of weeds.

His misfortune has been losing both his parents when almost an infant; and having been master of himself and a noble fortune, at an age when the passions hurry us beyond the bounds of reason.

I am the only person on earth by whom he would ever bear to be controlled in any thing; happily for Lucy, I preserve the influence over him which friendship first gave me.

That influence, and her extreme attention to study his taste in every thing, with those uncommon graces both of mind and person she has received from nature, will, I hope, effectually fix this wandering star.

She tells me, she has asked you to a masquerade at Temple-house, to which you will extremely oblige us all by coming.

You do not tell us, whether the affair of your majority is settled: if obliged to return immediately, Temple will send you back.

Adieu! Your faithful

Ed. Rivers

I have this moment your last letter: you are right, we American travellers are under great disadvantages; our imaginations are restrained; we have not the pomp of the orient to describe, but the simple and unadorned charms of nature.

LETTER 212 NOV. 4: Sir William Verville is come back to town; I was with him this morning; he desires to see the child; he tells me, his brother, in his last moments, mentioned this story in all the agony of remorse, and begged him to provide for the little innocent, if to be found; that he had made many enquiries, but hitherto in vain; and that he thought himself happy in the discovery.

He talks of settling three thousand pounds on the child, and taking the care of educating him into his own hands.

I hinted at some little provision for the amiable girl who had saved him from perishing, and had the pleasure to find Sir William listen to me with attention.

I am sorry it is not possible for me to be at your masquerade; but my affair is just at the crisis: Bell expects a particular account of it from Mrs Rivers, and desires to be immediately in the secret of the ladies' dresses, though you are not: she begs you will send your fair cottager and little charge to us, and we will take care to introduce them properly to Sir William.

I am too much hurried to say more.

Adieu! my dear Rivers!

Your affectionate

J. FITZGERALD

LETTER 213 NOV. 8: Yes, my dear Bell, politeness is undoubtedly a moral virtue.

As we are beings formed for, and not capable of being happy, without society, it is the duty of every one to endeavour to make it as easy and agreeable as they can; which is only to be done by such an attention to others as is consistent with what we owe to ourselves; all we give them in civility will be re-paid us in respect: insolence and ill-breeding are detestable to all mankind.

I long to see you, my dear Bell; the delight I have had in your society has spoiled my relish for that of meer acquaintance, however agreeable.

'Tis dangerous to indulge in the pleasures of friendship; they weaken one's taste too much for common conversation.

Yet what other pleasures are worth the name? what others have spirit and delicacy too?

I am preparing for the masquerade, which is to be the 18th; I am extremely disappointed you will not be with us.

My dress is simple and unornamented, but I think becoming and prettily fancied; it is that of a French *paisanne*: Lucy is to be a sultana, blazing with diamonds: my mother a Roman matron.

I chuse this dress because I have heard my dear Rivers admire it; to be one moment more pleasing in his eyes, is an object worthy all my attention.

Adieu!

Your faithful

EMILY RIVERS

TO MRS RIVERS, BELLFIELD, RUTLAND

LETTER 214 LONDON, NOV. 10: Certainly, my dear, friendship is a mighty pretty invention, and, next to love, gives of all things the greatest spirit to society.

And yet the prudery of the age will hardly allow us poor women even this pleasure, innocent as it is.

I remember my aunt Cecily, who died at sixty-six, without ever having felt the least spark of affection for any human being, used to tell me, a prudent modest woman never loved any thing but herself.

For my part, I think all the kind propensities of the heart ought rather to be cherished than checked; that one is allowed to esteem merit even in the naughty creature, man.

I love you very sincerely, Emily: but I like friendships for the men best; and think prudery, by forbidding them, robs us of some of the most lively as well as innocent pleasures of the heart.

That desire of pleasing, which one feels much the most strongly for a *male* friend, is in itself a very agreeable emotion.

You will say, I am a coquet even in friendship; and I am not quite sure you are not in the right.

I am extremely in love with my husband; yet chuse other men should regard me with complacency, am as fond of attracting the attention of the dear creatures as ever, and, though I do justice to your wit, understanding, sentiment, and all that, prefer Rivers's conversation infinitely to yours.

Women cannot say civil things to each other; and if they could, they would be something insipid: whereas a male friend—

'Tis absolutely another thing, my dear; and the first system of ethics I write, I will have a hundred pages on the subject.

Observe, my dear, I have not the least objection to your having a friendship for Fitzgerald. I am the best-natured creature in the world, and the fondest of increasing the circle of my husband's innocent amusements.

A propos to innocent amusements, I think your fair sister-in-law an exquisite politician; calling the pleasures to Temple at home, is the best method in the world to prevent his going abroad in pursuit of them.

I am mortified I cannot be at your masquerade; it is my passion, and I have the prettiest dress in the world by me. I am half inclined to elope for a day or two.

Adieu! Your faithful

A. FITZGERALD

TO CAPTAIN FITZGERALD

LETTER 215 BELLFIELD, NOV. 12: Please to inform the little Bell, I won't allow her to spoil my Emily.

I enter a caveat against male friendships, which are only fit for ladies of the *salamandrine* order.

I desire to engross all Emily's *kind propensities* to myself; and should grudge the least share in her heart, or, if you please in her *friendship*, to an archangel.

However, not to be too severe, since prudery expects women to have no propensities at all, I allow single ladies, of all ranks, sizes, ages, and complexions, to spread the veil of friendship between their hearts and the world.

'Tis the finest day I ever saw, though the middle of November; a dry soft west wind, the air as mild as in April, and an almost Canadian sunshine.

I have been bathing in the clear stream, at the end of my garden; the same stream in which I laved my careless bosom at thirteen; an idea which gave me inconceivable delight; and the more, as my bosom is as gay and tranquil at this moment as in those dear hours of chearfulness and innocence.

Of all local prejudices, that is the strongest as well as most pleasing, which attaches us to the place of our birth.

Sweet home! only seat of true and genuine happiness.

I am extremely in the humour to write a poem to the household gods.

We neglect these amiable deities, but they are revenged; true pleasure is only to be found under their auspices.

I know not how it is, my dear Fitzgerald; but I don't find my passion for the country abate.

I still find the scenes around me lovely; though, from the change of season, less smiling than when I first fixed at Bellfield; we have rural business enough to amuse, not embarrass us; we have a small but excellent library of books, given us by my mother; she and Emily are two of the most pleasing companions on earth; the neighbourhood is full of agreeable people, and, what should always be attended to in fixing in the country, of fortunes not superior to our own.

The evenings grow long, but they are only the more jovial; I love the pleasures of the table, not for their own sakes, for no man is more indifferent on this subject; but because they promote social, convivial joy, and bring people together in good humour with themselves and each other.

My Emily's suppers are enchanting; but our little income obliges us to have few: if I was rich, this would be my principal extravagance.

To fill up my measure of content, Emily is pleased with my retirement, and finds all her happiness in my affection.

We are so little alone, that I find our moments of unreserved conversation too short; whenever I leave her, I recollect a thousand things I had to say, a thousand new ideas to communicate, and am impatient for the hour of seeing again, without restraint, the most amiable and pleasing of womankind.

My happiness would be complete, if I did not sometimes see a cloud of anxiety on that dear countenance, which, however, is dissipated the moment my eyes meet hers.

I am going to Temple's, and the chaise is at the door.

Adieu! my dear friend!

Your affectionate

ED. RIVERS

LETTER 216 NOV. 14: So you disapprove male friendships, my sweet Colonel! I thought you had better ideas of things in general.

Fitzgerald and I have been disputing on French and English manners, in regard to gallantry.

The great question is, Whether a man is more hurt by the imprudent conduct of his daughter or his wife?

Much may be said on both sides.

There is some hazard in suffering coquetry in either; both contribute to give charms to conversation, and introduce ease and politeness into society; but both are dangerous to manners.

Our customs, however, are most likely to produce good effects, as they give opportunity for love marriages, the only ones which can make worthy minds happy.

The coquetry of single women has a point of view consistent with honour; that of married women has generally no point of view at all; it is, however, of use *pour passer le tems*.

As to real gallantry, the French style depraves the minds of men least, ours is most favourable to the peace of families.

I think I preserve the balance of argument admirably.

My opinion, however, is, that if people married from affection, there would be so such thing as gallantry at all.

Pride, and the parade of life, destroy all happiness: our whole felicity depends on our choice in marriage, yet we chuse from motives more trifling than would determine us in the common affairs of life.

I knew a gentleman who fancied himself in love, yet delayed marrying his mistress till he could afford a set of plate.

Modern manners are very unfavourable to the tender affections.

Ancient lovers had only dragons to combat; ours have the worse monsters of avarice and ambition.

All I shall say further on the subject is, that the two happiest people I ever knew were a country clergyman and his wife, whose whole income did not exceed one hundred pounds a year.

A pretty philosophical, sentimental, dull kind of an epistle this!

But you deserve it, for not answering my last, which was divine.

I am pleased with Emily's ideas about her dress at the masquerade; it is a proof you are still lovers.

I remember, the first symptoms I discovered of my *tendresse* for Fitzgerald was my excessive attention to this article: I have tried on twenty different caps when I expected him at Silleri.

Before we drop the subject of gallantry, I must tell you I am charmed with you and my *sposo*, for never giving the least hint before Emily and me that you have had any; it is a piece of delicacy which convinces me of your tenderness more than all the vows that ever lovers broke would do.

I have been hurt at the contrary behaviour in Temple; and have observed Lucy to be so too, though her excessive attention not to give him pain prevented her shewing it: I have on such an occasion seen a smile on her countenance, and a tear of tender regret starting into her eyes.

A woman who has vanity without affection will be pleased to hear of your past conquests, and regard them as victims immolated to her superior charms: to her, therefore, it is right to talk of them; but to flatter the *heart*, and give delight to a woman who truly loves, you should appear too much taken up with the present passion to look back to the past: you should not even present to her imagination the thought that you have had other engagements: we know such things are, but had rather the idea should not be awakened: I may be wrong, but I speak from my own feelings.

I am excessively pleased with a thought I met with in a little French novel:

"*Un homme qui ne peut plus compter ses bonnes fortunes, est de tous, celui qui connoît le moins les faveurs. C'est le coeur qui les accorde, & ce n'est pas le coeur qu'un homme à la mode interesse. Plus on est prôné par les femmes, plus il est facile de les avoir, mais moins il est possible de les enflammer.*"

To which truth I most heartily set my hand.

Twelve o'clock

I have just heard from your sister, who tells me, Emily is turned a little natural philosopher, reads Ray, Derham, and fifty other strange old fellows that one never heard of, and is eternally poring through a microscope to discover the wonders of creation.

How amazingly learned matrimony makes young ladies! I suppose we shall have a volume of her discoveries bye and bye.

She says too, you have little pets like sweethearts, quarrel and make it up again in the most engaging manner in the world.

This is just what I want to bring Fitzgerald to; but the perverse monkey won't quarrel with me, do all I can: I am sure this is not my fault, for I give him reason every day of his life.

Shenstone says admirably, "That reconciliation is the tenderest part of love and friendship: the soul here discovers a kind of elasticity, and, being forced back, returns with an additional violence."

Who would not quarrel for the pleasure of reconciliation! I shall be very angry with Fitzgerald if he goes on in this mild way.

Tell your sister, she cannot be more mortified than I am, that it is impossible for me to be at her masquerade.

Adieu! Your affectionate

A. FITZGERALD

Don't you think, my dear Rivers, that marriage, on prudent principles, is a horrid sort of an affair? It is really cruel of papas and mammas to shut up two poor innocent creatures in a house together, to plague and torment one another, who might have been very happy separate.

Where people take their own time, and chuse for themselves, it is another affair, and I begin to think it possible affection may last through life.

I sometimes fancy to myself Fitzgerald and I loving on, from the impassioned hour when I first honoured him with my hand, to that tranquil one, when we shall take our afternoon's nap *vis-à-vis* in two arm chairs, by the fire-side, he a grave country justice, and I his worship's good sort of a wife, the Lady Bountiful of the Parish.

I have a notion there is nothing so very shocking in being an oldish gentlewoman; what one loses in charms, is made up in the happy liberty of doing and saying whatever one pleases. Adieu!

LETTER 217 BELLFIELD, NOV. 16: My relation, Colonel Willmott, is just arrived from the East Indies, rich, and full of the project of marrying his daughter to me.

My mother has this morning received a letter from him, pressing the affair with an earnestness which rather makes me feel for his disappointment, and wish to break it to him as gently as possible.

He talks of being at Bellfield on Wednesday evening, which is Temple's masquerade; I shall stay behind at Bellfield, to receive him, have a domino ready, and take him to Temple-house.

He seems to know nothing of my marriage or my sister's, and I wish him not to know of the former till he has seen Emily.

The best apology I can make for declining his offer, is to shew him the lovely cause.

I will contrive they shall converse together at the masquerade, and that he shall sit next her at supper, without their knowing any thing of each other.

If he sees her, if he talks with her, without that prejudice which the knowledge of her being the cause of his disappointment might give, he cannot fail of having for her that admiration which I never yet met with a mind savage enough to refuse her.

His daughter has been educated abroad, which is a circumstance I am pleased with, as it gives me the power of refusing her without wounding either her vanity, or her father's, which, had we been acquainted, might have been piqued at my giving the preference to another.

She is not in England, but is hourly expected: the moment she arrives, Lucy and I will fetch her to Temple-house: I shall be anxious to see her married to a man who deserves her. Colonel Willmott tells me, she is very amiable; at least as he is told, for he has never seen her.

I could wish it were possible to conceal this offer for ever from Emily; my delicacy is hurt at the idea of her knowing it, at least from me or my family.

My mother behaves like an angel on this occasion; expresses herself perfectly happy in my having consulted my heart alone in marrying, and speaks of Emily's tenderness as a treasure above all price.

She does not even hint a wish to see me richer than I am.

Had I never seen Emily, I would not have married this lady unless love had united us.

Do not, however, suppose I have that romantic contempt for fortune, which is so pardonable, I had almost said so becoming, at nineteen.

I have seen more of the world than most men of my age, and I have seen the advantages of affluence in their strongest light.

I think a worthy man not only may have, but ought to have, an attention to making his way in the world, and improving his situation in it, by every means consistent with probity and honour, and with his own real happiness.

I have ever had this attention, and ever will, but not by base means: and, in my opinion, the very basest is that of selling one's hand in marriage.

With what horror do we regard a man who is kept! and a man who marries from interested views alone, is kept in the strongest sense of the word.

He is equally a purchased slave, with no distinction but that his bondage is of longer continuance.

Adieu! I may possibly write again on Wednesday.

Your faithful

ED. RIVERS

TO COLONEL RIVERS, BELLFIELD, RUTLAND

LETTER 218 LONDON, NOV. 18: Fitzgerald is busy, and begs me to write to you.

Your cottagers are arrived; there is something very interesting in Miss Williams, and the little boy is an infant Adonis.

Heaven send he may be an honester man than his father, or I foresee terrible devastations amongst the sex.

We have this moment your letter; I am angry with you for blaspheming the sweet season of nineteen:

"O lovely source
Of generous foibles, youth! when opening minds
Are honest as the light, lucid as air,
As softening breezes kind, as linnets gay,
Tender as buds, and lavish as the spring."

You will find out I am in a course of Shenstone, which I prescribe to all minds tinctured with the uncomfortable selfishness of the present age.

The only way to be good, is to retain the generous mistakes, if they are such, of nineteen through life.

As to you, my dear Rivers, with all your airs of prudence and knowing the world, you are, in this respect, as much a boy as ever.

Witness your extreme joy at having married a woman with two thousand pounds, when you might have had one with twenty times the sum.

You are a boy, Rivers, I am a girl; and I hope we shall remain so as long as we live.

Do you know, my dear friend, that I am a daughter of the Muses, and that I wrote pastorals at seven years old?

I am charmed with this, because an old physician once told me it was a symptom, not only of long life, but of long youth, which is much better.

He explained this, by saying something about animal spirits, which I do not at all understand, but which perhaps you may.

I should have been a pretty enough kind of a poetess, if papa had not attempted to teach me how to be one, and insisted on seeing my scribbles as I went on: these same Muses are such bashful misses, they won't bear to be looked at.

Genius is like the sensitive plant; it shrinks from the touch.

So your nabob cousin is arrived: I hope he will fall in love with Emily; and remember, if he had obligations to Mrs Rivers's father, he had exactly the same to your grandfather.

He might spare ten thousand pounds very well, which would improve your *petits soupers*.

Adieu! Sir William Verville dines here, and I have but just time to dress.

Yours,

A. FITZGERALD

TO CAPTAIN FITZGERALD

LETTER 219 BELLFIELD, NOV. 17, MORNING: I have had a letter from Colonel Willmott myself to-day; he is still quite unacquainted with the state of our domestic affairs;

300

supposes me a batchelor, and talks of my being his son-in-law as a certainty, not attending to the probability of my having other engagements.

His history, which he tells me in this letter, is a very romantic one. He was a younger brother, and provided for accordingly: he loved, when about twenty, a lady who was as little a favourite of fortune as himself: their families, who on both sides had other views, joined their interest to get him sent to the East Indies; and the young lady was removed to the house of a friend in London, where she was to continue till he had left England.

Before he went, however, they contrived to meet, and were privately married; the marriage was known only to her brother, who was Willmott's friend.

He left her in the care of her brother, who, under pretence of diverting her melancholy, and endeavouring to cure her passion, obtained leave of his father to take her with him to France.

She was there delivered of this child, and expired a few days after.

Her brother, without letting her family know the secret, educated the infant, as the daughter of a younger brother who had been just before killed in a duel in France; her parents, who died in a few years, were, almost in their last moments, informed of these circumstances, and made a small provision for the child.

In the mean time, Colonel Willmott, after experiencing a great variety of misfortunes for many years, during which he maintained a constant correspondence with his brother-in-law, and with no other person in Europe, by a train of lucky accidents, acquired very rapidly a considerable fortune, with which he resolved to return to England, and marry his daughter to me, as the only method to discharge fully his obligations to my grandfather, who alone, of all his family, had given him the least assistance when he left England. He wrote to his daughter, letting her know his design, and directing her to meet him in London; but she is not yet arrived.

Six in the Evening

My mother and Emily went to Temple's to dinner; they are to dress there, and I am to be surprised.

Seven

Colonel Willmott is come: he is an extreme handsome man; tall, well-made, with an air of dignity which one seldom sees; he is very brown, and, what will please Bell, has an aquiline nose: he looks about fifty, but is not so much; change of climate has almost always the disagreeable effect of adding some years to the look.

He is dressing, to accompany me to the masquerade; I must attend him: I have only time to say,

I am yours,

ED. RIVERS

TO MRS RIVERS, BELLFIELD, RUTLAND

LETTER 220 LONDON, NOV. 18, TWELVE AT NIGHT: Who should I dine and sup with to-day, at a merchant's in the city, but your old love, Sir George Clayton, as gay and amusing as ever!

What an entertaining companion have you lost, my dear Emily!

He was a little disconcerted at seeing me, and blushed extremely: but soon recovered his amiable, uniform insipidity of countenance, and smiled and simpered as usual.

He never enquired after you, nor even mentioned your name: being asked for a toast, I had the malice to give Rivers; he drank him, without seeming ever to have heard of him before.

The city misses admire him prodigiously, and he them; they are charmed with his beauty, and he with their wit.

His mother, poor woman! could not bring the match she wrote about to bear: the family approved him; but the fair one made a better choice, and gave herself last week, at St George's, Hanover-square, to a very agreeable fellow of our acquaintance, Mr Palmer; a man of sense and honour, who deserves her had she been ten times richer: he has a small estate in Lincolnshire, and his house is not above twenty miles from you: I must bring you and Mrs Palmer acquainted.

I suppose you are now the happiest of beings; Rivers finding a thousand new beauties in his *belle paisanne*, and you exulting in your charms, or, in other words, glorying in your strength.

So the maiden aunts in your neighbourhood think Miss Williams no better than she should be?

Either somebody has said, or the idea is my own; after all, I believe it Shenstone's, That those are generally the best people whose characters have been most injured by slanderers, as we usually find that the best fruit which the birds have been pecking at.

I will, however, allow appearances were a little against your cottager; and I would forgive the good old virgins, if they had always as suspicious circumstances to determine from.

But they generally condemn from trifling indiscretions, and settle the characters of their own sex from their conduct at a time of life when they are themselves no judges of its propriety; they pass sentence on them for small errors, when it is an amazing proof of prudence not to commit great ones.

For my own part, I think those who never have been guilty of any indiscretion, are generally people who have very little active virtue.

The waving line holds in moral as well as in corporeal beauty.

Adieu!

Yours ever,

A. FITZGERALD

All I can say is, that if imprudence is a sin, Heaven help your poor little Bell!

On those principles, Sir George is the most virtuous man in the world; to which assertion, I believe, you will enter a caveat.

TO COLONEL RIVERS, BELLFIELD, RUTLAND

LETTER 221 LONDON, NOV. 19: You are right, my little Rivers: I like your friend, Colonel Willmott vastly better for his aquiline nose; I never yet saw one on the face of a fool.

He is a fortunate man to be introduced to such a party of fine women at his arrival; it is literally *to feed among the lilies*.

Fitzgerald says, he should be jealous of him in your esteem, if he was fifteen years younger; but that the strongest friendships are, where there is an equality in age; because people of the same age have the same train of thinking, and see things in the same light.

Every season of life has its peculiar set of ideas; and

we are greatly inclined to think nobody in the right, but those who are of the same opinion with ourselves.

Don't you think it a strong proof of my passion for my *sposo*, that I repeat his sentiments?

But to business: Sir William is charmed with his little nephew; has promised to settle on him what he before mentioned, to allow Miss Williams an hundred pounds a year, which is to go to the child after her death, and to be at the expence of his education himself.

I die to hear whether your oriental Colonel is in love with Emily.

Pray tell us every thing.

Adieu!

Your affectionate

A. Fitzgerald

TO CAPTAIN FITZGERALD

LETTER 222 TEMPLE-HOUSE, THURSDAY MORNING, 11 O'CLOCK: Our masquerade last night was really charming; I never saw any thing equal to it out of London.

Temple has taste, and had spared no expence to make it agreeable; the decorations of the grand saloon were magnificent.

Emily was the loveliest *paisanne* that ever was beheld; her dress, without losing sight of the character, was infinitely becoming: her beauty never appeared to such advantage.

There was a noble simplicity in her air, which it is impossible to describe.

The easy turn of her shape, the lovely roundness of her arm, the natural elegance of her whole form, the waving ringlets of her beautiful dark hair, carelessly fastened with a ribbon, the unaffected grace of her every motion, all together conveyed more strongly than imagination can paint, the pleasing idea of a wood-nymph, deigning to visit some favoured mortal.

Colonel Willmott gazed on her with rapture; and asked me, if the rural deities had left their verdant abodes to visit Temple-house.

I introduced him to her, and left her to improve the impression: 'tis well I was married in time; a nabob is a dangerous rival.

Lucy looked lovely, but in another style; she was a sultana in all the pride of imperial beauty; her charms awed, but Emily's invited; her look spoke resistless command, Emily's soft persuasion.

There were many fine women; but I will own to you, I had, as to beauty, no eyes but for Emily.

We are going this morning to see Burleigh: when we return, I shall announce Colonel Willmott to Emily, and introduce them properly to each other; they are to go in the same chaise; she at present only knows him as a friend of mine, and he her as his *belle paisanne*.

Adieu! I am summoned.

Your faithful

Ed. Rivers

I should have told you, I acquainted Colonel Willmott with my sister's marriage before I took him to Temple-house, and found an opportunity of introducing him to Temple unobserved.

Emily is the only one here to whom he is a stranger: I will caution him not to mention to her his past generous design in my favour. Adieu!

TO MRS FITZGERALD

LETTER *223*   TEMPLE-HOUSE, THURSDAY

MORNING: Your Emily was happy beyond words last night: amongst a crowd of beauties, her Rivers's eyes continually followed her; he seemed to see no other object: he would scarce let me wait till supper to unmask.

But you will call me a foolish romantic girl; therefore I will only say, I had the delight to see him pleased with my dress, and charmed with the complaisance which was shewed me by others.

There was a gentleman who came with Rivers, who was particularly attentive to me; he is not young, but extremely amiable: has a very fine person, with a commanding air; great politeness, and, as far as one can judge by a few hours' conversation, an excellent understanding.

I never in my life met with a man for whom I felt such

305

a partiality at first sight, except Rivers, who tells me, I have made a conquest of his friend.

He is to be my cavalier this morning to Burleigh.

It has this moment struck me, that Rivers never introduced his friend and me to each other, but as masks; I never thought of this before: I suppose he forgot it in the hurry of the masquerade.

I do not even know this agreeable stranger's name; I only found out by his conversation he had served in the army.

There is no saying how beautiful Lucy looked last night; her dress was rich, elegantly fancied, and particularly becoming to her graceful form, which I never saw look so graceful before.

All who attempted to be fine figures, shrunk into nothing before her.

Lucy carries her head, you know, remarkably well; which, with the advantage of her height, the perfect standard of women, her fine proportion, the native dignity of her air, the majestic flow of her robe, and the blaze of her diamonds, gave her a look of infinite superiority; a superiority which some of the company seemed to feel in a manner, which rather, I will own, gave me pain.

In a place consecrated to joy, I hate to see any thing like an uneasy sensation; yet, whilst human passions are what they are, it is difficult to avoid them.

There were four or five other sultanas, who seemed only the slaves of her train.

In short,

"She look'd a goddess, and she mov'd a queen."

I was happy the unassuming simplicity of the character in which I appeared, prevented comparisons which must have been extremely to my disadvantage.

I was safe in my littleness, like a modest shrub by the side of a cedar; and, being in so different a style, had the better chance to be taken notice of, even where Lucy was.

She was radiant as the morning star, and even dazzlingly lovely.

Her complexion, for Temple would not suffer her to wear a mask at all, had the vivid glow of youth and health, heightened by pleasure, and the consciousness of universal admiration.

Her eyes had a fire which one could scarce look at.

Temple's vanity and tenderness were gratified to the

utmost: he drank eagerly the praises which envy could not have refused her.

My mother extremely became her character; and, when talking to Rivers, gave me the idea of the Roman Aurelia, whose virtues she has equalled.

He looked at her with a delight which rendered him a thousand times more dear to me: she is really one of the most pleasing women that ever existed.

I am called: we are just setting out for Burleigh, which I have not yet seen.

Adieu! Yours,

EMILY RIVERS

TO CAPTAIN FITZGERALD

LETTER 224 BELLFIELD, THURSDAY, TWO o'clock: We are returned: Colonel Willmott is charmed with Burleigh, and more in love with Emily than ever.

He is gone to his apartment, whither I shall follow him, and acquaint him with my marriage; he is exactly in the disposition I could wish.

He will, I am sure, pardon any offence of which his *belle paisanne* is the cause.

I am returned.

He is disappointed, but not surprized; owns no human heart could have resisted Emily; begs she will allow his daughter a place in her friendship.

He insists on making her a present of diamonds; the only condition, he tells me, on which he will forgive my marriage.

I am going to introduce him to her in her apartment.

Adieu! for a moment.

Fitzgerald!—I scarce respire—the tumult of my joy— this daughter whom I have refused—my Emily—could you have believed——my Emily is the daughter of Colonel Willmott.

When I announced him to her by that name, her colour changed; but when I added that he was just returned from the East Indies, she trembled, her cheeks had a dying paleness, her voice faltered, she pronounced faintly, "My father!" and sunk breathless on a sofa.

307

He ran to her, he pressed her wildly to his bosom, he kissed her pale cheek, he demanded if she was indeed his child? his Emily? the dear pledge of his Emily Montague's tenderness?

Her senses returned, she fixed her eyes eagerly on him, she kissed his hand, she would have spoke, but tears stopped her voice.

The scene that followed is beyond my powers of description.

I have left them a moment, to share my joy with you: the time is too precious to say more. To-morrow you shall hear from me.

Adieu! Yours,

ED. RIVERS

TO CAPTAIN FITZGERALD

LETTER **225** TEMPLE-HOUSE, FRIDAY: Your friend is the happiest of mankind.

Every anxiety is removed from my Emily's dear bosom: a father's sanction leaves her nothing to desire.

You may remember, she wished to delay our marriage: her motive was, to wait Colonel Willmott's return.

Though promised by him to another, she hoped to bring him to leave her heart free; little did she think the man destined for her by her father, was the happy Rivers her heart had chosen.

Bound by a solemn vow, she concealed the circumstances of her birth even from me.

She resolved never to marry another, yet thought duty obliged her to wait her father's arrival.

She kindly supposed he would see me with her eyes, and, when he knew me, change his design in my favour: she fancied he would crown her love as the reward of her obedience in delaying her marriage.

My importunity, and the fear of giving me room to doubt her tenderness, as her vow prevented such an explanation as would have satisfied me, bore down her duty to a father whom she had never seen, and whom she had supposed dead, till the arrival of Mrs Melmoth's letters; having been two years without hearing any thing of him.

She married me, determined to give up her right to half his fortune in favour of the person for whom he designed her;

and hoped, by that means, to discharge her father's obligations, which she could not pay at the expence of sacrificing her heart.

But she writes to Mrs Fitzgerald, and will tell you all.

Come and share the happiness of your friends.

Adieu!

Your faithful

ED. RIVERS

LETTER 226   TEMPLE-HOUSE, FRIDAY: My Rivers has told you—my sweet friend, in what words shall I convey to you an adequate idea of your Emily's transport, at a discovery which has reconciled all her duties!

Those anxieties, that sense of having failed in filial obedience, which cast a damp on the joy of being wife to the most beloved of mankind, are at an end.

This husband whom I so dreaded, whom I determined never to accept, was my Rivers.

My father forgives me; he pardons the crime of love: he blesses that kind providence which conducted us to happiness.

How many has this event made happy!

The most amiable of mothers shares my joy; she bends in grateful thanks to that indulgent power who has rewarded her son for all his goodness to her.

Rivers hears her, and turns away to hide his tears: her tenderness melts him to the softness of a woman.

What gratitude do we not owe to Heaven! may the sense of it be for ever engraven on our hearts!

My Lucy too; all, all are happy.

But I will tell you. Rivers has already acquainted you with part of my story.

My uncle placed me, with a servant in whom he could confide, in a convent in France, till I was seven years old; he then sent for me to England, and left me at school eight years longer; after which, he took me with him to his regiment in Kent, where, you know, our friendship began, and continued till he changed into another, then in America, whither I attended him

My father's affairs were, at that time, in a situation

which determined my uncle to take the first opportunity of marrying me to advantage.

I regarded him as a father; he had always been more than a parent to me; I had the most implicit deference to his will.

He engaged me to Sir George Clayton; and, when dying, told me the story of my birth, to which I had till then been a stranger, exacting from me, however, an oath of secrecy till I saw my father.

He died, leaving me, with a trifle left in trust to him for my use from my grandfather, about two thousand pounds, which was all I, at that time, ever expected to possess.

My father was then thought ruined; there was even a report of his death, and I imagined myself absolute mistress of my own actions.

I was near two years without hearing any thing of him; nor did I know I had still a father, till the letters you brought me from Mrs Melmoth.

A variety of accidents, and our being both abroad, and in such distant parts of the world, prevented his letters arriving.

In this situation, the kind hand of Heaven conducted my Rivers to Montreal.

I saw him; and, from that moment, my whole soul was his.

Formed for each other, our love was sudden and resistless as the bolt of Heaven: the first glance of those dear speaking eyes gave me a new being, and awaked in me ideas never known before.

The strongest sympathy attached me to him in spite of myself: I thought it friendship, but felt that friendship more lively than what I called my *love* for Sir George; all conversation but his became insupportable to me; every moment that he passed from me, I counted as lost in my existence.

I loved him; that tenderness hourly increased: I hated Sir George, I fancied him changed; I studied to find errors in a man who had, a few weeks before, appeared to me amiable, and whom I had consented to marry; I broke with him, and felt a weight removed from my soul.

I trembled when Rivers appeared; I died to tell him my whole soul was his; I watched his looks, to find there the same sentiments with which he had inspired me: that transporting moment at length arrived; I had the delight to find our tenderness was mutual, and to devote my life to making happy the lord of my desires.

Mrs Melmoth's letter brought me my father's commands, if unmarried, to continue so till his return.

He added, that he intended me for a relation, to whose family he had obligations; that, his affairs having suffered such a happy revolution, he had it in his power and, therefore, thought it his duty, to pay this debt of gratitude; and, at the same time hoped to make me happy by connecting me with an amiable family, allied to him by blood and friendship; and uniting me to a man whom report spoke worthy of all my tenderness.

You may remember, my dearest Bell, how strongly I was affected on reading those letters: I wrote to Rivers, to beg him to defer our marriage; but the manner in which he took that request, and the fear of appearing indifferent to him, conquered all sense of what I owed to my father, and I married him; making it, however, a condition that he should ask no explanation of my conduct till I chose to give it.

I knew not the character of my father; he might be a tyrant, and divide us from each other: Rivers doubted my tenderness; would not my waiting, if my father had afterwards refused his consent to our union, have added to those cruel suspicions? might he not have supposed I had ceased to love him, and waited for the excuse of paternal authority to justify a change of sentiment?

In short, love bore down every other consideration; if I persisted in this delay, I might hazard losing all my soul held dear, the only object for which life was worth my care.

I determined, if I married, to give up all claim to my father's fortune, which I should justly forfeit by my disobedience to his commands: I hoped, however, Rivers's merit, and my father's paternal affection, when he knew us both, would influence him to make some provision for me as his daughter.

Half his fortune was all I ever hoped for, or even would have chose to accept: the rest I determined to give up to the man whom I refused to marry.

I gave my hand to Rivers, and was happy; yet the idea of my father's return, and the consciousness of having disobeyed him, cast sometimes a damp on my felicity, and threw a gloom over my soul, which all my endeavours could scarce hide from Rivers, though his delicacy prevented his asking the cause.

I now know, what was then a secret to me, that my father had offered his daughter to Rivers, with a fortune which could, however, have been no temptation to a mind like his, had he not been attached to me: he declined the offer, and, lest

I should hear of it, and, from a romantic distinterestedness, want him to accept it, pressed our marriage with more importunity than ever; yet had the generosity to conceal this sacrifice from me, and to wish it should be concealed for ever.

These sentiments, so noble, so peculiar to my Rivers, prevented an explanation, and hid from us, for some time, the circumstances which now make our happiness so perfect.

How infinitely worthy is Rivers of all my tenderness!

My father has sent to speak with me in his apartment: I should have told you, I this morning went to Bellfield, and brought from thence my mother's picture, which I have just sent him.

Adieu! Your faithful

EMILY RIVERS

TO MRS RIVERS, BELLFIELD, RUTLAND

LETTER 227 LONDON, SUNDAY: No words, my dear Emily, can speak our joy at the receipt of your two last letters.

You are then as happy as you deserve to be; we hope, in a few days, to be witnesses of your felicity.

We knew from the first of your father's proposal to Rivers; but he extorted a promise from us, never on any account to communicate it to you: he also desired us to detain you in Berkshire, by lengthening our visit, till your marriage, lest any friend of your father's in London should know his design, and chance acquaint you with it.

Fitzgerald is *Monsieur le Majeur*, at your ladyship's service: he received his commission this morning.

I once again congratulate you, my dear, on this triumph of tenderness: you see love, like virtue, is not only its own reward, but sometimes entitles us to other rewards too.

It should always be considered that those who marry from love, *may* grow rich; but those who marry to be rich, will *never* love.

The very idea that love will come after marriage, is shocking to minds which have the least spark of delicacy: to such minds, a marriage which begins with indifference will certainly end in disgust and aversion.

I bespeak your papa for my *cecisbeo*; mine is extremely at your service in return.

But I am piqued, my dear. "Sentiments so noble, so peculiar to your Rivers—"

I am apt to believe there are men in the world—that nobleness of mind is not so very *peculiar*—and that some people's sentiments may be as noble as other people's.

In short, I am inclined to fancy Fitzgerald would have acted just the same part in the same situation.

But it is your great fault, my dear Emily, to suppose your love a phoenix, whereas he is only an agreeable, worthy, handsome fellow, *comme un autre*.

I suppose you will be very angry; but who cares? I will be angry too.

Surely, my Fitzgerald—I allow Rivers all his merit; but comparisons, my dear—

Both our fellows, to be sure, are charming creatures; and I would not change them for a couple of Adonises: yet I don't insist upon it, that there is nothing agreeable in the world but them.

You should remember, my dear, that beauty is in the lover's eye; and that, however highly you may think of Rivers, every woman breathing has the same idea of *the dear man*.

O Heaven! I must tell you, because it will flatter your vanity about your charmer.

I have had a letter from an old lover of mine at Quebec, who tells me, Madame Des Roches has just refused one of the best matches in the country, and vows she will live and die a batchelor.

'Tis a mighty foolish resolution, and yet I cannot help liking her the better for making it.

My dear papa talks of taking a house near you, and of having a garden to rival yours: we shall spend a good deal of time with him, and I shall make love to Rivers, which you know will be vastly pretty.

One must do something to give a little variety to life; and nothing is so amusing, or keeps the mind so pleasingly awake, especially in the country, as the flattery of an agreeable fellow.

I am not, however, quite sure I shall not look abroad for a flirt, for one's friend's husband is almost as insipid as one's own.

Our romantic adventures being at an end, my dear; and we being all degenerated into sober people, who marry and *settle*; we seem in great danger of sinking into vegetation: on which subject I desire Rivers's opinion, being, I know, a most exquisite enquirer into the laws of nature.

Love is a pretty invention, but, I am told, is apt to *mellow* into friendship; a degree of perfection at which I by no means desire Fitzgerald's attachment for me to arrive on this side seventy.

What must we do, my dear, to vary our days?

Cards, you will own, are an agreeable relief, and the least subject to pall of any pleasures under the sun : and really, philosophically speaking, what is life but an intermitted pool at quadrille?

I am interrupted by a divine colonel in the guards.

Adieu! Your faithful

A. FITZGERALD

TO MRS FITZGERALD

LETTER 228 BELLFIELD, TUESDAY: I accept your challenge, Bell; and am greatly mistaken if you find me so very insipid as you are pleased to suppose.

Have no fear of falling into vegetation; not one amongst us has the least vegetative quality.

I have a thousand ideas of little amusements, to keep the mind awake.

None of our party are of that sleepy order of beings, who want perpetual events to make them feel their existence : this is the defect of the cold and inanimate, who have not spirit and vivacity enough to taste the natural pleasures of life.

Our adventures of one kind are at an end; but we shall see others, as entertaining, springing up every moment.

I dare say, our whole lives will be Pindaric: my only plan of life is to have none at all, which, I think, my little Bell will approve.

Please to observe, my sweet Bell, to make life pleasant, we must not only have great pleasures but little ones, like the smaller auxiliary parts of a building; we must have our trifling amusements as well as our sublime transports.

My first *second* pleasure (if you will allow the expression) is gardening; and for this reason, that it is my divine Emily's : I must teach you to love rural pleasures.

Colonel Willmott has made me just as rich as I wish to be.

You must know, my fair friend, that whilst I thought a fortune and Emily incompatible, I had infinite contempt for the former, and fancied that it would rather take from, than add to, my happiness; but, now I can possess it with her, I allow it all its value.

My father (with what delight do I call the father of Emily by that name!) hinted at my taking a larger house; but I would not leave my native Dryads for an imperial palace: I have, however, agreed to let him build a wing to Bellfield, which it wants, to compleat the original plan, and to furnish it in whatever manner he thinks fit.

He is to have a house in London; and we are to ramble from one to the other as fancy leads us.

He insists on our having no rule but inclination: do you think we are in any danger of vegetating, my dear Bell?

The great science of life is, to keep in constant employment that restless active principle within us, which, if not directed right, will be eternally drawing us from real to imaginary happiness.

Love, all charming as it is, requires to be kept alive by such a variety of amusements, or avocations, as may prevent the languor to which all human pleasures are subject.

Emily's tenderness and delicacy make me ever an expecting lover: she contrives little parties of pleasure, and by surprize, of which she is always the ornament and the soul: her whole attention is given to make her Rivers happy.

I envy the man who attends her on these little excursions.

Love with us is ever led by the Sports and the Smiles.

Upon the whole, people who have the spirit to act as we have done, to dare to chuse their own companions for life, will generally be happy.

The affections are the true sources of enjoyment: love, friendship, and, if you will allow me to anticipate, paternal tenderness, all the domestic attachments, are sweet beyond words.

The beneficent Author of nature, who gave us these affections for the wisest purposes——

"Cela est bien dit, mon cher Rivers; mais il faut cultiver notre jardin."

You are right, my dear Bell, and I am a prating coxcomb.

315

Lucy's post-coach is just setting off, to wait your commands.

I send this by Temple's servant. On Thursday I hope to see our dear groupe of friends re-united, and to have nothing to wish, but a continuance of our present happiness.

               Adieu! Your faithful

                             ED. RIVERS

BIBLIOGRAPHY

Baker, Ernest A. *The History of the English Novel* (London, 1934), vol. v, 144–146.

Blue, Charles S. "Canada's First Novelist," *The Canadian Magazine*, LVIII (November 1921), 3–12.

[Brooke, Frances.] *The History of Emily Montague*. With an introduction and notes by Lawrence J. Burpee and an appendix by F. P. Grove. Ottawa: Graphic Publishers, 1931.

———. *The History of Julia Mandeville*. 2 vols., 2nd ed. London, 1763.

Brooke, Frances. [Letter to Dodsley, 1769.] [Add. MS. 29747, f. 68, in the British Museum.]

Burwash, Ida. "An Old Time Novel," *The Canadian Magazine*, XXVIII (January 1907), 252–256.

Chateauclair, Wilfrid. "The First Canadian Novel," *The Dominion Illustrated*, IV (January 11, 1890), 31.

———. *The Dictionary of National Biography* (London 1921), vol. II, 1328–1329.

Dobson, Austin. *Fanny Burney*. "English Men of Letters Series" (London, 1904), pp. 61–63.

Edwards, Thomas. *The Canons of Criticism . . . and Sonnets* (London, 1765), p. 348.

LeMoine, James. *Picturesque Quebec* (Montreal, 1882) pp. 375–378.

[Maseres, Francis.] *The Maseres Letters 1766–1768*, edited with an Introduction, Notes, and Appendices by W. Stewart Wallace (Toronto, 1919), especially pages 25, 25n, 46, 46n, 80.

Morgan, Henry J. *Bibliotheca Canadensis* (Ottawa, 1867), p. 50.

[Murray, James.] Dr Burpee, Dr Doughty, and Dr Lanctot reported their findings from records in the Public Archives of Canada in Ottawa (i.e. from the Murray Papers, the *Army List, State Records*, and the *Quebec Gazette*) in the Graphic Publishers edition of *The History of Emily Montague*, 1931, pp. 327–333.

Nichols, John. *Literary Anecdotes of the Eighteenth Century, comprising Biographical Memoirs of William Bowyer. . . .* 6 vols. Vol. II, 346–347.

Pacey, Desmond. "The First Canadian Novel," *The Dalhousie Review*, XXVI (July 1946), 143–150.

[Acknowledgments: to Dr Elizabeth Waterston and Mr Carl Ballstadt.]

THE AUTHOR

MRS FRANCES BROOKE, daughter of the Rev. William Moore, was born in Stubton, Lincolnshire, in 1724. The foundations of her career were laid in the literary circle of Samuel Richardson; under the pseudonym of "Mary Singleton, Spinster," she edited her own periodical, *The Old Maid* (1755–56). Play-writing (*Virginia*) came next; then translating of a French novel by Madame Riccoboni; and, in 1763, publication of her own *History of Julia Mandeville*. At this time, the Rev. Dr John Brooke, whom she had married in 1756, became chaplain to the British garrison at Quebec, a post which he held until late in 1768. Mrs Brooke joined her husband in Quebec City and stayed through a period of approximately five years, broken probably by one trip home beginning in November 1764. *Emily Montague* was published by T. Dodsley in London after her return to England (1769). It was followed by *Memoirs of the Marquis of St Forlaix*; a translation of the Abbé Milot's *History of England*; *The Excursion* (a novel, 1777); *The Siege of Sinope* (a tragedy); *Rosina* (a very successful light opera); and *Marian* (also at Covent Garden). Mrs Brooke died at Sleaford, Lincolnshire, on January 23, 1789.

SELECTED NEW CANADIAN LIBRARY TITLES

Asterisks (*) denote titles of New Canadian Library Classics

McCLELLAND AND STEWART LIMITED
publishers of The New Canadian Library
would like to keep you informed about
new additions to this unique series.

For a complete listing of titles and
current prices – or if you wish to be added
to our mailing list to receive future catalogues
and other new book information – write:

BOOKNEWS
McClelland and Stewart Limited
25 Hollinger Road
Toronto, Canada M4B 3G2

McClelland and Stewart books are
available at all good bookstores.

Booksellers should be happy to order from our catalogues
any titles which they do not regularly stock.